DANCE WITH THE DEVIL

DANCE WITH THE DEVIL

The Saga of Doc Holliday

Book Two

A Novel

VICTORIA WILCOX

TWODOT®

GUILFORD, CONNECTICUT
HELENA, MONTANA

For Ronald Carl Wilcox, D.D.S.
The real Doc in my life.

A · TWODOT® · BOOK

An imprint and registered trademark of The Rowman & Littlefield Publishing Group, Inc.
4501 Forbes Blvd., Ste. 200
Lanham, MD 20706
www.rowman.com

Distributed by NATIONAL BOOK NETWORK

British Library Cataloguing in Publication Information available

Library of Congress Cataloging-in-Publication Data available

Names: Wilcox, Victoria, author.
Title: Dance with the devil : the saga of Doc Holliday / Victoria Wilcox.
Other titles: Gone West | Saga of Doc Holliday
Description: Guilford, Connecticut ; Helena, Montana : TwoDot : Distributed
   by National Book Network, 2019. | Previously titled Gone West, published
   by Knox Robinson (London), 2014. The second volume in the Doc Holliday
   trilogy. |
Identifiers: LCCN 2019018108 (print) | LCCN 2019018841 (ebook) | ISBN
   9781493044726 (e-book) | ISBN 9781493044719 (pbk.)
Subjects: LCSH: Holliday, John Henry, 1851-1887—Fiction. | GSAFD:
   Biographical fiction. | Western stories. | Historical fiction.
Classification: LCC PS3623.I5327 (ebook) | LCC PS3623.I5327 G66 2019 (print)
   | DDC 813/.6—dc23
LC record available at https://lccn.loc.gov/2019018108

∞™ The paper used in this publication meets the minimum requirements of American National Standard for Information Sciences—Permanence of Paper for Printed Library Materials, ANSI/NISO Z39.48-1992.

Printed in the United States of America

Contents

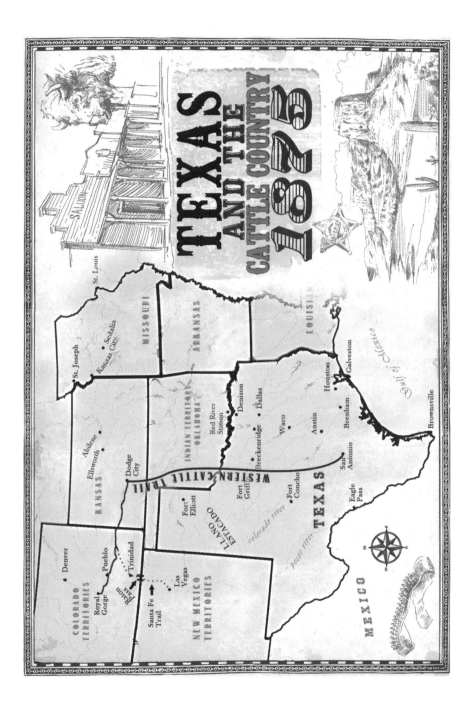

Chapter One

TEXAS, 1873

THE LAST THING ON HIS MIND WAS A TRAIN ROBBERY. ALTHOUGH HE knew about the $100,000 in gold rumored to be aboard, enough to make any outlaw eager, no one had ever robbed a moving train west of the Mississippi before. As long as the Rock Island Line's passenger train No. 2, bound from Council Bluffs to Des Moines, kept up its dizzying speed of forty-miles an hour, horsed bandits would have a hard time catching up with her.

But as the train neared Adair, Iowa, it slowed for a grade and a curve, and the engineer hollered out that something was slung across the tracks. He slammed the engine into reverse and the train shuddered and groaned, then jumped the rails. The locomotive thundered down the muddy bank of Turkey Creek spewing smoke and cinders from the chimney and lolling to one side, twisting the couplers and throwing the passenger cars skyward. The ground shook with the impact as steam rose from the troubled creek bed. And waiting alongside the bridge to greet the terrified passengers as they struggled from the wreckage was a white-robed gang of train robbers brandishing pistols and rifles and shouting the Rebel yell . . .

"You gonna buy that paper, Mister, or just stand there readin' all day?" the newsboy on the Galveston Strand complained as John Henry lost himself in the details of the West's most daring train robbery. The engineer had been killed, thrown from the locomotive then crushed to death as it rolled over him. But the conductor had lived to testify against the James gang that had derailed the Rock Island Line and held up its passengers.

Until that summer, the gang had kept their outlawry to holding up banks in the Missouri back country. This enterprise with the railroads was a whole new kind of crime, and newspaper sales soared whenever there was a report on the search for the elusive Jesse James. Aside from the gruesome death of the train's engineer, it would have been a perfect robbery had the money actually been on board and not delayed until later, leaving the gang only $6,000 in cash and jewelry taken from the express messenger and the passengers. But it was a thrilling attempt, even so, and folks took to the story like a dime novel come to life. Not since the long-ago legends of Robin Hood had there been such a popular outlaw, and ladies openly hoped that Jesse might show up in their own quiet towns, bringing adventure and his handsome gang with him. But that was the tenor of the times in 1873: the War was over and the new West was wild, and the country was ready for some entertainment.

But to John Henry Holliday, late of Georgia by way of a fast ride across Florida and a sailing ship to Galveston, the story of Jesse James was more of a relief than anything else. For with the newspapers filled with tales of the dashing outlaw, there was little chance that a shooting on a river in South Georgia would be reported. Not that there was all that much to report about such a commonplace crime: a young black man gunned down by a young white man. But it was John Henry's crime, and though he had run from Lowndes County before the law could catch him, then spent a long night in anguished prayer repenting of his sin and begging for God's forgiveness, he knew that repentance alone would not satisfy the State of Georgia. If the law decided to come after him, he could still hang for murder. So he anxiously read every newspaper he could get his hands on searching for any mention of violence on the Withlacoochee River, and was relieved to see the name of Jesse James, not John Henry Holliday, spelled out across the front page. Let the James Gang get the fame; he'd be happy if his own name never made the headlines.

There was certainly nothing else about him that would draw attention. He was of average height and average build, although a little on the lean side on account of a bout of pneumonia he'd had while spending two cold winters in dental school in Philadelphia. His coloring was fair, his eyes china blue, or so said the girls back home who'd called him handsome, though mostly it was his cousin Mattie Holliday calling him handsome that had meant something to him. And though there were other, less pleasing, things that Mattie had called him, as well—stubborn, selfish, arrogant—if those had been his only sins, he wouldn't be in Texas now, reading the paper and watching for any mention of his name or what had happened on the Withlacoochee.

Truth was, he was running from more than just the law. His father had thrown him out of the house and ordered him never to return, the result of a disagreement over his plan to marry his cousin Mattie, though Mattie had already wrecked those plans herself by telling him through her tears that her Catholic faith would not allow first cousins to marry. She loved him but she could not be with him, not ever. And the pain of those two denials, his sweetheart's love and his father's affections, had driven him into a drunken stupor and an unthinking shooting that sent him west fleeing for his life.

Yet other than a few bad dreams, a haunting worry over the long reach of the law, and a still-healing heart, he was in hopeful spirits, having stepped off the ship at Galveston Island sunburned and wind-blown from the sea voyage, and feeling amazingly well. While most of the other passengers had spent their time onboard the tall ship *Golden Dream* leaning over the rails and vomiting into the turquoise waters of the Gulf of Mexico, the sailing had actually seemed to agree with him. The fresh sea air had cleared his lungs and the prospect of starting a new life in Texas enlivened his mind. And though he had only the vaguest of plans for his immediate future, his long-term goal was set: he would find his way to his Uncle Jonathan McKey's plantation on the Brazos River and beg the family favor of a place in his Uncle's household. For surely his mother's eldest brother, a wealthy cotton planter, would welcome a long-lost nephew from back home in Georgia and be happy to offer him a home in Texas. And once he was settled, he would open his trunk-full of dental equipment and set up a profitable practice in some nearby town, and prove to his father and Mattie both that he was still a fine professional man and not someone to be sent away.

That was the plan anyhow, but first he had some obstacles to overcome. He had little money to pay for room and board in Galveston, having spent nearly all he had on the ocean voyage from Florida to Texas. He had no trunk-full of dental tools with which to practice his paying profession, having left Georgia in too much of a hurry to arrange for its shipment. And he had no idea of where his Uncle Jonathan McKey lived, other than the recollection that his property was somewhere in Washington County. Still he was glad to be in Texas at last, the place he had heard about and dreamed of since he was a child—though Galveston looked little like the rough and wild Texas of his childhood imaginings.

Galveston glittered at the edge of the ocean like some fancy-dressed lady decked out in jewels. This was no frontier town where cavalry soldiers fought wild Indians, but the richest city on the Gulf of Mexico and the second richest port in the whole United States. The streets were paved with crushed oyster shells that sparkled in the summer sun and gleamed at night under the glow of gaslights. The mansions of the leading men of Texas society lined Broadway Street, surrounded by gardens of flowering Oleander and fragrant groves of orange and lemon trees. The Strand, on the north side of the island where the wide harbor faced the mainland, was crowded with brick business houses and the traffic of port commerce, while the sand beach on the south of the island was filled with the carriages of pleasure-seekers enjoying the balm of the Gulf breezes. In fact, if it hadn't been for the lingering legend of the Karankawas, civilized Galveston wouldn't have seemed like wild Texas at all.

The Karankawa Indians were cannibals, so the story went, roaming the Gulf islands long before the shipping trade had turned Galveston into the leading port city of the West, and even before the legendary pirate Jean Lafitte had stopped by to bury his stolen booty. When the fishing wasn't good, the Karankawas turned to eating human flesh, and it was rumored that their campfires were heaped with the bones of their supper guests. The fact that they had stalked around the island stark naked, their bronzed bodies glistening in alligator grease to ward off mosquitoes, only added to the allure of their legend. Galveston was, after all, a beach and bathing resort where even very proper Victorians went nude into the waves.

John Henry learned about that surprising island custom on one of his first nights in Galveston when a drink in a Strand saloon led to an invitation to join an outing of men and ladies for a swim in the ocean.

"Though I don't have any bathing clothes with me," he remarked, and one of the other men answered with a laugh.

"Don't need 'em! City Ordinance says you can swim in the altogether between ten at night and four in the morning. They figure all the children are asleep by then."

"You mean you swim naked with ladies along?" John Henry asked in amazement. While he'd grown up going skinny-dipping in the green waters of the Withlacoochee, he'd never gone undressed in open public view—and certainly not with ladies.

"Well, I wouldn't call 'em ladies, exactly!" the gent replied. "It's usually only these saloon girls who are bold enough to accept the invitation. But once they've got their pantaloons off, the barmaids and the ladies all look pretty much alike, anyway. Care to come along?"

And that was how John Henry Holliday found himself in the company of several young sports and a few of their female friends, riding out in a hired dray toward the sand beach on the south side of Galveston Island. They could have walked the two miles to the shore, as it was a warm and brightly moonlit night, but the dray would be a convenient place to stow their clothing while they did their bathing in the surf.

The other young men seemed accustomed to watching women disrobing at a hardly discreet distance, although with the moon shining down so bright no distance would have been quite discreet enough. But John Henry was not accustomed to such a sight and had a hard time averting his eyes, as a gentleman should. The spectacle of those laughing young women loosing their hair and shedding shoes and stockings, skirts and bodices, petticoats and corsets and shimmies and pantaloons until they were standing bare-skinned under the summer moon took away all his mannerly reserve—though it wasn't just the eroticism of the scene that compelled him to shed his own clothes and join them in the waves. It was the freedom of the night, the wild abandonment of the life he'd left behind and the thrill of the world that lay ahead, that made him dive naked into the warm waters of the Gulf. It was Texas that made him do it, not the girls, and he felt not the slightest bit of remorse because of it.

No remorse, but a little regret later on when morning neared and the party tired of the ocean frolic, and found that the dray had disappeared with all of their clothing in it. There was momentary laughter over the missing horse and buggy until they all realized that they would have to make their way back into town on foot—and wearing nothing but their sandy, salty nakedness. Next time, John Henry vowed, he'd leave his own clothing somewhere more reliable than in the back of a rented dray. But in spite of the embarrassing early morning walk back to the livery stable where the horse had taken itself and the dray full of discarded attire, he wouldn't have traded away that night of emancipation for a lifetime of proper memories.

He was in Texas at last, and glad of it.

The rest of his days in Galveston were less romantic as he turned his attention to the more mundane matter of finding employment, which turned out to be a harder task than he'd thought it would be. Although he had a fine education as a graduate of the Pennsylvania College of Dental Surgery and professional experience with one of the most respected dentists in Atlanta, he had no way of proving it. And at one Galveston dental practice after another, the conversation was always the same:

"I'd be happy to have some extra help, busy as things are these days. Could use another trained man in the office, if you did indeed have the credentials . . ."

"Too bad about the diploma, and all. I've been thinking of advertising for a qualified partner . . ."

"One can't be too careful in our line, of course. My patients would want to know the background of someone new to town. It's all about trust, in our profession . . ."

Then would come the polite apologies, adding that when the doctor received his diploma that had been mistakenly left behind in Georgia, along with a letter of recommendation from his former employer, he'd be welcome to come by and inquire after a position again. . .

But John Henry couldn't afford to wait on the arrival of his diploma or anything else, short on money as he was. So he took the first job that seemed at all suitable: working for a Market Street barber who advertised bloodletting, leeching, and tooth extractions "promptly attended to" on the side of a hairstyling business, and who had a room to rent in the back of his shop, as well. John Henry did the work, took the money, and consoled himself that he wasn't planning on staying in town long, anyhow. As soon as he made enough to outfit himself properly for the journey to come, dressing like a gentleman instead of a ragged refugee from the law, he would leave the barber business and travel on to the Brazos River plantation of his wealthy Uncle Jonathan McKey, where he could live a life more befitting his station.

Of course, along with the new clothes, he'd need to have a new scabbard made for his Uncle Tom McKey's big knife that had come to Texas with him. Since the Hell-Bitch had started out as a plowshare on the McKey plantation before being forged into a sidearm, his Uncle Jonathan might recognize it and wonder how John Henry had come to carry it unholstered—and begin to ask questions about why his nephew had left home in such a hurry. In spite of the family connection, his uncle would be under no obligation to take in a man on the run, and might even turn him away if he knew the circumstances of John Henry's hasty departure from Georgia.

His earnings from the barbershop were slow in adding up, however. What he needed was some seed money, just a little loan to get himself started—and he knew just the person to ask. His Uncle John Holliday, a doctor in Atlanta, was the most well-off man he knew and could certainly afford to share something with his favorite nephew, if John Henry could just find the right words to say in asking him.

It took all the skills of composition he had learned in his school days at the Valdosta Institute to craft a letter that said just enough without saying too much, asking for the loan without explaining why he couldn't ask his own father for the money. But he must have done well in writing it, for within two weeks he received a reply—the small loan he had requested, along with a letter of introduction to a dentist living in the north Texas town of Dallas.

The dentist was a Dr. John Seegar, a former Georgian and old friend of the family. Dr. Seegar had married a girl from Campbell County, just over the line from Fayette County, and had made his home for a while in the Holliday's hometown of Fayetteville. Uncle John was well acquainted with him and was pleased to offer a letter of introduction which John Henry might want to use should he ever find himself in Dallas. But John Henry had no intention of using the recommendation, having heard enough about Dallas to know that he wasn't much interested in presenting himself there. Dallas was just another upstart farm town enjoying a little boom from the arrival of the railroads, but nothing much to brag about beyond that, and he had another kind of life in mind for himself— one of ease and comfort on his Uncle Jonathan's big cotton plantation on the Brazos River. So he put the letter away in his traveling bag and spent the loan money buying a new wardrobe for his trip: a vested wool suit and two white linen shirts, two stiff collars and two pairs of paper cuffs, a pair of soft leather ankle boots and a new felt hat, promising himself that he would repay the loan just as soon as he got settled again. And by the time he stepped aboard the Houston & Texas Central Railroad headed northwest toward Washington County, he almost believed that he really was just a young gentleman traveler off to see the world.

He was lucky to get out of Galveston when he did, on one of the last trains across the railroad bridge before a Yellow Fever quarantine went into effect. The city had reason to be wary: the epidemic of 1867, just six years before, had killed nearly a thousand people, and since no one knew what caused the fever, no one knew how to stop it. The only certainty was that the Fever always followed a season of heat and rain, and that early summer had been particularly hot and rainy. The oyster shell streets filled and flooded, the open ditch sewers overflowed, and the city reeked of human waste and stagnating tide water. When the rains finally cleared and the island dried out in the summer sun, pools of fouled water remained in all the low-lying places breeding mosquitoes that hatched and swarmed and made life miserable for the citizens of Galveston. The city fathers tried every known remedy to remove the noxious fumes that rose up from those mosquito pools, even spreading lime powder on the streets as a disinfectant, but the Yellow Fever came anyway. By the time the quarantine was ordered, seven souls had already died and the news-papers were reporting a new death every day, and fear stalked the island.

So John Henry was glad to be gone, leaving the sand beach and the Oleander gardens behind as the steam engine rumbled across the Gal-veston Bay Bridge and over the swampy mainland into the piney woods and Post Oak belt of east central Texas. He didn't even bother getting off the train in the little village of Houston, quaint on the banks of Buffalo Bayou, for Washington County was only another sixty miles past that and he was eager to get there.

He knew something of the place already, as he knew of Davy Crock-ett and Jim Bowie, as he knew of the Texas fight for freedom and the war cry, *Remember the Alamo!* For Washington-on-the-Brazos was the birthplace of the Texas Declaration of Independence from Mexico fol-lowing the massacre at the Battle of the Alamo, something every school boy knew about. The Declaration had been signed in a wooden shack on a muddy track that led up from the Brazos River, as primitive a beginning as there ever was for a new nation. But Washington County didn't stay the seat of the new government for long. The Mexican General Antonio López de Santa Anna was hot on the trail of the rebels, and five days after its birth the new government moved to the safer, more settled regions of east Texas.

When the Texans finally won their freedom at the Battle of San Jacinto, the Brazos River country started to fill up with settlers planting cotton and corn in the rich river bottoms. The Brazos was a natural pas-sage through the unsettled countryside, and soon steamers and freighters were carrying thousands of bales of cotton from the new plantations along the river to the coast and Galveston. By the time the Republic of Texas voted to become part of the United States of America, Washington County was on its way to being the leading cotton growing region in the entire South. Although secession and Civil War put a temporary end to the cotton prosperity and the big slave-run plantations were broken up into smaller farms, cotton was still King along the Brazos and there were still wealthy landowners sending barges downriver heavy-laden with raw white bales.

John Henry got off the train at the county seat of Brenham, asked around for directions to the McKey plantation, then hired a horse for the ride out to the Brazos River. He'd imagined his uncle's place in every detail: the tall white house facing the river, the acres of cotton fields stretching beyond, the horse lots farther out where long-tailed Texas mustangs waited impatiently for riding. But when he got to the end of the road where the McKey plantation ought to be, he saw nothing but a tangle of trees along the river's edge with a rough wooden farmhouse fronting furrowed fields. In the field nearest the road, two young girls in worn cotton dresses were working at the crops, and they stopped to stare as he reined in the horse.

"Afternoon, Ladies," he said, tipping his hat. "Can you tell me the whereabouts of the McKey plantation? I seem to have taken a wrong turn somewhere."

He waited for an answer, but the girls just kept staring up at him in silence, so he asked the question again.

"I said, can you point out the way to the plantation of Mr. Jonathan McKey?"

The older girl answered then, looking up and shading her face with her hand. "What do you want to know for?"

"I have business there," he replied, uncomfortable at being interrogated by a child. With her thin body and old rag of a dress, it was hard to guess her age.

"What kind of business?" the girl asked.

"That is my own affair, Miss," he answered sharply. It was clear the girl came from poor circumstances to be so rudely inquisitive of an adult. "Now can you point out the way to the McKey place or not? It's gettin' late and I've been travelin' a long way."

"Maybe I can, maybe I can't," she replied. "If I knew what your business was, I might could say. How do I know you're not a Yankee revenue agent or somethin'? We don't like Yankees much in these parts."

"Do I sound like a Yankee?" John Henry drawled.

"Well, not exactly. But you don't sound like you're from these parts, neither."

He took a slow breath, trying to hold back his irritation. "I have come a long way to find Mr. McKey. Now, if you don't know where he is, maybe your folks do. Is your mother at home?"

"Ma's dead," the younger girl blurted out, then hung her head.

"Hush up, Eula!" the older girl chided. "How do we know he's not a Yankee, anyhow? Pa'd whip us sure if he thought we was talkin' to a Yankee."

"I am not a Yankee!" John Henry repeated, about ready to give up on his search for the afternoon and ride back to Brenham and try again in the morning. But as he pulled back on the reins, he saw a tall man come out of the treeline along the river, shotgun in hand.

"That's Pa," little Eula said. "He don't like Yankees."

"And he don't like us talkin' to strangers, neither," the older girl said. "You better git, Mister, unless you're a better shot than my Pa."

"I doubt he'd let loose with y'all standin' right here beside me," John Henry answered coolly, the sight of the shotgun not bothering him nearly as much as those two unmannerly children.

"Eula! Lotti!" the man called as he walked toward them through the cornfield. "You girls get inside right now!"

The younger girl turned quickly and ran toward the house, but the older girl—Lotti, John Henry reckoned—hesitated a moment, almost smiling.

"Better not be a Yankee, Mister. My Pa don't much like Yankees," she said again. Then she turned, too, and ran through the fields toward the shelter of the farmhouse.

The girls' father was a tall man, thin like most farm workers but better dressed than most, and he wore a felt hat that looked like it had once been meant for better things than farm work. He stopped short of the edge of the road, the shotgun held loosely in the crook of his arm.

"What can I do for you?" he asked, as he closed the breech of the gun.

"I'm lookin' for Mr. Jonathan McKey. I understand he owns a big plantation down this way."

"He used to, 'till the damn Yankees stole it away."

"Then can you tell me where I might find him?" John Henry asked, afraid that his journey had all been for nothing, that he had come west only to find his uncle moved on or dead.

"That depends on who's askin'. I don't recall you introducin' yourself."

John Henry sighed. These Texas country people were a difficult lot, almost as suspicious as Georgia folk had been after the War.

"Jonathan McKey is my mother's older brother. I'm his nephew, John Henry Holliday. I've come all the way from Georgia to find him. Do you know where he is?"

The man pushed the hat back off his face, and for the first time John Henry could see the man's eyes clearly, sandy lashed and china blue like his own. "Why, you're lookin' at him, son. I'm Jon McKey. And I sure never expected to meet family out here in Texas."

John Henry was speechless. His uncle was nothing but a poor dirt farmer, no better off than any Georgia cracker! But more surprising than Jonathan McKey's poverty was the look of age about him. Though Jonathan was only a couple of years older than his sister Alice Jane, he somehow looked much older than John Henry had expected he would. His thick sandy blond hair was heavily streaked with gray, his face tanned to leather from long hours of working in the hot Texas sun, his blue eyes wreathed in wrinkles. He looked to be nearly sixty years old, though he must have been only in his late forties that year, and John Henry realized with a start that his own mother would be getting old now, too, if she had lived. He always liked to remember her the way she looked in photographs—her white brow smooth and unlined, her eyes clear and serene—before the illness that had overtaken her and drained her life away in that hard, bloody cough.

"So you're Alice Jane's son, are you?" Jonathan said. "Why, I haven't heard from her in years, seems like, not since she moved down to south Georgia during the War. I'm a poor correspondent, I'm afraid. How's she doin' these days?"

John Henry cleared his throat, holding back the cough that suddenly tried to come up from his lungs.

"She's passed on, Sir. She died in '66 after the War."

"Ah, poor Sis!" Jonathan McKey said, shaking his head. "I reckon the War years were hard for her. You favor her, though there's somethin' of your father in your face, as well. What brings you all the way to Texas, John Henry?"

"I'm here to practice dentistry, Sir," he said, giving as much truth as he dared. "I graduated from the Pennsylvania College of Dental Surgery last year. Heard tell Texas is full of opportunity for a young man like myself. I'm aimin' to set up somewhere around these parts, so I thought to pay a visit on my kin along the way."

Jonathan looked at him carefully. "I'm surprised you could find us way out here."

"I almost didn't. Those girls didn't seem too happy to give me directions."

"They're just mindin' my orders. We've had our share of trouble with Yanks here, so I make them be careful."

"But there wasn't any fightin' all the way out here was there?"

"Not durin' the War, no. Our trouble came after, with the Reconstruction. The Yankees near to ruined Washington County, burned half of Brenham then took our land and gave it away to the Nigras." He nodded to the farm across the road where fields of cotton fought against the encroaching line of trees. "That used to be my land over there. Had two-thousand acres, mostly all in cotton, before the Yankees came through. They stole most of it away, gave it to the coloreds I had working on my place, like they had a right to it. What was left they sold to some German immigrants. Mighty hard to see my land run by Nigras and folks that can't even speak English—land my father's inheritance money paid for."

He stared off into the distance, then shifted the shotgun in the crook of his arm.

"I hate them Nigras," he said sullenly. "But I hate the Yankees worse, dirty land-stealin' bastards. I'll get my land back one day, or there'll be hell to pay. Well, come on in the house, then, John Henry. Can't leave my own kin standin' out in the road all day."

It was clear that Jonathan McKey was a bitter man, but he had good reason to be. He was the oldest son of the oldest son of a wealthy Southern family and had been raised to expect that life would treat him well, and for a while it had. When his father, John Henry's grandfather William Land McKey, had died, Jonathan took his inheritance money and went west to Texas buying up those two-thousand acres of prime cotton land along the Brazos River. But then the War came, and Jonathan signed on as an officer with the Second Texas Cavalry, leaving his wife behind with two small children and another on the way. When the War ended, Jonathan came back to Washington County to find his plantation ruined, his wife Emma and her baby both dead of Yellow Fever, and his two small daughters being tended by neighbors.

Lotti and Eula, Jonathan's girls, must have taken after their mother, John Henry thought, since they didn't bear much resemblance to the McKeys, though they had enough McKey in them to give them that natural Southern pride he had taken as arrogance. Jonathan never let them forget that they were Southern ladies, though his circumstances were too poor even to send them into Brenham for schooling. Still, he had hopes that they might find good husbands and help to raise the family back up from poverty. Lotti was fifteen that year, close enough for marrying age, and shy little Eula was thirteen and would be old enough soon. But the possibility of them finding well-off husbands in that part of Washington County was pretty slim, and chances were they would both end up married to sons of German immigrant families with almost as little as they had. Until they did marry, they kept house for their father and helped out in the fields, and looked less and less like Southern ladies every year.

But they did their best to entertain their new-found cousin in a genteel manner, even setting the supper table with the few remaining pieces of their mother's china dinnerware. And if it weren't all so pathetic, John Henry might have laughed at the irony of it. He had come all the way from Georgia looking for a hand-out from his wealthy uncle, and Jonathan's family was so destitute that they hardly had enough food to pass around the table. It was funny, all right, and too sad for words.

There were only two beds in the McKey house: Jonathan's downstairs in a little bedroom behind the kitchen, and the one the girls shared upstairs in the attic. John Henry would have been content to just ride on back to

Brenham to spend the night in the hotel there and forget all about Washington County, but Jonathan insisted that he had to stay the night at least as he was family and all. So the girls made themselves a pallet out of blankets by the kitchen hearth, and John Henry took their bed upstairs.

But he found it hard to sleep on that lumpy old mattress, with the rope-strung bed creaking every time he rolled over and tried to get comfortable and the air so close in the windowless attic that he could hardly breathe. It was no wonder that he started to coughing, with that stale air and the dust of the attic and the summer heat sweltering in.

He had a strange dream that night as he tossed and turned in his troubled, fitful sleep. He dreamed he was back in Georgia again, a fairhaired boy sitting beside his mother at the piano in the parlor. She was young again too, and as beautiful as the Franz Liszt music she played.

"Here, honey," she said, laying his little hands on the keyboard. "You try it. You know how Mother loves to hear you play."

But before he could make a sound, he heard his father's voice calling to him from somewhere outside, and the music and his mother both disappeared.

"Leave that nonsense now, there's work to do," Henry Holliday said, and John Henry followed the sound of his father's voice. Henry was busy building a sapling box and he handed John Henry a hammer and nails. "See if you can make some use of yourself," his father said, as John Henry began to hammer at the wood. And as he worked, the sound of the hammering grew louder and louder until he wasn't a boy anymore, but a man, full grown, and standing at the end of a long drive of trees in front of a beautiful home.

It was his own home, he knew, though it looked like some Peachtree Street mansion, and he walked up the drive toward the wide front stairs. The door was open and he stepped into a house full of light, sunlight reflecting off oiled wood and polished brass, with every long window open to the air. But the beautiful rooms were empty, still and silent as a tomb.

Then another sound came out of the silence, a sound sweet with memory and affection: Mattie's voice speaking from behind him in the open doorway.

"You've come home, John Henry!" she said, but when he turned to face her, it was an auburn-haired child who looked up at him with Mattie's eyes and Mattie's smile. He reached out to touch her, but she turned and ran away from him back down the tree-lined drive and into the wild fields beyond, laughing and calling him to follow.

He ran after her, laughing too, but when he reached the end of the drive, he saw a railroad track stretching out between him and the field. The child Mattie stood in the tall grass beyond the track, smiling and waiting for him to cross over to her, but he was too winded to run any farther and stopped to catch his breath.

And then he heard the train coming, the sound of it growing louder and louder until it filled his ears with a roaring and rushing, and he tried to call out to the child to wait for him. But when he opened his mouth to speak, his words turned into a pain that tore at his lungs like a fire in his chest. He stumbled to the ground, coughing and gasping as the train roared on by.

When he could finally lift his head, the train was gone and so was the child. And all that was left before him was an open, empty field that stretched out forever, endless, alone.

He woke with a start. Someone was standing over him in a dim shadow of light and it took him a moment to realize where he was. The light came from the attic stair, and his little cousin Eula was by his bedside, a candlestick in her hand.

"You sick, John Henry?" she whispered. "You been coughin' all night long."

"No," he started to say, but he had to clear his throat just to get the word out.

"You sure sound sick to me," she said, leaning closer, and as she did the light of the candle fell over him.

"What's that all over your face, John Henry?" she asked, then she pulled back and gasped. "Why, you' got blood all over you!"

And in the flickering light of the candle, John Henry looked down and saw that his pillow was splattered with blood, dark red and drying where his head had been. Then he put his hand to his face, wiping his mouth. *Tell me if there's ever any blood*, his Uncle John Holliday had told him once, and the hand that touched his mouth was streaked blood-red, too.

"I think maybe you're real sick, John Henry," Eula said, slowly backing away from him. "You want me to get Pa?"

But John Henry didn't answer her. He was staring at the blood that stained his pillow and remembering how his mother had coughed up blood that stained her bed linens blood-red.

"No," he said, "I'm not sick. I am not sick."

"But you're bleedin'," Eula said. "I'll go get Pa."

"No!" he said, pulling himself up. "Get my horse, I'm leavin' here!"

"Right now? But it's hardly daybreak even."

"Get my horse!" he said, the words rasping out, and Eula took the candle and hurried down the attic stair.

He was not weak. He would not be ill. Illness was weakness, and he was not weak. But there was blood all over his pillow, blood on his hand.

It was the sea voyage that had made him sick, he told himself, or the Yellow Fever that had quarantined Galveston, or the choking black smoke of the steam engine on the ride to Washington County. Anyone would get sick breathing in all that coal smoke. Or maybe it was the air in that stuffy little attic room, or vapors from the Brazos River. Vapors brought on the Yellow Fever, vapors could make a man cough up blood . . .

But when he tried to get up, he found that he was drained of all energy like he'd coughed up part of his life with that blood. He had no choice but to stay in bed in that airless little attic while Eula and Lotti brought him broth and tea and sponged his head with wet rags. And every time he closed his eyes to sleep, he had an awful fear that the train would come back again and take him with it, coughing and gasping his life away.

It was days before he was well enough to travel again, and by then he'd convinced himself that it was indeed the Yellow Fever that had caused the bloody coughing fit and he was lucky to be away from Galveston before the Fever killed him. And blaming his troubles on Galveston and the Fever, he decided to follow his Uncle John Holliday's advice, after all, and take himself off to Dallas to ask for a position with Dr. Seegar. What other option did he have, anyhow? He couldn't go back to quarantined Galveston, nor could he stay with his Uncle Jonathan McKey on that miserable remains of a cotton plantation. So once again, he was on the run, buying another train ticket north and heading on to Dallas.

Chapter Two

DALLAS, 1873

THE CITY HAD BIG PLANS FOR ITSELF, BUT A LONG WAYS TO GO STILL TO get there. Although a new red brick courthouse cast a substantial shadow, Dallas was mostly board sided buildings lining prairie sod streets, with as many saloons as dry good stores and merchant shops in the one mile stretch between the train depot and the Trinity River—the liquor likely making up for the fact that there was no public water fit to drink. Yet there was a sense of excitement to the place that pleased John Henry, in spite of the herds of pigs and cows that crowded Main Street.

It was the coming of the railroads that had turned Dallas from farm town to cowtown, with the Houston & Texas Central building north from the coast and the Texas & Pacific Rail Line laying tracks west from Shreveport toward Fort Worth and on to California. In a few years, the whole of Texas would be crossed by rails, part of a great transcontinental railroad system—or so the plans went. For now, Dallas was end-of-the-line and the place where planters brought their cotton to ship and cattlemen brought their stock to market, making the dirt streets a noisy, smelly mess.

Dr. Seegar's office was located in the middle of the busiest part of town, on Elm Street halfway between Market and Austin, in a second-floor suite above a druggist. And though he'd never heard of young Dr. John Henry Holliday before, other than the letter of recommendation he carried with him, the doctor had been cordial enough.

"So what brings you to Dallas, Dr. Holliday?" Dr. Seegar asked, looking up from the letter and studying him. "According to what your uncle writes, you had a good career ahead of yourself in Georgia."

"Opportunity," John Henry replied easily, having practiced the answer all the way up from Washington County, another smoky twelve-hour train ride that had left him coughing again. "I hear that Dallas is boomin' and full of possibilities for a young man like myself."

"Oh, it's boomin' all right," Dr. Seegar said, and a moment later the board and plaster walls of the office began to shake and rattle as if to prove the point, and he raised his voice to go on. "There's a new hotel goin' up a block from here, so we get the blessin' of the sound and the fury both."

"Shakespeare," John Henry said with a nod.

"Pardon me?"

"You were quotin' Shakespeare. Macbeth: Fifth Act, I believe. I memorized a lot of the classics as a schoolboy." Then he finished the quotation, as Professor Varnedoe had taught him to do back at the Valdosta Institute:

"Out, out, brief candle!
Life's but a walking shadow, a poor player
That struts and frets his hour upon the stage
And then is heard no more: it is a tale
Told by an idiot, full of sound and fury,
Signifying nothing."

He smiled at his own performance, but there was no appreciative applause from Dr. Seegar as there had always been from his classmates in school.

"Well, you won't find much use for that kind of education around here," Seegar said, "unless you aim for a career on the stage."

The remark might have seemed like a criticism coming from someone else, but Dr. Seegar didn't seem the type to criticize. He was a mild-mannered fellow, slight of build, with a balding patch in the middle of his thin brown hair, and a brown beard and mustache to match, giving him the impression of being done all in sepia tone.

"But if you enjoy the theater," he went on, "we do get some good entertainment at the Opera House, though the show outside is often better than the show inside."

"I don't understand."

"It's the trouble with the dressing rooms. The owner forgot to put any in, so the actors are obliged to climb out the back window and run down the street to the Grand Hotel to change their costumes. Sometimes, when the show's a little dull, the audience goes outside to see the actors makin' an exhibition of themselves. But that's not nearly as entertainin' as the show Belle Swink puts on."

"Belle Swink?" John Henry asked. "Is she one of the actresses?"

"Certainly not. Belle's a mule, one of the team that pulls the Dallas Street Railway car. She's well behaved, as mules go, until the rains come and this prairie sod turns to mud. Then Belle gets stuck and the railcar comes off its tracks and the passengers have to climb out and right it again. The operator tried to rectify matters awhile back by layin' down planks of Bois D'Arc wood from the banks of the Trinity, but they just sank down into the mud like everything else does. You may wonder why I am tellin' you these colorful stories."

"Yessir, I am."

Dr. Seegar nodded toward the window with its view of Elm Street business buildings and cattle-filled roads. "Dallas is pretty rough around the edges still. I wouldn't want you to settle here expectin' the kind of life you had in Atlanta. But you are right about there bein' plenty of opportunity for a man who's willin' to work. Of course, there are some personal conditions I would expect you to meet should we become partners."

"Yessir?"

"As a family man, the moral climate of this community is of great concern to me. That's why I've accepted the position of President of the Dallas Temperance League. I would expect that my partner be willin' to hold with my stand against drinking. Would that be a problem for you?"

John Henry shifted uncomfortably, feeling the weight of the whiskey flask in his coat pocket. He'd refilled it just before his interview, finding a liquor store conveniently close on the corner of Elm Street.

"No, Sir, that wouldn't be any problem at all."

"And I would naturally expect my partner to be a church-goin' man, as well. My family and I attend the Baptist Church. I assume you have a chosen denomination?"

That answer came more easily, trained into him over long years by his mother. "Yessir, I was raised a Methodist-Episcopalian."

Seegar smiled as though satisfied. "Well, if what your uncle writes of you is true, you come well qualified to join my practice—Pennsylvania College of Dental Surgery, associate of Dr. Arthur Ford in Atlanta, attendee of the Georgia Dental Society Convention. We seldom see such professional dental practitioners in this locale. Most of the other dentists in town are home-trained barber surgeons. But that is what has made my practice successful: professionalism. I have worked for ten years to build a quality name in this part of Texas. I would expect you to uphold that level of service to the community."

John Henry glanced around the well-appointed office, knowing that it would be some time before he could afford such a space of his own, much less equip it adequately. He needed Dr. Seegar and his successful practice, whatever sacrifice he had to make—even if that meant keeping his drinking private and making a public show of being a temperance man. But hadn't he come to Texas to make a fresh start for himself, after all?

"It would be an honor to work with you, Dr. Seegar," he said. "And I look forward to walkin' the paths of rectitude here in Dallas."

He had some letters to write once he'd gotten himself settled in a boarding house room nearby to the dental office. His wrote to his Uncle John Holliday in Atlanta, thanking him for the recommendation and telling him of his new partnership with their old family friend. He wrote to his Uncle Tom McKey in Valdosta, asking him to send along the personal items he'd left behind in his hurried departure, most particularly the trunk full of dental tools and books that he would need in his new business. And he wrote to Mattie, telling her that he had chosen to establish himself in Dallas where he planned to make a fine career and prove himself the man she had always wanted him to be, and that he hoped she might someday be able to visit him there. To his father, he sent a short note saying that he had moved to Texas.

Dr. Seegar wore a frock coat to work, presenting a professional appearance as well as keeping his suit clothes clean from the spittle and drill filings that flew from the open mouths of his patients, and he expected his new partner to dress in similar fashion. So John Henry's first purchase in Dallas, after paying a month's rent in advance to the landlady at his boarding house, was a new black wool coat made by the Jewish merchant, Emmanuel Kahn.

It was Dr. Seegar's suggestion that he visit E.M. Kahn's Gent's Furnishing Goods on Commerce Street, though that might not have been John Henry's first choice for a clothier. To his knowledge, he had never before had any dealings with a Jew, only heard stories of them or seen them from a distance, like the long-bearded men he had watched walking to their Synagogue in Philadelphia. "Hebrews," his mother would have called them, saying in hushed tones that they were not Christian and had crucified the Lord, though his Aunt Permelia had always had more generous views, commenting that the Jews were the best business people she had ever known, Christian or not. In fact, his Aunt had caused a minor scandal in Fayetteville, the year the War started, by traveling to Atlanta to buy silk from a Jewish merchant to be sewn into a battle flag for the Fayette Rifle Grays. The ladies of the town weren't entirely sure if the Lord would bless their efforts in making the flag and, thereby, not bless the boys who carried it into battle, considering the source of the material. But silk was silk, his Aunt Permelia insisted, and the Jewish merchant's price was the best to be found—as long as one didn't mind a little haggling. In the end, the ladies sat demurely in Aunt Permelia's parlor, stitching the flag together and embroidering its brave motto: *We come back in honor, or come not again.* The fact that the flag did come home again, and without a tear or tatter, seemed to show that the Lord had accepted it, after all.

So it was with a mix of his mother's caution and his aunt's practicality, along with his own curiosity, that John Henry stopped into Emmanuel Kahn's store to be measured for his new wool frock coat—and found the man to be almost nothing like what he'd expected. Instead of a dour-dressed rabbi like the Jews he'd seen in Philadelphia, Emmanuel Kahn was a dapper young man with a fashionable French accent.

"I was born in the Alsace-Lorraine," Kahn explained. "And the French, as you know, are gifted with a sense of style."

"Seems like a long way from France to Texas," John Henry commented. "And from what I can see, Dallas isn't a city to appreciate style all that much."

"Ah! But that is where the opportunity comes!" the merchant said with a smile. "As the first retailer of men's clothing in this city, it is my style the men of Dallas will wear. And may I suggest that this black frock would look more finished if you carried a cane?"

"I'm sure it would, but as I'm plannin' to wear the coat at work, I won't have much use for a walkin' stick."

Emmanuel Kahn sighed as he rolled his measuring tape and slipped it into the pocket of his own coat. "A pity. I was hoping to interest you in one of my new shipment from Paris, a gold-headed cane fit for a Southern aristocrat."

"And what makes you think I'm an aristocrat, anyhow?" John Henry asked with some amusement. Surely, the man was only speaking flattery to get him to buy that gold-headed cane—a needless bit of luxury.

"It is in your tone," Kahn replied, "and in the way you carry yourself: neck proud and shoulders squared. Your bearing shows you to be a man of substance, satisfied with his place in the world. A clothier notices things like that."

John Henry didn't disagree, though he knew himself to be neither an aristocrat nor satisfied with his place in the world. The only aristocrat he had ever known was his Grandfather McKey, with his thousands of cotton acres at Indian Creek Plantation and his hundreds of slaves to work the place. That kind of aristocracy had disappeared after the War and John Henry would never know the equal of it.

"And what about yourself?" he asked, changing the subject. "You don't seem all that Jewish, for a Jew. I mean, you don't look like any Jews I ever knew."

"Oh, I am thoroughly an Israelite, I assure you. I was, in fact, trained to be a cantor. My parents died when I was still a boy, and my relatives—well meaning, certainly—thought it best to train me for the synagogue. I served there for a year before a life of trade beckoned me. Some would say, however, that trade is a religion to the Jew. So tell me, a frock coat of this quality, of such fine material and exquisite tailoring, what would you like to offer me for it?"

John Henry had to hide a smile, remembering his Aunt Permelia's story of the haggling silk merchant in Atlanta. "Whatever I offer will be far too little," he said with mock cordiality, "and I'd hate to insult you with a price you couldn't accept. Why don't you just decide what price you'd like to be paid, and I'll decide if I'd like to pay it."

Emmanuel Kahn sighed heavily and shook his head. "That is the only trouble with doing business in Dallas," he said with disappointment, "no one wants to barter the price. Just hang a tag on the merchandise and take in the money. What an impersonal way to do business! I might as well bring in a railcar loaded with ready-made suits and give up on the tailoring business entirely. Of course, then you'd never know the pleasure of wearing a frock coat custom made to your particular measurements, a style selected to suit your aristocratic *joie de la vie.*"

John Henry had to laugh at the man's imaginative enterprise.

"All right, Mr. Kahn, you win. Tell me your price and I'll tell you it's too much. Then we can duel it out all night until one of us goes home with a frock coat. But I'm not buyin' that gold cane, so you can save your breath."

"No, no, of course not," Emmanuel Kahn replied. "It is far too expensive for you, being newly into business yourself. I wouldn't dream of taking your money for something so frivolous, so *modèle élève.* The cane is entirely forgotten."

He might not look like the Jews that John Henry had seen in Philadelphia, but Emmanuel Kahn knew how to haggle a sale.

The Jews had first arrived in Dallas twenty years before the railroads came, fleeing from revolutions in their European homelands, then planting their cemetery on the rolling prairie sod and gathering together in Congregation Emanu-El. They had hopes of building a Temple and bringing in a rabbi for regular services as their numbers grew, though they already had a bigger community than the Catholics whose scattering of Irish families were served by a traveling priest from the parish of St. Paul in Collin

County, forty miles away. But as a Southern city, Dallas had more Protestants than any other denomination, with Disciples of Christ and Baptists and Cumberland Presbyterians and the four-hundred members of the Methodist congregation the most numerous of all.

John Henry had told Dr. Seegar that he was raised a Methodist-Episcopalian, so that was the sect with which he chose to affiliate himself. But it wasn't just for Dr. Seegar's sake that he was trying to make a show of being a churchgoing man. It was for his own sake and salvation, as well, being haunted still by the horror of what had driven him from Georgia. He would never forget the face of the faceless boy and the blood on the Withlacoochee River, but he hoped that by attending to his worship, God might be willing, someday, to forget and forgive.

So he took his place on the log pews of the one-room chapel of the First Methodist Church, and offered his devotions along with the rest of the congregation. The minister preached the grace of God from a pulpit at one end of the cramped building, the pump organ played at the other, and between them the worshippers sang hymns and knelt for prayers. The Methodists had always been great hymn singers, likely one of the reasons John Henry's musical mother had favored them, and the Sunday music brought back memories of his childhood in Georgia and of the need of a sinner like himself for a redeemer:

> Rock of ages, cleft for me,
> Let me hide myself in thee!
> Let the water and the blood
> From thy wounded side which flowed,
> Be of sin the double cure,
> Save from wrath and make me pure!

According to one Sunday's sermon, the number of sins a man might commit in his life could run to over two million possible digressions, surely more than any mortal being could atone for and numerical proof of the need for divine intervention. But John Henry had only committed a handful of sins, not counting his youthful follies, so surely God's grace would be sufficient to cover his few real failings—including a murder he hadn't meant to commit. And with that hope, he joined in reciting the Lord's Prayer and sang the hymns with all the gusto of the good Christian he knew he should be. Texas was his new beginning, after all.

In October, the North Texas Agricultural, Mechanical & Blood Stock Association Fair opened in a pretty grove of hardwood trees out past the tracks of the Texas & Pacific and the Houston & Central railways. Though the event was promoted as the "First Great State Fair of Texas," and promised to bring a boom of business second only to the coming of the railroads, it looked more like a circus than business to John Henry. There was a livestock ring at the center of the fairgrounds and a circle of red-striped tents around that, and with the First Texas Artillery Corps firing off their big guns every time a prize was announced, and prize competitions in fifty categories, the air thundered with salutes all day long.

At Dr. Seegar's suggestion, John Henry had entered some of his dental school projects in the Scientific Exhibitions as advertising for their new partnership. A frontier town like Dallas rarely saw such fine work, so he easily won three blue ribbons and a cash prize of $15 for his display: a set of teeth in cast gold, a set of teeth in porcelain, and a denture made of carved ivory and vulcanized rubber. And along with the ribbons and the money, he won his own noisy cannon salute and the admiration of a pretty young girl.

"Hello Dr. Holliday!" she called as she appeared, breathless and beaming, out of the crowd on the midway at the end of the awards ceremony.

"Why, Lenora Seegar," John Henry said, smiling down at Dr. Seegar's daughter, "I didn't expect to see you here today. Where's your folks?"

"Mother's over there," she said, pointing toward the Home Crafts tent. "We've entered some of our baked goods in the contest. Mother thinks my cobbler may take first prize. I made your favorite," she added with a shy flutter of lashes, "least the one you always say you like so well when you come for Sunday supper."

John Henry had stayed with the Seegars his first few days after arriving in Dallas before taking a boarding house room, and he still had supper there once a week, much to the delight of Lenora. She was thirteen-years old and too naïve to know how to hide her adolescent infatuation for her father's young dental partner. But John Henry didn't mind the attention, considering it an innocent form of flattery, and he always tried to treat her kindly.

"Well, I bet you do take first place. You're the best cook I know in Dallas."

She blushed at the compliment, and John Henry realized that she looked different somehow.

"What is it you've done to yourself, Lenora? You look all grown up today."

"It must be my hair," she said, putting her hand to the ringlets at the back of her head. "Mother let me wear it up for the fair. Do you like it?"

"Very much. Shows off those pretty eyes of yours."

"Oh!" she said, and John Henry had to hold back a laugh. She was no older than he'd been when he first knew he loved Mattie, and the feeling had been so overwhelming he could hardly contain it. The carnival barker must have seen that same look on Lenora's face, for he called out:

"Win your sweetheart a prize, Sir? Lasso yourself one of these pretty celluloid dolls and it's yours. Just toss this wooden hoop and ring a doll. It's so simple, a child could do it."

"And how much to buy a hoop?"

"A nickel, Sir, just a nickel and the prize is yours."

"Would you like me to win you a doll, Lenora?" John Henry asked, reaching for the change. "You pick the one you want and it's yours."

"Oh, no," she said, biting her lip, "I couldn't . . ."

"Why not? It'll be a souvenir, somethin' to remember the fair by."

"But isn't tossin' the ring a game of chance?"

"I reckon so."

"Then father would never approve. He says all games of chance are gamblin', and gamblin' is a sin . . ."

"A sin? Throwin' a nickel hoop around a little doll? I don't believe it!"

"Oh, yes, he's very firm about all forms of gamblin'. He says that little games of chance just lead to all kinds of other things, terrible things like card playin' and horse racin', and . . ."

"And drinkin'?"

"And drinkin'," Lenora answered meekly. "Mother was a preacher's daughter, you know, and Father promised him to always keep the Lord's word about such things."

"Well, I consider gamblin' a gentleman's sport, and I happen to be very good at it." Then he put the nickel in the barker's hand and took the wooden hoop, giving it a light toss and watching with satisfaction as it settled down easily onto the prettiest of the painted dolls. "In addition to being a good dentist, I am also a fine aim. Now, do you want the prize or shall I find another girl to give it to?"

He spoke sharply, though he wasn't really angry at Lenora—it wasn't her fault that Dr. Seegar had ridiculous views on gaming. But he hated to be criticized in public, and the doll was suddenly more than just a prize to him.

"Well," he said, pressing the point, "do you want it or not?"

Lenora looked like she might start to cry, torn between her Father's dictates and the power of her adolescent infatuation. But love got the better of her, and when John Henry held the doll out to her, she took it.

"Thank you," she said softly.

For a moment, John Henry felt almost ashamed of himself for forcing Lenora to take the prize. It didn't really mean all that much to him, anyhow, and it might bring trouble for her.

"What's that ring you always wear?" Lenora asked, interrupting his uncomfortable thoughts. "The one you're always playing with? It's so small, it hardly fits you. Did you have it as a child?"

He held out his hand and the gold Irish Claddagh ring caught the light. He still wasn't used to the feel of it on his little finger or the way it stuck halfway past his knuckle, and he did catch himself twisting at it from time to time.

"It was a goin' away gift from my cousin," he said, remembering how Mattie had given it to him on their last day together. *Two hands for friendship and a heart for love*, she had said, describing the ancient symbols on her grandmother's heirloom ring that would be a kind of promise between them. "I have never taken it off since."

"Then you must be very fond of her. Is she—beautiful?" Lenora asked, and John Henry looked at her quizzically.

"How did you know it came from a woman?"

"Well, it's too tiny to be a man's ring, and—there was somethin' in your face, I guess."

Woman's intuition, John Henry thought with amazement. Even though she was mostly a child still, Lenora seemed to have that same kind of insight that Mattie had always had, seeing into his heart somehow and knowing what he was feeling.

"She is beautiful to me," he answered. "I miss her very much." And fighting back the lonely memory, he took Lenora's hand in his. "Come on, I've got to get you back to your mother. She must be worried about you by now."

Lenora went willingly, her little hand soft in his, the doll held close against her. And for a few wistful moments, John Henry thought that if only Lenora were just a few years older they might be able to share company long enough for him to forget about Mattie for awhile.

But he didn't want to forget Mattie, not ever. The memory of her still shone as bright in his heart as that gold Claddagh ring, and he intended to be faithful to it.

While he couldn't fault Dr. Seegar for having conservative views on drinking, he didn't think it fair that he should have to keep himself to such puritanical ways in regards to gambling. He'd been raised playing cards and considered gaming a proper gentleman's pastime. Back in Atlanta, the biggest saloon and gambling house in the city had been owned by the Mayor, and the best men of Southern society spent their evenings there, discussing politics and the War they should have won. So with little else to fill his after-work hours in Dallas, a friendly game seemed a welcome and suitable entertainment for a Southern gentleman like himself.

The city of Dallas didn't agree with his opinion, however, having made gaming in a house of spirituous liquors a legal offense. A man could drink until he was senseless and gamble until he was flat broke, but he couldn't do both in the same establishment without fear of being arrested—a ridiculous statute which most of the Main Street saloons got around by having one room for drinking and another room for gaming.

But as the saloon patrons tended to drift from one room to another carrying drinks and poker chips along with them, the drinking and the gambling generally ran together and kept the local police busy and the police coffers full.

There were other places where a man could play a few cards and have a few drinks without fear of being found out, as long as he didn't mind lowering himself some. Down on the muddy banks of the Trinity was Frogtown, filled with brothel shacks and shanties, and south of the railroad tracks was the Negro tent city called Freedman's Town where even the law didn't bother to go. But John Henry was only looking for a little distraction, not a whole different kind of life, and he couldn't imagine himself in such surroundings.

So he kept his card playing to hands of solitaire or the occasional penny-ante poker game against the other residents of his boarding house, and spent his evenings writing letters to Mattie, telling her about his sailing voyage on the Gulf of Mexico, the crushed Oyster shell streets of Galveston Island, the sad circumstances of his Uncle Jonathan McKey's cotton plantation, and his decision to settle in Dallas and go into partnership with Dr. Seegar. He told her about the Fair and his blue-ribbon winning display of dental work, his regular Sunday attendance at the First Methodist Church, and his occasional visits to the Dallas Temperance Union—not that she'd believe he'd turned temperance himself, but knowing that he was a man of the community would make her happy. He told her what a fine Southern town Dallas was, how there was a public outrage when a girlie show opened at the Variety Theater, and how the local fire brigade, good family men all, stood aside while the citizens of Dallas set fire to the place and joined in cheering as the theater burned to the ground. He even wrote to her about Belle Swink and the herds of pigs and cattle that crowded the dirt streets. But the one thing he didn't tell her, could never tell her, was the real reason he had left home and couldn't come back.

Her own letters came regularly, nearly every week, though he walked to the post office at the Depot almost daily in case she'd sent something extra. He'd gotten to be such a regular visitor there, in fact, that he was on a first name basis with the postmaster and several of the railroad employees, and they liked to fool with him, telling him there was nothing for him when there really was. Then they'd pull out his anticipated letter and laugh at how he'd tuck it quickly into his coat pocket, waiting until he was alone to read it. He wasn't about to share his love letters with railroad men, for to him, they were love letters, though Mattie said little that was romantic. It was the fact that she kept writing so regularly and the things she wrote about that proved her affection. In every letter she mentioned something they had done together in days past, reminding him of the special friendship they had shared. Then she'd go on about what was happening in Atlanta, chatting away as though he were there in the room with her and could hear her every word. And every letter would end with the same gentle question: would he be coming home again soon? Would he be back in time for Christmas? Oh, how she would love to have his company for this Christmas, especially. . .

One year it would be, come Christmas, since Mattie's father had died, taking ill with pneumonia in the middle of the coldest Georgia winter in memory. One year since John Henry had made a daring ride on icy roads, racing from Jonesboro to Atlanta to fetch the Catholic priest to give Uncle Rob his last rites. One year since he'd saved a man from Purgatory, only to find himself cast out of paradise and fighting perdition.

Of course, he couldn't go home, though there was nothing he would like better, and his own Christmas would be spent with the Seegars at their new brick house on Ross Avenue. He was grateful for the invitation as he had nowhere else to go for the holiday, though he suspected it was mostly Lenora's idea. And when the day arrived and he found his favorite peach cobbler for dessert along with the traditional pumpkin pie, he made a point of thanking Lenora for her thoughtfulness and she smiled and blushed and said he was most truly welcomed. But though he did, indeed, feel welcome in the Seegars home, being there for Christmas only made him remember the things he was missing: his own home and his own family, his country, his kin. And Mattie, always Mattie.

By the time the Christmas meal was done and the Christmas carols had been sung, John Henry was ready to be away from the Seegars' fine new house that was filled with the old memories he'd carried in with him. But as he said his goodbyes and stepped out into the early December twilight, the winter chill of the prairie wind cut right through him, catching his breath and setting him off into a sudden fit of coughing.

It was a half-mile walk back to town, and even the trolley mule Belle Swink was taking Christmas night off and wasn't around to offer him a ride, and the exercise left him wheezing, with his heart racing like it would never slow down. *Damn Texas cold!* he swore to himself. And wishing that he had more than a sip of whiskey left in the bottle tucked under his bed pillow, he stood in the dusky darkness considering. If he went back to his boarding house now, his coughing would surely disturb his landlady who was entertaining some family of her own. If he stopped into one of the nearby saloons just to buy a quick drink, someone might see him and pass the word to Dr. Seegar and cause him trouble with his employer.

Then he laughed at the thought. Who would see him in a saloon on Christmas night, anyhow? All the fine folk in Dallas were home by now, the members of the Methodist Church and even the Catholics and the Jews all safe and warm around their hearths. Only sports would be in a saloon on a night like this: gamblers, drinkers, men who didn't have families around to care about them.

Like himself.

He turned his collar to the wind and headed toward Main Street where the saloons stayed open all night long.

Only the few downtown streets of Dallas were lit by gas, with the rest of the town being so dark one had to carry a lantern to see by. But against the winter darkness, the dim lights of Main Street seemed like a blaze, and he felt cheerier already just walking under their yellow glow.

His cheer continued as he pushed open the swinging doors of the Senate Saloon and was greeted by a fragrant cloud of cigar smoke and the lively music of an upright piano. And all at once, he felt at home, with the cigar smoke and the music mixing together to bring back bittersweet memories: his father, smelling of tobacco every night after supper, his mother laying graceful hands on the piano keys. And with those memories, he was home at last for Christmas, if only for an evening in a Dallas saloon.

It was only for one night, he reminded himself, as he found an empty seat at a poker table and joined in the game. Just one night of whiskey and poker, and once it was over he'd be back again to his proper and professional self. He was a dentist, after all, with a reputation to uphold, and not really a gambler like the other men at the table that Christmas night. But they were good company, easy with the wagers and a raucous joke, and happy to make John Henry feel like part of their society. It was a pleasure playing with them, and almost made him forget that he'd been melancholy just a few hours before.

But once the evening was over and he'd walked back to his boarding house in the thin light before dawn, the melancholy came flooding back. It wasn't the start of a whiskey hangover coming on, though he would surely have one of those in the morning. It was something more powerful than liquor that he was lacking: it was the comfort and the camaraderie of the saloon, the elation of putting down wagers and picking up winnings. It was the games that he needed to keep his loneliness at bay, and he had to find a way to keep playing.

Chapter Three

DALLAS, 1874

EAGLE FORD WAS SIX MILES WEST OF DALLAS, ACROSS THE TRINITY River and out into the prairie where the unfinished roadbed of the Texas & Pacific Rail Line ran out. The town had one cheap hotel, two good saloons, no police to speak of, and was both close enough and far enough away for a young man who wanted to do a little gaming and not have word get back to Dallas. He could hire a horse for a pleasant Saturday ride across the Trinity and be back in time for a good night's rest before Church the next day.

But once he'd made the trip a few times, John Henry reckoned that an afternoon in Eagle Ford was hardly worth the expense and effort of getting there. If he were going to have a chance of turning a real profit at the poker table, he'd need to invest a little more time along with his money. So he started spending his Saturday evenings there as well, and as Saturday evening games led to Saturday night games, he started staying over to save himself a trip home in the dark. He was only being cautious, as the Trinity River crossing could be dangerous at night with the riff-raff of Frogtown lurking in the shadows of the railroad bridge and who knew what kind of criminals waiting to waylay a traveler. And as long as he was staying over Saturday nights, he might as well take in a Sunday morning game, too, before heading out of town, praying in his heart while his hands were busy with the paperboards. He was likely doing the Dallas First Methodist Church a favor anyhow, freeing up a seat in their crowded chapel.

He knew that he was living a duplicitous life, making a pretense of being a temperance man during the week, then spending his weekends in Eagle Ford wagering on cards. But what other choice did he have? When he was playing cards, he didn't think about how far he was from home, or how tired he often felt, or how the cough he'd picked up during two hard winters in Philadelphia was still plaguing him. The gambling made him happy and wasn't hurting anyone as far as he could see, and as long as Dr. Seegar didn't get wind of it, what was the harm? So his weekly pay from the dental office went into the games, and the money he won gambling paid his living expenses. And on the few weekends when he lost more than he made, he just wrote out a voucher with a promise to pay up before the next weekend was over—and most of the time he did.

The only trouble with his gambling excursions was that sometimes the games ran long and he got back to Dallas later than he should have, and his late arrival on Sunday nights meant a short sleep after which he'd have to brace himself with so much black coffee that his hands were shaking while he held the dental drill the next day. He generally dreaded those Monday mornings, so it was a nice distraction to see little Lenora Seegar sitting in the office the first day of the first week in March after a particularly tiring weekend in Eagle Ford. The games hadn't gone well, on account of some sports who passed themselves off as cowboys and ended up being sharps instead, and he'd come away in rather compromised circumstances. But it would all work out soon enough, once he had a chance to make some more wagers and earn back what they'd taken from him.

"Why, Lenora! How nice to see you here," he said, though instead of answering with her usual smile, Lenora hung her head and gazed down at the wood plank floor. "Have you come to help your father?" he said, wondering what could be troubling her.

"She has," Dr. Seegar said, and John Henry looked up to see the older man watching him, hands behind his back in a military stance. Like his father, John Henry thought uncomfortably, when he was about to give a lecture. And like his father, Dr. Seegar had a cold look in his eyes.

"Tell him why you're here today, Lenora," he said.

"No," she answered, her voice small as a child's. "I can't."

"You can't what?" John Henry asked. "What's all this about?"

"Tell him, Lenora. Tell him about our visitors this morning."

And when she raised her face, her little mouth trembling, John Henry had a sudden sick feeling in the pit of his stomach. "What visitors?" he asked quickly, and Lenora started to cry.

"Friends of yours," she said in a voice so soft that he could hardly be sure he was hearing her correctly. "Two men from Fort Worth. They were . . ."

Her voice trailed away, but John Henry didn't have to hear anymore.

"Gamblers," Dr. Seegar said in disgust. "Two vulgar men who claim to be friends of yours. Desperate characters, if ever I saw any, smelling of liquor and using profane language."

"They're no friends of mine!"

"Indeed. Then can you explain how they came to be holders of two notes from you promising payment of a poker debt from the profits of this dental practice?"

John Henry went suddenly weak at the knees, and when he didn't answer immediately, Dr. Seegar's voice rose in anger.

"How dare you, Dr. Holliday! I have worked for ten long years to build this business, and I have never once sullied the name of the firm with any kind of debt! And now this! Bad enough that you should obligate our business for anything without first consulting me, but to bring on a debt like this—gambling!" He spat the word out as if it were a profanity. But when he heard Lenora's little gasp and fresh run of tears, his voice softened. "And worse than all of this, you have brought the filth right into my home. My own daughter was the one to answer the door and have to suffer the language and the abuse of those two men."

"Lenora," John Henry said weakly, looking down at her. "I am so sorry, Lenora . . ."

"It's too late for apologies, Dr. Holliday. The damage has already been done. She'll never forget this, I'm afraid, though perhaps it's better if she doesn't forget it. She has gentle emotions and can be easily swayed in matters of the heart. I'm sure you've noticed that she's been taken with you ever since you arrived in Dallas."

John Henry couldn't help shooting a glance at Lenora, but she kept her eyes lowered. All he could see was the crimson blush spreading across her cheeks.

"Hopefully now she will choose more carefully where she puts her affections," Dr. Seegar went on. "Look at him, Lenora. See how gambling can ruin a man."

"I am not ruined," John Henry protested. "I'll pay back the debt."

"I don't know how you're going to do that, Dr. Holliday, being out of a job."

And for the first time, he realized what Dr. Seegar planned to do. "You're—firin' me?"

"I have no choice. You've brought disgrace on this firm. If I had it in my power, you'd never practice in this city again, but that is entirely your own affair now. Get your things and go. Our partnership is dissolved, Dr. Holliday."

"But what will I do?" he asked, stunned and bewildered.

"Go back to Georgia. Tell your uncle that he made a poor choice in recommending you. The last thing Dallas needs is another damned gambler."

It was the only time John Henry had ever heard Dr. Seegar swear, and it hit him harder than all the profanity those Fort Worth sharps had flung around. And worse than that was the look on Lenora Seegar's sweet face, heartbroken and disillusioned all at once and older by far than her thirteen years.

"What are you waiting for, Dr. Holliday?" Seegar said sternly, stepping in front of his daughter so that John Henry couldn't see her cry. "Leave now. We don't want you here anymore."

Texas was supposed to have been his new beginning, not his downfall. When he'd stepped off the sailing ship at Galveston Island, he'd thought himself on the way to a life of ease and comfort on his Uncle Jonathan McKey's big cotton plantation on the Brazos. Now he was worse off than he'd been when he first arrived, with no money and no job and even bleaker prospects than before. But there was one benefit to being fired by Dr. Seegar: he didn't have to hide his gambling anymore. As long as the Dallas police didn't catch him at it, he could play cards anytime he wanted and not have to worry what anyone thought.

Mattie would have been so very disappointed in him, had she known about his unfortunate situation, but he couldn't bring himself to tell her about it. His being fired wasn't really his own fault, anyhow. If those Fort Worth sharps had just waited the week they'd promised before coming to collect, he'd have had their money for them and everyone would have been satisfied. It was their greed that had driven them to seek out Dr. Seegar and ask for an early reckoning, and he placed the blame for his troubles squarely on them where it belonged.

The real worry was how to start up a new dental practice in the midst of the country's worst depression, for though the North Texas Fair had been intended to celebrate a new era of prosperity, it turned out to be the last hurrah before a nationwide economic panic. The railroad boom that had started after the War had finally slowed, with nearly every railroad in the country cutting back or closing down, and when the big New York investment house of Jay Cooke and Company collapsed a string of banking failures followed, bringing the worst depression the country had ever seen. Five-thousand businesses closed that year and whole towns seemed to just dry up and blow away altogether.

John Henry had no money for the expenses of opening a business and all the Dallas County Bank would offer in the way of a loan was a good deal for an empty office on the second floor of their own bank building. So he set out his kit of dental school tools, hooked a portable headrest to a slat-backed arm chair, and spent his gambling winnings ordering a foot-pedal driven Morrison Dental Engine drill. But after a whole long day of sitting in the dental office waiting for patients to arrive, he'd have only a dollar or two to show for his efforts, and that wouldn't even buy him a seat at a Frogtown poker game.

The owner of the Elm Street liquor store where he bought his whiskey had a suggestion for him, when he mentioned that work was slow and not showing signs of improving anytime soon.

"There's always work if a man's willing to go looking for it," Thomas Miers said as he refilled John Henry's silver flask. Though the whiskey was more expensive than his meager purse could allow, the liquor helped to soften his worries and calm the cough that was still troubling him. Dallas was a dusty town when it wasn't muddy from rain.

"I can't exactly go lookin' for toothaches," John Henry replied. "And toothaches don't generally make much money, anyhow. It's crowns and such that bring in the profit. But seems like nobody's got any money for fancy dental work, these days."

"I'm not talking about dentistry," Miers said, leaning across the counter like a friendly bartender. "I'm talking about butchering, which is near the same thing according to some folks. The slaughterhouse up in Denison is hiring, paying good money and not much experience needed. The manager is one of my customers, if you'd like me to put in a good word for you."

"I am not a butcher!" John Henry said, affronted. "I am a professional man, trained in Philadelphia!"

"Not much use in having a profession no one's paying for," Miers said with a shrug. "Or time to change careers, maybe. That's what I did, leaving my calling behind to be a liquor dealer. I set out to be a preacher, but alcohol pays better than God does in times like these. What a man begrudges the collection plate, he's more than happy to pay for a bottle of whiskey."

"So why is Denison in such need of butchers when everyone else is layin' off?" John Henry asked, though he still wasn't inclined toward slaughterhouse work.

"It's the Refrigerated Car Company that's behind it, the way of the future, that's what. You see all these cattle herds coming through town? Ever wonder where they're going?"

"To market, I reckon," John Henry replied, "by way of the railroad."

"That's right. But it's a pricey enterprise paying the cowboys for the drive and the railroad for the rest of the trip. So the Refrigerated Car Company came up with a plan: slaughter the cattle before they're transported and pack the meat on ice to ship east. Built special cars even to keep the ice cool. More expensive than your usual cattle cars, but they can pack a hell of a lot more beef than if the beeves were still on the hoof, and without any dying along the way. First refrigerated cars went out last year and more planned for this year. Which is why they're hiring men for the slaughterhouse. Like I said, sometimes you got to change professions if you want to make a living."

John Henry shrugged. "I reckon as long as I can pay to keep this flask filled, I'm not interested in a change of careers." He was sure he'd never lower himself to butchering cattle for a living, no matter how empty his flask ran.

There were other ways to make money in a cowtown, like joining a Keno tournament, a game so embarrassingly easy to play that it could hardly be called gambling, except that wagering was the whole reason for it. The house kept an empty water barrel filled with numbered billiard balls, and the gamblers wagered on which balls would be pulled at random from the barrel. There wasn't any strategy to it at all, no calculating the odds or remembering the cards like there was in Faro or poker. A gambler just had to pick a lucky four to ten numbers each round to win whatever was in the pot, and the only thing that increased his chances of winning was betting on more numbers.

John Henry couldn't afford to place more than a few wagers, but he also couldn't afford not to make a bet. Silly as the game seemed, there was a big pot to be won—enough to pay the rent to his landlady and the Dallas County Bank both. He was a month behind at the boarding house and about to go into arrears to the bank, as well, which would mean losing his home and his dental office all at once, and he didn't relish the idea of being on the streets. All he needed was a little luck to turn things around.

But luck was avoiding him that night as it had been ever since he'd arrived in Texas. He had only just placed his opening bet, taking a numbered card to represent his wager, when a voice rang out from the doorway of the saloon.

"Hands up! This saloon is now closed, and all of y'all are under arrest!"

Of course, the police would arrive just as the bets went down, giving the Dallas police department a quick profit for their night's work. But it was one lawman against a whole saloon full of sporting men, and his order was answered by a round of laughter until the officer fired off his pistol, flaming out the gaslight hanging from the board ceiling.

"I said hands up, and put 'em high! Y'all know the law: No gaming in a liquor saloon. Save your excuses for the Judge."

The gamblers grumbled as they made their way to the swinging doors of the saloon, but they were orderly enough. Most of them had been arrested for gaming before and knew the ropes: sign in at the County Courthouse, spend a night or two in jail until the bond hearing came up, then pay off the sheriff and go free to gamble again. The trial would come later with another fine to pay, but the courts were so overloaded with the nightly collection of charges that the date could be two months away or more—and that was plenty of time to raise the money for a fine or skip town and turn into a fugitive from the law. Most of the gamblers just paid the fine and stayed around.

But John Henry wasn't as nonchalant about being hustled off to jail like a common criminal. If the arrest had been for something serious, like the shooting of that boy on the Withlacoochee River, he could have reasoned it away as God's just punishment. But spending a night in jail for something as inconsequential as Keno was an insult to his pride. And when his night in jail turned into ten while he waited for the bond hearing to come up, he swore he'd never set foot in a Keno saloon again.

The Dallas City Jail was a bad place to spend all that time, cooped up as he was in a tiny iron-barred cell with two other prisoners. The whole jail building was less than twenty-feet square with four cells and a jailer's office. There wasn't even a washroom inside, so the prisoners had to be escorted under armed guard to the outhouse to relieve themselves, as if they would try to escape with their pants down around their legs. The only escape John Henry managed was to sleep away the days, curled up on a hard cot and dreaming that he was anywhere but where he was. But the sleep felt good and helped to ease the discomfort of suddenly going without his daily dose of whiskey. Though the jailer provided three meager meals a day, he didn't oblige his guests with alcohol, which was a real shame. Being drunk would have made being in jail a little more tolerable.

Then, after the humiliation of being locked up in jail, came the added indignity of the bond hearing at the red brick County Courthouse when his name was called out by the bailiff for all of Dallas to hear:

"Case Number Two-two-three-six, The State of Texas versus Dr. Holliday."

The whole state of Texas coming after him for a foolish little Keno game! And though he was prepared to plead guilty and have it all over with, he was having a hard time feeling like he'd done anything wrong. Where he came from gambling wasn't a crime, just a gentleman's sport. If Dallas had hopes of becoming a real city, it was going to have to lose its backwards views on gaming.

But the judge of the Criminal District Court of Dallas City saw things differently, and he evidently hoped to make an example of the young doctor who had strayed from the straight and narrow.

"A doctor, eh?" the judge said, peering down from the bench like a preacher staring down from a pulpit. "You don't look like much of a medical man to me."

John Henry shifted uncomfortably in his rumpled suit and stained white shirt. He knew he didn't look as professional as he should, but how could he? There'd been no bathtub in the jailhouse, just a bowl of water and a razor offered to him that morning for a hasty shave. Although his mustache was neat and his face was smooth of the blonde beard that had been growing there for a week, he was still unbathed and wearing the same suit of clothes he'd slept in since his arrest.

"Well?" the judge questioned again. "Are you or are you not a medical man?"

"No Sir," he replied carefully, "I am a dentist, a graduate of the Pennsylvania College of Dental Surgery."

The judge raised silver brows. "Ah, then you are an educated man. I assume you understand what law is."

"Law, Sir?"

"Law, Doctor. The rules that govern our society and keep us from tearing each other apart like jungle creatures."

"Yessir, I believe I know what Law is."

"And do you know what the law of Dallas is in regards to gaming, Dr. Holliday?"

He took a breath and let it out slowly before answering, feeling like a rabbit headed into a trap. "Gaming in a liquor saloon is against the law, Sir."

"Very good, Dr. Holliday. Then can you tell me why an educated professional man like yourself, a man who should be one of the pillars of our new society, a man who ought to be an example to all young men, should be found breaking the law by gaming in a saloon?"

And all at once, he saw the trap for what it was. This was only a bond hearing, not a trial. There was no jury to decide his guilt or innocence, only the judge who held his freedom in hand. The wrong answer, and he could be denied bail and sent back to jail until his trial did come up—whenever that would be.

"No Sir, Your Honor, I can't think of any reason why an educated man should be found gaming in a liquor saloon."

"Well, you'll have plenty of time to think of a good reason. As I believe an educated man ought to be able to change his ways when he sees the error of them, I am setting your trial for one year from now to give you a chance to improve your habits before coming back into this courtroom. In the meantime, you'll be under bond and under my watch as well. And if I see you back in this criminal court before that time, you can put your money on this: your sentence will not be light. Bond set at $100. Have you a surety to stand for you?"

"That'd be me, Judge," a voice spoke from the spectator gallery. "Thomas M. Miers of Miers and Caldwell, Wholesale Dealers in Foreign and Domestic Liquors and Cigars, Sir. Elm Street at Poydras, Your Honor."

The judge peered at the portly storeowner, then looked back at John Henry with a sigh. "Is this the best you can do for yourself, Dr. Holliday? A liquor dealer? Have you no more reputable acquaintances to bring on your behalf?"

"No, Sir," John Henry replied heavily, "not anymore." And his own words condemned him more than any judgment the court could have given.

Chapter Four

THE TOWN ON THE ROLLING HILLS SOUTH OF THE RED RIVER WAS SO
new that most of the inhabitants still lived in tents, drawing water from
communal wells and cooking over open campfires. The only real business
was the meat packing plant alongside the tracks of the Kansas & Texas
Line Railway, and even the tracks were new, laid the year before when the
K&T had planted Denison and contracted with the American & Texas
Refrigerated Car Company to ship beef from there across the Indian
Territory to markets in the east.

The closeness of the Indian Territory, only four miles north on the
other side of the Red River, gave a thrill of danger to the place. For
although the Five Civilized Tribes of the Choctaw, Chickasaw, Seminole,
Creek, and Cherokee who occupied the land north of that part of Texas
were generally peaceful, the Southern Plains tribes farther to the west were
not. The Cheyenne and Comanche had refused to retreat to their Government ordered reservations, and the Army was fighting a war all along the
Red River to keep them contained. As the booming of Denison proved,
civilization was moving west and the savages must make way for it.

Denison looked more like adventure than civilization to John Henry,
when he arrived that summer after the embarrassment of his trouble in
Dallas. Though his arrest hadn't even made the back pages of the Dallas
Herald, somehow everybody knew about it anyway. It seemed to him
that everywhere he went folks suddenly looked at him differently. Walking down Elm Street, he saw ladies to whom he used to tip his hat now
cross to the other side of the street, pretending not to see him. Even the

supposedly charitable members of the Dallas First Methodist Church shunned him, stepping aside as he walked into church two days after his bond hearing—and him only trying to set himself straight with God. Well, God was everywhere, so his mother had told him, and he could do his repenting just as well in Denison as in Dallas.

He still had no intention of trading his dental tools for a butcher's knife, however. What brought him to Denison was the news that there were five small hotels along Main Street, three passable restaurants, and a twenty-four hour post office—and not a single dentist as of yet. So he packed up his things, left word at the Dallas County Bank that he was relocating elsewhere, and took the train north to Denison for another fresh start at being a professional man. And he was pleased to find, soon after his arrival, that the owner of the Alamo Hotel needed some dental work done and would be willing to trade a month's rent for a couple of extractions, so all he needed was a paperboard sign hung in the window to announce that J.H. Holliday, Dentist was in business again.

But he only stayed in his hotel room dental office until mid-afternoon each day before turning his sign and heading down to Skiddy Street, the shallow ravine behind Main Street where most of the saloons and gambling dens were located. For although he'd sworn off Keno, he had no intention of giving up on other games of chance. Betting money on cards and watching them come up winners still gave him a thrill that drove away all his other worries.

Denison was a dark town by night as gas hadn't yet come to that part of the country. The only illumination came from candlelight and kerosene oil, yet for John Henry, the darkness had something like a familiar feel to it. Valdosta had been dark at night, too, with no streetlights and surrounded by tall over-reaching pines that shadowed the moonlight. Even the smell of the place reminded him of Valdosta: a mix of wood smoke and outhouse and a green dampness from off the river. But where Valdosta's dark nights were silent except for the sound of katydids chirping, Denison was raucous all night long. In the open-windowed heat of August and Indian summer, families said their prayers to the sound of dance hall pianos, and children were lullabied by the God-profaning curses of gamblers. And now and then, shots rang out in the darkness as some of the boys got out of hand, and Red Hall, the town marshal and former Texas Ranger, would step in to calm things down.

It was the darkness that brought John Henry his best, if not most pleasant patient—a butcher from Dallas who'd come to work at the slaughterhouse next to the meat packing plant. His name was Charlie Austin, a small man with a big opinion of himself, and he had better things in mind than butchering. Charlie wanted to be a saloonkeeper, pouring drinks across the bar in some fine establishment—not that there were any such places in Denison. He planned on going back to Dallas once he'd made some good money at the slaughterhouse, though first he'd have to pay a chunk of his earnings to John Henry.

"Damn Injuns!" Charlie said, when found his way to the dental chair after being assaulted outside one of Denison's groggeries. He'd need several new teeth to replace the ones he'd lost and make himself presentable again; pricey work that the only dentist in town was happy to oblige.

"What makes you think it was Indians?" John Henry asked as he inspected the result of Charlie's midnight run-in with an unseen assailant. If the butcher had been passable-looking before the attack, he wasn't anymore with his torn and swollen lip and toothless grimace. "Did you hear any whoopin' or hollerin'?"

"Didn't hear nothin' once I got hit on the head," Charlie said, whistling through the bloodied space in his mouth. "Who else would slip up so quiet and slip off without nobody seein'? Comanche braves, mor'n likely, scoutin' the town. And likely back across the river by now. Colbert's too damn easy with who he lets on his ferry boat."

John Henry knew the man Charlie was talking about, as he'd taken Ben Franklin Colbert's ferry across the river himself just to say he'd been in the Indian Territory, though there was nothing much to see but more empty land and switch grass and the flat waters of the Red River. The Indians weren't allowed off their reservation and generally kept themselves to their own towns out of sight. But white men could enter to trade or cross over to Kansas or Missouri, and for them, Colbert kept a general store on the south side of the river near the ferry landing. He called his place the "First and Last Chance": first chance to buy a drink coming down from the Territory and last chance to buy a drink before crossing into the Territory, as it was against the law to sell alcohol to the Indians. But the Indians got the liquor somehow, just the same.

"But the wild Indians aren't even on this part of the river," John Henry said reasonably. "It's Choctaw near here. The Comanche and Cheyenne are up in the Panhandle fightin' the Army. I doubt they'd bother comin' this far. What've we got here that Indians would want?"

"Beef, I'd say," Charlie Austin replied with a grunt. "They're starvin' half the time, now they've lost their buffalo huntin' grounds. Let 'em starve, damned red heathens, knockin' me on the head!"

Which brought John Henry back to the real question at hand:

"So what did these mystery assailants take from you, other than your good looks? You didn't happen to have any beef on you, I reckon."

"Just my poker winnin's, damn 'em," Charlie said, wiping a drool of bloody spittle from his mouth. "Money I was gonna use to buy me a whore for the night. Ought to pay Colbert to take me over to the Indian Territory so's I can use a squaw instead. Teach 'em all a lesson."

Though John Henry shared some of Charlie Austin's distrust of the Indians, he didn't think raping their women would solve anything. That kind of lesson might just bring on the Indian attacks Charlie was already imagining and overwhelm Denison's little police force of Marshal Hall and his three deputies. The police were mostly for show, not staving off Indians, dressed as they were in their brass-buttoned blue uniforms and wide Panama hats, and spending their time breaking up saloon fights or collecting the $5 per week license fees from the brothels.

"So can you fix me up?" Charlie asked, as John Henry finished the exam and wiped his soiled hands on a waiting piece of toweling. "Can't be 'Champagne Charlie Austin' lookin' like this. That's the name I'm plannin' to use in Dallas once I get myself a saloon job there: 'Champagne Charlie,' just like the vaudeville song. Suits me, don't you think?"

He could fix Charlie's teeth for a price, but it would take more than fancy dentistry to turn Charlie Austin into anything finer than corn liquor.

He wrote to Mattie, of course, telling her that he had moved his practice to booming Denison, though he didn't mention the embarrassing circumstances of his leaving Dallas. Mattie would be distressed to know that he'd been arrested, even for something as inconsequential as betting money on a gambling game. So it was good to have a patient like Charlie Austin who needed several visits and some careful dentistry to straighten out the mess of his teeth, and giving John Henry something interesting to say in regards to his professional life. Since being fired by Dr. Seegar and not finding much work on his own in Dallas, his letters of the past months had been mostly travelogue, avoiding the subject of how he spent his days. But although he chose to keep some parts of his life from her, he still found that he could talk to Mattie more easily than he'd ever been able to talk to anyone else, and for the hour or so that he spent writing each letter, recounting the colorful atmosphere of the Texas frontier and the fine work he was doing in Denison, he didn't feel so very far away from her.

It was one thing doing expensive dentistry, however, and another thing entirely getting paid for his efforts, as he discovered too late. For once Charlie Austin had teeth in his mouth again, he suddenly forgot that he still owed money to his dentist—John Henry's fault, partly, for allowing Charlie to pay for the work in installments as he collected his own pay from the slaughterhouse. And though John Henry didn't want to go collecting the money at gunpoint like some swindled gambler, he didn't want to give his services away for free, either. But before he could call on Marshal Hall for assistance with the matter, Charlie Austin was gone, taking his new teeth and leaving John Henry unpaid and unsatisfied.

Charlie's skipping town was just the start of the trouble, for as the sultry Texas summer cooled at last into fall, the noise of Denison disappeared, silenced by the same depression that had sucked the life out of the rest of the country. The American & Texas Refrigerated Car Company, whose eight-acre meat packing plant beside the railroad tracks had been Denison's major industry, lost its financial investors and went bankrupt. There would be no more big cattle drives into Denison, no thousands of head of livestock loaded onto the railcars or thousands of pounds of slaughtered Texas beef shipped out on the Kansas & Texas line. And without the cattle business, there was little to keep Denison alive, and it quickly turned from the last boomtown of Texas to yet another victim of the Panic of 1873.

The personality of the place changed almost overnight as the thousands of single young men who had come to work on the railroad or at the slaughterhouse drifted off to greener pastures. By Christmas, the only folks remaining in town were the homesteaders and the depot workers, as well as a few sporting men and bawdy house girls, though most of the bawdy houses had closed down, too. And maybe because of the sudden quiet, or because of the sudden lack of whorehouse license fees, even Marshal Red Hall packed his bags and left Denison behind. The fact that even the law wasn't interested in Denison anymore only proved the point that the town was drying up.

There was no reason to stay in a town that couldn't support a dentist. So by New Year's Eve, John Henry was back in Dallas in time to watch the fireworks over the Trinity River and the First Texas Artillery shooting off cannonades from the fairgrounds, the festivities seeming more a celebration of the old year ending than of the new one just coming in, considering how bad 1874 had been for most folks. And seeing the old year go, John Henry had hopes that his own hard times of the past few years were finally behind him.

It was a sign of good luck and better times to come when he started the new year by opening the *Dallas Herald* and finding Charlie Austin, as the advertisement for the saloon at the new St. Charles Hotel read: *Champagne Charlie is a rollicking fellow who fixes up the smiles and hands them out smilingly.* What the advertisement didn't mention was that it was John Henry who'd put Champagne Charlie's smile back together again and who was still owed more than he'd been paid.

The saloon took up the entire first floor of the St. Charles Hotel, and it was already crowded with cowboys and farmers up from Cleburne and Tyler and Waxahachie when John Henry stepped in out of the January cold still coughing from the smoke of the train trip and a little foggy from his New Year's Eve drinking of the night before, but looking forward to collecting on that Denison debt. If he were to try his hand at dentistry in Dallas again, he'd need some money to get himself set up in business, and Charlie's payment would help.

But Charlie Austin didn't look like he was in the mood for discussing finances as he muttered to himself and poured the drinks.

"Cowhands are one thing," Charlie was saying to one of the saloon girls as John Henry approached him through the crowd. "They've been around some at least. But these farmers, they don't even know how to handle the liquor. Serve 'em and souse 'em, that's all I do, then call the bouncer to throw 'em out if they don't puke on the floor first, which I have to clean up."

"Howdy, Charlie," John Henry said affably. "I see you found your true callin'."

Charlie looked up at him with surprise, then narrowed his eyes. "What are you doin' in Dallas?"

"Same as everybody else, I reckon, enjoyin' the festivities. Thought I'd stop by and have a visit with my old friend from Denison. At least, I thought we were friends. You didn't even bother sayin' goodbye when you left town."

"I got a job offer," Charlie said gruffly. "Didn't see as that was any of your business."

"I disagree, since it was your job offer that hurt my business. You owe me some money, Charlie, and I mean to collect."

"Go to hell," Charlie said.

"I well may, someday," John Henry replied, "but there's no cause for angry words just now. I only want what's rightfully mine. And considering it's partly my work that got you this job, I'm probably entitled to more than what you owe. But I'm willin' to settle for what's on your tab."

"Well, I haven't got it. The slaughterhouse closed up before makin' the last payroll on account of the Refrigerated Car Company goin' bankrupt and not payin' them. So take a number and you can get your money when I get mine."

"I won't be dissuaded, Charlie," John Henry said, standing his ground. "It's the principle of the thing . . ."

But Charlie Austin had a laugh at that, showing off his new teeth and saying to the crowd of rowdies around him: "Did you hear that, boys?

This man's got principles!" Then he pulled something from beneath his apron and said: "Well, I've got a pistol. Let's see who wins."

He should have left the saloon then and come back later when things were quieter. He should have left and never come back at all. But there was something infuriating about being laughed at like that, at gunpoint and in front of a whole saloon, and him only trying to make things right. And with that righteous indignation rising in him, John Henry pulled the Colt's Navy revolver from his own pocket and leveled it at Charlie Austin.

"Pay me for my work or lose it," he said, taking aim at Charlie's fading smile.

"What the hell are you doin'?" Charlie asked in surprise. "Customers aren't allowed firearms in the saloon, you know that!"

"I'm not a customer. I'm a debt collector. Or the angel of death, maybe. You choose."

He cocked the hammer of his revolver and the pistol in Charlie's hand wavered.

"You plannin' to kill me over a dentist bill?" Charlie asked, incredulous.

"Not yet," John Henry replied. Then he took aim at Charlie's hand and fired a shot that sent the bartender's pistol flying and discharging into the board ceiling.

Charlie screamed, the saloon girls screamed, then a gruff voice commanded:

"Drop it! You boys are both under arrest."

Of course, there were police patrolling the saloons on the day after New Year's Eve. The police were always around when they weren't wanted.

"Me?" Charlie cried as the deputy stepped forward to take them both into custody. "Why me? He's the one did the shootin'. He could have killed me!"

"I could have, if I'd wanted to," John Henry said under his breath, as he grudgingly turned his pistol over to the officer. "But you're not worth repentin' over, Charlie. And you're sure as hell not worth goin' to jail for."

As for getting paid for his work, that was probably never going to happen.

The Dallas City Jail had been uncomfortable lodgings when he'd spent a long spring week there the year before. But with the bitter winter wind of a Blue Norther blowing in through the unplastered chinks in the log walls, it was dangerous as well. A man could catch his death of chill there, even if he'd had strong lungs before he started. But John Henry had already been through two winters of pneumonia and taken a glancing blow from the Yellow Fever, and his health wasn't up to spending any more time in jail.

So it was with surprise and relief that he learned he had a visitor the morning after his arrest. He'd been hoping that Thomas Miers, the friendly liquor dealer, would hear of his predicament and come to bail him out again. It wasn't Miers who came to help him that January afternoon, however, but Dr. John Seegar.

"You would have done well to have taken my advice and left Dallas permanently, Dr. Holliday," Seegar said, and John Henry was too amazed at the sight of him to disagree. After that unfortunate incident with the Fort Worth gamblers, he'd never expected Dr. Seegar to speak to him again, let alone come to see him in jail.

"I don't know how to thank you, Sir," he said, reaching his hand through the cell bars to Dr. Seegar, but the older man just glared at him.

"Don't bother thankin' me. I'm not here to pay your bail. As far as I'm concerned, you can rot in this jail cell until your trial comes up. I'm just here to make sure that when you are tried, you get acquitted. That's why I've hired you a lawyer, one of the best in Dallas. Name's J.M. McCoy, a personal friend of mine."

John Henry caught his breath. Having Seegar put up money for bail would have been one thing. Having him pay to hire a lawyer was a gesture he couldn't comprehend.

"But I don't understand, Sir. Why would you do such a thing for me?"

"It's not for you, Dr. Holliday. I wouldn't waste a penny on your behalf. I'm doin' this for my own reputation. Because if you are convicted, everyone will have somethin' to say about my choice of professional partners, and I haven't worked all these years to build a practice just to have your criminal behavior destroy it. Well? Aren't you even interested in knowin' how I found out about your incarceration?"

"I reckon someone told you . . ." John Henry said with a shrug.

"Someone told all of Dallas," Seegar replied sharply. Then he snapped open the newspaper he'd carried with him, holding it up to the bars for John Henry to see. "It's all right here on the front page of the *Dallas Herald*," and he read the awful news aloud:

Dr. Holliday and Mr. Austin, a saloon-keeper, relieved the monotony of the noise of fire-crackers by taking a couple of shots at each other yesterday afternoon. The cheerful note of the peaceful six-shooter is heard once more among us. Both shooters were arrested.

"So much for your reputation, Dr. Holliday," Seegar went on, sliding the newspaper through the bars to John Henry. "You have managed to make a fool of yourself, and that is a real shame. Because you are a fine dentist, the best clinician I ever saw. But you are also one sorry excuse for a man."

"But you don't understand," John Henry said. "I was just collectin' on a debt. Charlie was my patient, up in Denison . . ."

"I don't want to hear your excuses, Dr. Holliday. I just want you to get out of town before you cause me any more embarrassment or my daughter any more heartache."

"Your daughter?" John Henry asked, looking up from the paper. "What's Lenora got to do with this?"

"Nothin'," Dr. Seegar replied heavily. "Or rather, she should have nothin' to do with this. But for some reason, she still thinks you hung the moon, and learnin' of your arrest will break her heart. But I don't guess you'd understand about that, bein' so heartless yourself. My lawyer will be by to see you in the mornin'."

But he wasn't heartless as Dr. Seegar had said. For if he were, his heart wouldn't be paining him the way it was now, knowing he'd hurt little Lenora again.

John Milton McCoy, Dr. Seegar's lawyer, had come to Dallas from Indiana just two years before as a grief-stricken young widower looking for a fresh start. But his mourning was short-lived when a friendly correspondence with his late wife's best friend blossomed into love, and John Milton found himself a married man again. And though he vowed to his new bride that he would use his legal profession to help civilize the plains of Texas, the economic depression had forced him to compromise his vow a little. With money short and collections slow in coming in, he was obliged to take whatever cases offered themselves—even that of a drunken dentist who had taken a couple of wing shots at a local barkeep named Austin.

But if J.M. McCoy had qualms about taking on his case, John Henry had more doubts about Lawyer McCoy. Though he was a genial enough man, rosy-cheeked and round about the middle, McCoy hadn't had much experience in the trial setting. He practiced real estate law, trusts and guardianships and such, and John Henry was going to need a good criminal lawyer to get him acquitted of the charges made against him— Assault with Intent to Commit Murder.

It was all nonsense, of course. If he'd meant to kill Charlie Austin, he could have done it easily enough. He'd only meant to knock the gun from Charlie's hand and put a scare into him, and he'd succeeded on both counts. But knowing he was innocent of the charge didn't ease his mind any. As his uncle William McKey had told him once, there was a difference between what a man could prove and what he got accused of, and oft times the accusation was all it took to ruin a man's good name. Though if the jury decided John Henry was guilty as accused, he'd have more than just his good name to worry about. The penalty for attempted murder in the state of Texas was two to twenty years in the State Prison—a prospect that left him downright scared.

So while Lawyer McCoy put together the case, interviewing witnesses and visiting the shooting scene, John Henry spent two sleepless weeks in the drafty Dallas City Jail waiting to see what would come of it. And by the time his trial came up on the frosty morning of January 28th, he was worn out from worry and lack of sleep, and coughing from the cold so hard that he kept interrupting the judge during the proceedings. But that was the one bright light of the entire affair: Lawyer McCoy had managed to get his case before a new judge in town, one who hadn't heard of John Henry's earlier arrest and arraignment, so at least that much hadn't gone against him.

For all John Milton McCoy's corpulent geniality, however, he turned out to be a formidable attorney. He knew the law and knew how to explain it to a jury, and when the panel of twelve men returned from their sequestered room, they brought a happy verdict with them: In the case of The State of Texas vs J.H. Holliday, the defendant was found not guilty.

It was the best news he'd heard since coming to Texas.

He still had his dental equipment, which he'd used in Dallas and then taken on the train to Denison and back, so he set up again in a cheap rented room and hung out his sign, hoping to draw business. But he still had the cough that had come on him in jail, as well, and a weariness that wouldn't let go. Most days, he was too tired to do more than a few hours of work, and some days he didn't bother opening his door at all, staying in bed to sleep off the lingering effects of what was surely another close brush with pneumonia. Come spring, he told himself, he'd be feeling better, once the winter chill had lifted and the days started to warm again. Come spring, he'd be back on his feet and busy at his practice again.

But when March came with balmy days and April followed with signs of an early summer, his weariness remained and his work continued to suffer. He was making enough for living expenses and not much more, and the last thing he wanted to spend money on was a visit to the doctor for something as inconsequential as a cough and a little tiredness, until one morning when he woke with a tearing pain in his chest and a strangling gasping for breath and felt something like vomit rising up in his throat. But as bent over the china bowl on his washstand he saw that it wasn't vomit, but blood coming up, bright red and foamy and filled with pus.

"Oh God!" he whispered hoarsely, with hardly enough breath to say the words, "don't let me be sick, please don't let me be sick!"

Then he started coughing and vomiting again, until he couldn't talk, or pray, or even think anymore.

The doctor sat behind a dark oak desk in his medical office, staring down at the papers in front of him and saying nothing at all. Behind him, a tall apothecary case was filled with medicine bottles, amber and blue glass reflecting the golden afternoon light that filled the little room. He took a deep breath, then looked up at John Henry who sat across the desk from him.

"When did these symptoms first start?" he asked.

"A few years back, in Georgia. I had a little spell then and another one when I first got to Texas. But nothin' like this . . ."

"And when did the bleeding start again?"

"Mornin' before last. I woke up feelin' sick, coughin' up blood."

The doctor pushed his chair back and stood slowly, turning to face the apothecary case.

"There's a few medications we could try, of course," he said, more to himself than to John Henry, "remedies that have some claim to usefulness. Most of them are just mixtures of whiskey, but they help with the pain, at least. And there are some medical men who claim a dry climate can be beneficial. Colorado is becoming quite popular with victims . . ."

"But it's just the pneumonia again, isn't it? It's just the pneumonia?"

The doctor shook his head and turned back to face him. "No, Dr. Holliday. I don't believe it's pneumonia."

"Then—what?"

"Consumption," the doctor said lightly, as though the word had no weight at all, no heavy burden of death to drag it down. "Pulmonary consumption, likely the acute form. It's a—fairly common ailment of the lungs . . ."

"I know about consumption," John Henry said quickly. "My mother died of it. But she was always weak, especially after the War. Surely, you're mistaken . . ."

But the doctor went on as though John Henry had not spoken at all.

"We are still unclear about the mode of transmission, but the symptoms are quite well known. There is lack of appetite, loss of weight at first . . ."

"I've always been thin," he objected.

"Then there's the quickened pulse, the tiredness you've described, the night sweats. Then the coughing starts, just in the morning at first, but getting worse with time until the patient starts to bring up blood from the lungs."

"But I've had the pneumonia . . ."

"The blood comes from cavitary lesions in the lungs, areas of infection that swell, burst, bleed, then scar over. Eventually, the entire surface of the lung is involved, scarred, leaving little viable tissue left for respiration. The patient . . ." The doctor stopped, cleared his throat, started again. "The patient—dies of asphyxiation, usually delirious at the end. There is no known cure. It is—always fatal."

"But I'm just a little sick," John Henry said. "I'm a little tired, that's all. If you can just give me somethin' to clear up this cough so I can sleep . . ."

"I wish you had come to see me sooner, Dr. Holliday, when I might have been able to do something. I wish you hadn't waited so long . . ."

The doctor's words ran out into a long silence.

"I can't be dyin'," John Henry said, as though arguing could change things. "I'm only twenty-three years old! I've just started out. I've got plans for my life . . ."

"You can still have plans. You'll have years yet ahead of you, if you take care of yourself. Consumption is a slow illness."

"A slow death, you mean?"

"We all die, son. It's how you live that counts, no matter how long you have. And if there's anything at all that I can do . . ."

"You can go to hell!" John Henry said, voice shaking as he fought against angry, anguished tears. "You can go to hell!"

His father had taught him responsibility, drilling it into him from childhood, and only because of that training did he bother showing up in court for the one legal affair he still had to attend to: his trial for the year-old Keno arrest.

It was the first case heard that morning of April 13th, and he didn't even go to the expense of hiring Lawyer McCoy to represent him. He was guilty of the gambling and pled such, and took his ten-dollar fine without making a comment—though the Dallas County Sheriff had a word of caution for him as he received the payment for the fine and court costs.

"You ought to have a doctor take a listen to that cough," the Sheriff remarked. "Sounds downright unpleasant."

John Henry didn't even reply.

The Dallas First Methodist Church held choir practice on Tuesday afternoons, the sound of the singing carrying out through the open chapel doors like an invitation, but John Henry hadn't come for the music. He was looking for a miracle, for some sign that what the doctor had told him wasn't true. His mother had taught him to believe in miracles, in signs and wonders and the mercies of God. And as he took off his hat and found a seat on a wooden pew, the words of the old hymn seemed to ring right through him:

> Depth of mercy, can there be
> Mercy still reserved for me?
> Can by God his wrath forbear
> The chief of sinners spare?

Salvation had always been waiting for him, willing to give him time—time for remorse, time to repent, time to sow his wild oats and wander a bit. Even after his greatest sin, God could be forgiving if only he sought forgiveness with a broken and contrite heart. That was the Gospel his mother had taught him and that he had always believed. That was the legacy she had left him in her testimony written down by the minister before she died: God was good, in spite of trials; God was loving, in spite of losses. God heard each heartfelt prayer and answered accordingly.

But though John Henry had repented, though he had done his best to change his life and live according to God's plan with only a few minor failings, he hadn't earned salvation, but damnation. He had killed a boy and God was punishing him for it, a life for a life. There was no mercy, only justice, and the Lord would have His vengeance.

He knew all about the consumption. He'd watched his mother die of it, the pain-wracked body and horrible bloody cough that tore her apart and wasted her away before his very eyes. His beloved mother, taken from him so young. His own life, being taken too soon. How could he have faith in such an unfaithful, vengeful God?

"Damn you!" he cursed, and the choir's director turned around and stared. "Damn you all! Damn your heaven and your hell and your pitiful, painful earth! Damn you all!"

Then, before anyone could ask him to quiet his blasphemous words, he rose and strode from the church, turning his back on the music and the mercies of God both.

There were other places where comfort came easier. Dallas was full of saloons and he would visit them all, getting so roaring drunk that he couldn't feel a thing: not pain, not despair, not the anger that was raging inside of him. Damn the whole world for giving him life at all! Tonight, he just wanted to bury himself in a bottle of whiskey and never wake up again.

And then came a faint memory of another confused and drunken night when he had stood in the dark with Mattie and recited Hamlet's soliloquy:

> ". . . To die—to sleep,
> No more; and by a sleep to say we end
> The heart-ache and the thousand natural shocks
> That flesh is heir to: 'tis a consummation
> Devoutly to be wished. To die, to sleep . . ."
> To die . . .

Everybody died sooner or later. He didn't have to wait for the consumption to torture him down to his grave when there were other, more pleasant, ways to go. How much liquor did it take for a man to drink himself to death? How long before he stopped thinking altogether?

He ordered a bottle of whiskey and poured his tumbler full.

Chapter Five

Llano Estacado, 1875

There was a sea of grass on the far western reaches of the Texas frontier. There was a sky so wide it seemed to swallow up the earth. There was a land so flat that the moon lay down to sleep at night on the far horizon. There was air so dry it could suck the breath out of a man, or give him the breath of life again.

There were parts of that year that he didn't remember at all, like how he'd gotten himself from Dallas to a frontier town a hundred miles west of the last railroad stop and how he'd ended up in bed with an ugly prostitute called Hurricane Minnie. The woman remembered more than he did, saying that she'd met him in a saloon owned by a man named Johnny Shaughnessey, who turned out to be a friendly Irishman who warned him that he didn't hold his liquor well, then poured him a whiskey and gave him the lay of the land.

Fort Griffin Flat, as Shaughnessey called the place, was the main outfitting point for the western buffalo hunts, with one wide excrement-filled main street and a tumble of shacks and saloons along a pecan-shaded bend of the Clear Fork of the Brazos River. Above the Flat, on a high bluff overlooking the river, was the military outpost of Fort Griffin, though just because there were soldiers nearby didn't mean the place was orderly. The soldiers were posted there to keep the Indians at bay and protect the buffalo trail; the town was mostly left to its own devices. So with the nearest law at Jacksboro, seventy miles away, the Flat was as wild as any town on the frontier and as good as hell for a young man who'd meant to kill himself anyhow.

He might have stayed there forever, awash in liquor and still trying to end his sorrows, if the Law hadn't come along with a new sheriff sent over from the county seat of Albany. The sheriff decided to shine up his badge by cleaning up the Flat, arresting the gamblers and the prostitutes and collecting on their jail fines, and the sorrowful young drunk from Dallas was arrested along with the rest of them. In his former life, he'd have stayed around to answer the charges and make a show of responsibility for his actions. But what did responsibility matter when a man was dying? So as soon as the jail spat him out, he skipped town, taking the stage west from Fort Griffin and not caring where he ended up.

And so he came to the Llano Estacado, the Staked Plains, the Americans called it, a thirty-thousand square mile stretch of emptiness where the Seminole and the Comanche lost themselves before the army could trail them to their camps, and even the great buffalo herds seemed to disappear into the red dust. It was downright spooky how that land of so much nothing could hide almost anything.

There was something else disappearing in the arid emptiness of the Staked Plains: the bloody cough that had sent him, terror filled, into a liquored fog of forgetfulness. The dry air was drying out his lungs, and by the time he laid over awhile at Fort Concho, then took the stage to San Antonio and the Alamo where Jim Bowie and Davy Crockett had died glorious deaths, he began to think that maybe he wasn't dying after all. He was still tired, but still alive as well—and not sure what to do about it, living a sort of shadow life and waiting to see what would happen next.

He crossed over the border at Eagle Pass, made some money pulling teeth for the Commandante at Nuevo Laredo, and practiced target shooting with the soldiers at the Mexican presidio. At night, he played Spanish Monte until he could best the Mexicans at their own game, his hands getting to be so agile with the cards that he could almost feel the markings. But it wasn't until he started swearing with the soldiers in their own language, his smattering of childhood Spanish learned from Francisco Hidalgo, his father's Mexican serving boy, turning almost to fluency, that he knew it was time to go home—or back to Dallas, at least.

It was one thing taking a leisurely wander across the Staked Plains and the border country, and another taking a hard stagecoach ride all the way from Mexico to north Texas. By the time the Butterfield Overland reached Fort Griffin on the last long stretch to Dallas, John Henry was worn out and ready for a layover before going any farther. With all the jostling over rough roads, his body was aching and his nerves were as tight-drawn as the springs of the coach, and he feared the illness was coming back on him again. So he was already in an irritable mood when he climbed out of the stage and saw a crowd of blue-coated Negro soldiers parading the streets and said as much to the driver, commenting that there were altogether too many Yankees in town for his liking.

"Leave day," the driver remarked. "They've been away chasing horse thieves and Comanches, so the commander gave 'em some time off as a reward. Guess the whores in town'll make some money tonight."

John Henry bristled at the thought, though he didn't begrudge the soldiers their amusement. After what he'd seen of the Llano Estacado, he knew that Indian service on the Staked Plains was worthy of whatever reward the Army wanted to offer. It was the color of those leave-day soldiers that rankled him. Most of the prostitutes in town were white, and the thought of those black men having the pleasure of them went against his well-trained Southern ways. It wasn't right, that kind of intermingling, no matter how eager the girls were for some federal pay. But distasteful or not, the soldiers' couplings were none of his affair. All he needed to concern himself with was getting a glass of whiskey and a place to sleep before continuing on with his journey back to Dallas.

The red-haired Irish saloonkeeper welcomed him back like an old friend, with a free drink and a cheap room for the night upstairs.

"Why the favors, Shaughnessey?" he asked, taking the whiskey, "you don't hardly know me."

"Well, lad, maybe I'm just a do-gooder at heart. But more likely it's that Claddaugh ring you've got on your little finger there. Either you're Irish yourself, or there's an Irish girl who's got your heart, and either way, you're countryman to me. Now empty that drink and I'll pour you another glass you can pay me for. You look like you could use a whole bottle full after that long ride."

The whiskey was good and quickly made him forget the pains of the road as he found his room at the top of the stairs, pulled off his boots, and slumped down onto the lumpy mattress ready for a blessed long nap. By morning, his nerves would be unwound and he'd think about a bath and a shave, but for now, only sleep. But he'd only just drifted off when he was startled back to wakefulness by a loud pounding on the bedroom door, followed by the louder sound of a man's laughter.

"Open up the door, whore, and lemme in! I'se ready and able, iffen you know what I mean."

The sudden awakening left him shaking, and he picked up one of his discarded boots and threw it at the closed door. "Wrong door!" he said angrily, then rolled over and tried to go back to sleep.

"Shanssey say this door," the man called back at him, "so you move it on out and lemme in. I only got jest so much time fo' leave, and I need's a woman."

"You've got the wrong room, boy," he said derisively, recognizing the sound of a colored voice. "But you keep knockin', and I'll give you somethin' to remember me by. My pistol's loaded and it's ready and able, too."

But his threat only got a laugh from the man on the other side of the door.

"Well, suh, I got more'n a pistol out here, more like a Sharps Fifty rifle. You ask that whore which gun she'd rather have goin' off. 'Cause I ain't never seen a white woman didn't prefer a big buffalo gun to a white boy's little derringer."

In one fast move, he lunged from the bed to the door, his pistol cocked and ready to fire. The man had not only insulted him, but all white women as well, and deserved to be taught a lesson. But as he swung the door open and took a fast aim, his pistol hand wavered.

The intruder was the biggest black man he had ever seen, filling the doorway and casting a shadow that darkened the whole hall. He looked more like a big farmhand on a Georgia plantation than a United States soldier, though he wore the blue uniform of the Tenth Cavalry. And the arrogant way the man stood there, laughing in Yankee blue, turned John Henry's angry irritation to rage. The man might be big enough to swat him down with one massive hand, but his own loaded pistol evened out the odds.

"I said this is the wrong door, boy," he repeated imperiously. "You git or get what you deserve."

But the man clearly didn't understand the seriousness of the situation, because instead of retreating as he'd been told to do, he threw back his head and let out a mocking laugh. Then foolishly, the soldier dropped his right hand down to his coat pocket going for a gun.

John Henry didn't wait to see the man's pistol. With all the speed of weeks of Mexican target-practice, he let loose with his Colt's and sent a blast of smoke and lead into the soldier's blue-coated chest.

The gunshot and the sound of the man's heavy fall to the wood plank floor brought Shaughnessey's girls rushing out of their rooms, and the Irishman bounding up the stairs close behind them.

"Dear mother of Mary!" Shaughnessey cried, crossing himself. "What's happened here?"

"Damned Nigra tried to pull his pistol on me, so I shot him!"

But Shaughnessey's words made his rage go cold. "How could he have pulled on you? Buffalo Soldiers aren't allowed to take weapons off the post. They're never armed in town. Everyone knows that." And to prove the point, he reached into the man's coat pocket, pulling out nothing more than a folded bit of paper with a number scrawled across it.

"His girl's room number," Shaughnessey remarked. "Looks like I gave him your room number by accident. Sometimes I get confused when things are busy down at the bar. Did anyone else see the shooting?" Then another of the girls came out into the hall and started to scream. "Stop that!" Shaughnessey commanded. "We don't want to make a scene here. There's just been a little accident, that's all. Now go on back in your rooms, girls, and stay there."

"What do we do?" John Henry asked, staring at the big man's body in disbelief. Had he killed an unarmed man over nothing more than irritation and mixed-up numbers?

"*We* don't do anything," Shaughnessey replied. "You're getting out of here, right now, before any of his companions finds out about this."

"But where will I go?" he asked, still standing dazed, the gun hot in his hand.

"Out of Texas! And mighty fast, too. The law here in the Flat might not pay much attention to a darky getting his in a saloon, but you can bet the military authorities will pursue the matter. Now go and get yourself together while I move the poor man's body out of the way. Once you're gone, I'll say I never saw the fellow who did it—maybe the army will even think it was one of their own men in a fit of jealousy over one of these girls."

But John Henry stood motionless in the hall, staring blankly at the soldier's body and trying to believe what he was looking at. He knew he wasn't a killer, but he'd killed his second man. He was no killer—but the body on the floor showed that he was.

"I said *go!*" Shaughnessey whispered harshly, "or there'll be hell to pay for sure!"

He couldn't go back to Dallas now, at least not until news of the soldier's shooting died down. He couldn't go much of anyplace else without having an income to support himself, and as his dental office equipment was still back in Dallas, he'd have a hard time practicing without asking for a loan to get himself setup somewhere. But where could he go? And from whom could he beg the price of a dental chair and all that went with it? The answer came to him soon enough, spurred on by his desperation. And all he needed to reach the source of that loan was a twenty-dollar train ride on the Kansas & Texas Line, cutting north across the Indian Territory and east across Missouri to where the city of St. Louis rose up in smoky splendor on the banks of the Mississippi River.

He hadn't seen Jameson Fuches in four long years, not since taking a sudden departure from St. Louis after losing a high-stakes poker game down on the Levee—and the poker game was reason enough for him to avoid St. Louis altogether now. But if the friendship they had developed in their time at the Pennsylvania College of Dental Surgery still counted for anything, Jameson would be willing to help him out of his current difficult circumstances, and that was worth the risk. Jameson Fuches had saved his life once before, nursing him through a bout of pneumonia in

Philadelphia, and making him a loan to save his skin now should be a reasonable enough thing to expect.

But the more John Henry thought of it on the long train ride from the Red River to the Mississippi, the less he liked the idea of telling Jameson why he was running from the law. He still remembered how Jameson had gone white-faced at hearing his preceptor Dr. Homer Judd's tale of gold-rush greed and murder in California. Even with Jameson's idol-worship of Dr. Judd, the older man's confession had been a hard thing for the young dentist to hear. Jameson had talked about Dr. Judd's shooting of the gold-panner for many evenings after that, as though by talking about it he could somehow come to accept the crime. But at least that killing was something long done, having happened years before Jameson had ever met Dr. Judd. It was in the past, and could be forgotten.

John Henry's own dilemma was still smoldering, and telling Jameson about it would only make matters worse. Better not to mention it at all and come up with some other plausible excuse for his sudden reappearance in St. Louis after being away all those years, and the explanation seemed obvious: he'd finally tired of rural life after having tasted the pleasures of the city in Philadelphia and St. Louis. So he was leaving the South behind and taking a gamble on the Gateway City of the West, hoping to make St. Louis his home for awhile—if Jameson would consider taking him in as a partner.

That was what he planned to say, anyhow. But when he arrived at the Fourth Street house where Jameson and his German aunt had lived, his plans fell apart. It wasn't a kindly old woman who answered his knock at the door, but an old man who apparently spoke even less English than Tante had.

"*Ja? Was wollen Sie?*" the man asked.

"Dr. Fuches?" John Henry replied, hoping that perhaps the man was another of Jameson's German relatives and would understand the request.

But the man stared at him suspiciously from under overgrown gray eyebrows.

"*Doktor Fuches?*" the man asked. "*Nein, da ist kein Fuches heir. Nein.*"

"Dr. Jameson Fuches," John Henry said, trying again before correcting himself and using his friend's German name: "Dr. Auguste Fuches?"

The man's suspicious stare continued as he closed the heavy door to just a crack. "*Nein, nein,*" the man repeated, then added something under his breath that could have been a curse.

John Henry felt like cursing as well, frustrated at not finding Jameson where he should have been. For though he, himself, had spent the last four years moving from one place to another, somehow he'd always envisioned Jameson in the same snug little front-parlor office. But he couldn't very well just wander the graveled macadam streets of St. Louis calling out Jameson's name, hoping someone would understand and point him in the right direction.

The only thing he could think to do was pay a visit on Dr. Judd at his office as Dean of the Missouri Dental College. Surely, Dr. Judd would know where his protégé had relocated, and it was even possible that Jameson was teaching there at the dental school. After all, Jameson's scholarly ways had earned him the nickname "Professor Fuches" while he was still just a first-year dental student himself. And in spite of his own difficulties, John Henry had to smile at the memory of it.

Then he remembered Jameson's disapproval of his evening diversions in St. Louis, and a pair of memories swept back: Hyram Neil, the Levee gambler who'd tried to steal his inheritance; and Kate Fisher, the hot-blooded Hungarian actress who'd almost stolen his heart. Kate might be in the city, too, if her performing company wasn't out on tour somewhere. And though he'd never responded to any of her letters and had done his best to sweep her lusty image from his heart in devotion to Mattie, he suddenly found himself hungering to see her again. But Kate wouldn't be able to offer him any help in finding Jameson or getting himself established in business, so he pushed the tempting thought of her to the back of his mind, and made his way to Nineteenth Street and the Missouri Dental College.

But Jameson, it turned out, wasn't even in St. Louis anymore. According to Dr. Judd, he had returned to Philadelphia to study medicine at the Jefferson Medical College, one college degree not being enough for someone with his abilities.

"I did the same thing myself, of course," Dr. Judd explained, "though the other way around: Medical degree first, then the Dental degree. But

I understand Auguste's desire for further education. The first thing one learns in medicine is how much more there is to know."

"Yessir," John Henry replied, feeling somehow inadequate with his single college diploma. He had never given a thought to going back to school once he was finished, and had happily started into practicing what he had learned. As far as he could see, the purpose of his education was to give him a career, and he had already attained that.

Except that his career was back in Texas with his dental tools and he was in sore need of some means of supporting himself. Finding Jameson gone and unavailable to help him out came as a hard blow.

"How long are you staying in St. Louis?" Dr. Judd asked politely.

"I don't know," he said with a shrug. "Not long. I was hopin' to see Jameson before movin' on . . ."

There must have been something telling in his unfinished thought, for Dr. Judd looked at him quizzically a moment.

"So you are traveling without plans, then?"

"I reckon so . . ." he said hesitantly.

"And you mentioned having left Texas rather hurriedly."

"That's right," he said cautiously. He'd had to make some excuse as to why he didn't know where his friend was, and had come up with the story of a misplaced bit of correspondence before a hasty trip. But though the explanation sounded plausible enough to John Henry, Dr. Judd seemed to be seeing right through it.

"And you traveled here by way of the Indian Territory?"

"That's the way the railroad runs," he replied uncomfortably. "It's either take the train or take the stagecoach, and both of them run through the Territory."

"True, true," Dr. Judd said with a nod. "And all rails lead to St. Louis, to coin a misused phrase. How convenient that the transportation from Texas to the Mississippi is so obliging, and how unfortunate that you left home without so much as noting your friend's whereabouts."

John Henry shifted in his hard-seated chair, feeling the same scrutiny that had made Jameson squirm in Dr. Judd's too-observant presence. There was a long silence as he tried to think of something to say, with Dr. Judd waiting patiently for him to answer some unasked question. And as he'd been trained to give a reply when a professor asked for one, he felt compelled to tell something of the truth.

"I had some difficulty there, Sir, and wasn't really thinkin' about much but leavin' Texas. The fact is, I didn't know until I got into the Indian Territory which way I was even goin'. St. Louis was sort of an afterthought, under the circumstances, but I was hopin' to see Jameson while I was here. I was hopin' maybe he would be in a position to help me out a little and let me work in his practice for awhile."

Dr. Judd nodded and stroked his neat gray goatee.

"I'm sure Auguste will be happy to have your assistance once he returns to the city. But sadly, he won't be arriving for some weeks still. He plans to stop in Illinois for a visit on the way back. There's a young lady there, I understand, for whom he has developed a certain fondness. I believe he may even be thinking of making a marriage proposal before returning to St. Louis."

Of course, Jameson would have found himself a young lady and be thinking of marriage. It was the right and proper thing to do at his age and in his position. An unmarried medical doctor might have difficulty in establishing a practice with female patients, as the bachelor status was viewed with suspicion in polite society. So in his usual thoughtful way, Jameson would allow himself to fall in love with just the right young woman and marry her at just the right time. His life would always be one of order and propriety.

"Then I don't reckon I can wait around for his return," John Henry said. For though he was across the Indian Nation and clear to the banks of the Mississippi River, he still felt too close for comfort to Texas and the United States Army that was no doubt looking for the man who'd shot a Buffalo Solider in Fort Griffin. He needed to be moving on, with or without financial aid from Jameson.

"And what will you do for traveling money?" Dr. Judd asked, as if reading his thoughts.

"I don't know," John Henry replied honestly. "I spent my last Double Eagle on the train fare here."

"I thought as much," Dr. Judd said, though there was thankfully no sound of criticism to it. In fact, he seemed to have something like a look of sympathy in his placid gray eyes. "I have been on your road myself, as I may have mentioned at our first meeting. I told you of my experience in the California gold fields?"

"I remember somethin' of it, Sir, but I don't see as how my situation compares to yours. I didn't shoot anyone." Of course that was a lie, but he couldn't let Dr. Judd think he had a killer sitting in his office and decide to call the authorities. Besides, he hadn't meant to kill that Buffalo Soldier. It had just happened, that was all.

"I didn't say that you did. I only meant that I have been running from difficult circumstances myself, and see something of that in your own face. As a physician, I have spent a great deal of time observing my patients in an effort to answer their needs. And it shows, the look of a desperate man. You have that look, under all your admirable restraint. But I am not one to judge a man, having been worthy of judging myself. I only hope to teach and warn, and caution against the sort of reckless behavior to which I succumbed."

"I accept the caution, Sir," John Henry said evenly, though his heart was racing. If Dr. Judd could see through him so easily, would others do the same?

"Then I hope you will also accept my making you an offer of financial assistance, in lieu of what your friend Dr. Fuches would no doubt offer. Shall we say $200?" he asked, and pulled open the center drawer of his sturdy mahogany desk. "I'll write you a draft against my bank here in St. Louis, to cash at your convenience. We'll consider it a loan, payable on demand."

"And when might that be?" John Henry said uneasily. Though he did indeed need the money, he'd had no plan of asking for Dr. Judd's help.

"Whenever you've settled yourself again. For like your friend Auguste, I have a great deal of faith in human nature and the ability of the individual to overcome these tribulations." Then he dipped his pen in a crystal inkwell and signed his name with a flourish on the promised bank draft, dusting it with sand and blowing it dry.

John Henry took the paper note and stared at it, feeling something between regret and relief. Taking the money was a humiliation, of course, as it meant that Dr. Judd was right about him, in spite of his denials. He was a man on the run who needed a handout and a safe getaway from his reckless deeds. But having the bank draft in his hand made him feel halfway to safety, at least.

"And where will you go now?" Dr. Judd asked, when John Henry had expressed his embarrassed gratitude.

"I don't know, Sir."

"Back to Georgia, perhaps?"

"No, not Georgia," was all he could bring himself to say. There was no thought of going home now, not with a second killing on his conscience. For if Dr. Judd, who knew him only by acquaintance, could see what trouble he'd brought on himself, surely Mattie would see right through him as well.

But as quickly as the thought of Mattie came to him, another one came following after it, pushing it out of his mind: Kate Fisher. Of course he knew where he was going next; he'd known it ever since he'd decided to take the train to St. Louis. He was going to see Kate Fisher and find out if the feelings she had engendered in him were still as powerful as they had once been. And if they were. . .

He'd been an innocent when they'd first met, and wary of her passions. But he was well past innocence now.

"I do appreciate your generosity, Dr. Judd," he said, pulling his thoughts away from Kate and back to the business at hand. "And I assure you that I will return the loan as soon as possible. And Dr. Judd, Sir?"

"Yes?"

"Don't mention this to Jameson, if you don't mind. I'd rather him not be concerned about me, what with his new practice and a new bride and all. In fact, you don't even need to tell him that I came through town."

"To tell you the truth, I hadn't planned on telling him anything of it. And I commend you for wanting to shield your friend from your own troubles. Auguste thought very highly of you. I'd hate to ruin that memory for him."

Dr. Judd's words stung at his heart, but he deserved to hear them. And it wasn't really a judgment against him that Dr. Judd was offering, just the truth: his actions had consequences, and others might also suffer for what he had done. But he wasn't in a mood for truth or lectures, just a quick way to forget the humiliation of taking money from a man he'd once admired. Charity was all well and good when one was on the giving end. Getting it was another experience altogether.

The fastest way to forgetfulness in St. Louis was a walk down to the saloons along the levee, but he didn't dare take himself there. If the gambler named Hyram Neil still held court in the Alligator Saloon—and still remembered the poker debt that had never been repaid—he'd no doubt be happy to have John Henry back for a reckoning. So he stayed clear of the levee and headed for the shabby elegance of the Comique Theater, instead, where there was sure to be a varieties show playing and the mindless entertainment of comedians and minstrel singers and dancing girls in scanty costumes.

But there was no Kate Fisher to be seen, not even her name on the board that listed the theater company players. And according to the stage manager, she'd been gone from the Comique for some time.

"Left after Mazeppa closed, as best I can recall."

"She went to New York then?" John Henry asked, remembering her dream to become an actress on the legitimate stage.

"Not that I've heard," the manager replied, "unless he had business that away."

"He?"

"Her husband. She got married right in the middle of the run, hurried like. Met a salesman from out of town who come to see the show and fell for him right off, I guess. Must have been love at first sight, 'cause she was single one minute and off and married the next. Last I heard, they was headed to Kansas. But maybe it was New York. You got some special interest in asking?"

John Henry shrugged. "Nothin' much. Miss Fisher and I knew each other some awhile back. I just thought I'd look her up and say hello."

And though he turned away with nothing more than a nod, he had a peculiar sensation of having lost something. Not that he'd ever really had Kate, of course. Their affair had been far more restraint than passion. But the memory of what it could have been, if he hadn't bridled himself around her, still haunted his dreams. Kate's willingness had promised him that he might have all the passion he wanted, if he ever returned. Now he was back and she was gone, and worse than that, she was married as well, and his frustrated dreams of her would have to remain just that. Well, his loss would be some other girl's luck that night, now that he'd cashed Dr. Judd's bank note and was carrying enough money to buy himself whatever he wanted. But what he wanted was Kate, at least for that one night, and she was gone.

He left St. Louis and headed west with little thought of where he would go, other than away from Texas and the reach of the Army there. But once he was aboard the Missouri & Pacific Railroad and headed out across the Great Plains, the beauty of the prairie land turned his escape into something more like a pleasure trip. It was the widest green he had ever seen—endless miles of grass that moved like waves in the breezes of late spring. If it hadn't been for the savage Sioux waylaying stages and scalping travelers, the plains might have seemed like paradise.

It was the gold rush in the Black Hills of the Dakotas that had put the Indians in a fighting mood. The Black Hills were part of the Indians' Holy Wilderness, a sacred hunting ground given to the Sioux people by the Great Spirit himself. And for awhile, the United States Government had protected the Indians' right to their land, making a treaty that promised to keep the white men out. But then a scattering of prospectors, trespassing on the treaty land, discovered gold in the Black Hills. The United States was still recovering from the Panic of 1873, and that Black Hills gold would be a welcome help to the American economy. So the government changed its policy toward the Holy Wilderness of the Sioux. The Indians would have to share the Black Hills or be killed if they resisted. To the Sioux, it was a holy war, to the Americans, it was a defense of civilization, and both sides were willing to fight to the death.

Fighting meant soldiers, and Cheyenne was full of them, and the sight of all those blue-coats reminded John Henry that this was no pleasure trip, after all. He was still running from the Army and wary of staying too close around, so he left the Union Pacific at Cheyenne and took the first train south headed into the Colorado Territory.

But it wasn't Dr. John Henry Holliday who arrived in Denver City that warm afternoon in June, only someone who looked like him: a fair-haired, blue-eyed gambler named Tom McKey who didn't have the United States Army following after him. He hoped his uncle wouldn't mind him borrowing the name.

Chapter Six

Denver City, 1876

The first order of business was finding himself a job that didn't demand credentials or references, but would pay enough for room and board and other living expenses. When he'd been in similar circumstances in Galveston, he'd taken a job pulling teeth in the back room of a barber shop. But there were more pleasant ways to make a dollar in a busy city like Denver, especially for a man who was clever with cards. And Tom McKey, Faro dealer, was born.

He took a position dealing in the gambling hall of Charlie Foster, located above Babb's Variety House on Blake Street, then found a room to rent above Long John's Saloon just down the road. Babb's was one of Denver's finer sporting establishments, competing for customers with Big Ed Chase's famous Palace Theater, and both places boasted stage performances and dance halls along with fine dining restaurants. But mostly they were casinos, built for the entertainment of the Denver gambling community.

As the last stop on the trail to the Rocky Mountains, Denver had become a wealthy town even before the gold and silver rush began. Pioneers crossing the Great Plains stopped there to buy supplies and catch a breath before heading into the thin air of the mountains, traveling on toward their distant promised lands. But some weary travelers decided that the supply town at the confluence of Cherry Creek and the Platte River was promised land enough, and stayed to turn Denver into the Queen City of the Plains.

Tom McKey wasn't sure it deserved such an accolade. Compared to Atlanta or St. Louis, Denver looked pretty rough around the edges still. Its two-storied brick buildings faced board sidewalks and dirt streets, and Cherry Creek regularly flooded over with snowmelt from the mountains, washing out the footbridges and sweeping sewage into town. Along the banks of the creek, where Larimer Street crossed the temperamental waters, a hanging tree still dangled a rope noose, ready to be used again. But while Denver wasn't quite as polished as it pretended to be, it did have its charms—the chiefest being the busiest gambling district west of Texas where a man who needed to lay low could lose himself amongst all the other sports. Like Tom McKey, who made his $10 a day dealing cards at Babb's Variety House and did his best to stay out of trouble—and for the most part, he did.

He wrote to Mattie from his room above Long John's Saloon, sitting at the lop-legged desk and doing his best to put into words the confusion of the past year while leaving out whatever he thought would offend her. For how could he put into words all that had happened in his life? So finally, he settled on telling her the best parts of the truth: that he'd been diagnosed with consumption, but was feeling so much better that he was sure the doctor had been wrong; that he'd been traveling in the west looking for a better climate than Texas offered; that he was living in Denver for the foreseeable future and enjoying the mountain scenery; that he was using his uncle's name for privacy sake and that she should write to him in care of Tom McKey; that he loved her and always would and hungered for the chance to see her again. And with any luck, he'd never have to tell her the rest.

That was the Centennial Summer when the whole country commemorated the one-hundredth birthday of the American nation. In Philadelphia, there was a grand exhibition in Fairmount Park and a reopening of the renovated Independence Hall. In Washington, New York City, and San Francisco, there were parades and fireworks. Even the former Rebel states observed that historic July 4th, in their own fashion, by hoisting the Stars and Stripes alongside the Confederate battle flag.

Denver had double reason for celebration as the Colorado Territory had just voted to ratify a new constitution making it the 38th American state. But although President Ulysses S. Grant had yet to approve the document, with Colorado's Republican leanings and Grant's need for Republican votes in the upcoming Presidential election, there was little doubt that he would welcome the new state into the Union. So Denver celebrated both the Centennial Fourth of July and Colorado's impending statehood with the biggest parade the territory had ever seen.

Tom McKey wasn't one to miss such a revel, and he joined in the crush of the cheering crowd as the parade made its noisy way along the wide dirt streets of Denver. The parade featured the usual assortment of marching bands, flag-waving politicians, bunting-covered carriages, and volunteer fire companies showing off their shiny pumper cars, with the highlight being the horse-drawn "Centennial State" float, a haphazardly connected train of wagons carrying thirty-eight ladies dressed in costumes representing the thirty-eight states of the Union. The float seemed as unstable as the Union itself had been just before the War, ready to pull apart at any moment and send ladies and horses careening across 16th Street—though the danger only made the crowd press closer for a better look.

Tom saw the accident coming before it happened: the lead horse frightened by a blast of water from a pumper car, the startled rider yanking the horse to a sudden halt, the second wagon following too close behind and turning into the crowd to avoid running over the horse, the screaming onlookers stumbling backward to keep from being crushed by the wagon wheels, and the golden-haired girl who slipped and fell and would have been trampled by the crowd if Tom hadn't seen and reached a fast hand to pull her to safety. It was just a reflex, reaching out to grab ahold of her the way he did, the whole thing happening too fast to even allow him the pleasure of having performed a gentlemanly act of heroism. But she looked up at him like he was a hero anyway, her thanks coming in gasps as she tried to catch her breath.

"Oh Sir! You saved me!" But as he helped to steady her on her feet, she winced and gasped again.

"Are you injured?" he asked quickly, his voice rising to be heard above the crowd and his eyes glancing over her for any sign of violence. She was a pretty thing, with a tumble of golden curls and a frock entirely too fancy for daytime attire, though her costume seemed somehow appropriate for the Centennial parade.

"It's my ankle," she replied. "I think I've turned it." And with immodesty surely born of pain, she lifted her ruffled petticoats to peer at the troublesome ankle laced into scuffed leather boots.

"We'll have to take off the boot to see if it's broken," he said, and was surprised when she lifted her skirt even higher. He hadn't really meant that he would be the one removing the boot, but as she seemed to expect it of him, he obliged.

"There's no break in the bones," he said, gingerly pressing his fingers against her stockinged ankle. "Likely just a strain. You'll have to stay off it for a few days while it heals. Where's your escort? Have you a ride home?"

"No," she replied, looking puzzled, then quickly pulled her skirts back down again as though suddenly remembering her modesty. "I always walk."

"Well, you won't be walkin' anywhere today, so I reckon I'll have to get you there myself."

"You're going to take me home?" she asked in surprise.

"I couldn't very well consider myself a gentleman if I left a lady in her hour of need," he said reasonably. And though he'd been thinking more of his own pride than of her trouble, he was touched by her response.

"Then you are a gentleman, truly," she said in a voice barely audible above the din of the crowd, "and I thank you for calling me a lady."

He had no time to wonder about her words as he led her limping through the press of the crowd. But after they'd gotten away from the cheering throng and he asked directions to her home, her words came back to haunt him.

"It's not far," she said, "just a few blocks from here, down Holladay Street."

"Holladay Street?" he asked in surprise, though it wasn't the familiar name that caught him. Denver did indeed have a street that shared his surname, though misspelled, in honor of old Ben Holladay, the founder of the overland mail. His surprise came from the nature of the Holladay Street neighborhood. It was just one street over from Blake Street where he lived and worked, and right in the middle of the saloon district.

"But that's just gamblin' halls and such," he commented, "and no real houses. Perhaps you've gotten yourself all turned around, what with the fall and all."

"Oh, I know where I am," she replied, "but it's all right if you don't want to walk me there. I'll understand."

And all at once, a picture came together in his mind: the gaudy dressed girl, the ankle too easily shown, the surprise at being called a lady...

His face must have betrayed his thoughts, for before he could say what he was thinking, she said it for him.

"I'm just a working girl. I don't expect a gentleman like yourself to bother about the likes of me."

He shouldn't have been surprised, but he was. For though Denver was full of fallen angels, as it was full of the sporting men who gave them employment, this girl was nothing like the prostitutes he'd known in Fort Griffin. In spite of her gaudy dress, there was something almost innocent about her, something that was somehow familiar and endearing.

"I thought you knew right off," she said. "Most men know right off..."

"Of course, I knew," he said, lying to put her at ease. "But that doesn't mean you don't deserve an escort home. It's that twisted ankle that concerns me, not your choice of a profession."

And when she put her hand on his arm, accepting the help, he almost believed the words himself.

Her home turned out to be a parlor house, and one of the nicer brothels in the saloon district that clustered around Holladay and Nineteenth Streets. She'd come to be living there after being thrown out of her own home, she said, sharing a story that was probably all too common.

She'd once been as virtuous as any other Victorian girl, until her father died and her mother remarried and the new stepfather felt he had a right to take liberties with her. She was horrified at first and shamed as things continued, but altogether too frightened to do anything to stop the situation. Then one afternoon her mother found her with the stepfather, and put her out into the street. Her protestations that it was all his doing and none of her own fell on deaf ears. The stepfather called her a scheming strumpet who had planned the seduction to discredit him in the eyes of his beloved and worthy wife, and her mother chose to believe the lie. So all at once, the girl found herself homeless and moneyless with no training to become anything other than what she was.

She was fortunate to have found herself a position in that Denver parlor house, as there she had the security of a house mother who made sure she was dressed and fed as long as her customers paid up. The streets were full of girls who didn't fare so well. There were hurdy-gurdy dancers who wore short skirts and showed themselves off in the saloons, streetwalkers who enticed men out of passing carriages, whores in dingy shacks called "cribs," and billboard girls who sat holding advertising signs and doing business from the stools they sat upon. Parlor house prostitutes didn't have to lower themselves to such baseness to make a living, only open their well-appointed bedrooms to men who paid them good money for what some girls had to do for free. That was the way the girl looked at it, anyhow, considering her present circumstances better than the horror of being regularly molested by her mother's husband.

After hearing her sad story, Tom couldn't quite bring himself to accept the offer she made him in repayment of his kindness. She'd called him a gentleman and he felt compelled to behave as one, though he was sorely tempted not to be. Why not accept such an offer and take an available girl when there was no hope for a future with the one he loved? Mattie would never be able to give him such pleasure, and neither would Kate. . .

It was the unbidden memory of Kate Fisher that made him take a hasty leave of the golden-haired parlor house girl and head for the first saloon he could find. Thinking of Kate in St. Louis, where he was surrounded by memories, was understandable. But thinking of her now, and in the same thought with Mattie, seemed like a sacrilege. It was Mattie he loved and Mattie he'd vowed to remember always and, in his own fashion, he was trying to be faithful to her, but having Kate Fisher's memory insinuate itself into his mind made him feel more unfaithful than sleeping with a whole host of fallen angels.

It took a tumbler of whiskey to wash away the uneasy memory of Kate Fisher, but by the time he'd headed back to his little room above Long John's Saloon, he could hardly remember what had made him so distressed in the first place. Kate had been nothing but a diversion to him, and was less than nothing to him now. Mattie was his love and always would be, and he felt a sudden need to write to her again, filling three pages with stories about the Union Pacific Railroad, the rampaging Sioux, and the Centennial excitement in Denver. And by the time he'd signed his name and dried the wet ink with a dusting of sand, he almost believed himself that his life was nothing but a pleasant travelogue.

Almost. There was still a weight on his soul that wouldn't let go, a weight of watching two men die at his hand and knowing that he could never go back to being the man that he had once been. He wasn't a gentleman anymore, at least not the kind of gentleman that Mattie had known. He was Tom McKey, Faro dealer, and he couldn't think of any good reason not to take the parlor house girl up on her tempting offer. It was convenient that she lived just one street over from Long John's Saloon, so he wouldn't have to wait long for the pleasure.

There was a newsboy at the corner of Holladay and 16th Streets, like there was at every major intersection in town, hawking the *Rocky Mountain News*. But unlike most days when the newsies had to scramble to sell off their load of freshly printed papers, the lad on Holladay Street was scrambling to keep from being knocked down by a crowd of men fighting to get a copy of the paper. The headlines he hollered out explained the frenzy:

"Satanic Sioux! General Custer's command slaughtered like sheep! Seventeen commissioned officers and Custer family killed! The battlefield a slaughter pen in which lie three-hundred and fifty boys in blue!"

The paper was filled with the rest of the story and Tom McKey could imagine it all as he read those first reports out of the Black Hills. Custer was already a hero before he died and became a legend immediately after. But he was less than one month dead when another hero fell and entered into Western legend right behind him, making that Centennial Summer a summer of legends—and the papers were full of the stories.

Wild Bill Hickok was a different sort of hero than George Armstrong Custer—a gambler, gunfighter, and sometime lawman who was known for his flashy cross-draw and flashier clothes. But even Custer, for whom Hickok had once been a scout, recognized Wild Bill's finer qualities, calling him, "One of the most perfect examples of physical manhood I ever saw . . . entirely free from bluster and bravado . . . his skill with rifle and pistol unerring." Skillful as Hickok was, however, he couldn't see behind his back, which was how the cowardly Jack McCall was able to shoot him to death at a card table in Deadwood, South Dakota.

Wild Bill had gone to the gold-gulch of Deadwood to do a little prospecting and a lot of card-playing, as he was doing on an August night at the Number Ten Saloon. The poker game had been going on for hours already and Bill was about to play the winning hand when a shot from a Colt's revolver shattered the smoky air. The bullet hit Wild Bill in the back of the head and he toppled over backwards before he could put down that winning hand—a pair of aces and a pair of eights that quickly became known as "The Deadman's Hand."

The ignoble death of Wild Bill Hickok might have inspired Tom McKey to keep his own pistol loaded and ready to pull, but he was wary of getting himself into trouble as Denver had a gun ordinance and thirteen overzealous policemen who liked to enforce the law. So he left his pistol packed away in his traveling case and kept the Hell-Bitch with him for protection instead, slid neatly down into the leather shoulder holster he'd had made for himself in Galveston.

And if what Mattie wrote was true, in the letter he received in answer to his own, the real danger wasn't in Denver anyhow—but all the way back in Georgia.

Mattie must have written to him as soon as she received his own letter, as hers was dated just a week later, though he didn't get the letter for another month after that. The trouble was, he hadn't gotten used to his alias yet, and didn't notice the name T.S. McKey listed in the Advertised Letters column of the newspaper. It was the parlor house girl who pointed it out to him when he brought the paper along with him one hot summer afternoon.

"Why, that's you, Tom," she said with something like surprise. "What's the 'S' stand for?"

"Sylvester," he replied, figuring he might as well give his uncle's middle name since he was already using the rest of it. And as long as he was using all of that, he might as well add to the charade by giving a place of residence as well. "Thomas Sylvester McKey, late of Valdosta, Georgia."

"Valdosta. That sounds lovely," she said, as she helped him out of his jacket and herself out of a ribbon-tied chemise. "What does it mean?"

"Nothin', really. It's a play on the name of the Governor's plantation: Val d'Aosta. Which was named after a castle in Italy, so I hear. I reckon namin' the town after the Governor's place was meant to curry his favor. But all Valdosta seems to favor is bugs. Summers are mighty humid and natty there, not like here. Used to be, the air felt so close you couldn't catch a breath in August."

"I'm glad you like it here," she said, smiling. "I like having you here."

She certainly seemed to, the way she welcomed him whenever he felt like stopping by and only charged him half her usual fee. She would have given her time for free, she said, if her house mother would have allowed it. But she was a working girl and had to show a profit for her favors, and Tom didn't mind paying the price. Besides, not paying her would have made the visits seem like something more than he was willing to make them—and she was, after all, just a prostitute. And knowing there was a letter waiting for him, most likely a letter from Mattie, reminded him that he was only in the parlor house for a little pleasure, and nothing beyond that.

The letter made him forget the golden-haired girl, or anything else, with the news it brought from Atlanta. For behind Mattie's affectionate words was a warning he hadn't expected. Though he had tried to hide the killing in Fort Griffin from her, she'd heard all about it already—from a Pinkerton's Detective who came calling at the Hollidays' home in Atlanta.

We didn't believe him, of course, Mattie wrote in her delicate and feminine hand, heart-felt words still believing the best of him.

Who could believe such a story? For though I have sometimes chastised you for being reckless and quick-tempered, I know, dear cousin, that you would never do such a thing as the man from Pinkerton's has accused you of. So, knowing that he was mistaken in his charges against you, charges which I do not have the heart to here repeat, I felt it no wrong in keeping from him that which he came seeking, which was a photograph of you. Of course, I have one, the daguerreotype you had made in Philadelphia, and which I cherish as a memento of you.

So thinking it then the best thing to do, I lied straight out when he asked if we had any such possession, and told him we had nothing to help him. He seemed disatisfied to hear the news, as the Detectives Agency has been commissioned by the Army to aid in finding you, and without a proper portrait of you they cannot accomplish much. Mother was fearful of displeasing the man, after what we have heard of that company's dealings in Missouri, and would have shown the portrait to him herself, if Lucy hadn't shushed her. I have never seen my sister Lucy shush Mother before, so you can imagine the family's astonishment—and my own grateful feelings for having such a loyal and clever sister.

It has been a blessing to have my family here with me. I say here and by that I mean Atlanta, as Mother has let our house in Jonesboro and moved with my sisters and Jim Bob here to be near Uncle John and his family. Her circumstances have been very difficult, as you might imagine, since her widowhood, being left with a large and helpless family and no means of support for her household. Uncle John has been kind, as always, in helping to provide for us here, taking a house for us just down the road from his own home. We are happy here, as much as can be without our dear father to provide for his loving children and wife. Mother still grieves, though she tries to hide it from the children.

She cannot hide it from me, as I have a heavy heart of my own, worrying over you every day. How I long to have you back home again, safe from these awful charges which I cannot bring myself to believe! I will not believe them, unless you tell me in your own hand that they are true.

Please write soon, and tell me that all is well with you. Until then, my prayers are with you always, as my love is always, dear John Henry.

He read the letter over twice to make sure he had understood her properly, then tried to settle his shaken thoughts. The Army had followed him after all, at least far enough to know that he wasn't in Texas anymore, and had trailed him all the way to his relatives in Georgia. But thankfully, no one but Mattie knew of his whereabouts, and she would never tell them that he was far off in Colorado. He was safe for awhile in his life as a Denver Faro dealer, though it wasn't only his own safety that concerned him, but that of Mattie and her family.

They had reason to be fearful of the Pinkerton Agency, as Mattie's mother was surely well aware. The detectives had caused a national outcry earlier that year trailing the outlaw Jesse James and his gang, hounding them day and night and putting an armed guard around the home of Jesse's mother. Jesse wasn't there, but his young half-brother was, and when the Pinkertons threw a bomb into the house, it was the brother who died and the mother who lost an arm in the explosion. It was an unfortunate accident, the Agency said, but worth the cost if the outlaw was captured in the end.

They hadn't caught the James gang yet, but with their dogged determination and their motto *We Never Sleep*, they would probably catch them soon enough. And what if the Pinkertons went after John Henry like they'd gone after Jesse James? What if they went back to Mattie's home, waiting for his return that she was always hoping for, and made some awful mischief there? What if it were Mattie who ended up paying the price for his misdeeds the way Jesse James' family had paid for his? The thought that his own actions might cause her any harm left him shaking and sick at heart.

The solution was obvious: leave his alias and his Colorado safety behind and go back to Texas where the Army could have their shot at him. Then the Pinkertons would have no wanted man to trail nor any reason to molest his relatives back in Georgia. The solution was obvious—but he couldn't bring himself to consider it. Going back to Texas now, if the Army were still looking for him, would likely mean hanging for that unintentioned killing of the Buffalo Soldier. If he'd meant to kill the man, he might have been willing to take the consequences of his actions. But it had been nothing more than a drunken mistake, and he wasn't ready to throw his life away for that. The best he could do was to ease Mattie's concerns by writing and telling her what she wanted to hear—that the Army was wrong in their charges against him and that soon enough the Pinkertons would realize as much and give up their search. As for easing his own concerns, he'd send a letter back to Fort Griffin asking Shaughnessey to find out what he could about the Army's plans and to let him know when things settled down some there. And in the meantime, he'd have to keep on pretending to be Tom McKey, with nothing but Faro and parlor girls on his mind.

The world of a Denver sporting man covered only a few city blocks, encompassed by the winding bed of Cherry Creek to the west and 16th Street to the east, by Curtis Street to the south and the tracks of the Union Pacific Railroad to the north. Most of the saloons and brothels, the gaming halls and varieties theaters lay within those confines, making the sporting district a little world of its own. Unless a gambling man had important business elsewhere, he could spend all his days and nights on Wynkoop or Wazee, Blake Street or Holladay Street, Larimer, Lawrence, or Arapahoe and never venture out into the more proper neighborhoods of the city.

The unofficial boundary line between sporting district and city proper was the brick bastion of the Inter-Ocean Hotel occupying half a block at 16th and Blake Street. The Inter-Ocean had claim to be the swankiest hotel west of the Mississippi with its only competition being its sister hotel, the Inter-Ocean in Cheyenne, since both boasted gentlemen's saloons, billiard parlors, basement barbershops, and annexes that housed bathrooms with real indoor plumbing just a short walk from the guest rooms. But what really set the Inter-Ocean apart from any other hotel in the West was that its millionaire owner, Mr. Barney Ford, had started out life as a slave—a story that all of Denver couldn't help rumoring about.

He'd been born on a Virginia plantation in 1822, but as soon as he went to work in the tobacco fields, Barney knew he was meant for better things. Past the fields and up where the smell of manure on the tobacco didn't foul the night air, Barney's white master lived in easy elegance in a sprawling manor house on a hill. Barney spent his days pulling tobacco and gazing up at that house, and promised himself that someday he would have a house even grander than his master had. But other than running away, there was little hope for him to ever break free of his slavery. So young Barney determined that as soon as the chance came, he would run for his life and become a free man.

The chance was slow in coming, though. Barney's master sold him down south to a Georgia hog-farmer, an ignorant man who hardly knew how to manage his own affairs, much less care for his Negro slaves. The one thing the master did do well was to beat his slaves whenever he'd been drinking too much mountain whiskey. But he wasn't a discriminatory man; he beat his own wife about as hard as he beat his slaves, and his children only a little less.

Then one year when the hog business was going slow, the farmer hired Barney out to a gold camp in the north Georgia mountains, and Barney got his first case of gold fever. Men were getting rich just by filling tin pans full of gold-laden water from the cold mountain streams. It didn't seem to take any talent to get that gold—just patience and a little luck. Barney had patience, he figured; living in slavery had taught him that. And as for luck, he figured he could get a little of that, too.

But first he had to get his freedom, and in Barney's mind that meant getting out of Georgia. So when the hog-farmer hired out some of his Negroes to a man who ran a riverboat on the Mississippi River, Barney made sure he was one of the ones who went. They said the Mississippi was a wide watery road that led from the slave states in the South to the free states in the North, and Barney was headed for freedom. When the riverboat dropped anchor at Quincey, Illinois, he jumped ship and made for the Underground Railroad and didn't stop running until he got to Chicago.

He was twenty-six years old when he started life as a free man, but he felt like he was just being born. For the first time in his life, he could decide for himself what he wanted to do and who he wanted to be. He had no surname—slaves didn't need one, being property instead of people—so his first task was to choose a name for himself. Near the house where he was staying in Chicago was the Baldwin Locomotive Company which had just unveiled its newest engine, the Lancelot Ford. Barney didn't much care for the name Lancelot, but he liked the sound of the name Ford, and he liked the idea of naming himself after something that was going places, like that locomotive engine, so the slave boy named Barney became a man named Mr. Barney L. Ford.

The next thing he needed was an education, so he taught himself to read and write, and devoured every book he could find. He had a naturally quick mind and a hunger to learn everything all at once, and by the time the California Gold Rush started, Barney Ford was better educated than most of the white men he knew. So with the gold-fever still in his blood and that dream of a big house on a hill still in his heart, he headed west.

But going west wasn't easy for a runaway slave in those dangerous years before the War. The trail led across Southern territory where he could be arrested and returned to his master, or hung. So he took the long way around, from Chicago to New York City, then by ship to Central America and the Nicaragua crossing. Nicaragua was a free republic and would give passage through the jungles—for a price. Barney paid the price, most of the little money he had, then took sick in the jungle and couldn't go any farther. But he was patient, and once he recovered his strength, he opened a little tourist hotel in Nicaragua City and started saving his money for another try at the California Gold Rush. He might have even made it if Nicaragua hadn't rescinded its anti-slave laws and forced him to flee for freedom once more.

He took passage back to Chicago and went to work for the Underground Railroad helping other slaves to freedom and making friends with abolitionist politicians. The North was full of men who wanted to show their moral fiber by being friendly with a former slave, and had Barney stayed there, he might have become one of the leading black men in the abolition movement like the fiery young Frederick Douglass.

But Barney still had gold-fever in his blood, and when the Colorado Gold Rush started in 1859, he headed west again. This time, he made it to the gold fields and did some prospecting in the diggings around Central City. Rumor had it he even found a promising strike, until he learned from an armed party of white miners that territorial law didn't allow a colored man to file a mine claim. It was bad luck, all right, but Barney didn't plan to give up so easily.

There were other ways to make money in a gold rush. Denver was in its first boom and almost every kind of business was turning an easy profit. Barney started out by opening a barbershop, then took the money he made from that to open a restaurant, and when the restaurant proved a success, he turned his money around again and opened a big hotel. And Barney Ford, the runaway slave, finally had a house as big as his master's on that Virginia tobacco plantation. It was some years later that he built the first of his Inter-Ocean Hotels, when he was a wealthy man with influential friends, but it was that first hotel in gold rush Denver that was the fulfillment of his dreams.

A success like that would never have happened in Georgia, Tom McKey knew. But Colorado wasn't like the South, tied up with traditions so old that no one even remembered how they'd started. Colorado was brand new and full of opportunity and so empty of people still that the local paper quoted an eastern editor as saying, "Colorado consists of Denver, the Kansas Pacific Railway, and scenery."

Tom didn't know much about the scenery himself, having never ventured up into the wall of mountains that rose to the west, peak after peak disappearing into a blue distance, but he'd heard tell of it. There were gorges up there that could swallow a wagon train whole, and forests where a man could get lost and never be heard from again. There were also gold mining towns where a man might find a fortune if he didn't mind working for it. But Tom was content for the time being to make his money more easily, dealing the cards and betting on the games in his off-hours, profiting from the gold-dust dreams of others.

It was during one of those after-hours card games, while he was playing poker in the gentleman's saloon at the Inter-Ocean Hotel, that Tom first met the famous Mr. Barney Ford. The Inter-Ocean's saloon was a cut above the usual gaming rooms, with linen tablecloths and waiters serving drinks that came from the restaurant upstairs and a clientele that was expected to act accordingly. Playing cards there made Tom feel something like a gentleman again in spite of his present circumstances. But Bud Ryan, a local gambler who happened into the Inter-Ocean that same afternoon, evidently didn't know the rules of polite society. He complained, in a voice loud enough that all the other gentlemen there could hear and words that would offend everyone, that the tablecloth was getting in the way of his cards, that the waiter was excessively slow in bringing his drinks, that the banker was slighting him on his chips—complaints which demanded an answer from the hotel staff.

The answer came in the person of Mr. Barney Ford, himself, who suggested that Ryan might be happier playing cards elsewhere.

"The Cricket Club has a card room without tablecloths, I understand, and the Lucky Break doesn't even employ waiters. You can stand up to the bar with your fellows imbibing cheap whiskey until your boorish insides rot."

His words were meant to be sarcasm, but seemed almost pleasant instead, coming as they were from the mellifluous voice of Mr. Ford. It was a voice that took Tom by surprise, considering the source. The slave boys he'd known, growing up in Georgia, spoke in an accent all their own: part Africa, part Appalachia, but always recognizably colored. "Nigra talk," his father had called it, and proof that the black man could never be the cultural equal of his white masters.

But Barney Ford's words slid off his tongue like warmed honey, rich and resonant. His carefully modulated baritone sounded something like Shakespeare and Schubert put together, poetry and music all mixed up, and if Tom hadn't been looking right at Barney's black face and nappy gray-streaked hair, he would have sworn the man was white. Except that he had never heard a white man who sounded so elegantly cultured—completely disproving his father's provincial beliefs.

Bud Ryan seemed less impressed. He scowled and threw out an ugly epithet, then made the mistake of reaching into his pocket for a pistol to make his point, for in a moment he was set upon by an irate throng of hotel guests and sporting men, all scrambling to grab his handgun away. All except for Tom McKey, who found himself suddenly standing in front of Barney Ford and brandishing the Hell-Bitch like a shield, as though the beveled blade could stop a bullet in mid-air. From across the room, Bud Ryan glared at him.

It was the first time Tom had ever defended a colored man, and for the life of him he couldn't imagine what had brought him to it. But Barney Ford accepted his uncharacteristic gesture with a half-bow.

"I am in your debt, Sir," he said, "but you can go ahead and put that weapon away. I doubt our gambling friend will be causing any more trouble with half the Denver sporting community holding him back."

Tom sheathed the knife, feeling suddenly foolish for his needless show of bravado.

"No debt at all, Mr. Ford," he said with a shrug, "just hate to have my card game interrupted, that's all . . ."

A look of something like amusement passed over Barney Ford's dark face, then he waved a hand toward the crowd that surrounded Bud Ryan.

"Put him out please, gentlemen. This hotel will not abide riffraff."

And as bidden, the sports gathered Bud Ryan and hustled him out of the saloon, while Barney Ford watched with untroubled eyes as though there were nothing unusual at all about a colored man giving orders to white men and having them quickly obey.

Barney Ford believed in paying his debts, as he had paid in full the first loan advanced him for his first restaurant in Denver—$9,000 repaid with interest before it was due. So John Henry shouldn't have been surprised that Barney Ford made a point of paying back what he considered a debt on his life to the man who had stepped between him and a gunman's aim. But it was the way the debt was repaid which confounded John Henry. For somehow finding out where he worked, Barney Ford had a long box delivered to Babb's Variety House, and inside it a fancy gold-headed cane and a note that said only, *For doing a gentlemanly job. B.L. Ford.* And John

Henry wasn't sure who was more the gentleman—himself, or the former slave. One thing he did know: Emmanuel Kahn, back in Dallas, would have been pleased to see him carrying that cane and looking downright fashionable.

He wrote to Mattie about Barney Ford, hoping that she would understand something of his own amazement. Mattie was a forward-thinker, for a proper Southern girl, but she had surely never seen a colored millionaire nor a black man who could command such instant respect. She wrote back that she would like to meet a man like Mr. Barney Ford someday, and that his rise to prominence only underscored the importance of education, for if a run-away slave could turn his life to such profitable use, what things might a white man accomplish? Their Uncle John, she pointed out, had been the first man in the Holliday family to attain a college education, and he was not only well-off but had set an example of accomplishment for his sons—and his favorite nephew, as John Henry had proven by his own professional education.

It was her mention of his education that ruined the rest of the letter for him, reminding him that he was living a life below both his own station and her expectations. As far as Mattie knew, he was still just touring around the countryside, enjoying a little adventure before returning to Texas and his dental practice there. Sooner or later he'd have to go back, or explain to her why he couldn't go. But until he knew that the Army had given up its search for him, he didn't dare, though at least the Pinkertons seemed to have lost interest in him, as Mattie said they hadn't yet returned to Forrest Avenue.

The Pinkertons had trouble enough elsewhere, that fall, in the James boys' retribution for the murder of their half-brother. While the ex-Confederate outlaws had always before confined their train robbery and bank hold-ups to Northern businesses operating in Southern territory, their new exploit took them north of the Mason-Dixon Line where they planned to rob a bank full of hard-earned Yankee cash. Mr. Allan Pinkerton was, after all, a Yankee supported by Yankee money, and a strike at a bank in his own country would leave a message that the James Gang was not to be trifled with—and would bring them a tidy $200,000 as well, retribution and reward all rolled together.

But they were mistaken in thinking that the mild-mannered Swedes of Northfield, Minnesota would stand aside meekly as outlaws stole the town's hard-earned savings. While Jesse and the boys tried to get the unwilling bank teller to open the safe, the townsfolk gathered in the streets bringing whatever weapons they could find: handguns, shotguns, canes, meat-cleavers. And when one of the outlaws took a shot at the uncooperative teller, the people of Northfield went into bloody action.

Frank James caught a slug in the leg. Charley Pitts took a bullet in the ankle before a blast from a Remington shattered his shoulder. Cole Younger took a shoulder hit too, and Bob Younger was shot in the thigh and the wrist. Their brother Jim got half his upper jaw torn away. Bill Chadwell got both eyes shot out, and Clell Miller had his face blown off. Only Jesse James, himself, was left uninjured, and he led what remained of his gang on a ragged run from town and the posse that would surely be following.

Gruesome as it was, the story of the street fight seemed somehow consoling to Tom McKey as he read the gory details afterwards in the *Rocky Mountain News*. For if he wasn't the man Mattie thought he was, at least he wasn't an outlaw like Jesse James and his gang, robbing banks and waylaying trains and killing innocent bystanders for the greed of gold. He was, for the time being, just a gentleman gambler with an unlucky streak of trivial arrests and a temper that occasionally got the better of him—and the unintentioned deaths of two black men still weighing heavy on his soul.

The snows began the first of November, coming on all at once in an early-season blizzard that left the dirt streets of Denver a mess of ice and mud. Tom had seen snowy weather before, having passed two frozen winters in Philadelphia, but Denver snow was different, the flakes as big as shiny silver half-dollars, the air so dry he could hardly draw a breath. Mountain air, folks called it, and said it was bracing, but for Tom the air was too dry, leaving him with red chapped skin and burning lungs. His only recourse was staying as well-lubricated as possible, downing more than his usual daily dose of whiskey while he watched the snow pile up.

With the sudden change of climate, the streets emptied and the saloons and gambling houses filled up with sporting men coming in from the cold and making it hard to find an empty seat at a gaming table. Of course, every gambler wanted the same seat at each table: back to the wall, facing the door. No one wanted to repeat Wild Bill's deadly mistake in having his back to the door when an enemy came along. But for Tom McKey, having his back to the door would have been better—especially when the quarrelsome Bud Ryan showed up again.

It happened on the Saturday after Thanksgiving in a Holladay Street saloon where Tom had stopped to play on his way to the parlor house. The place was crowded, but somehow he found that choice back-to-the-wall seat at a table facing the door. It was cold there, with the wind blowing snow into the saloon every time the door opened, which probably explained why the seat was free. But Tom turned his coat collar up and drank a tumbler of whiskey down and let the heat of it warm him as he joined into the poker game, quickly losing himself in the play of the cards. There was nothing like a gambling game to make a man forget everything else—even the importance of being wary in a crowded saloon.

So Bud Ryan saw him first as he came in from the cold after being thrown out of another saloon up the street. Ryan had already drunk his share of liquor, by the smell of him, and was already in a wrath when he spotted the man who had stepped between him and Barney Ford and seemed glad to have an opportunity to make amends, striding straight to Tom's poker table.

"Damned if this day ain't turnin' out all right after all!" Bud said with a snarl of a smile, leaning over the other players and putting his hand to his hip. He had his pistol back, Tom could see, and was playing toward it with eager fingers.

There was a sudden clamor around the table as the other players pushed their chairs back, scrambling to be away from the coming fight. But Tom had nowhere to run, his own chair already flush against the cold wall of the saloon, his heart gone as suddenly cold as the brick. Bud Ryan's hand inched closer to the pistol as he leaned forward, his whiskey breath hot and angry.

Tom's heart stopped, but his body reflexed in self-defense, his hand sliding into his coat and the Hell-Bitch slicing out and up into flesh and bone. The knife flayed open neck and cheek and brow, one gaping red wound that tore across Bud Ryan's face and nearly took out his eye as well. The gambler caught at his pistol then let it go, his hand slapping at his face as though he'd been mosquito-bit, before he realized that blood was pouring out of him. He gasped then started squealing like a butchered pig, all the fight gone out of him. The rest of the saloon had gone as quiet as a graveyard, all eyes on the man with the monster knife in his hand.

Tom started shaking in mingled horror and relief, then dropped the bloodied Hell-Bitch onto the table. There was no reason to run, and nowhere to go if he did. Everyone in the saloon had seen him knife Bud Ryan, and soon enough the Denver City police would arrive to arrest him. His only consolation was the hope that Ryan would be arrested as well for provoking the incident in the first place. Then another, more interesting thought swept into his mind. His Uncle Tom had been right when he'd first introduced John Henry to the Hell-Bitch in his boyhood days back in Valdosta. You didn't throw a knife that big, you cut with it, cross-draw from the shoulder holster, slicing up the enemy like slaughtering a hog. The Hell-Bitch had, after all, started out as a meat cleaver on his grandfather's cotton plantation, where the children used to sit in the shade of a dogwood tree and drink sweet curdled syllabub.

The memory made John Henry smile.

Justice Whittemore called the case of the Holladay Street incident into court the Tuesday following Thanksgiving, but Tom never made an appearance. Tom McKey was back in Valdosta where he belonged, living his honest and upstanding life while the man who had stolen his name made bail and took the first train out of Denver. For whatever else John Henry Holliday was, he wasn't so low as to sully his Uncle's good name with an undeserved jail sentence for assault with a deadly weapon. His Uncle Tom was still a gentleman, after all, and deserved better than that.

Chapter Seven

DALLAS, 1877

TEXAS MIGHT HAVE SEEMED LIKE THE LAST PLACE HE SHOULD GO WITH the Army and Pinkerton's Detectives still looking for him, except that he wasn't a wanted man in Texas anymore, at least according to the most recent letter he'd received from Mattie:

> I have asked our cousin Robert to make some inquiries, quietly of course, and have learned that the detective agency is no longer looking for you and has closed their absurd investigation. They had to do so eventually, as it was all ridiculous and just a case of mistaken identity, I am sure. You would never have done the thing they accused you of, dear John Henry, and I am so relieved that they will finally leave us all alone. And now that I am feeling less fearful for you, I will tell you the details of what my clever sister Lucy did when they came here looking for a photograph of you. She took your portrait, the one you sent me from Philadelphia, and hid it down the laces of her corset, and the detectives would have to have made a much more thorough investigation than they did to discover it! Lucy and I laughed about it privately after they were gone, but Mother was quite unsettled by the whole affair. I have never doubted you for a minute.

So he was free at last to return to Dallas and reopen his dental practice, pretending that he'd never been anything but a well-educated professional man with a run of bad luck. And Mattie and his father could be proud of him once more.

But Dallas didn't seem inclined to forget his previous misfortunes there, and his inquiries for a partnership or even an available office space were met with polite disinterest, or worse. And when he turned to his other profession to support himself, he drew the attention of the ever-vigilant Dallas police, being arrested for gambling three times in his first three weeks back in the city. With all that vigilance, however, the Dallas County Court docket was so crowded with gambling cases that John Henry's charges wouldn't be heard for months. So while he waited to pay his fines and clear his record yet again, he decided to try his luck in someplace more friendly—like the town of Breckenridge, one-hundred miles to the west and celebrating its first birthday with fireworks and picnics and wide-open poker games.

He arrived in Breckenridge on the afternoon stage, took a room at the new Drake House Hotel, then dusted off his suitcoat and felt-brimmed hat and headed down Walker Street with Barney Ford's gold-headed cane in hand, and looking downright dapper. He went unheeled, of course, not eager to break the Texas gun law after his previous trouble in Fort Griffin, and still so unnerved by that self-defense knifing in Denver that he didn't dare carry the shoulder-holstered Hell-Bitch either. But Breckenridge was a tame enough town, by the looks of it, for a man with no enemies and nothing but cards on his mind.

There were a couple of saloons and gambling halls in town, the most convenient to the Drake House being the Court Saloon, which stood at the end of a bit of board sidewalk across from the County Courthouse lot, though there was no courthouse there yet. The lot was still just a mess of mesquite, as was most of the town, with official county business being conducted in a box-pine hall across from Marberry's General Store and Veale's Law and Land Office. But rustic as the place seemed, the saloons were as boisterous as any in Dallas with the influx of gamblers come for the town's birthday celebration.

The Court Saloon had all the usual games going on that hot afternoon: poker, Faro, keno, Red and Black, High Dice, Over and Under

Seven. John Henry ordered a whiskey at the bar, then joined in the crowd around the Faro layout as he waited for a seat at the poker table. After his time dealing Faro in Denver, he'd lost interest in being a mere player in the game. The real money, he knew, went to the banker and the gambling hall. The players only thought they were wagering on Lady Luck and had a chance of winning, a fantasy that a good dealer encouraged. The trick was to keep the players thinking they'd beat the system by dealing them just the right amount of wins to make it seem like they had. All in all, dealing Faro was far more interesting than playing Faro when it was done with skillful sophistication.

The Faro dealer at the Court Saloon was neither skillful nor sophisticated, as he kept turning every card for the house and driving away the players he should have been seducing into the game. He was either stupid or greedy, or both, and John Henry said as much to a gentleman standing beside him in the crowd.

"More likely greedy than stupid," the man replied, "him being a Jew and all. Name's Henry Kahn, a bad man around these parts."

John Henry took a long look at the Faro dealer, trying to see any resemblance between the man and the elegant Emmanuel Kahn of Dallas, and couldn't see anything aside from the sleek black hair and prominent nose. But all Jews had that profile, from what he'd seen, and that didn't mean that this Kahn was related to the other one. He certainly didn't have Emmanuel Kahn's refinement or sense of style, as the gambler sat in a cloud of cigar smoke and crude language, swearing at the players for not betting high enough.

"Seems to me," John Henry said, addressing the dealer, "that you'd do better to let them win a little, encouragin' them to put down their money instead of badgerin' them into it."

"And what the hell business is it of yours?" Kahn asked, looking up in irritation.

"None. But it should be yours, if you play the game right. Give a little to get a lot was the way I learned the game when I was dealin' in Denver."

"Is that right? Then you can go the hell back to Denver. I'm banking this game, and I'll play it anyway I want."

"Suit yourself. But you're a shame to the Hebrew nation if you don't learn to deal Faro better than you're doin' right now."

That remark made Kahn pause in mid-deal, and he looked up at John Henry with angry black eyes. "You a Jew-hater?"

"Not at all. In fact, I have the greatest respect for the wanderin' children of Israel. But one of their finest traits, it always seemed to me, was an innate understandin' of finance and a natural ability to drive a hard bargain. Hagglin' Hebrews—one of God's most interestin' creations."

"What are you driving at?" Kahn asked. "'Cause I'm getting tired of this prattle of yours. I've got a game to deal."

"Which is precisely my point. You've got the game, but you're not dealin'. Any Faro dealer worth a copper knows you've got to let the bettors win a time or two. Looks to me like you've got the whole thing rigged for the bank, and these gentlemen are never going to see any increase for their hard-earned investments. Seems like a natural born Jew would understand that and give up a win from time to time to curry things along. The way you play, you're either too greedy to be a Jew, or not greedy enough, and I'll be damned if I can tell the difference."

He wasn't trying to be ugly, just informative, and his little speech pleased him so much that he smiled at the end of it, accepting the appreciative nods of the other gamblers. But Henry Kahn was not so pleased, and he shoved back from the layout, knocking the coppers awry.

"You take that back," Kahn growled.

"I will not. I meant every word of it. You should consider it instructional."

"I consider it an insult, and you'd better take it back, or . . ."

"Or what?" John Henry asked, having all confidence that in a well-policed place like the Court Saloon, the Faro dealer wasn't likely to be armed. But Kahn didn't need a gun. With a curse on his breath, he lunged forward and slapped John Henry hard across the face.

He hadn't been slapped in years, not since his father had knocked him down and thrown him out of the house, and the old memory and the new pain swirled together into a sudden fury. In one unthinking move, John Henry grabbed his gold-headed cane and swung it hard against Henry Kahn's head, knocking him to the floor.

He was surprised by the violence of his own emotions, and more surprised by the surge of satisfaction he felt. But the satisfaction didn't last long, as Kahn pulled himself up from the floor and reached for the derringer he'd had concealed in his vest pocket.

It was the last thing John Henry saw before the world went black.

Dying. He heard the word from somewhere outside himself, and struggled against it. He wasn't dying, not yet, just dead tired from the ride to Atlanta and back, riding hard to bring the Priest to save Uncle Rob's soul. It was Uncle Rob who was dying, laid out in the parlor downstairs like a corpse already, cold and still as death, cold as the wind that blew against the broken window and came in through a hole in the roof. So cold outside, but so hot beneath the old quilts Mattie laid over him that he was sweating in spite of the chill.

"It's all right, honey," he heard her say. "It's all right. Mattie's here." But there was something sad in her sweet voice, and when she leaned down to kiss him, a tear fell on his face.

"I love you, Mattie," he murmured, "I love you." And though he was too weak to do more than whisper the words, he knew that she was there, sitting close beside him and giving him the strength to get well. Then she put her hand on his face, cool and comforting, and brushed the perspiration-damp hair from his brow, and he slept again.

When the fever finally broke and he woke again, it wasn't Mattie who was caring for him so tenderly, laying a cool hand on his forehead, but a woman he didn't know. He moved his lips to ask who she was and found his throat too dry to make the sounds, then lost the thought as she turned toward the dark shadowed corner of the room and spoke words that made no sense to him.

"He's coming around, Mr. Holliday," she said, and John Henry's eyes followed her gaze to the darkened corner where the dusk was beginning to gather itself into the form of a man.

Mr. Holliday, she had said? A confusion of ache and anger swept over him. His father, here in Texas? His father come to find him at last?

But it wasn't Henry Holliday there in the shadows, only someone who bore a family resemblance to him.

"Hello, John Henry," his cousin George Holliday said. "We thought we'd lost you. Welcome back to the world of the livin'."

George looked substantial enough, with the well-fed weight of happy marriage on him, but John Henry knew he had to be nothing more than another dream. George wasn't in Texas. George was back home in Atlanta, tending to his father's store and raising a houseful of Holliday kin.

But this dream didn't fade and seemed determined to keep him awake.

"You almost bled to death, the doctor says, taking that shot so near to the belly. Lucky for you, the doctor in this town's a poker player and happened to be in the saloon at the time."

"I got shot?" he asked, the words coming out in a whisper. Then he remembered the derringer. "Kahn . . ."

"That's what they called him. He left town before I got here, so I didn't have the pleasure of meetin' him myself. To tell you the truth, I didn't expect I'd be meetin' you again this side of the Pearly Gates after that wire your landlady sent."

"My landlady?" He was too dizzy, too breathless to follow the story.

"At the hotel, where you left your things. She found a letter from Mattie in your bag and telegraphed with the news that you were dyin' and she didn't know what to do about the body. Mattie came to us straightway, hopin' we'd come along with her here. We made her stay home, of course. Collectin' the dearly departed's remains seems like men's business, more like. If I'd have known you'd still be breathin' when I got here, I'd have brought her along, after all, to do the nursin'. You've cost a bit in medical care."

George's practical little speech proved he was no dream after all, but raised more questions than it answered.

"Why you?" John Henry asked hoarsely, and meant, *Why not my father?* Surely if the family thought he were dying, his father would have come . . .

"I got elected, that's why, though Mary wasn't too happy about it. We had a new baby last month, and she thought I ought to stay home with her and the boy. You heard we had a son this time?"

John Henry shook his head, and the room spun around him. He didn't know if he knew that or not. Had Mattie mentioned it in her letters?

"Robert would have come, but he's up in Virginia at a dental convention. So that left me. Lucky for us both, the Texas & Pacific goes straight through from Atlanta to Fort Worth now, so it didn't take me too long."

But still no explanation of why Henry Holliday hadn't come himself, and John Henry forced out the painful words.

"Does my father know?"

George shrugged. "We wired him and he sent some money for a coffin. I reckon he was too tied up with business to get away just then. He's Mayor of Valdosta now, you know."

John Henry closed his eyes and let the dizziness lift him—away from the groaning pain in his side, away from the aching knowledge that his father didn't care if he lived or died. All his struggles to become something, to somehow earn back Henry's respect and affection, had been for nothing, after all.

"You sleep awhile, John Henry. You've got some healin' to do before I take you home."

He had some healing to do, all right, and it would take longer to mend than just the wound in his side. So in spite of George's generosity in taking a room for them at the new Transcontinental Hotel in Fort Worth and staying with him three weeks while he got his strength back, in spite of an emotional letter from Mattie praising the Lord for his life and saying that she was praying for his safe return, he knew he couldn't go home. Not now, maybe not ever. He still had his pride, after all, and until that was completely gone, he couldn't go back to his father's world knowing he wasn't wanted there.

As for giving up the long anticipated reunion with Mattie, he laid that disappointment at his father's door, as well.

He went back to Dallas intending to stay just long enough to answer the court cases against him—and ended up getting arrested again in yet another flush of the gambling district. But this time he didn't even bother waiting around for the trial. He was done with Dallas and done with trying to be his father's son.

There were other towns less judgmental of a man's recreations, and where he could live the life of a sporting man without excuses. So he packed up his things and took the train back to Fort Worth and the stage from there to the banks of the Clear Fork of the Brazos River, looking for a place with a little less constraining civilization—though on first sight, Fort Griffin looked to have become almost civilized itself. Gone were the rows of shacks along the wide muddy track called Griffin Avenue, their place taken over by two-storied saloons and false-fronted shops and stores. Gone were the buffalo hides drying in the putrefactioned air. For in the year since he'd last seen it, Fort Griffin had grown from buffalo town to cattle town and the premier outfitting point on the newly opened Western Cattle Trail from Brownsville to Dodge City.

Fort Griffin's transformation from frontier hellhole to the rowdiest cowtown in Texas had come as a side benefit of the Kansas quarantine against Texas Longhorn cattle. The trouble was that the Longhorns carried a sickness that had the unfortunate effect of killing off the shorthorn cattle of the plains. All along the old Chisholm Trail, from the cattle ranches of south Texas to the railheads in Kansas, shorthorns died while Longhorns grew fat and healthy. So the legislature of Kansas placed a quarantine on the whole eastern side of the state, forcing the Texas cattle drovers to find another way to the railroad besides Wichita and Kansas City.

They found their way on the Western trail that led right past Fort Griffin toward Doan's Station and north to Dodge City. In one spring month, more than 50,000 head of Texas cattle passed by Fort Griffin, herded up the trail by thousands of south Texas cowboys.

"'Tis the best thing that ever happened to business here," red-haired Irishman Johnny Shaughnessey said, as he welcomed John Henry back with a drink at the shiny new bar of his newly repainted saloon. "The cowboys are carousers, but as it's carousin' I'm here to profit from, I don't mind the disturbance. And what brings you back to the Flat? I thought maybe I'd seen the last of you after that little skirmish in the upstairs."

"I reckon I'm here to profit from the cowboys too, by way of the poker cards. Unless you're lookin' for a Faro dealer. I got to be pretty handy with the layout up in Denver. I'd think about opening a dental office here if I weren't still wary of the soldiers up at the Fort."

"The soldiers aren't so much of a problem as they used to be," Shaughnessey said, "not since we got our own law in the County: Sheriff

John Larn. A regular Robin Hood, he is, but he takes care of the folks around town."

"A Robin Hood?"

"Aye, that's right. Takes from the rich and gives to the poor, or rather he takes from the cattlemen and gives to his friends. 'Course, his bein' a cattleman too, you might call that rustlin'. But you won't call it anything at all, if you know what's good for you."

"So aren't you playing it chancey, telling me about this new Sheriff's philandering?"

"I figure tellin' you is as safe as tellin' the Priest," Shaughnessey said, "if we had one in this God-forsaken place, seein' as you've got your own secrets I'm holdin', as well. We might as well be blood-brothers, you and me, for the trust we hold in each other."

John Henry wasn't sure whether he should be flattered or alarmed, but chose flattery.

"I appreciate your confidence, Shaughnessey. And I'd appreciate another shot of this Irish whiskey. You always could pick the liquor."

"And the women, if you'll recall. I'm thinkin' of havin' a sign painted to hang over the front door: Shaughnessey's Saloon: Shacklesford's Best Whores. What do you think about that?"

"I think it's bound to get you a fine from the County Sheriff," John Henry said with a laugh, "advertisin' your business like that!"

But the laugh brought a pain from the still-healing wound in his side, making him catch his breath, and Shaughnessey gave him a worried look.

"Are you all right, then?"

"I've been better. I took a gunshot awhile back, and it still troubles me some. My misfortune for holdin' to the gun law and not heelin' myself properly while travelin'. A walkin' cane isn't much use when the other man's carryin' a derringer."

"Pshaw! Texas gun law! Makin' good men go unarmed when every outlaw's got himself heeled to the teeth! That only gives bad men an unfair advantage in a fight."

"So I noticed," John Henry replied, and was going to add that he no longer held with the gun law since his altercation in Breckenridge, and had his own Colt's revolver safely tucked into his pocket. But before he could get the thought out, the conversation was interrupted by a commotion from the second floor of the saloon where a woman's shriek was followed by a man's holler, then both voices joining together into a duet of obscenities.

It was such fine cussing that John Henry had to stop and listen and was disappointed when it ended as abruptly as it had begun, followed by something that sounded like bedsprings squeaking in the room overhead.

"That's Katie Elder and her cowboy," Shaughnessey said apologetically. "They get a little loud when they're lovemakin'."

"She one of your whores?" John Henry asked, going back to his drink.

"Nothing so cheap as that," Shaughnessey replied, "more's the pity. I've had plenty of offers to pimp for her, but I'm the one that has to pay. Katies's a dancer in my floorshow. I had a real stage built for it out behind the gamin' room. Come back tonight and you'll have a treat. Until then, you might go lookin' for a room over at the Occidental Hotel. Nicest place in town, and Mrs. Smith makes a good meal for her boarders, as well. As for me, I mostly take my meals down at Lottie Deno's place. She's not much of a cook, but she's got her charms."

"Lottie Deno? Now that is a name I know. Isn't she the lady gambler?"

"That she is, and more besides. Keeps the biggest brothel in town, so you might say she's competition. But I don't mind losin' a little money her way as long as she doesn't charge me for my own time with her. 'Tis a tricky business bein' in love with the madam of a whorehouse, but when there's nothin' but whores in town, a man doesn't have much of a choice in the matter, now does he?"

Everyone in Texas had heard of Lottie Deno, though where she came from or what her past was, no one knew for sure. She'd arrived in Fort Griffin one afternoon on the stage from Jacksboro and immediately went about setting up a quality house of prostitution. She hired only the most experienced girls and wouldn't sully the reputation of her establishment by bringing in the virgin runaways other madams liked to employ. Lottie claimed that she didn't want to be responsible for tarnishing a young lady's good name until the young lady had tarnished it for herself. So most of Lottie's girls were divorcees or fallen angels who'd been disowned by pious families in the east. And unlike other madams, she didn't frown upon her employees falling in love with the customers and going off to start families of their own. Made her feel like a proud mother, she said, when she got to throw a wedding party for one of her girls.

"Aye, she's a good woman," Shaughnessey went on, "and a good business woman, besides. I gave her a gift of some new bedroom furniture, awhile back, and she stopped chargin' me for her own services. 'Course, she still sees her other clients. It's business, you know. But I'm her favorite and she lets everyone know it. Ah, Lottie, darlin'!" he said, getting moony thinking about her. "The love of a good woman is a glorious thing!"

John Henry didn't bother pointing out that, as a successful madam, Lottie couldn't really be termed a good woman. Shaughnessey was obviously too in love with her to care about the technicalities.

In the midst of Shaugnessey's fawning, John Henry hadn't noticed that the bedsprings had stopped squeaking upstairs until the hollering started up again.

"Sounds more like fightin' than lovemakin' up there," he commented. "What's the argument?"

"Katie's not fond of her cowboy's line of work. He's been in the employ of Sheriff Larn since he showed up here from Travis County. They say he shared a jail cell down there with that killer, John Wesley Hardin. He's killed a man or two himself, in the Mason County Range Wars, but mostly, he's just a cattle thief. Katie wants him out of it, but he's proud of his work. You'll likely run into him around town. Name's John Ringgold, but folks call him Ringo."

And as if he'd heard the introduction, the cowboy came down the wooden stairs with a clatter of boots and spurs and still buttoning his trousers from the tumble with Katie Elder. He wasn't bad looking for an outlaw, John Henry noted, with a lanky walk and drooping auburn mustaches and a face a lady might have called pensive.

"Looks more like a poet than a killer," he commented.

"That's the funny thing about looks," Shaugnessey replied, "you never can guess what they're hidin' inside. Take you, for instance. I'd never have taken you for a killer, either, but you did the deed."

John Henry couldn't argue the point, though he didn't much like the turn of the conversation.

"So what time's the show tonight?" he asked, paying for his liquor with two silver pieces slid across the bar. "I think I'd like to take a look at that new dancer of yours."

"Starts at eight, but you don't have to wait that long. She's comin' downstairs just now. Ringo must have forgotten to kiss her goodbye."

John Henry followed Shaughnessey's glance toward the staircase where a woman in a red satin dressing gown descended the steps with something almost like queenly grace, imperious in spite of her undress and loose hair hanging like a dark cloud around her shoulders hiding her face. John Henry watched her, amused, as she waited for her cowboy to come back to her and then shouted a profanity at the door when he did not.

"She's got a bit of a temper, as you can see," Shaughnessey said with a laugh. Then he called to the girl. "Katie, m'darlin', come over here. I'd like you to meet someone."

"I'm not interested in meeting anyone just now," she said, not bothering to look his direction. "I'm going back to bed for a nap. You can send my supper up before the show." Then she tossed her hair out of her face and turned and glided back up the stairs as gracefully as she had come down, like undressed royalty in that satin robe of hers.

"So what do you think?" Johnny Shaughnessey asked with a smile. "Do I have a prima donna on my hands?"

John Henry nodded in mute agreement, unable to put his thoughts into words. She was a prima donna, all right, too fine for a place like Shaughnessey's Saloon, with her tantalizing mix of worldliness and refinement, her tumble of glistening dark hair, her skin the color of golden honey, her voice that sounded like something exotic and intoxicating. Too fine for this place or even for the Comique Theater in St. Louis where he'd first laid eyes on her.

For Katie Elder, the cowboy's lover and Shaughnessey's dance hall girl, was his Kate.

Chapter Eight

FORT GRIFFIN, 1877

HOW MANY LUSTY DREAMS HAD HE DREAMT OF HER SINCE LEAVING St. Louis, dreams he'd at first felt guilty over? For he'd left her, after all, running away without so much as a proper farewell, then burning all her letters that followed him home. But he hadn't been able to burn away the memory of her or make the dreams stop coming. And after a time, he'd found himself looking forward to the nights he spent with her, imagining himself back in St. Louis, imagining Kate in his arms, imagining Kate's bed . . .

But there was someone else there now, the cow-thief called Johnny Ringo, and from what John Henry had seen that night at Shaughnessey's place, Kate was glad to have him there. Would she be as glad to see John Henry again, if he could bring himself to speak to her? Or would she turn the same angry words on him that had filled her last letters, calling him a coward and worse for leading her on and then leaving her? Would she want him again, now that fate had brought them back together? Or would she laugh at him, flaunting her new love affair with the outlaw cowboy?

It was the thought of her laughter that kept him from making himself known, though he asked after her so often that Shaughnessey began to suspect something more than just prurient interest on his part. And hearing what the Irishman had to say about her, John Henry was even more unsure of what he should do. For Kate's life had not gone well since he'd left her there in St. Louis—and he feared that he may have had some part in her downfall.

Shaughnessey had a barkeep's knack of knowing how to talk to people and for getting them to talk to him, and he knew all about Kate's sad story. As he retold it, she'd been a fine actress once with a grand career ahead of her until she found herself both pregnant and unwed. The father of the child was a married man, unfortunately, which left Kate no choice but to find herself another man and marry him to give herself and the baby a legitimate name. It didn't hurt that Mr. Elder, her new husband, had a good income as a traveling salesman, since a pregnant actress couldn't find all that much work. But when her new husband soon died in a fever outbreak, Kate was again left to fend for herself, and this time with an infant to care for. That was when she started onto the dance hall circuit, trying to rebuild her old career—though some folks said she'd turned to whoring for awhile, as well.

But it wasn't her whoring that most surprised John Henry; it was the name of the man who'd fathered her child.

"An odd name it was," Shaughnessey said, pausing to remember what she'd told him. "Sounded like Shamus, as I recall, but it wasn't a good Irish name like Shamus."

"Silas?" John Henry asked, and Shaughnessey nodded.

"Aye, that's it. Silas it was that fathered the baby, the shameless adulterer that he was, getting her in the family way when he already had a family of his own. It's one thing to go a-whoring, I always say, and another to go adulterin'. A blessing it was that the wee little thing left this earth before it ever knew the scoundrel that gave it life."

"You mean the baby died?"

"'Tis true, sad to say. So after all that, Katie had nothin' left in the end. No adulterin' lover, no baby, no kind man to be a husband to her. Nothin' but her career, what there was left of it. And to tell you the truth, she's not all that much of a dancer, either. She says she used to do an act with a horse, but the horse got sold when the baby came to help pay expenses. I told her I'd get her another horse, if she wanted one, and she could do her act for my customers here. But she says there'll never be another horse like the one she had. A wonderful horse, she said it was."

"Wonder," John Henry mumbled into his drink. "The horse was named Wonder . . ."

"What's that you're sayin', Doc?" Shaughnessey asked. "Do you know somethin' of our Katie Elder, then?"

But John Henry answered with a shake of his head. "No, I never met your Katie Elder. It was an actress named Kate Fisher I was thinkin' of. I knew her for a time, back in St. Louis . . ."

For the Kate he knew would never have had a love affair with the likes of Silas Melvin, and he began to think that maybe he had never known her at all.

He took a room at the Occidental Hotel, as Shaughnessey had suggested, a comfortable place run by Fort Griffin merchant Hank Smith and his Scottish-born wife, Elizabeth Boyle. The enterprising Smiths had a notion that Fort Griffin might become a real civilized community one day, and ran their hotel as if it already were. The ledger books were carefully kept, recording each guest's daily expenses, and Mrs. Smith made a point of not allowing drunken men into the dining room. That didn't stop John Henry from drinking, however. He just bought his bottle at the bar and took it up to his bedroom where he could drink as much as he liked without the landlady's disapproving gaze to disturb him.

He could have done his drinking elsewhere and would have preferred to have taken his liquor at Shaughnessey's Saloon where the conversation was often more interesting than the card games. But Shaughnessey's had the uncomfortable presence of Kate, whom he was doing his best to avoid. Since his return to the Flat, when he'd learned in quick succession that she was in Fort Griffin, was bedding a cowboy, and had lowered herself to sleep with Silas Melvin, he'd had ambivalent feelings for her. His attraction to her was still there, as it had been from the first time he saw her on the day of the St. Louis storm. But his estimation of her had fallen so far that he was almost angry at himself for feeling attracted and wasn't sure he even wanted to see her again.

But Fort Griffin being the smallish town that it was, he couldn't avoid Kate forever. So he wasn't surprised to run into her when he did, while she was mailing a letter at the post office. He knew she was a letter-writer, of course, having been the uncomfortable recipient of all those passionate epistles she'd sent to Valdosta after his hasty departure from St. Louis. But somehow, he'd never pictured the exotic Kate doing something as ordinary as buying postage.

His own letter was addressed to Miss Martha Anne Holliday, Forrest Avenue, Atlanta, Georgia, and he had just handed the letter over to the postmaster at the Butterfield Overland Stage post office when he turned around and came face to face with Kate. She must have heard his surprised catch of breath and sudden cough, for even the postmaster commented on it.

"You all right?" the man asked, and John Henry nodded quickly.

"Just fine, thank you," he replied, then regained his composure enough to tip his hat to Kate, a common courtesy to cover his sudden awkwardness.

He had two thoughts as he looked down into her rouged and powdered face: she had grown a little thinner over the years, and she was even more striking than he had remembered her to be.

"Afternoon, Miss Fisher," he said, and added with practiced manners, "It's nice to see you again."

"Good afternoon, Dr. Holliday," she replied, though he noticed that she didn't add the same mannerly comment.

"I'm stayin' here in Fort Griffin awhile," he said, as though he needed to make some explanation for his presence, and she answered with a nod of her head, making her gold earrings dance against her honey-gold throat.

"So I heard," she said blandly. "Shaughnessey mentioned there was a dentist in town. I thought the name sounded vaguely familiar."

Her chill reply was unnerving. He'd expected heat when they met again, anger or tears or something other than this cool propriety, but she looked at him from under the brim of her narrow bonnet as though she had never had any interest in him at all.

"I was just sending off a letter to my cousin . . ." he said, finding that he had nothing really to say.

"Well, I'm sure he'll be pleased to hear from you," she replied, then added with an unmistakable tinge of sarcasm, "I thought perhaps you didn't know how to write."

The postmaster must have been listening in, for he laughed at her comment then added with a smile, "Caught your show the other night,

Miss Elder. Mighty fine acrobatics you do up there. You're a helluva performer, if you don't mind my saying so."

At the sound of the praise, a smile swept across Kate's face and she curtsied toward the postmaster, her stiff taffeta skirts rustling against the floor. Quicksilver she was, mercurial. She was also an actress, John Henry reminded himself, her enigmatic behavior all a show. Had her willing behavior with him, in those weeks in St. Louis, been all a show as well?

"You are too kind," she said to the postmaster, gushing, and held out one gloved hand to his, turning all the heat that John Henry had expected for himself onto the stranger at the mail window. Then she went about her business, seeming to ignore him completely as she bought postage and sent off her letter.

He could have turned and left the stagecoach office then, and probably should have, as Kate clearly had no interest in continuing their conversation. But her aloofness somehow made him stand his ground instead.

"Kate," he said, as she finished her postal business and turned around to face him once more, "we need to talk . . ."

"Really?" she said, slipping her coin purse into a tassled handbag. "I can't imagine what we'd have to talk about, Dr. Holliday. My teeth are just fine. Now if you'll excuse me . . ."

But as she brushed past him and stepped to the door, he said lightly: "I hear you're with Ringo now."

And finally, she gave him something like a smile.

"That's right," she said. Then she turned regally and swept out of the post office.

As much as Kate's coolness bewildered him, her smile bedeviled. What had it meant? he wondered, pondering on it when he should have been concentrating on the cards or living a life of pleasant, mindless abandon. Was she pleased to be with Ringo, or pleased that he had noticed? And the more he pondered on it, the more he came to dislike the cowboy he'd never met, though that didn't mean he was having any renewed feelings for Kate. Of course, he wasn't. His pride wouldn't allow it.

His pride wouldn't allow him to keep hiding out from her either, now that they had finally crossed paths again, so he proved his disinterest by returning to his old place at Shaughnessey's Saloon. Why should he deny himself the company of the friendly Irishman just because there was a troublesome woman living in the rooms upstairs? And what difference did it make to him if he could hear Kate and Ringo going at it on the squeaky bed overhead while he sipped at his whiskey down below? There was hardly a saloon in town that didn't have a brothel attached to it, the squeaking of bed frames as much the music of Fort Griffin as the clamor of honky-tonk pianos playing out of tune.

Shaughnessey's piano was an exception, however, as he'd paid good money to have a nice instrument hauled out from Dallas. Shaughnessey had dreams of turning his watering hole into a real varieties house one day—the reason he'd paid good money for Katie Elder, as well, who knew something about the theater. Unfortunately, there weren't all that many good piano players on the Texas frontier, so Shaughnessey's spinet took the same abuse as the lesser instruments on the Flat, gathering prairie dust and cigar smoke on its ivory keys and going slowly out of tune.

John Henry's mother would have been pained to see the way that piano-forte was treated, a fine piece of workmanship being worn out by the wild frontier. She would have dusted the keys and oiled the rosewood cabinet until it gleamed and had the strings tightened and tuned again. She would have played it as it was meant to be played, making something lovely out of it instead of letting it go to waste the way it was. And thinking of her made him feel a sudden yearning to have her music in him again. So, late one night after the stage show had ended and the back room had cleared out, he took his whiskey with him and sat down at the spinet, thinking he might play a bit.

His hands were still agile, with all the card playing and dealing he'd done in the last few years, but his memory for the music had faded some. The only piece he remembered well was the one his mother had most loved, the little waltz she'd been playing the night Mattie had taught him how to dance . . .

"Franz Liszt," a voice said, giving the name the proper Hungarian pronunciation, and from out of the shadows of the darkened dance hall stepped Kate. She was wearing the red satin dressing gown, her glossy dark hair loosed from its hairpins and hanging down around her shoulders, and without the fashionable bonnet and bustle she looked smaller, somehow, and fragile almost. Then she moved toward John Henry and the dressing gown fell open a little showing a glimpse of bare white skin beneath the satin.

"I had forgotten you knew Liszt," John Henry said, his pulse quickening at the unexpected sight of her.

"I'd thought you'd forgotten me altogether," she replied. "You never wrote back to me, not once."

"I was busy," he said, lying. "I had my work in the dental office, and more helping around my father's place. And I've been sick since then . . ."

"You left without saying goodbye. You didn't even care enough to answer my letters. You have no heart, and I was fool enough to think myself in love with you."

Her words took him by surprise, though she'd said almost as much in her letters. But since his arrival in Fort Griffin, she'd done nothing to show that she'd had such feelings for him, only offended his pride by her frustrating aloofness.

"And what of Silas?" he asked, his pride speaking out. "Doesn't seem like you waited too awful long to fall in love again—or to fall into Silas Melvin's bed. I remember you once claimed to have more refinement than that."

There was a sudden hot light in her eyes and an unexpected anger in her voice.

"At least Silas was there in St. Louis! At least Silas didn't leave me!"

"Silas was there, all right. Silas was always there as I recall, ignorin' his wife to spend his nights makin' indecent proposals to you. Which were finally accepted, so I hear. I imagine it must have been quite the talk around the theater: the famous Kate Fisher and her married lover, makin' a baby . . ."

He hadn't meant to be cruel, but her own words had driven him to it.

"You don't know anything about it!" she cried, her voice rising with emotion. "You don't know . . ."

"I don't need to know. It's clear that I was mistaken in my estimation of you, back in St. Louis. It's clear you were nothin' grander then than you are now, a cowtown whore sleepin' with a cow thief."

"How dare you!" she screamed, then at the sound of her own voice she suddenly drew herself back in, the actress taking over again. "I am not a whore. Ringo doesn't pay me. He doesn't have to. I'm with him because I want to be."

"So why aren't you with him now?" John Henry asked.

"Because he's drunk. He drinks too much, sometimes, when the nightmares come. He watched his father die with half his head blown away by a shotgun. Johnny gets mournful sometimes when he remembers it and there's nothing that will soothe him."

John Henry paused a moment before replying, then he said slowly, "What I meant was, why are you here with me?"

She hesitated a moment before answering, "I heard the music, that's all. It was beautiful. And there is so little in life that is beautiful anymore."

Then she turned and walked away, leaving him alone in the darkness.

The music had lost its attraction for him, so he went back to the barroom for another shot of whiskey and found the bar closed and Shaughnessey nowhere in sight. It was, after all, so far past midnight that even the drunks had gone off to sleep the night away. So he helped himself to the liquor and sat down in a round-backed armchair for a nightcap, sipping at the whiskey and toying with his loaded Colt's. He spun the chamber and cocked the pistol, spun the chamber again and uncocked it. Curse Johnny Ringo, he thought. And curse Kate, as well.

Then he heard a scream and knew without a second thought that it was hers.

He leaped to his feet with the pistol still in his hand, crossed the barroom in three steps and bounded up the narrow wooden staircase, kicking in the locked bedroom door at the top of hall.

"No, Johnny!" Kate was crying. "Please don't, I was only trying to help you!"

Kate was lying in the middle of the bed with Ringo crouched above her holding a revolver to her face.

"What would it feel like to die that way?" he was saying in a slurred whiskey voice. "Why don't you try it for me, and tell me all about it?"

"Drop the pistol, Ringo, or you're a dead man!" John Henry commanded, and Ringo looked up in drunken confusion.

"Who the hell . . ."

"I said drop it now and let the lady go. Or you'll learn for yourself what it feels like to get your head blown off."

Kate used the moment of distraction to pull away from Ringo, rolling off the far side of the tumbled bed.

"He doesn't know what he's doing," she said. "He would never hurt me, in his right mind."

"But he'd likely kill you with the mind he's in now. You're a fool, Kate, throwin' your life away on trash like this!"

"I was just doing a little experiment," Ringo said to himself, "just having a little demonstration . . ." He swayed on his feet and put out a hand, reaching for the air.

"You're not worth wastin' a bullet on," John Henry said in disgust. Then he grabbed the drunken man by the arm and pushed him out the open door. "Sleep it off in the street, Ringo. The lady is through with you."

And Johnny Ringo, driven by his own private demons, gave Kate a sorrowful look before he stumbled down the stairs.

John Henry turned back to where Kate stood holding onto the brass bed frame and breathing fast.

"He said he was going to shoot me," she whispered. "He wanted to show me how his father died . . ."

"He's crazy, Kate. And you're crazy for bein' with him."

Then she looked up at him with tear-filled eyes.

"Hold me!" she cried, trembling and reaching out to him. "Please hold me . . ."

But when she went into his arms, John Henry felt the soft rise of her body under the satin dressing gown, and he forgot that she was frightened and only needed comfort.

"Kate," he said hoarsely, "Kate . . ." and he bent his head and kissed her.

And somehow, he wasn't surprised when Kate slipped the dressing gown from her shoulders and slid her arms around his neck.

"Why don't you close the door?" she said in that sultry voice he had dreamed about for so long. "And you can put that pistol away, as well. I won't be giving you anymore fight."

Making love to Kate was like no kind of lovemaking he had ever known. She had a hunger about her, a seemingly insatiable need to please and be pleased that kept him hungry, too. And though he had thought that one night with her would satisfy him, he found himself wanting her again every night. She was like some sweet, heady liquor to him; once he got started drinking, he couldn't seem to stop.

For the convenience of their affair, Kate moved into his room at the Occidental Hotel. But she was only there a week before the hotel's proprietress, the virtuous and very Presbyterian Mrs. Smith, discovered that the doctor's new companion wasn't his legally wedded wife and made a fuss about them staying there together, waking them early one morning with a brisk knock on the door and a voice filled with righteous indignation.

"Honeymooner's, I thought you were, the way you've been spendin' all day and night in the bedroom! Then one of my other guests says to me, 'They may be honeymoonin', but she ain't no doctor's wife. That's Katie Elder, the dance hall girl. Well, I'll not be allowin' any such things under my roof, Dr. Holliday! The Occidental is a fine hotel, not some cheap bawdyhouse where harlots and such can ply their trade. Shame on a fine man like you, bringin' disgrace upon yourself by such fornications!"

It was the same sort of speech that his mother would have given him, had she known about his sins, and once it would have made him feel guilty enough to beg forgiveness. There was a time when the memory of one night with a prostitute had driven him into fits of remorse. Now here he was living in sin, and he hardly felt any guilt at all. Even the thought that by taking a mistress he was somehow being unfaithful to Mattie didn't trouble him too much, for though Kate had his body, Mattie still had his heart.

He found it interesting, in fact, that while he and Kate were making love, he could still summon up visions of Mattie's sweet face smiling at him. And sometimes, holding Kate's soft, perfume-scented body close to his, he let himself imagine that it was Mattie who was there beside him in his bed. And if that meant that it were really Kate he was being unfaithful to, well, that was the chance a woman took when she left a life of chastity.

"So you're throwin' us out, Mrs. Smith?" he asked, standing in the open doorway of his room while his landlady finished her tirade. She'd roused him from a pleasant sleep and he hadn't had time to do more than pull on his trousers and undershirt and run his fingers through his sleep-tousled hair.

"You give me no choice, Dr. Holliday. I'm pleased to have your own business, but I can't allow such wickedness in my house. So until you put that harlot out or marry her and make an honest woman of her . . ."

"Marry Kate?" he said, laughing at the very thought of it. "She may be my mistress, Mrs. Smith, but she will never be my wife!"

"Who is that you're talking to, darling?" Kate called from the bedroom behind him, and Mrs. Smith took a quick glance past him to where Kate was still lying in bed, undressed under the rumpled bedcovers.

"Harlot!" Mrs. Smith said with a scowl. "I want her out of my house today, Dr. Holliday! And don't forget to pay your bill on the way out. It's $20 for the room and $22 for the liquor from the bar." Then she turned on her heel and swept down the hall.

"Well, Kate," John Henry said with a sigh, as he stepped back into the room and closed the door behind him. "It appears we're gonna have to find ourselves other accommodations. Our hostess doesn't approve of our livin' arrangement."

Kate sat up and pulled the sheets around her, her glossy dark hair tumbling over bare shoulders.

"To hell with her, then," she said, lifting her chin in that proud, haughty way of hers. "I've been thrown out of better places than this."

"Have you?" John Henry asked as he crossed the room and sat close beside her on the bed. Though they'd spent half the night making love, the sight of Kate with nothing but a bed sheet wrapped around her was still mightily arousing.

"And just what fine establishments have you been thrown out of, Kate?" he asked, bending to kiss her neck. "I'd hate to have a bad woman ruin my good reputation."

"What do you care about your reputation? All you need in this town is fast hands at the card table."

"Oh, I've got fast hands, all right," he said with a smile. "Shall I show you again?" And as he spoke, he slipped his hands under the sheet and slid his fingers over her breasts, and Kate shivered with pleasure at his touch.

"I thought we had to leave the hotel," she said. "It will take me some time to get dressed."

"And who the hell wants to see you dressed?" he asked, pulling the sheet aside and pushing her back down on the bed. "If I wanted a lady, I sure wouldn't be lookin' for one in Fort Griffin, Texas.

"And where would you look, my love?" Kate asked, smiling up at him with smoky blue eyes.

"Georgia," he replied, mumbling the word against her lips as he leaned down to kiss her. "Georgia . . ."

If Kate heard, she made no reply except to sigh and pull him closer.

The owner of the old Planter's Hotel wasn't nearly so particular about the personal lives of his guests, especially when they paid the room rent in advance and ran up a big bar tab on top of it, and he was pleased to have Dr. Holliday and his lady friend staying there.

They took two rooms at the hotel, one for a bedroom and one to use as a dental office so that John Henry could start practicing again. Though it had been more than two years since he'd done any real dentistry at all, it came back to him fast enough, and once he put up a signboard in the hotel window, he had all the patients he could handle as he was still the only dentist in Fort Griffin Flat. "Doc" Holliday, the locals took to calling him, and he could have made dentistry a full-time job again with all the cattle-drive cowboys coming through town, but he'd come to Fort Griffin to gamble and he didn't want to lose too much time at the tables.

He started most nights with a round of Monte, picking up a little extra cash before moving onto a game of draw poker with anyone who had enough money to make an attractive pot. It was high stakes gambling he was interested in; penny-ante was for gutless cowboys who didn't know how to play the game. And he found that Kate made a surprisingly good companion for a gentleman gambler. With her dramatic looks and full-bosomed figure, she was stunning in the new gowns he bought her, and standing by his side at the gaming tables, elegant and aloof, she was a natural capper and often all the distraction he needed to pull a winning card out of a losing hand. The other gamblers were too busy looking at her to pay attention to the game the way they should have been when they were playing with a man like Doc Holliday.

And after a successful night in the gambling halls, Kate liked to count up their winnings while lying in bed before making love again. It made her feel so safe, she said, having Doc taking such good care of her, that she hardly even thought about Johnny Ringo anymore. As for sharing a bed with a man who was suffering from the consumption, that didn't seem to worry her much. There'd been worse things to catch than a bad cough in her life as an actress.

Chapter Nine

FORT GRIFFIN, 1878

KATE MAY NOT HAVE BEEN THINKING ABOUT RINGO ANYMORE, BUT John Henry had an uncomfortable run-in with him one night after a long game of poker at the BeeHive Saloon when he found the cowboy lingering in the shadows outside the gambling hall.

"Looks like Katie's got herself a damned lunger these days, the way you been coughing in there all night," Ringo said, taunting. "Hope she don't kill you off before I get a chance to do it myself. She's a regular cyclone in the sheets." Then he slipped a revolver from his pocket and gave the barrel a spin. "You stole what's mine, Holliday, and I want it back."

"I didn't steal your woman, Ringo," John Henry said contemptuously. "She came of her own accord. Not that a cow thief like you would understand such a thing."

"I'd watch what I say, if I was you, or they'll be more than one pistol drawing a bead. I got high-up friends in this town."

"Is that a confession or a threat?" John Henry answered cooly, though his hand moved toward his own pistol pocket. He was sure he could beat a drunken cowboy in fast-draw, but had no desire to hang another murder on his conscience.

"Just call it a warning," Ringo replied. "This here's a hanging town for men who make trouble. Like you."

For a moment, they stood staring each other down, pistols ready, until John Henry forced a laugh. "If you want Kate, why don't you come ask her yourself? But I'd take a bath before you do. You reek of cow manure."

Then he turned on his heel and walked down the center of the muddy street. If the cowboy wanted to take a shot at him, he'd have to do it plain sight.

Ringo didn't bother him again, spending his time making trouble with the cattle ranchers of Shackleford County instead. Rumor had it that he and his friend Pony Diehl had thrown in with Hurricane Bill Martin's gang of cow rustlers, making night raids on the local ranches and running off branded cattle. But although the rustlers were the ones doing the lawbreaking, they were just hirelings in the employ of the real outlaw of Shackleford County: former Sheriff John Larn.

The Vigilance Committee, the old law before there was law in Fort Griffin, suspected that Larn was behind the rustling as he was the only rancher in the county who wasn't losing any of his own cattle to the rustlers, but until he made some move himself, there was little the vigilantes could do against him. The longer he succeeded in stealing from his neighbors, the more arrogant John Larn became, even handing out one-hundred dollar bills to men who'd lost their cattle to him. But he never got too brash to stop watching his back, and he started traveling with an armed guard whenever he went into town.

Larn didn't drink much that anyone knew, and he rarely gambled, but when he did feel like taking in a game, he did his playing at the Beehive Saloon where his favorite henchman, Hurricane Bill, had an interest. John Henry had played against Larn at the Beehive a few times and found him to be a bad poker player but a good loser, which made him good company for a night of cards. Hurricane Bill, himself, had joined them on occasion, and the rustler duo made a comically ill-suited couple: John Larn in an expensive suit of clothes and fancy tooled leather boots, and Hurricane Bill in a matted buffalo hide coat to match his heavy matted beard. But on one warm summer evening, they were joined by an even odder looking pair of sports—Lottie Deno, the red-haired lady gambler and whorehouse madam, and a fidgety young man with a tangle of curly hair who was introduced as Billy Brocious.

"But we call him Curly Bill on account of his pretty hair," Hurricane said as John Henry and Kate made their entrance. "Curly's working with me and Mr. Larn these days."

"That's enough, Hurricane," cautioned John Larn. "We don't need to talk business in front of company. I'm sure the doctor has more interesting things on his mind than cattle ranching."

"Would that be Doc Holliday?" the lady gambler said with a lift of a brow. "I believe Johnny Shaughnessey's mentioned your name to me. And this must be the talented Miss Elder," she added, giving Kate a generous smile. "I was disappointed to hear you're not dancing anymore."

"I'm with Doc now," Kate replied. "He makes enough off the gambling for both of us, don't you my love?"

"I do my best. But you are an expensive woman to keep, Miss Elder. I am often forced to desperate means to pay your bills." And so saying, he reached a hand to his vest pocket, making the other players freeze in their places.

"Hold on, Doc!" Hurricane Bill said quickly, "you know there's no weapons allowed in here!"

But John Henry laughed. "I'm not plannin' to rob you fine gentlemen! I'd just like to ante into this game, if you'll have me. I was only reachin' for my money purse." And as he pulled his hand from his vest, he opened it to show a wad of greenbacks. "How does two-hundred sound for starters? I think a healthy pot makes for a more interesting evenin', don't you? Five card draw, nothin' wild, and no limit on the bets?"

Then he tossed the bills onto the table and noted with satisfaction that even wealthy cattleman John Larn seemed impressed.

"I hear you're the best poker player in Texas, Dr. Holliday," purred Lottie Deno, as John Henry settled himself between her and Hurricane. "Is that true?"

"No Ma'am, I don't believe that's true. I reckon I'm the best poker player in the whole Wild West. Kate darlin', why don't you make yourself comfortable? This may be a long evenin'."

And by reply, Kate slowly dropped the lace shawl from her shoulders, showing off her figure in a low-cut satin dress, and letting the men have a good long look at her before taking a seat behind John Henry.

"Hell, Holliday!" Curly Bill Brocious said, letting out a wolf whistle. "Your woman's looking damn fine tonight!"

"Keep your trousers on, Curly," Hurricane Bill warned, "this is just poker tonight. Deal the cards, Lottie. I'm running out of time to beat you at this game."

"Oh, you'll never beat me," Lottie said with a smile. "I cheat, remember?"

But though Lottie Deno claimed to be playing a crooked game, John Henry somehow kept coming up with good cards himself, like the straight flush and the full house he took an hour later. And if he hadn't known better, he might have thought that Lottie was purposefully dealing him better hands than she was giving the other men who were soon played out of the game.

"Although losing to you is always a pleasure," Larn told Lottie as he bent to kiss her cheek after throwing in his last losing hand.

"You're a fool with your money, Larn," Hurricane Bill complained. "If you want to give your winnings to a whore, you might as well get some whoring for it."

"I would, if I weren't such a faithful married man," Larn replied. "Not that you'd understand the concept of fidelity, Hurricane, being married to a whore yourself."

"Save your piety for the preacher. Everybody in the county knows you been sweet on Lottie Deno for years. I'll bet your wife wondered why you laid out your flower garden in the shape of playing cards. Did you know about that, Lottie? He even put a queen of hearts in the middle, just for you."

And something almost like a blush ran over John Larn's handsome face when Lottie smiled up at him.

"Did you really, Sheriff? How very sentimental of you! I'll have to think of you from now on whenever I play the red queen."

But Larn had quickly regained his composure and he glared at Hurricane Bill. "I should have let the Vigilance Committee have you last time they came looking around. Good night, Lottie. Mr. Martin and I have some ranching to do. Come along, Billy."

"Interesting man," John Henry said when Larn and his bodyguards had left the saloon. "Do you reckon he really planted a flower garden in the shape of playing cards?"

"Sure he did," Lottie replied. "It's famous in these parts. I rode out to take a look at it myself when he wasn't around. There's a queen of hearts in the middle of it, all right, though I didn't know he put it there for me. But I'm not much of a flower lover. Flowers always die sooner or later." Then she collected the scattered cards and ruffled them expertly, "So I guess this leaves just you and me now. Mind if I deal?"

"As a matter of fact, I do, Miss Deno. The other gentlemen may not have noticed you palmin' a card or two, but I did. If you were a man, I'd have had to shoot you for cheatin'. So why don't we start this hand with a fresh deck, and let Miss Elder deal for us? Kate, open up that pack of playin' cards I bought just today, will you?"

"Now Doc," Lottie said disappointedly, "you don't really expect me to fall for that old game, do you? Even I've resealed a marked deck and pretended it was new!"

"Have you indeed, Miss Deno? Then you're a worse cheat than I thought you were."

"And I'd say that makes us two of a kind."

"Well then," John Henry said with a slow smile, "it appears we are at an impasse. Neither one of us can be trusted to play square. However are we going to finish this game? I don't think I can let you just walk away with all that money of mine." Lottie's winnings were piled high on the table in front of her, cash and chips and several notes for credit at the local bank.

"Why don't we let this hand decide it?" Lottie said. "Your mistress can deal, and you can pretend not to notice if I palm a card. That way, we can both do a little cheating and still be playing fair with each other."

Kate opened the sealed deck of carefully marked cards and shuffled and dealt them as John Henry had taught her to: three jacks to him, his favorite hand, and a couple of high cards to Lottie. The high pair gave the competition a sense of security, but his three of a kind was enough to win most games and could turn into a full house or even four of a kind on a lucky draw. But though he knew that Kate had given Lottie a high pair, he didn't know for sure what kind they were. Even when he cheated, he liked to have some element of chance left in the game. That was what made gambling a thrill, after all.

But Lottie Deno was a cool player as she opened with that pair— aces, John Henry figured, from the fact that she wagered so high. Unless she was bluffing, of course. It was hard to tell, her being a woman and not the kind of competition he was used to. He could read most men, but Lottie Deno seemed inscrutable, and maybe even unbeatable, until the wagering ended and he called.

As Lottie laid her cards face up on the table, John Henry let out a whistle. She had two pair, all right, just as he'd thought, but what a two pair hand she had: Aces and eights and a queen kicker.

"The Deadman's Hand!" he said with admiration. "Wild Bill Hickok's last play. I'm surprised you had the nerve to keep it, Lottie. They say no man has ever left that hand alive."

"But I'm not a man, as you may have noticed. And how about your own hand?"

"It's not as impressive," he said, turning his cards over, "but it beats your two pair, anyhow: three-of-a kind jacks."

But Lottie smiled as if she were the real winner. "Well, at least I can say I lost to the best card player in the whole Wild West! Though I have a confession to make. Those chips of mine can't be cashed in, not here in the saloon, at least. I'm afraid I've left my handbag at home tonight. Hurricane gave me the chips on credit, at Mr. Larn's request."

"Then I suppose I can carry your credit, too," John Henry said, "though I usually like to collect my winnin's directly."

"But I'm not asking you to carry me," Lottie said. "I've got the money at my house, if you'd just walk me down there. Do you mind loaning him out for a bit, Miss Elder? You know what my part of town is like, not safe for a woman walking alone."

"I suppose I don't mind," Kate replied, as she pulled the last of the cash into her velvet handbag. "Doc's taught me how to use a knife as well as how to deal the cards. I ought to be able to get back to the hotel without losing all our money." Then she stood and gave John Henry one long, lingering kiss. "Just don't take too long, my love," she said in that sultry Hungarian voice of hers. "You know how I hate to go to bed alone."

Lottie lived at the end of the main street of town, down by the banks of the Clear Fork of the Brazos where the prostitutes had their shanties, though her house was nicer than the rest. It was built of white-washed pickets, willow timbers laid side by side and bound together to make boards for the walls.

"I'd never seen a willow picket house before I came to Fort Griffin," Lottie said, as she stood on the doorstep in the thin midnight light, her dyed red hair looking a little less garish in the darkness. "But it makes a nice, comfortable home, and I do like my customers to be comfortable. I suppose that's why I do so well here. Men know they can always have a nice time at Lottie's place."

"You said you had the money?" John Henry asked, feeling uncomfortably conspicuous standing on the front step of Lottie Deno's brothel. He knew plenty of men who were regular customers at the houses of prostitution down by the river, but he'd never had the need to venture into that part of town before. Shaughnessey's girls had always been happy to offer, and now that he had Kate for company, he didn't need to go looking for amusement.

"What I meant is, I can pay you what I owe you here," Lottie replied. "But as I'm a little low on cash right now, I was hoping maybe you'd accept something in trade."

"In trade?"

"I'm talking about a business transaction, Doc," Lottie said coolly. "You come in and let me work off my debt. Prostitution is my business, after all. Why not let me give you some of what I sell in payment for my debt? I promise you'll be satisfied with the arrangement."

"You mean sleep with one of your girls and forget the money?" he said in surprise.

"Not one of my girls, Doc," Lottie said with a friendly smile. "Spend the night with me, and call my poker debt even."

But when he hesitated, she put her hand on his arm and looked up into his face. "What's the matter, Doc? You're not married to that Elder woman, are you?"

And John Henry thought of Kate, back in their hotel room counting up his gambling winnings and drinking the liquor his gambling money bought. Then he touched the gold Claddagh ring on his little finger, and he said softly:

"No, I'm not married to Kate."

"Well then, will you accept my payment?"

And when Lottie smiled and reached her hand out to his, he took it, and followed her inside.

It was the sound of screaming down by the river that woke him in the early hours of the dawn, long after he and Lottie had finished settling her gambling debt. She'd been as good as her word about paying off to his satisfaction, and he was deep asleep in her comfortable bed when the noise began, a terrified wailing that sounded more animal than human.

"What the hell?" he said, rolling over and reaching for his revolver on the night stand, his reflexes amazingly quick for a man who hadn't had much rest.

"A hanging, I expect," Lottie replied, as she pulled the sheet around her nakedness and climbed out of bed, peering through the curtain at the window. "The vigilantes like to leave us a man for breakfast every morning, strung up in the trees there by the river. They're hanging the wrong men, though, if you ask me, just poor cowboys. It's John Larn who deserves to be strangled. He's the one who's behind it all."

"I thought Larn was a friend of yours," John Henry said, rolling back over and laying his pistol down.

"I'm friends with any man who loses a game of poker to me."

"And what about me? I beat you."

"Oh, you only thought you beat me, Doc. I still had an Ace up my sleeve, if I'd wanted to play it."

"You mean you let me win?" he asked, puzzled. "Why would you do such a thing?"

"Well, honey," she said, lying back down beside him and running her hand over the fair hair on his bare chest. "I figured that was the only way I'd ever get you into my bed. I took a liking to you the minute you walked into that saloon last night. And why shouldn't I have some fun myself from time to time?"

"You are a bad woman, Lottie Deno!"

"I know I am," she replied, "but at least I'm good at being bad!"

"You are that," he agreed, remembering how much he'd enjoyed collecting on that debt. "It's a shame we've settled up already."

"We can always cut the cards again. I've got time for another quick go 'round, if you're feeling ready to ante up."

And if he hadn't started into a fit of morning coughing just then, he might have taken her up on the offer. But it was a few minutes before he could even catch his breath, and by then, Lottie was looking more concerned than amorous.

"That's a bad cough, Doc. Have you seen a doctor about it?"

"Sure, I've seen a doctor. He told me to try a dryer climate. So I went to the Staked Plains and dried out."

"You've got the consumption? That's a shame, Doc, that's a real shame. I'll probably die of some social disease myself, if I don't die in childbirth first. Though I've done fine in that department so far."

"You have children?" he asked in surprise, though the news shouldn't have startled him too much. Prostitutes were always getting pregnant by their customers and having babies who would never know their fathers. The west was littered with illegitimate children and their working-girl mothers. But he didn't picture Lottie Deno being in that situation. "So where are they?"

"Far away from here, you can bet. No baby of mine is ever going to know what his mother does for a living. That's why I work as hard as I do, so I can have enough to send to them and something left over for me, as well. So now you know my secret, Doc. Do you still think I'm a bad woman?"

"No," he replied, suddenly seeing Lottie in a softer kind of light. "I think you're a real nice woman. No wonder John Larn has such a fancy for you."

"John Larn . . ." she said on a sigh, sitting up and shaking out her tangled red hair. "He did come to me once, right after I moved here. I think he'd had a big row with his wife, and figured he was losing her anyway. We had a good time together, that once. It might have even been his baby boy I had awhile later—he was a real pretty baby. But there's no telling, working the line the way I do. I like to think that maybe he was John Larn's, though. The queen of hearts," she said wistfully, "what do you think of that?"

"I think you're a queen, all right, Lottie," he said, pulling her back to him. But before he could do more than hold her close, the bedroom door flew open. Kate was standing in the doorway, her face wild with anger and the Hell-Bitch in her upraised hand.

"Come away from her!" she said in a fury. "Come away, or I'll cut her open!"

"Why, Kate, whatever are you doing with that blade?" John Henry asked in surprise, though he was less startled by the weapon than by Kate's sudden appearance in Lottie Deno's brothel.

"How could you do this?" she demanded. "You know she's Shaughnessey's woman. I thought Shaughnessey was your friend!"

"Shaughnessey knows what I do for a living," Lottie said, pulling the sheet back around her. "It's none of his business who I do it with."

"We were just settlin' our gambling debt," John Henry explained. "Miss Deno got herself in a little deeper than she planned."

"Oh, I think it's you that got in deep, Doc!" Lottie said with a bawdy laugh, and Kate screamed and rushed at her.

"Whore! I'll kill you!"

But when she raised her hand to strike at Lottie, John Henry grabbed his revolver and leveled it at her.

"Don't make me shoot you, Kate. This isn't worth dyin' over." And when he cocked the pistol with a click of the hammer, Kate froze in her steps.

"Would you really kill me?"

"Not if you behave yourself and give me that knife. Come now, Kate. You can't beat a bullet, can you?"

And slowly, Kate's arm fell back to her side, the huge knife clattering onto the wooden floor.

"I thought you said you weren't married, Doc," Lottie commented, as she slid off the bed and pulled on a dressing gown. "But she sure looks like a jealous wife to me."

"Why don't you give us a moment here alone?" he asked her.

"Sure, Doc. Just don't let her kill you in my house, all right? I've got customers coming in pretty soon."

"There now, Kate," John Henry said evenly, after Lottie had closed the door. "It's all over now. Shaughnessey doesn't ever need to know . . ."

But Kate turned to him with sudden tears in her eyes.

"I don't care about Shaughnessey!" she cried. "I care about you! How could you do this? How could you do this to me?"

"This had nothing to do with you. I was just collectin' on a gambling debt, like I said . . ."

"But why this way? Don't I give you what you need? Aren't I a good enough lover to you? Why did you have to go to someone else's bed?" Then she sat down beside him and said with surprising passion: "Love me, Doc! Make love to me!"

"I'm tired," he said, turning away from her and reaching for his clothes. "I want to go home."

But Kate was already unfastening the buttons on the bodice of her dress, and she reached for his hands and pulled him toward her.

"Love me!" she said hungrily. "I need you to love me!"

And feeling the softness of her skin under his fingers, John Henry felt the urgency rising up in himself.

"Kate," he said hoarsely, "I don't want to do this here. Not in Lottie's bed . . ."

But Kate was laughing as she lay down and pulled him to her.

"Yes, in Lottie's bed!" she said. "I want you to remember me in Lottie's bed! I want you to remember me . . ."

And after they had finished making love and had walked back to their hotel through the early morning quiet of Fort Griffin Flat, Kate was as cool and calm as if nothing had ever happened at all.

A man for breakfast, Lottie had called the vigilante lynchings down by the banks of the Clear Fork. There weren't enough sturdy trees for hangings anywhere else in that dry cattle country, so the pecans along the riverbank became a kind of public gallows for the Vigilance Committee. And though it wasn't every morning, there were still so many bodies swinging from those shady branches that Fort Griffin was getting a reputation as a hanging town.

But in spite of the vigilante's efforts, the cattle rustling in Shackleford County went on, drawing in more and more cowboy drifters looking for a way to make a fast dollar. The local law couldn't seem to do anything to stop the rustling either, as newly appointed Sheriff Bill Cruger had his hands full just keeping the gambling dens of Fort Griffin under control. Whenever the cowboys got bored out on the range, they came in to run the town, gambling away their wages and shooting up the saloons. John Henry even saw Johnny Ringo in town a time or two with his friends from Hurricane Bill's gang. But Ringo always seemed more interested in getting drunk than in looking up the woman he'd spent a few weeks with at Shaughnessey's Saloon.

Shaughnessey's was still John Henry's headquarters, in spite of the fact that he got uncomfortable whenever the Irishman mentioned Lottie Deno's name. It might not be any of Shaughnessey's business who Lottie slept with, but John Henry couldn't forget Kate's angry accusation. Shaughnessey was the first friend he'd made in Fort Griffin and had saved his life once, and he owed the Irishman some kind of loyalty, at least. Sleeping with Lottie had been a mistake and he didn't mean to repeat it.

He was in Shaughnessey's dance hall one cool November afternoon, having a drink and taking in the show before going back to his hotel to get ready for a night of cards, when the Irishman motioned to him from his office behind the long walnut bar.

"Doc, there's somebody I'd like you to meet, an old friend of mine from my boxing days. He's here looking for a job, and I thought maybe you could help him to find one."

"Why me? I'm not lookin' to hire anyone."

"He's after a law job," Shaughnessey said with a wink, "and I told him you know more about the law around here than anybody else!"

"Very amusin'. And where is this friend of yours?"

"He's right over there," Shaughnessey said, "the big fellow at the far end of the bar," and he nodded toward a tall man in a long white duster coat, his flat-brimmed hat pulled down low over his eyes. "His name's Wyatt Earp. Why don't you go on over and introduce yourself?"

But John Henry lingered a moment, thinking that he might just finish his whiskey and leave without bothering to meet the man at all. Kate was waiting for him at the hotel and he ought to get back to her. She hadn't been feeling well lately, with a sick stomach and edgy nerves, and she didn't like to be left alone too long. Then he sighed and threw back the rest of his drink. He owed Shaughnessey, after all.

"Mr. Earp?" he said as he took a place beside the man at the bar, but before he could introduce himself, he started into a fierce fit of coughing Finishing a drink too fast always started him off like that; usually he just sipped at his liquor, letting it go down slow. He grabbed the handkerchief from his vest pocket and coughed hard into it, then folded it quickly to hide the red-flecked sputum that stained the cloth.

"That's a bad cough," Wyatt Earp observed. "You a Lunger?"

"For the time bein'," John Henry replied, clearing his throat and pushing the handkerchief back into his pocket. "I reckon I'll get over it, sooner or later."

"Oh? I thought the consumption was fatal," Earp said, and John Henry sighed—the man obviously had no appreciation for sarcasm.

What he did have was the broad-shouldered, hard-muscled look of a man who'd spent a lifetime on the frontier. His face was square-jawed and tanned, his hair and heavy mustache a russet-gold, making him seem like a big mountain lion, poised and powerful. A man's man, John Henry thought enviously, and probably a lady's man, too.

"You Doc Holliday?" Earp asked, as he took off his hat and pulled a cigar from his coat pocket, lighting it and taking a long, deliberate draw. "I seem to remember that surname on a poster from Pinkerton's Detective Agency. Wasn't the army chasing after you awhile back?"

"I had some trouble with the law at one time. Why? Are you plannin' to arrest me?"

"Not today," Earp replied, letting out a slow cloud of cigar smoke and a familiar aroma of some Havanna blend, "there's no money in it. The army's got a short memory where Buffalo Soldiers are concerned."

The conversation was taking an uncomfortable turn, and John Henry quickly changed the subject away from himself. "That's an interestin' name you've got, Mr. Earp. Are you a Southern man?"

"Hell, no. I was born in Illinois. My brothers fought for the Union. I would have too, if I'd been old enough to fight. Why do you ask?"

"I knew of some Earps back home in Georgia. It's not a common name. I thought maybe you were kin to them: Daniel Earp and his wife Obedience?"

"Daniel Earp?" Wyatt repeated. "There was a Daniel in the family, my father's older brother. I haven't heard of him since before the War."

"Well, I reckon you wouldn't have, bein' a Union man," John Henry drawled. Then he added with a smile. "Daniel Earp was the biggest slave trader in Griffin, Georgia. Which may come as hard news to your Yankee family."

"Do you think you're funny, Holliday?"

"Sometimes."

"Well, I don't," Wyatt Earp said disdainfully. "But Shaughnessey says you're the man to talk to about the lay of things around here. He says you play cards with everybody in town, so maybe you can give me the lead I'm looking for. I came down here trailing some rustled cattle, but it seems those beeves have already been sold to market. Now I'm looking for another job. I figured maybe your sheriff here could use a little help fighting the rustlers. I'm good at handling cowboys."

"You're barking up the wrong tree, Mr. Earp. It's not Sheriff Cruger who's taking care of the rustlers. It's the Old Law Mob, and they won't be asking for help from a stranger like you."

"The Old Law Mob?"

"The local Vigilance Committee. They've been around since before there was any real law in this county, even before the military came in.

They're old Shackleford County boys who don't trust anyone but themselves. You try to break into the vigilantes, and they'll string you up right along with the rustlers."

"And if they're so tough, why haven't they got this county cleaned out yet?"

"They're chasin' the wrong men," John Henry said, repeating Lottie's words. "Until they get the rustler boss, the cattle thievin' won't stop."

"And who's this rustler boss?" Earp asked, giving him a steady blue-eyed stare. "I get the feeling you know something about him."

"I do," John Henry replied, "but my life wouldn't be worth very much around here if I told you who he was. You'd best just leave it alone, Mr. Earp, and look for a job somewhere else. The Vigilance Committee won't take you, and Sheriff Cruger doesn't have the goods to bring the rustlers in."

"And suppose I find out for myself who's behind the rustling and bring him to justice? I guess the county might be so grateful, they'd make me sheriff."

"You dream big, Mr. Earp!" John Henry said with a laugh.

"I do, for a fact," Wyatt Earp agreed without a trace of brag about it. "I've been a deputy in all the cowtowns: Ellsworth, Wichita, Dodge City. Summer work, mostly, during the cattle season. But that kind of lawing doesn't pay, not like being a county sheriff pays. I figure I just need to find the right county and make myself known. So how 'bout we make deal, Holliday?"

"Such as?"

"You put me in touch with somebody who's willing to talk, and I'll pay you a reward once I get made sheriff. And nobody will ever know I got the lead from you. How's that sound?"

"Sounds suspicious," John Henry answered. "Why would a lawman like you trust an outlaw like me, anyhow?"

"We've all done things we regret," Wyatt said with a shrug. "Your past doesn't concern me too much."

"And why should I trust you? What if you get drunk some night and mention to the wrong people that you got your information from me? It could shorten my already short life."

"I'm not much of a drinker," Wyatt Earp replied, "nor much of a talker, neither." He paused and looked into his glass. "Laconic, my folks called me—that means spare on words."

"I know what it means," John Henry said. "I just want to make sure you stay that way as long as you're in Fort Griffin."

"So, what do you say about my offer, Doc? Can we deal?"

While he waited for an answer, Earp took another draw on his cigar and blew out another cloud of smoke, and John Henry realized where he'd smelled that kind of tobacco before: it was the same Havanna his father had smoked, an aroma that brought back too many memories. He was about to turn Wyatt Earp down when he remembered the debt he owed to Shaughnessey, and reconsidered.

"All right," he said, "I reckon you've got yourself a partner, Wyatt Earp."

"Good," Wyatt replied with a quick flash of a smile against his frontier tan. Then, as he put out his hand to shake on the deal, he added: "Oh, and tell Katie I said hello."

"Katie?" John Henry asked in surprise. "You know Kate?"

"I knew a little Hungarian pistol who called herself Katie Elder back in Wichita when I was lawing there. She worked in my sister-in-law Bessie's brothel for awhile."

He was less surprised by the news of Kate's Wichita career than he was by Wyatt Earp's family connection to it. "Your sister-in-law ran a bordello? Didn't that put you in a compromisin' position, being a lawman?"

"Not much. Bessie ran a good place and paid her fines regular. I figured the house was her business, hers and Jim's. Besides, having a brothel in the family had its benefits. I met my wife there."

"You married a girl on the line?" John Henry asked in surprise. Marrying a woman of negotiable virtue seemed to him like a needless thing to do. Why buy the cow, folks always said, when the milk was free—or cheap, anyhow? Not that Kate didn't cost him some money with her expensive gowns and extravagant taste, but at least he wasn't tied to her the way he'd be tied to a wife. They were both free to pack up and leave anytime either one of them got tired of their living arrangement.

"We're not married exactly," Wyatt explained. "I didn't sign anything legal. But Celia Ann knows how things are with me. She knows I don't plan on ever taking a marriage vow again . . ."

Wyatt stopped in mid-sentence as if he suddenly realized he'd revealed too much of himself, and for a moment his eyes were unguarded, filled with pain, and John Henry felt he'd had a glimpse of the man behind the brave facade. Wyatt had lost someone, too, he sensed, and carried the pain of that loss as John Henry carried the pain of losing Mattie. Then Wyatt's eyes shaded again, closing over the emotion. A man's man, all right, John Henry thought—the kind of man he wished that he could be.

"Why don't you have Katie come by the hotel," Wyatt went on after that momentary pause. "I'm sure Celia would enjoy a visit from her. The two of them used to be friendly back in Wichita."

"I think Kate might like that."

"So Doc, are you really as good as they say you are with the cards?"

"Why don't you join me for a game tonight, and find out for yourself? I'll be down at the Beehive Saloon where all the rustlers play."

"The Beehive? I think I'd like to meet some of those card players."

"Oh, speakin' of that," John Henry said almost casually, "there is one rustler in particular I'd like to see run out of this county, if you happen to come across him some dark night. His name is Johnny Ringo."

"Ringo," Wyatt repeated. "I'll keep that in mind, Doc."

"I met an interestin' man today," John Henry told Kate when he got back to their room at the Planter's Hotel. Kate had been taking one of her afternoon naps, but she woke with a lazy yawn when she saw him.

"Who's that?" she asked, stretching languidly.

"He's a lawman from Kansas," John Henry replied, as he pulled off his jacket and vest and poured wash water into a china bowl on the dressing table. "He wants me to help him with a law job here in Fort Griffin."

"You?" Kate asked, reaching for the lady's magazine she'd been reading before falling asleep. "Why should you help a lawman? The law's no friend of yours, is it?"

"Not generally. But there's something about this particular lawman— he seems like a man you could trust. And it didn't seem to bother him that I've had some troubles with the law myself. He seems accepting, somehow, open-minded . . ."

He stopped a moment and looked at his reflection in the mirror over the dressing table and had the sudden notion that with his sandy blond hair and mustache and his clear blue eyes, he looked like a smaller, thinner version of Wyatt Earp himself. Then he shook his head and said with a laugh, "Imagine that; me having a lawman for a friend!"

"Friend?" Kate said in surprise. "What are you talking about? You don't even know this man."

"I knew some of his family back in Georgia. His uncle lived in Griffin when I was growing up there. And I hear he's an acquaintance of yours, as well. His name is Wyatt Earp."

And looking back into the mirror, he saw a sudden movement behind him as Kate dropped her magazine and stared at him.

"What did you say?"

"I said I met your friend Wyatt Earp today," he repeated, wondering why Kate always seemed so jumpy these days. "He says he knew you in Wichita."

"Wyatt Earp is no friend of mine! He's no friend to anyone but himself! He had a hard reputation around Kansas . . ."

"Well, he's gonna need a hard reputation around here," John Henry said, drying his hands and pulling a fresh linen shirt from the dressing table drawer. "He's got big plans for himself, cleanin' up the county and gettin' himself elected sheriff for it. But if anybody can do it, I reckon he can."

Kate said with a sarcastic laugh, "And while he was telling you all his brave plans, did he happen to mention that he was dismissed from the Wichita police for roughing up his prisoners?"

"Is that right?" John Henry asked, giving her a questioning gaze. "And is that how you knew him, Kate? Did he arrest you for whoring?"

"No," she said quietly, looking away. "He didn't arrest me."

"Then what gives you the right to judge him, anyhow? I should think you'd be pleased to have me find a friend with any redeeming qualities at all. Johnny Shaughnessey aside, most of the men I know would as soon kill me as lose a game of cards to me. And speaking of that, Earp and I will be goin' out to play some poker together tonight, if you'd like to come along."

It was the first time since they'd taken up together that he hadn't just assumed Kate would be his companion for the evening, and she said bitterly:

"Why should I? You've got a new friend now, don't you? What do you need me for?"

And John Henry, bewildered by Kate's sudden belligerence and a little hurt as well, snapped back at her. "I need you for the same thing I always have, Kate. But if you'd rather not be accommodating, I reckon I can always get what I need down at Lottie Deno's place. She seemed happy enough to have me in her bed."

For a moment, Kate looked up at him with a hot Hungarian pride in her eyes. Then she took a long breath and said in that sultry voice of hers, "You don't need to go back to Lottie, my love. Whatever you want, you can get right here from me," and she lay back on the bed, waiting for him to come to her.

But John Henry wasn't interested in making love just then, and pretended not to notice Kate's willingness as he pulled writing paper and a pen from the dressing table.

"What are you doing?" she asked in surprise.

"I'm writin' a letter. I think my cousin will be interested in hearing about my day, even if you're not."

"Your cousin?" Kate said with a haughty laugh. "Well, tell him hello from me!"

He ignored Kate's contemptuous comment as he sat down at the small table in front of the long windows that looked out over raucous, rowdy Fort Griffin, and began writing:

My Very Dearest Mattie,

Do you remember that summer Sunday back in '72 when Aunt Permelia made us all a picnic at the Ponce de Leon Springs? You asked me then if I needed a hero, and I said I guessed that I did. Well today, I think I may have finally found a real one. His name is Wyatt Earp.

The night of cards with the Kansas lawman turned out to be two weeks of nightly card games, and John Henry got to know a lot about

Wyatt Earp, though getting Wyatt to talk about himself wasn't an easy thing to do. He was laconic, all right, and surprisingly shy, as well, which seemed funny for a man as brave and daring as he was. Even his mannerisms seemed on the shy side, the way he hunched his shoulders in his big duster coat and pulled his hat so low down on his face that his eyes were always half-hidden in shadow, keeping himself to himself. But Wyatt was a man of action, not a man of words, and he'd lived the kind of adventurous life that most men only dreamed of.

He was born on an Illinois farm, the son of a Mexican War veteran and named after his father's commanding officer, a fighting man named Wyatt Berry Stapp. It was a big name to hang on a little boy, but young Wyatt Berry Stapp Earp soon proved equal to it, growing tall and strong as his family moved on from Illinois to Iowa, Missouri, Kansas, and finally across the plains to California. And by the time Wyatt was eighteen-years-old, he was on his own and working his way back across the country again, driving freight wagons over the mountains from California and laying rails for the Union Pacific Railroad across the Wyoming wilderness. He settled for a time in Missouri, taking a job as a constable in the little town of Lamar, but settling down didn't seem to suit him, and soon he was off again, hunting buffalo on the great plains, guarding stage coaches of gold bullion out of the mines of the Black Hills, and controlling rowdy cowboys in the cowtowns of Kansas. He'd done just about everything there was to do in those wild western territories, and done it all well enough to live to tell the story. And the more John Henry heard of Wyatt's life, the more sure he was that he'd finally found himself a real American hero.

But hero or not, Wyatt couldn't seem to catch the trail of the Shackleford County rustlers, and after two fruitless weeks in Fort Griffin, he packed up and headed east to Fort Worth. They were hiring police officers there, he'd heard, and until his summer hitch in Dodge City started up again, he needed a paying job. John Henry could have given Wyatt a break and told him who the rustler boss was, but John Larn wasn't a man to cross. If John Henry divulged what he knew about the rustlers, his own life would be on the line, and he already had enough trouble to worry about. It seemed his card playing fame had spread from Fort Griffin all the way back to Dallas, where the local law heard of it and sent a warrant out for his arrest on the old gambling indictments.

It was Sheriff Bill Cruger who brought the warrant, though he was sorry to have to do it.

"I got no quarrel with you, Doc," he said apologetically, as he stood in the doorway of John Henry's room at the Planter's Hotel. "But the law's the law, and I got to honor this warrant. I'm afraid I got to take you in and send you back to Dallas to stand trial."

"But it's just a gamblin' charge, Sheriff," John Henry argued amiably, "surely you don't intend to inconvenience us both over such a triflin' matter!"

"Got to, though where the hell I'm going to put you until the next stage leaves for Dallas, I don't know. The jailhouse at Albany is already full, and so's the guardhouse up at the Fort."

It was clear that the Sheriff wasn't going to shirk his duty and ignore the papers from the Dallas County court, and John Henry knew better than to try to offer the county's leading lawman a bribe. But maybe there was another way to avoid going back to Dallas . . .

"Tell you what, Sheriff, why don't you put me under house arrest right here in the hotel? That'll keep you from overfillin' your jail, and give me a chance to pack up and get ready for the ride to Dallas. It'll take me awhile to get my dental equipment put together, and I don't dare leave it here unsupervised while I'm gone. I'm gonna need it when I get back to take care of that bad tooth of yours. I wouldn't want you to start hurtin' again like you were last week . . ."

It was an obvious play, but the only one he could think of on such short notice. Sheriff Crueger had been mighty grateful when John Henry had opened up that badly decayed tooth and taken out the throbbing, rotting nerve. And by the way the sheriff winced at the reminder of it, John Henry could tell that he still remembered the pain.

"Guess you're right, Doc," Sheriff Cruger said, rubbing his jaw at the memory. "I guess I could leave you here with one of my deputies to guard the door. I'd hate for you to lose anything valuable just to make a court date."

"Why, that's real kind of you, Sheriff," John Henry drawled in his most gentlemanly manner, "and I'll be sure to have myself ready in time to catch the stage." Of course, the stage had other destinations besides Dallas, and it would be easy enough to change his itinerary once he got out of Fort Griffin . . .

"Oh, I know you'll be on time, Doc," Sheriff Cruger said in parting, "'cause I'll have my deputy take you to Dallas himself. Just in case you forget the way."

And before John Henry could think of another ploy to avoid being sent back to Dallas to stand trial again, he had an armed deputy posted at his door and another in the lobby of the hotel.

Kate had missed all the excitement of John Henry's arrest, as she had spent the afternoon up at the military fort on the hill seeing the post doctor. After weeks of being sick at her stomach, she still wasn't getting any better, and the usual remedies of liquor-laced elixirs only made her feel worse. So when she took a notion to try the post doctor for a cure, John Henry had been more than happy to pay for the visit. Kate's illness had taken its toll on their lovemaking, and if she didn't get well soon, he'd have to find himself another mistress.

"And where am I supposed to go while you keep Dr. Holliday incarcerated?" she demanded of the deputy at the door when she returned. "This is my room, too! All of my things are here."

"Sorry, Ma'am," the deputy apologized, cowering some before her haughty tirade. "I only got orders to keep the Doc here. Sheriff Cruger never said nothing about a lady being allowed in."

But Kate wasn't accepting any apologies, and she swore at the man in a most unladylike fashion. "You damned fool! Step aside at once, and let me in!"

"No, Ma'am," the deputy replied. "Like I said, I'm real sorry for the trouble, but ain't nobody going in or out of this room until I take the Doc down to the stage tomorrow morning. Sheriff says I got to take him to Dallas for trial, and that's what I'm going to do." He was a young deputy, still a little awestruck by the badge he was wearing, and firmly committed to honoring his appointment.

"You're taking him to Dallas?" Kate asked, startled for a moment out of her rage. "I thought you worked for the county sheriff."

"Yes, Ma'am, I do. But seems like Dallas has a long record on the Doc, and now they're after him for skipping town on a gambling charge. The way I hear it from Sheriff Cruger, the Dallas law don't forget too easy, and they're planning on making an example of him this time. Maybe even give him some jail time instead of just a fine like they usually give for gambling. I guess Dallas is getting real cosmopolitan these days, trying to clean up the streets."

"Well, they can start by cleaning out their courthouse!" Kate fumed. "I'll be damned if I'll let them put him behind bars again!" and if John Henry hadn't come to the door at that moment, Kate's anger might have ruined the plan that he was formulating.

"Why, Kate darlin'," he drawled, "has the deputy here done somethin' to offend you?"

"The deputy is exceedingly offensive! He won't let me into our room. He says he's keeping you locked up here alone until the stage leaves for Dallas."

"I am sorry, Kate, but that's the arrangement I made with Sheriff Cruger. House arrest seemed preferable to spendin' the night in jail."

"And where am I supposed to go?" she demanded again. "Where am I supposed to sleep? And what of my clothes? Am I to be turned out into the street?"

John Henry sighed and nodded to the deputy. "Might you let Miss Elder come into my room for just a moment? Perhaps, if she could just put a few things together, get a change of clothing? You can examine her bags if you like. She'll just have a dress or two, a corset and shimmy and pantalettes . . ."

And as John Henry had hoped, the young deputy turned crimson with embarrassment at the mention of women's underpinnings, and he sputtered: "No, Sir! That won't be necessary! I won't need to look into her bags! You go right ahead, Ma'am, and get your clothes and . . . and . . . things . . ."

He couldn't even finish his sentence, for blushing so badly, and Kate smiled triumphantly as she swept past him into the room.

John Henry winked at the guard as he pulled the door closed behind Kate. "You know how women are, don't you deputy?" he said in a confidential tone, though it was clear the deputy was thankfully an innocent still. A more experienced man wouldn't have been so distracted by the thought of a lady's scanties, and would have supervised the visit to make sure his prisoner didn't do anything suspect. But the young deputy stood in embarrassed silence outside the door, while John Henry grabbed Kate by the shoulders and spoke in hushed and hurried sentences. He had one last, desperate plan of how to get himself out of Fort Griffin before the stage left for Dallas, and it was going to be up to Kate to work it out.

It was three in the morning when the fire-alarm sounded, rousing everyone in Fort Griffin. A fire in a town made of picket houses and board-front stores could mean disaster unless enough water could be carried up from the river to put out the blaze before it spread. When the fire-alarm bell was rung, everybody in town was expected to come running, and that's what they were doing, pouring out of the saloons and bawdy houses and forming a bucket line that reached down the main street of town all the way to the Clear Fork of the Brazos River.

The only person in town not racing to answer the alarm was John Henry, who was pacing his hotel room waiting for a signal knock at his door. If Kate had set the blaze properly, lighting the woodshed behind the Planter's Hotel on fire as he had instructed her to do, soon everyone in the place would be smelling smoke and running in a panic—hopefully even the steadfast deputy standing guard at his bedroom door. But if the guard were too foolish to save himself from a fire, Kate could always pull her derringer on him. She'd carried it out in her bag that evening, hidden away under her laciest garter belt, just in case the deputy had decided to take a look inside after all. That garter belt would have been enough to make even a worldly man a little modest, but the deputy had, thankfully, never bothered to open the bag. Still, the thought of Kate trying to overpower an armed guard didn't help John Henry's nerves any.

Outside his room, the darkness of the early morning sky was colored crimson from the flames of the burning woodshed in the horse lot behind the hotel. Kate's fire must be a regular conflagration to be making so much flame and ashy smoke, and he only hoped that she would be able to get to him before he suffocated right there in his room or died in the blaze if the fire spread to the hotel itself. It was a dangerous escape he'd planned for himself, but the only one he could think of under the circumstances.

His anxious thoughts were interrupted by three swift taps at the bedroom door, then another three—the code he'd given to Kate—and he let out a gasp of relief as she burst into the room.

"The guard's gone! I didn't want to have to shoot him, but I would have."

And in the noise and the confusion of the town crisis, no one noticed them leaving their room and running right down the front stairs and out through the lobby of the hotel along with the other boarders, some still wearing their nightshirts and bedclothes. John Henry's own clothes were packed into his valise along with Mattie's precious letters and a packet of dental hand tools. Everything else would have to wait until he could send a message to Shaughnessey asking him to send along his trunk. It wasn't the first time that Shaughnessey had kept his things for him, though this time he wouldn't be coming back to Texas to collect his belongings again. He was through with the Lone Star State and its overly-efficient legal system. Texas was a shame to the rest of the South, making such an awful fuss about guns and gambling.

John Henry had told Kate to hire him a horse and leave it saddled and waiting just up the street from the hotel, away from the fire that was distracting everyone's attention. With an hour's hard ride, he could be upriver into Throckmorton County and out of Sheriff Cruger's jurisdiction by the time he was missed. It would take several days for another warrant to be issued for his arrest there, and by then he'd be long gone on a stage headed north to Dodge City. It was a perfect escape and had worked out just the way he'd planned—except for the fact that there were two horses waiting in the early morning darkness and not just the one he'd counted on.

"Who's the extra horse for?" he asked, and Kate laughed as she gathered up her skirts and stepped into the stirrup of a pretty dappled gray.

"For me, of course!" she said. And as she straddled the saddle, John Henry saw that she was wearing men's trousers under her flounced skirt. "Don't look so surprised, Doc! Did you expect me to ride side-saddle?"

"I didn't expect you'd be comin' along at all," he said, tying his valise behind the saddle of the big black that Kate had left for him. "It's gonna be a hard ride, not a pleasure trip."

"I don't mind the ride," she said, twisting her glossy dark hair into a knot under a too-big cowboy's hat. "I've done harder things in my life. And you know I can handle a horse."

It was true that she was an expert horsewoman, but doing stage tricks on a trained horse wasn't the same as traversing the Texas panhandle and the Indian Territory beyond.

"No, Kate," he demurred, as he swung up into his saddle and gathered the reins with leather-gloved hands. "It wouldn't be fair to take you along when the law may be comin' after me."

"But I want to be with you. I love you, Doc! You know that I do!"

But John Henry looked down into her flushed face and shook his head. "Oh, Kate," he sighed, "this arrangement of ours isn't about love. It never was. We were just keepin' company, surely you know that. I never gave you cause to think it was anything more, did I? Stay here in Fort Griffin. A beautiful woman like you won't have any trouble findin' another man to take you in."

And for a moment Kate said nothing, her breath going out in a gasp as though she had just been hit by a blow. Then she put her head up proudly, and said with tears in her eyes:

"And who will want a pregnant mistress?"

His sudden jerk on the reins made the horse whinny and reel around.

"What did you say?" he demanded.

"I said I'm pregnant. The post doctor told me so this afternoon. It's not an illness I've been suffering from after all, only morning-sickness." Then her tears turned to laughter, and her words rushed out so fast that John Henry could hardly take them all in.

"I was told I would never be able to have another child after the hard time I had bearing my son. And when he died, I thought that I would never have another baby of my own. And after all these years, I never did conceive again. But now, I finally have! And I have your baby inside me, my love! I have your life within me!"

John Henry was speechless in his bewildered astonishment. Then something she had said struck him hard. "My life? But I'm dyin', Kate. You know I've got the consumption."

"No, my love, you're not dying!" And she reached for his gloved hand and laid it against the gentle swell of her belly. "You're alive in me! Feel how the life grows inside! Our baby, Doc, our child . . ."

He was still disbelieving, but as he looked down at Kate, he couldn't deny that there had been a change in her lately. Her breasts had grown fuller, the delicate veins across them faintly blue against the honey of her skin; her smooth and curving waist had grown wider; her flat stomach feeling fuller against his hips when they made love . . .

And suddenly, he knew that what she said was true. They'd been together almost every night since he'd returned to Fort Griffin, and many mornings as well, their affair so passionate that it had nearly worn him out.

"All right," he said finally, swallowing his pride and facing up to his gentleman's responsibility, "all right. I'll take you along with me. But I can't promise you anything once we get to Dodge. Hell, Kate, I don't even know if I'll get there alive myself."

"I'll take care of you, Doc. Don't I always take care of you? What better nurse could you have than a doctor's daughter? And we'll find another doctor there, one who will know what to do about your disease . . ."

"I said I can't promise you anything, Kate. Please don't ask me. But I will take you with me. It's the least I can do . . . and it's all I can do, for now."

"You won't be sorry, Doc! We'll get to Dodge City soon enough, and I'll bring your child into the world and everything will be fine for us. You'll see, my love. Everything is going to be just fine!"

But as they spurred the horses and rode off together into the crimson-skied darkness, John Henry had the feeling that nothing would ever be fine again.

Chapter Ten

SWEETWATER, 1878

THEY LEFT THE HORSES WITH A LIVERY STABLE OWNER IN THROCKMORTON County, then took the stage north across the Texas panhandle to Fort Elliott, two-hundred-fifty miles away, where the new Dodge City and Panhandle Line took on passengers. It was a long, hard trail even by coach—forty hours from Fort Griffin to Fort Elliott over roads so rough and rocky that the horses had to be changed out every twenty miles and the passengers arrived bruised and exhausted. Most travelers were thankful for the chance to layover a day or two at Sweetwater, close to Fort Elliott, before continuing on across the Indian Territory to Fort Supply and Dodge City, another grueling two-hundred miles away.

Sweetwater was the closest thing to a town that there was along the Dodge City Trail, with one general store, one dance hall, a scattering of saloons, and a combination restaurant and boarding house with a Chinese laundry next door. But though the Chinese laundry seemed like a sure sign that Sweetwater was about to boom and turn into a real little city, the truth was that the boom had ended when the buffalo had died out, and Sweetwater would never be anything more than what it was—just a collection of dirt-floored, sod-roofed adobe buildings huddled together in the windy, treeless waste of the Texas panhandle.

The only memorable thing about the little town was that it had been the scene, two years back, of the tragic killing of a pretty dance hall girl named Mollie Brennan. Mollie was the favorite among the "Seven Jolly Sisters," the saloon girls who entertained the soldiers and the buffalo hunters who visited the town. But being popular in a God-forsaken place like Sweetwater could be a dangerous thing, and Mollie Brennan had the misfortune of getting caught in a fight between two of her beaus: a soldier from Fort Elliott named Melvin King, and a young buffalo hunter and teamster called Bat Masterson.

Corporal King had a jealous streak, along with the mistaken notion that Mollie was his special girl, and when he learned one night that she was over in the dance hall entertaining one of the buffalo hunters, he loaded his six-shooter and went looking for a fight. If what he'd heard was true, and Masterson was trying to seduce Mollie and steal her away, Corporal King meant to do something serious. When he got to the dance hall and found his pretty Mollie dancing close in Bat Masterson's arms, he put his pistol into play without asking any questions.

Mollie caught sight of the soldier just as his thumb hit the hammer and she screamed and turned to throw herself between her partner and the bullet that was aiming for him, hoping perhaps that Corporal King wouldn't shoot if she were standing in the way. But the soldier was a fast draw and a quick shot, and he'd already pulled off his round before he saw Mollie spin herself into his line of fire. It was too late to do anything but watch in horror as the ball passed right through her and crashed into Masterson's pelvis, knocking him to the floor. But Bat Masterson was almost as fast as the soldier was, and as Mollie crumpled to the ground and his own legs went out from under him, he drew his revolver and fired off a shot that hit Melvin King square in the heart, killing him instantly.

The shooting was a clear-cut case of attempted murder and self-defense, so no charges were brought against Masterson, and as soon as he was recovered enough from his wound to make the trip, he went back to recuperate on his family's farm in Kansas. His buffalo hunting days were over, anyway, he said, since the herds were almost all wiped out, and he was thinking of going into some new line of work, law enforcement maybe, to protect other innocent people from the likes of Corporal Melvin King. And though he'd probably always have a limp from that bullet wound to the pelvis, he counted himself lucky to be alive at all—poor Mollie had bled to death in the back room of the saloon before anyone could call for the post surgeon.

If it hadn't been for the shooting of Mollie Brennan, Sweetwater wouldn't have had much of a reputation at all, good or bad. There were only thirty full-time residents in the town, not counting the Seven Jolly Sisters and the soldiers who came to visit from the nearby fort. But small and rough as it was, Sweetwater looked like paradise to John Henry after that long ride up from Throckmorton County, breathing in road dust all the way and shivering in the bitter January cold—though it was Kate who seemed to be taking the trip the hardest. The long hours riding over rough roads had left her with a dull aching in her back, an ache that didn't go away even after they'd spent a night at Tom O'Laughlin's Sweetwater Boarding House and Hotel.

By morning, Kate's backache had grown worse, reaching clear around her until it tore at her belly and made her cry out in pain. And then the bleeding started, a smear of bright red that stained her lacy underclothes, but soon the blood was darker and more profuse, gushing out of her with every gripping pain. And as she lay huddled in the bed, clutching a wad of sheeting to her bleeding body, Kate moaned and cried in despair. She knew she was losing her baby and there was nothing to be done but wait until the tiny life within her was swept away.

In spite of all his fine professional education, John Henry had no idea what to do with a woman in too-early labor. Outside of the physical intimacies that caused conception, he was as ignorant as any Victorian man about women's medical problems. His maiden aunts had never shared any such knowledge with him, nor had the embarrassing subject of childbirth ever come up in his proper conversations with Mattie. And though he'd gotten used to seeing his own blood coughed up from his diseased lungs, seeing Kate lying in bed with a bloody sheet drawn up between her legs left him feeling downright helpless, and painfully responsible as well. It was his child she was carrying, after all, a child he'd never meant to make, but having made it, he had decided to do right by it. Now the child was dying, and for all he knew, maybe Kate was dying, too. And though he didn't care for Kate enough to marry her, he certainly didn't want her death on his conscience, either. Selfishness, Mattie might have called it, but that was how his thinking ran as Kate lay bleeding and moaning in despair.

Finally, unable to bear Kate's misery any longer, he sent for the post surgeon from Fort Elliott to come care for her, and left the hotel room looking for a saloon and a drink to steady his nerves. A man didn't belong in a laying-in room, anyhow, and by the time he'd had a few tumblers of whiskey and played at cards a little, Kate's situation didn't seem like such a problem anymore. Loose women got pregnant all the time. Lottie Deno had admitted as much, saying that she'd had several children of her own and wasn't even sure who the fathers were. Maybe Kate's baby wasn't even his. Maybe it was Johnny Ringo's, conceived while Kate was still sharing her bed with the cow thief.

It was long after dark by the time he got back to the adobe-walled boarding house, feeling comfortably drunk and ready to be generous about Kate Elder and Ringo's baby she was having. Perhaps the doctor from Fort Elliott had been able to save it, and Kate would take it back to its real father and leave John Henry to finish his Dodge City trip in peace. He'd be happy to pay her way back to Fort Griffin, and even give her something to set her up again there. He could still be a gentleman, even if she was nowhere near being a lady.

But the sight that greeted him when he opened the door of the sod-roofed room pushed the comfortable cloud of liquor clear from his mind. Kate was still in bed, but she wasn't writhing and crying anymore. She was lying flat on her back, eyes closed and face as pale as white linen, her legs spread wide apart. And kneeling at the end of Kate's bed, a heavy-figured woman was reaching some kind of silver tool up inside her, pulling out wads of bloody tissue.

"What the hell's goin' on?" John Henry demanded, his hand flying to the pistol in his pocket. "What do you think you're doin'?"

"Cleaning up," the woman replied, not bothering to look up at him. "Lieutenant Finley sent me over when he realized it was just a stillbirth going on. The post doctor's too busy treating sick soldiers to bother with something as ordinary as a birthing, so he sent for me."

And something about the way Kate was lying there, so still and white against the dingy linen sheets, gave John Henry a sudden feeling of dread. "She's not—she's not dead, is she?" he asked slowly, almost afraid to hear the answer.

"No, she's not dead," the woman replied, "just passed out from the pain. This scraping hurts worse than the birthing, so they say. Poor little baby's dead, though. Are you the father?"

"So she said. I only found out last week . . ."

"Well, I guess she'd know," the woman said casually. "She's been around men enough to figure things out. Kate's no holy Virgin Mother, now, is she?" Then she turned and gave John Henry a knowing look, and he saw the garish paint on her eyes and cheeks, the hardened gaze of a woman who'd lived a hard kind of life. "Me and Kate worked together over at Charlie Norton's dance hall here last year," she commented, "when she first come down from Dodge City."

"Kate was here?" he asked. Kate had never mentioned Sweetwater to him—of course, she'd never said much about her past at all after St. Louis, and he hadn't asked. Her life was her own business, and none of his.

"Hell, Kate worked everywhere," the woman answered, "like we all do, following the cowboys and the cattle drives. Summer in Dodge, spring and fall in Texas, winter wherever we can find a job. You go where the men and the money are, in this business. I've known Kate ever since she hit Wichita. I never figured to see her like this, with another baby. She said she couldn't have any more children, scarred up like she was from the first childbirth. I'm surprised she got this one in her at all. Poor little fella never had much of a chance, I guess."

And something the woman said suddenly struck John Henry hard in the heart.

"Little fellow . . ." he repeated, looking up quickly from under his sandy lashes.

"Your son," the woman replied, "if you are the father." Then she laid the bloodied tool down on a dirty cloth beside her, and pulled the stained sheet back over Kate's bare legs. "It was a baby boy. Four or five months along, I'd guess. They're still mighty small at that age, but you can see what they're made of. Guess Kate don't have any more luck with babies than she do with men." Then she turned back to John Henry and nodded. "She'll be asleep awhile, if you want to clear out now. I'll stay here with her until she's ready to take care of herself, you won't need to worry yourself none. There'll be a new company of soldiers coming into the fort this spring, and plenty of work for whores like Kate and me."

But Kate wasn't like the coarse-talking whore with her bloody surgery. Lying there on the bed, so still and so pale, Kate looked as fragile and delicate as a fine china doll. Too fine, John Henry thought, for life in a coarse place like Sweetwater, Texas.

"No," he said quietly. "I won't leave her here. Kate's . . .needy," he said, trying to explain the way she was. If she woke up and found him gone there was no telling what she would do. Kill herself, maybe, or come looking to kill him. Why he would choose to stay with a woman like that he couldn't even explain to himself. Now that the baby was gone, he ought to feel freed of his responsibility to her, but somehow he did feel responsible still. It was his son she had lost, after all—and for a moment, something like sadness started to well up inside him.

"I won't leave her," he said again. "I'll stay until she's ready to go on to Dodge with me."

"Well, well," the woman said, looking up at him with a little envy in her painted eyes, "maybe Kate's bad luck has finally turned. Maybe she's finally found herself a husband, after all."

It was springtime before they left Sweetwater and headed on again to Dodge City after Kate's slow recovery from the stillbirth of her baby. She had lost a lot of blood between the birthing and the midwife's primitive surgery, and then an infection set in draining her strength even more, and for weeks she didn't even have the energy to leave her bed.

John Henry passed the time at first by playing poker and bucking the tiger at the one Faro game in town, but it wasn't long before he'd beaten all the regular townsfolk and couldn't find anyone foolish enough to go up against him again. So when the gambling ran out, he hired himself on as a contract dentist for the soldiers at nearby Fort Elliott, and collected in fees what he hadn't already taken in at cards. With four companies garrisoned there, and no other dentist for two-hundred miles, the post commander, Lieutenant Colonel Hatch, was grateful for the service at any price. A soldier with a bad toothache was as good as worthless, and the doctor did seem to do nice work.

But John Henry was restless to get moving again. The siren song of Dodge City kept calling to him from the end of the trail, and he was eager to answer it. The coming cattle season was going to be the biggest one Dodge City had ever seen, the biggest in all of Kansas for that matter, and there would be enough cowboys in town to make him two fortunes—one from the gambling and another from the dentistry. So when Kate was finally healed enough to face another forty-hour stagecoach ride, they packed up and left Sweetwater behind without even bothering to say goodbye. At least John Henry didn't leave with any sad farewells; Kate did cry a little when the stage pulled out of Sweetwater. Her baby was buried there, after all, in a tiny grave on a low rise just outside of town.

"But we'll have another, Doc," she said, sitting close beside him in the stage as they drove on up the trail. "Now that I know I can still conceive, I'll give you another son. You'd like that, wouldn't you, my love?"

But John Henry didn't answer her, as he stared out the window and into the rising cloud of dust. What he really wanted he would never have, and what he had he didn't really want anymore.

Chapter Eleven

DODGE CITY, 1878

IT WAS THE MOUNTAIN OF BONES THAT FIRST CAUGHT JOHN HENRY'S eye when the stage finally pulled into Dodge City that morning in early May.

"Looks like they're killin' men in Dodge faster than they can bury 'em," he commented to Kate as he looked out the window of the stage and got his first view of the town.

"Don't be ridiculous," she retorted, straightening the veil of her small hat and primping one last time, preparing for her entrance. "That's just buffalo bones left over from the big hunt. They'll be sending them off to make bone china soon. At least the bones smell better than the carcasses used to."

"Smells pretty bad around here, yet," John Henry said, taking a careful breath and thinking that famous Dodge City was just as rank as any other cowtown. For all its grand reputation as the Cowboy Capital, Dodge City seemed to be an ugly little town, not much bigger than Fort Griffin Flat and without Fort Griffin's interesting landscape of pecan-shaded river and rugged bluffs. Dodge City was as flat as the treeless prairie that surrounded it, with one wagon-wide main street and the tracks of the Atchison, Topeka & Santa Fe Railroad running right through the middle of town. South of the tracks, the muddy Arkansas River formed the boundary between the city and the open range country. North of town, past the few short side-streets of plain family homes, the only high ground was capped by a windswept cemetery.

It was a short walk along dusty Front Street to the Dodge House Hotel and Billiard Hall, a two-storied wooden building with a wide front porch and a hitching post outside. The Dodge House was billed as the finest hotel in town, though the two billiard tables in the lobby and the gang of cowboys huddled over their cues made it look more like a saloon than a nice hostelry. The cowboys looked up with appreciative stares as Kate accompanied John Henry into the hotel, and laughed as she pretended not to notice their attentions. Even dressed in sedate traveling clothes and with her rouged face hidden behind a demure veil, Kate was an eye-catcher.

"Hey there, honey," one of the cowboys called out with a lewd laugh, "want to play with my billiard balls?"

"Y'all settle down over there, ya hear?" the balding man at the front desk chided, looking at the cowboys over the top of his wire-rimmed glasses, then he nodded to Kate and John Henry. "Never mind them, folks. They just had a little too much sour mash last night, that's all."

"Sour mash?" John Henry asked. "I haven't heard that phrase in awhile. Are you from Georgia, Sir?"

"Yessir," the man said, putting out his hand. "The name's Deacon Cox, and I own this fine establishment. And whereabouts are you folks from? Maybe I know y'all's kin."

"I don't think so," John Henry said quickly. "I've been gone awhile, and the lady is from Europe."

"Is that right?" Cox said, giving Kate a once-over. "Why, no offense ma'am, but I could have sworn we've met before. You look a lot like a girl we used to have workin' over at Tom Sherman's Dance Hall. No offense intended, of course. She was a real looker."

"No offense taken, Mr. Cox," Kate replied with a silky voice and a restrained smile.

"We're lookin' for a room, Mr. Cox," John Henry said. "Something nice and quiet. I generally sleep late in the mornings and don't like to be disturbed. And I'll be needin' an additional room to use as a dental office, if you don't mind my practicin' here in your hotel."

"A dentist at the Dodge House?" Deacon Cox said. "Hell, no, I don't mind, be real good for business." Then he added with an apologetic nod to Kate, "Beggin' your pardon, Ma'am, for my language. I'm used to rougher folks, not doctors and such. I'd be happy to put you up and have your office here, too. Now, if you'll just sign the guest register . . ." and he handed the ink pen to John Henry. "You'll be in the room at the top of the stairs with a nice view of town."

John Henry laughed under his breath as he signed his name to the book. From what he'd seen so far, there wasn't any such thing as a nice view of Dodge, unless it was from the boot-end of a stage headed back out of town.

"I wonder, Mr. Cox, if you've heard whether Deputy Earp is back in town yet?"

"Which one?" Deacon Cox asked. "We got two Earps in Dodge."

"Two Earps?" John Henry asked in surprise.

"Sure do, Wyatt and Morgan both. They're brothers, you know, 'course Wyatt's the main one. Morgan just kind of drifts in and out as it pleases him, more of a gambler than a real lawman. Ain't neither one of them back in Dodge yet, though they'll probably be comin' in soon. We got a hundred herds of cattle headed up this way from Texas. Goda-mighty, you never saw a town boom like this one does in cattle season!" then he nodded to Kate, "beggin' your pardon again, Ma'am, for my language. Like I said, I ain't much used to fine folks at the Dodge House. Now how 'bout I help you carry up those bags? Stairs are kind of narrow and rickety, but hell, this ain't Chicago! You know what they call us back there in Chicago? *The Beautiful, Bibulous Babylon of the West*, that's what. Printed it in the Chicago papers! Now, I ain't sayin' we're beautiful, and I ain't never heard of bibulous, but they got the Babylon part right, I reckon. It's a real babel around here when the cowboys hit town!"

"It means having a heavy intake of alcoholic drink," John Henry said, growing weary of the man's voluble conversation.

"What does?"

"Bibulous. From the Latin verb 'bibere,' to drink. What they're sayin', in a rather florid fashion, is that this is one well-distilled town."

"Well, they got that right! Never seen liquor flow like it does around here. Hell, we got everything from Frenchy champagne to rot-gut to cold beer on ice . . ."

"And where might I find the Earp brothers when they do return to Dodge?"

"Any place there's trouble, I reckon, but mostly they hang around the Long Branch Saloon," then his eyes narrowed suspiciously behind his wire-rimmed glasses. "Say, you're not that fellow who's gunnin' for Wyatt are you?"

"Gunnin' for Wyatt?"

"The bounty hunter. I hear there's a thousand dollar price on his head put up by some Texas cattle-King who didn't like Wyatt sniffin' around his business."

"Me? A bounty hunter?" John Henry said with a laugh. "No Sir, Mr. Cox, I am just his dentist! Now if you'll kindly show us the way to our room . . ."

But though he laughed off the bounty hunter talk, John Henry had an uneasy feeling. Maybe Wyatt had learned something about the rustlers of Shackleford County, after all, enough to draw a bounty from the rustler-boss, John Larn. Wyatt had better watch his back if Larn's men were after him, and keep his pistol loaded up all around as well.

Kate only waited until the bedroom door was closed behind them before venting herself on John Henry.

"You didn't tell me Wyatt Earp was going to be here!" she said angrily.

"You didn't ask."

"I thought we were through with him! I thought we left him back in Texas!"

"As I recall," John Henry replied with a yawn, "it was him who left us when he went off to Fort Worth. But he did tell me to look him up if I ever happened to be passin' through Dodge City. Well, here I am in Dodge, and I plan to say hello. Now be a good girl and go draw the drapes. I'm gonna take a nap." Then he took off his jacket, pulled off his leather ankle boots, and stretched himself out on the brass-framed bed, pleased to find that it had a real feather mattress and soft linen sheets. The trip from Sweetwater to Dodge City had taken five days, the trail crossing the snake-infested Canadian River and the Kiowa Indian

Nation, and other than a night's layover at Fort Supply, he hadn't had a good bed under him in all that time.

Kate watched him for a moment in silence, then went to the window and stood staring out over the dirt streets of Dodge. "He'll bring you nothing but trouble, you know. He'll only break your heart one day."

"Whatever are you talkin' about, Kate?"

"I'm talking about Wyatt. You're getting your heart set on the wrong friend. He's not your kind, he's not quality like we are . . ."

"Quality?" John Henry said with a bitter laugh. "Is that what you think we are, quality? My dear, deluded consort, you and I have not been quality for a long time. You may be a doctor's daughter, but you are also a denizen of the lowest levels of the theatrical stage—I suppose Mr. Cox recognized you from a past sojourn in Dodge. And I, for all my fine professional education, am still a Texas outlaw. If it weren't for Wyatt Earp's very generous acceptance of me, in spite of my faults, I wouldn't feel even halfway respectable anymore. The truth is, Kate, you and I have both fallen so far from grace that we may never be able to claw our way back up again. Now take off your dress and come lie down and get some rest. We're gonna have a busy night ahead of us."

But Kate stayed at the window, neither drawing the drapes nor readying herself for a rest.

"I don't want to be here . . ."

"Well, it's a fine time to tell me that," John Henry replied irritably, "after all the effort I went through to get you here. But here is where we are, so either stop talkin' and let me sleep or leave me be and go out streetwalkin'. It makes no difference to me."

He half expected her to fly into a rage at his cold remarks, and was surprised when she turned to him instead, her face awash with a desperate light.

"Let's not stay here, Doc! Let's take the train east and get away from these cowtowns once and for all! Let's go back to St. Louis and start over again. You can open another practice there; I can find another role on the stage. Or let's go to New York! I've always wanted to act on the stage there, have a real professional career . . ."

"Ah, Kate," he said, "you really are an actress, imagining a world that can never be. I can't go back to St. Louis. I'm too tired to go anywhere, to even think of goin' anywhere. New York might as well be the ends of the earth . . ."

"I would go to the ends of the earth for you," she said, her sultry voice as sincere as he had ever heard it to be. "You must know how I love you. That's why I don't want you throwing in with Wyatt Earp. I don't want anything to come between us, ever."

It was no explanation of her animosity toward the quiet-spoken lawman, but it did explain her behavior in regards to Lottie Deno. He could still see the mad look in her eyes as she had stood in that Fort Griffin whorehouse, the Hell-Bitch in hand, and ordering him out of Lottie's bed.

"Come away or I'll cut her open!" she had screamed, and he knew that she'd meant what she said. What would she do if she felt that his friendship with Wyatt were a threat as well? Worse: what would she do if she ever found out about Mattie? Hell would have no fury like Kate's if she knew where his love really lay.

And fearing that she would somehow discover the direction of his thoughts, he said sleepily, "And what would we do in New York? We don't know anyone there."

"Who cares? As long as we're together, we'll make out all right. As long as you love me . . ."

He could have fought back sleep long enough to reply, but didn't.

The Long Branch Saloon was crowded with cowboys that evening, spurs jingling on their high-heeled boots and money jangling in their jeans' pockets as they lined up three-deep at the bar. A cattle drive had just hit town and the boys were ready to play, and Chalk Beeson, the jolly proprietor of the Long Branch, was happy to have them.

"Right this way, boys, belly up to the bar! We got plenty of booze to go around, plenty of girls, and the best games in town!"

Beeson's Long Branch Saloon gave a nod to gentility with a six-piece orchestra on an oriental carpet at one end of the narrow room, but gave a big howdy to the Texas cowboys with the "long branched" head of a Longhorn steer mounted over the white-painted bar. And the Long Branch was only one of the Texas-themed saloons in town, along with the Lone Star, the Alamo, the Nueces, and a dozen others, all ready to help those cowboys spend their newly made trail pay.

"Make yourselves at home, boys!" Chalk Beeson said cheerfully, "just make yourselves at home!"

And the cowboys were doing just that, adding their raucous laughter to the riotous sounds of the gaming tables, where roulette wheels whirred, poker chips clicked, dice clattered, and the dealers called out the odds. "Thirty-five to one! Get your money down, folks! Eight to one on the colors! Are you all down, gentlemen? Then up she rises!" There was no place as jolly as a saloon when the games were in play.

Kate had chosen to skip the evening's entertainments, saying that she was still tired out from the trip, though John Henry reckoned she was really just trying to avoid a reunion with Wyatt Earp. So he was on his own when he ran into an old acquaintance from Fort Griffin, a one-time buffalo hunter by the name of Jack Johnson who was just finishing off a huge plate of beef steak and fried eggs, and greeted John Henry with a belch and a smile:

"Howdy, Doc! You're lookin' dapper today! Gotcha a new sombrero?" he asked, nodding to John Henry's new black Stetson.

"I do," he answered, doffing the hat and giving it a quick brush off. Dodge was so dusty that the walk across Front Street had left him covered all over in a fine yellow powder—cow manure in the air no doubt, he thought with disgust. And though Kate said that his new hat made him look like an overdressed cowboy, her irritation made him like it even better somehow, in spite of the way it gathered dust across the wide brim and high crown. "Have you heard anything of Wyatt Earp being back in town?" he asked Jack, not bothering to make small talk.

"Not today. Only thing anybody's interested in talkin' about is this here writer we got amongst us," Jack replied, and he waved his fork in the direction of the orchestra.

"What writer?"

"Some fellar named Ned Buntline. He comes in here every evenin' when he's not too drunk to walk over from his hotel."

DANCE WITH THE DEVIL

"Well, I'll be damned!" John Henry said in amazement. "The real Ned Buntline? Why, I was weaned on his books! I must have read a hundred Buntline stories growing up, in between Shakespeare and the Bible. What's he doin' here in Dodge?"

"Writin' a new book, so he claims. Says he'll pay $50 gold to the man who can tell him a story worth puttin' in print."

"I don't believe it," John Henry scoffed. "Since when did Ned Buntline have to pay for a story?"

Ned Buntline wasn't just some writer. He was the most famous writer of his era, making a career and a fortune out of traveling the frontier and writing dime novels about his adventures, with over four-hundred published books and hundreds of magazine articles and short stories to his credit. There wasn't a newspaper in America that wouldn't pay top dollar for a serialization of his latest work, and there wasn't a reader in America who hadn't read his stories of the exploits of the Indian scout William F. Cody, whom he'd dubbed "Buffalo Bill," in his wildly successful plays and novels.

"Well, according to him," Jack said, "they ain't no more legends to write about. He says now they's just ordinary fellars like you and me, and nothin' much else. That's why he's payin' the reward, if he can hear a story good enough to put in his new book. Too bad I ain't never done nothin' worth talking about," Jack said with a shrug and a scratch at his scraggly beard. "I sure could use that $50 right about now."

"You and me both," John Henry admitted, as Kate's first afternoon of shopping in Dodge had already set him back some. As they'd left Fort Griffin with only what was in their saddlebags, they'd both needed some new clothes after the journey—especially Kate, who'd had a harder time of the traveling, all things considered, and always found shopping a calming diversion.

"Hell, I can tell a story," John Henry remarked. "My cousin Robert used to say I was all talk, anyhow, back in Georgia."

"And what story are you gonna tell, Doc?" Jack asked skeptically. "No offense, but ain't you just a dentist? What adventures have you had to talk about?"

He was only a little offended by Jack's blunt remark. Though he'd had plenty of adventures along the way, they weren't the kind to brag on.

His own life, he knew, would never be worth writing about, but he was generally smarter than anyone else around and that ought to count for something, at least.

"Well, I reckon I'll just have to make somethin' up."

"But Mr. Buntline's only payin' for true stories," Jack cautioned. "Make believe don't count."

"And who's gonna argue about my story bein' true when you're there to back me up with that big bowie knife of yours showin'?"

"Me?"

"It's a two-man story," John Henry replied with a conspiratorial smile, remembering a little bit of larceny he'd dreamed up on the long stage ride from Sweetwater to Dodge while Kate had been too uncomfortable for conversation. There'd been a rumor of stage robbers near the Cimarron crossing, which had all come to nothing, but had gotten him thinking about stage robbery in a theoretical sense and how one might make a profit without having to do the actual robbing. He'd never get to try the plan out, as it was at least unethical if not downright illegal, but it might make a good showing for the famous Ned Buntline.

But as he made his way, drink in hand and story playing in his mind, toward the crowd surrounding the great man's table, he was disappointed to find that Ned Buntline, or Edward Zane Carroll Judson as he introduced himself, was in reality just a small man with bloodshot eyes and a red whiskey nose. After all the press about the adventurous author—Civil War soldier, political activist, husband to eight women and philanderer with many more—John Henry had expected someone a little larger than life and more like the characters he wrote about. The Ned Buntline who sat slump-shouldered at a small table, wearily judging the entrants in his so far fruitless story contest, looked like any ordinary saloon drunk.

"I did have a start on something once . . ." Ned Buntline was saying to his liquor glass and anyone else who would listen. "The Adventures of Wild Bill Hickok, it was going to be. I followed him all the way to Deadwood, summer of '76, collecting my notes. I was there when Jack McCall shot him in the back while he was playing poker, and that was the end of my story. I haven't had the heart to write another one since.

Next?" he said, looking up with sorrowful eyes at John Henry. "And what is your name?"

"Dr. J.H. Holliday," he said, then he nodded to Jack Johnson who'd followed him along, "and this gentleman is my associate. We're recently returned from a profitable trip to Chicago, a trip which you may find rather amusin'."

"Doctor of what?" Ned Buntline asked, looking skeptical.

"Doctor of Philosophy," John Henry replied breezily. "My degree came from a very reputable German institution, the Jameson Fuches Academy. Perhaps you've heard of it?"

"No," Buntline said drearily, "and I very much doubt that it even exists. But go on, you've caught my attention, which is more than anyone else has done thus far."

"My story begins on the Deadwood stage," John Henry said, pulling up a chair and getting himself comfortable, "where my partner and I first met the Colorado bankin' man who made us our fortune. We got to talkin', as stage passengers do, and discovered that he had some money that needed investing—a happy coincidence, we told him, as we had just come into a certain amount of gold bars that needed to be reinvested, so to speak. The banking man was too greedy to care how we'd come into possession of the gold, and we weren't inclined to explain, though we did mention that this was government gold which needed to be disposed of quickly. In consequence of this difficulty, we'd be willin' to make the banker a good deal on the bars, if he'd take them off our hands discreetly. And all we asked in trade for this fortune of gold was a mere $20,000."

"Go on," said Buntline, pulling his liquor glass closer.

"As you can imagine, the banker was droolin' by now. A fortune in gold for only a fraction of its real value! Whatever loyalty he may have felt to the Federal Government quickly melted away in greed, though he wasn't quite ready to become a traitor to his country until he'd had a chance to check out the gold for himself. So we arranged to meet again at the end of our journey, where we showed him a sample brick from our stash and let him file shavings from it into a fine white silk handkerchief, which he then took to an isolated spot where he could apply acid to test the metal. The filings passed the test, of course, as along the way we'd exchanged handkerchiefs, making sure his silk was filled with the genuine metal."

"A common ruse," Buntline said, not overly impressed. "It's easy enough to switch false gold for the real thing."

John Henry nodded. "And so the banker himself said, demanding that we show him the entire stash of gold bricks. Which were, we told him, buried in the bottom of a mountain lake, but that he could watch us bring some of them up and test them again as he had tested the first brick. It wasn't much trouble to bring him a few bricks and let him file shavings from them, then switch the handkerchiefs again. And soon enough, the banker's greed for gold overtook his moral compunction, and he handed over the $20,000."

As he told the tale, an audience of cowboys and dance hall girls had gathered and began applauding loudly, but John Henry held up his hand.

"No, gentlemen, the story isn't over quite yet! You see, the banker was still bein' cautious about the deal, and he insisted that one of us accompany him all the way to Chicago, where he could arrange for the safe deposit of the gold bricks into the vaults of his bank's main office. My partner here kindly volunteered to be the man's guardian for the journey, and all went along fine at first until somewhere past the Missouri River a bearded United States Marshal came on board the rail car, threatenin' to arrest the banker as an accomplice in a theft of government gold. The banker was understandably terrified, so my partner suggested that maybe the Marshal could be bought off with a bribe. Well, of course, no United States Marshal would ever consider takin' a bribe . . ." he stopped there long enough to let the crowd around him howl a little.

"But in the end, the Marshal was convinced that he should take $15,000 to let the banker go. So the banker got his gold bars and his freedom, and my partner and I . . ." he looked up at his rapt audience and smiled, "we got $35,000 for a pile of worthless gold-painted clay bricks. The United States Marshal being myself in disguise, of course."

But before he could accept the ovation of the delighted audience, a voice of indignation spoke up from the doorway.

"And that's the closest you'll ever come to wearing a lawman's badge. Do you think you're funny, Holliday?"

"Sometimes," John Henry replied, and as he turned to answer the question he looked straight into the cool-eyed face of Wyatt Earp.

"Well, I don't," said Wyatt, standing solemn as a preacher in his black frock coat and sober tin star. "Doesn't Dodge have enough trouble of its own without more Texas trouble like you coming along?"

John Henry sat stunned. He hadn't expected Wyatt to greet him warmly, exactly, but he hadn't expected to be insulted, either. If he'd had a pistol on him, if it had been any other man who had thrown those insulting words . . .

Then a shadow behind Wyatt laughed and slapped him on the back. "Hell, Wyatt, why don't you cut him some slack? I thought it was a damn good story, even if it was a lie!" Then, moving forward into the dim saloon light with eager, outstretched hand: "I'm Morgan Earp. And you must be Doc Holliday. Wyatt's told me about you."

John Henry had never seen two men who looked more alike, or more different, than Wyatt Earp and his shadow, brother Morgan. They had the same broad shoulders and squared jaws, the same sweeping russet mustaches and steel-blue eyes, the same sun-bronzed faces. But where Wyatt could hardly find a smile to soften his somber expression, Morgan had a boyish grin that matched his ready laugh. And as Morgan took off his hat and shook the yellow dust from its brim, an errant lock of hair kept falling onto his face, refusing to stay neatly in place—no part of Wyatt Earp's disciplined person would ever dare to be so disobedient as that.

"I thought it was a good story, too," Ned Buntline said, leaning forward to refill his well-used liquor glass. "The best story I've heard in a long time, though undoubtedly a fabric of lies from beginning to end, and I'm only interested in true adventures. But it was literate at least. Are you a writer yourself by any chance, Dr. Holliday? Or are you even a doctor at all?"

"I am actually a dentist by profession. It's letters I write, mostly." Then he added with mock formality, "And have you met Mr. Wyatt Earp? One of Dodge City's finest, if not very sociable, peace officers. And this is his brother, Morgan."

"Men of heroic proportions," Buntline said, giving an appraising glance up at the two Earp brothers, both of them standing a head taller than any other men in the room. Then his eyes rested on the pistol holstered at Wyatt's side, and he laughed. "A man as big as you needs a firearm more his size, Officer Earp! That pistol looks like a child's toy on you!"

"Not just officer anymore," Morgan Earp said. "Mayor Kelley's just promoted Wyatt to Assistant Marshal, right under Charlie Bassett. That means Wyatt's just about the top dog around here now. Ain't that right, Wyatt?"

Wyatt shrugged his answer. "It'll do for now. Somebody's got to stand down these Texas boys when they cause trouble in town, show them the business end of a gun."

"Wyatt don't actually shoot 'em, though," Morgan said. "Mostly he just buffalo's 'em, knocks 'em over the head with his pistol butt, then drags 'em off to the cooler while they're unconscious."

"It works," Wyatt said, as laconic as ever.

"Mind if we join you for a drink, Doc?" Morgan asked, and without waiting for an answer he pulled up a chair and spun it around, straddling it cowboy style. "Come on and grab a seat, Wyatt, and we'll have a whiskey to celebrate your big promotion."

"I don't feel like celebrating," Wyatt said. "You have one for me, Morg. I've got police work to do. Jack, you better check that knife at the bar before I run you in for breaking the weapons law." Then he turned on his bootheel and walked out of the saloon and into the windy prairie night. Jack Johnson, cowed, took himself and his knife to the bar.

"What's vexin' him?" John Henry asked. "I know he's not one for conversation, but that was just plain impolite." Though it wasn't so much Wyatt's bad manners that bothered him, but his cool indifference.

"Give him time," Morgan said. "We just got back to town after hearing about Ed Masterson's shooting, and Wyatt's taking it kind of hard. He was friends with the Mastersons from back in their buffalo hunting days. He never did think Ed was the right man for Marshal, too good-natured and all, and I guess he feels like if he'd been here to help, Ed wouldn't have gotten killed."

"But that was just a common saloon-shooting, wasn't it?" Ned Buntline asked, "a drunk with a loaded firearm that went off too fast? What could he have done to prevent that?"

"Nothing, probably. But Wyatt's like that. Thinks everything is his responsibility. He's serious-minded, always has been. Not like me! I take things easy!"

"You said the Marshal was named Masterson?" John Henry asked. "Is that the same man who shot Corporal King down in Sweetwater?"

"Nah, that's his younger brother, Bat Masterson—he's our Ford County Sheriff now. It was Ed Masterson who was Town Marshal of Dodge. Wyatt was real close to both of them. That's why we burned the breeze getting back to Dodge as soon as he heard about Ed's death. I guess he wanted to do something to make up for it."

"You mean revenge, retribution?" Ned Buntline said with a melodramatic flourish and a shaky smile. "Now that would make a cracker-jack story! I can see it in print already: Ned Buntline's *The Deputy's Revenge*," and he launched into a stream of the kind of overblown prose that had made him famous. "*There was a steel-eyed resolve in the lawman's hooded eyes as he carefully drew his heavy revolver and leveled it manfully at the heartless murderer. Revenge! Retribution! Spent blood atoning for spent blood!*"

"Hell, no!" Morgan said. "Wyatt's not that crazy! He'd never take the law into his own hands like that! He just plans on keeping the peace a little better around here, so no more lawmen have to die."

"Ah, well!" Ned Buntline said with a sigh. Still, there may be something to it . . ." and he started scribbling on the stack of copy paper he kept beside him, whiskey stained and wrinkled.

"What about Doc's story?" Morgan asked. "You said it was a good one."

"It was," Buntline agreed. "I'll tell you what, Dr. Holliday. I'll buy your story, pay you the prize money of $50, if you'll promise to keep in touch with me by letter. I could use some Dodge City color to add to the Deputy's Revenge. I think this may turn out to be something interesting. Heaven knows my career could use the help!"

"All right," John Henry said, "as long as you don't use my name in your book. Maybe I'll still get a chance to try out that little gold-brick scheme . . ."

"Not as long as Wyatt is lawing in Dodge, you won't run that blazer!" laughed Morgan. "But I sure would like to hear that story again, if you've got the time to tell it."

"I've got all the rest of my life, such as it is."

And Morgan let out a laugh at that, slapping John Henry on the shoulder like they were old pals. "Wyatt said you had a sour sense of humor! But I don't mind. Hell, I don't mind much of anything! 'Cept for sitting around a saloon without a drink in my hand. Hey, bar dog! Send over a bottle of lightning, will you? Damn, it's good to be back in Dodge!"

When the eastbound Santa Fe out of Pueblo rolled into Dodge City four days later, it drew more than the usual crowd of curious spectators. Rumor had it that the killer Ben Thompson was on board that train, along with Bill Tighlman and Texas Jack Vermillion, and a hundred more of the toughest gunslingers out of Texas. But though it looked like Dodge was in for more trouble than even Marshal Wyatt Earp could handle, the Marshal didn't seem to be too alarmed.

The truth was that the Texas boys were just returning to Dodge after doing guard duty on the railroad works at Cañon City, Colorado, where the Atchison, Topeka & Santa Fe Railroad was battling the Denver & Rio Grande for the right-of-way through the Royal Gorge of the Arkansas River. The Royal Gorge, a three-thousand-foot deep, thirty-foot wide slash through the Rocky Mountains, was the shortest passage to the silver boom camps, and both railroads claimed the right to lay track through it. The dispute was mostly a legal one, with the Colorado courts wrangling over leases and contracts, but it had turned physical when the Denver & Rio Grande sent in three-hundred armed railroad workers to take the Royal Gorge by force. Not to be outdone, the Santa Fe sent to Dodge City for an army of its own, and the cowboys were quick to rally to the cause.

"Damn, Doc! Would you look at that?" Morgan Earp exclaimed to John Henry, as they stood together on the station platform watching the train come in, along with most of the rest of the citizenry of Dodge. The saloons and gambling halls had all emptied out as soon as the train's black chimney of smoke had appeared on the western horizon—it wasn't often that Dodge was descended upon all at once by so many famous and infamous characters. "Did you ever see so many six-guns in your life? Which one of those boys do you think is Bill Tighlman?"

"Your guess is as good as mine, Morg. I reckon one bad man looks about like any other. Where's Wyatt, anyhow? This crowd's gettin' feisty."

"Checking out the gambling joints, probably, making sure nobody's robbing the store while the clerk's away. You know Wyatt, duty first. He'll be here soon enough, though. Bat's coming in on the train, and Wyatt's been wanting to see him."

"You mean Masterson? What's he doin' riding with these cowboys? I thought he was County Sheriff."

"He is. But he does some work for the Santa Fe, too. He recruited these Texas boys for guard duty and went along to make sure they didn't get out of hand. Well, speak of the Devil, here's Wyatt now!" Morgan said, pulling off his hat and waving it in the air to catch his brother's attention. "Hey, Wyatt! Come on over here with me and the Doc!"

But Wyatt only nodded in Morgan's direction as he shouldered his way through the crowd to where a fist-fight had broken out among the spectators by the side of the tracks. Without saying a word to the brawlers, Wyatt pulled his six-shooter from the holster at his side and slammed it butt first over the heads of two of the combatants, who just as wordlessly slid to the ground, knocked unconscious by the marshal's heavy-handed blow.

"Like I said," Morgan grinned, "duty first!"

The buffaloing was startlingly brutal, but it seemed to do the trick as the rest of the crowd momentarily quieted down. Clearly, it wasn't just Wyatt Earp's cool presence that kept the peace in Dodge City, but his swift shooting arm as well—even when he used his revolver as a bludgeon.

"And who's that bandbox?" John Henry asked, turning his attention to where a dandy in a three-piece suit was stepping down from the train, limping as he leaned on a gold-headed walking stick. Surrounded by the denim and corduroy of the cowboys, the man looked amusingly over-dressed, with a derby hat set at a tilt and a fancy leather gunbelt carrying silver-mounted pistols.

"Why, that's Sheriff Bat, himself!" Morgan said. "If you think that's something, you should have seen the getup he wore when he first came to Dodge—red chaps and a fringed bolero, a big black sombrero with silver doo-dads all over it. He looked like a Mexican greaser going to a fiesta. He's got sophisticated living in Dodge. He used to be a mule-skinner, but you couldn't tell that by looking at him now."

But what John Henry could tell was that Bat Masterson and Wyatt Earp were fast friends, as the marshal ignored the revival of the fist-fight he'd just broken up and pushed his way through the crowd to the sheriff's side, taking his hand in a steady handshake. And as the two lawmen stood together, John Henry could see the shadow of a shared sorrow crossing their handsome faces.

"First time they've seen each other since Ed Masterson got himself killed," Morgan said. "Guess they'll have some commiserating to do." And for a moment, he was uncharacteristically pensive. "I wonder if Ed saw the light at the end."

"What light?"

"The heavenly light. My Ma says that right before you die, you see this light, the light of God reaching down to bring you home. All you have to do is follow the light to find your way to Heaven."

"And what happens if you don't see the light?" John Henry asked, intrigued to find a spiritual side to the otherwise worldly Morgan Earp.

"Then you end up in hell, I guess. That's what our Ma says. She says that some folks are so bad, they can't even see the light when it's right there shining on them. They go to hell when they could have just opened their eyes and gone to heaven instead. Do you suppose Ed saw the light, Doc? He was too nice a fellow not to get to heaven."

"I reckon I don't know much about heaven. Though I have been to hell and back a couple of times."

Morgan's pensive moment was over, as he laughed out loud and slapped John Henry on the back, setting him off on a coughing jag.

"You're a funny one, Doc, always kidding around! Been to hell and back!"

John Henry grabbed for the linen handkerchief in his vest pocket and quickly covered his mouth. Morgan Earp didn't know him well enough to realize that he rarely kidded around and meant most everything he said when he wasn't purposefully telling a lie. He had been to hell and back, as far as he was concerned.

"So what do you say we take in the show at the Varities?" Morgan said.

"Don't you want to give your condolences to the Sheriff? Maybe invite him and Wyatt along?" Much as he enjoyed Morgan's light-hearted company, it was still Wyatt that John Henry admired and with whom he wanted to strike up a friendship.

"Hell no! Bat's as bad as Wyatt is about drinking and such, a real temperance man. Dull as death! Leave 'em to their lawing, Doc. You and me can do the town plenty fine on our own!"

The June 14th edition of the *Dodge City Times* carried a report of the Santa Fe's hired gunslingers, a story from the *Pueblo Chieftain* calling Dodge *The Wicked City*, a report of Wyatt Earp's appointment as Assistant Marshal, and an advertisement for Dodge City's first dentist:

DENTISTRY

J.H. Holliday, Dentist, very respectfully offers his professional services to the citizens of Dodge City and surrounding country during the summer.

Office at room No. 24, Dodge House.

Where satisfaction is not given money will be refunded.

And with only that one printing of the advertisement, John Henry had more patients than he had time to see. Toothache was the most common complaint; he pulled so many rotten teeth that the whole office began to smell of disease and Kate regularly complained of the awful odor. He got more satisfaction from doing the fine gold work the cattle buyers were ready to pay for and making the porcelain crowns all the ladies in town wanted.

With the money he was making, he was able to order himself some new dental equipment, including a Pocket Dentist kit like the one Dr. Judd had described back in St. Louis—a little leather-covered box about the size of a daguerreotype case and filled with tiny gold-foil tools that attached to an ivory handle. Then he used the sharpest of the tools to carve his name into the eagle-headed medallion on the brass-hinged lid: *J.H. Holliday, 24 D.H., Dodge* along with a set of smiling teeth and the letters *au*, the chemical symbol for gold.

Kate watched his painstaking work, commenting that his hands wouldn't be so steady after the evening's gambling and liquor, and calling him foolish for putting his office address on the kit as if he meant to stay in Dodge City permanently. She was still yearning to be away from the dust and the dirt of the cowtowns and back on the theater stage where she knew she belonged, and Dodge wasn't her kind of theater. But John Henry was happy in Dodge, doing his professional work by day and his sporting work by night, and feeling himself almost settled again in a town where he had no bad reputation to hide.

It was his dental practice that brought Wyatt to pay him a visit at the Dodge House, much to Kate's irritation, though it wasn't for Wyatt, himself, that the services were needed, but for a hulking cowboy who'd taken the bad end of a brawl with the marshal.

"He tried to go across the Dead Line with his guns on," Wyatt explained as he dragged the moaning man into the dental office and dropped him unceremoniously into the wooden arm-chair that John Henry used for examinations. "Town law doesn't allow firearms north of the railroad tracks. I had to buffalo him to get his attention. He's been yelping like this ever since. I figure maybe he's got a bad tooth."

But one look at the man, with his face bruised and bloody and his mouth hanging crooked, told John Henry that this was no simple toothache.

"This man's got a broken jaw! What the hell did you hit him with, Wyatt? An anvil?"

"Just this," Wyatt said as he pulled open his frock coat to show the shiny new pistol at his side. It was the longest Colt's revolver John Henry had ever seen, ten-inches in the barrel at least, and box fit into its own custom scabbard. "Your friend Buntline sent it to me. Said I needed a bigger gun, and he appreciated the idea for *The Deputy's Revenge*, whatever that means. I didn't want to insult him by returning it."

"So you used that—cannon—on this man's face, just to get his attention?"

"Better to buffalo him than to shoot him."

"Shootin' him would have hurt less," John Henry said, as he carefully pried open the cowboy's disfigured mouth, making him howl in pain. "He's got some rotten teeth, all right, but they're the least of the trouble. I'll have to try splinting him, see if I can stabilize this mess. You did a day's work here, all right, Marshal Earp."

Wyatt pulled off his flat-brimmed hat and smoothed his well-oiled hair into place. "He was breaking the law, Doc."

"Well, he won't be breaking anything for awhile. I'll have to keep him here until I know he's on the mend."

"Keep him here? You mean you want to take custody of him?"

"Ironic, isn't it?" he said with a bemused smile. "I used to be a wanted man myself, until I met you. Now I'm practically a lawman."

"Now hold on, Doc. Leaving him here don't mean I'm deputizing you. He's still my responsibility . . ."

But John Henry shook his head. "The truth is, Wyatt, I reckon he's a little bit my responsibility, as well."

"What are you talking about?"

"I'm talkin' about your weapon of destruction there. That special pistol of yours was a payment for the story of your Dodge City exploits, provided by me."

"My exploits?"

"Buntline asked me to keep him informed of the doin's here in Dodge, anything colorful that would look good in print. I've written him a letter or two telling him how you handle the cowboys so well. I didn't think you'd mind."

"And why would Buntline be interested in me?"

"Why, Wyatt," John Henry drawled, "you're our hero, don't you know?" And though there was a sarcastic cut to his voice, he meant every word of it.

"Me? A hero?" Wyatt said, and his handsome, solemn face broke into the first real laugh that John Henry had ever seen on him. "Hell, I'm no hero! Ask Celia! Ask Morg!"

"Morg thinks you walk on water."

"Morg's my kid brother, he's supposed to think like that. Isn't that how brothers are?"

But John Henry didn't answer, pretending to be studying his patient's injury. It was going to take some doing to bring that dislocated mandible back into place, make the unfortunate cowboy's teeth match up again the way they should—though it wasn't just the dental work he was thinking of.

"I reckon I don't know much about brothers," he said at last, "as I never had any."

"No brothers?" Wyatt said, as though he could hardly fathom such a misfortune. "That's too bad, Doc. I'd be real lonely without any brothers. I've sure been looking forward to seeing everybody again, soon as they get to Dodge."

"As soon as who gets to Dodge?"

"The rest of the family. My folks are headed off to California again, coming out on the Santa Fe Trail. They'll be here any day now, I figure. Be quite a wagon train when the Earp outfit pulls into town."

And though John Henry should have been glad for Wyatt, he only felt a stab of jealousy. Wyatt had family, and he had no one but Kate.

"So Marshal," he said, "where do I send the bill? This is gonna be an expensive repair job."

"I guess you better send it to me. Much as this cowboy deserved what he got, I wouldn't want to get a bad reputation around Dodge."

"I reckon you've already got a bad reputation," John Henry said. "You know there's a bounty on your head? A thousand dollars to the man who can fill you full of lead."

"I heard of it."

"So what are you going to do about it?"

Wyatt shrugged his broad shoulders. "I guess I'll shoot first and ask questions later. I'm not much for talking things out."

"So I noticed," John Henry commented as the broken-jawed cowboy moaned in agreement. "Maybe you ought to hire yourself a bodyguard until this bounty thing blows over."

"Now who'd be crazy enough to want to take a bullet for me?" Wyatt said, his long mustache moving just a little over a momentary smile. "Only Morgan, maybe, and I'd never ask him to do it. My Ma's kinda fond of that boy." Then, the smile gone, he added quietly: "And I don't believe I could stand to lose him the way poor Bat lost his brother Ed. No, Doc, I figure I'm alone on this one." Then he put his hat back on, pulling it low over his eyes. "You keep track of that prisoner there. If it gets back to Charlie Bassett that I put you in charge of things, I'll be looking for another job fast."

But as John Henry watched Wyatt leave, the only lawman who'd ever treated him like he was worth talking to at all, he was surprised by the feeling that swept over him.

I'd be your bodyguard, Wyatt, he thought. *I'd be your brother, if you'd let me.*

But it was Morgan Earp who was treating him like another brother, inviting him along for evenings of drinking in the saloons and gaming in the gambling halls and spending time with the ladies. If Morgan didn't have one lovely sitting on his lap or fetching his drinks, he was looking for one who would do, and with his sun-bronzed good looks and white hot smile, the ladies were always plenty willing. Then after a long session at the tables, Morgan liked to end his night with a visit to the red-light district, spending some of his winnings relaxing with the bawdy house girls there. Morgan was a lively character, all right, and John Henry couldn't help being amused in his company.

Kate, however, was not so amused. She didn't mind Morgan's drinking and gaming, but his devoted whoring made her wary. Whenever Doc and Morgan were out late together, she was sure that Doc was following his lead and spending some of his own money in the cribs of Dodge City, and sometimes she was right. Mostly, though, she was offended because Morgan had become John Henry's favorite poker companion instead of her.

"Damn Wyatt Earp and all his family with him!" Kate said loudly when John Henry came home too late for her liking, loud enough for Deacon Cox to hear and ask her to quiet down some. The Dodge House had traveling families rooming from time to time, who didn't like to be woken by a marital row going on in the rooms above. "They're nothing but whoremongers, all of them! And look at what they're doing to you! You never sleep, you never eat . . ."

"I'd be asleep already, Kate, if you'd stop shoutin'. Now be a good girl and pour me some water. I'm feelin' dirty all over from this damn Dodge City dust."

"I should think you'd be feeling dirty after spending time with whores. Damn Wyatt!"

"It wasn't Wyatt I was with, Kate. It was just Morg. You don't hate Morg, too, do you? Sometimes I think you must hate every man in Kansas, but me."

"And what makes you think I don't hate you, too?"

"Then leave. There's the door. Nobody's stoppin' you."

But Kate never did walk out the door. Her tempers always passed once she and John Henry had settled their spat with a session of lovemaking. She just wanted to know that he still cared for her, she said, she just needed to know that it was her he wanted in his bed, and not some Dodge City floozy. She just wanted to hear that he loved her, though he never could bring himself to say it.

Wyatt disapproved of Morgan's womanizing as much as Kate did, a fact which John Henry found immensely amusing. That Kate should agree with Wyatt on anything at all was a marvel. For although Wyatt had done his own share of whoring, he was mostly a faithful husband to Celia—mostly, as Morgan recounted, except for a slip now and then while they were on the road together and Celia wasn't around to take care of his needs.

"But what the hell's a man supposed to do, anyhow?" Morgan said with a laugh. "Find a friendly cow, like these cowboys do?" Though Morgan's humor often ran to the ribald, at least he liked a good joke. John Henry rarely even saw Wyatt break a smile.

But Wyatt had a reputation to uphold, especially after he and Bat were enlisted as deacons for the new First Union Church. It wasn't a spiritual calling, exactly, as they were both asked to wear their sidearms to church—having the law there, armed and obvious, helped to keep things reverent during services and made the congregation feel a little more comfortable during the rowdy cattle season. But Wyatt's being made a deacon said a lot about how the people of Dodge felt about him: a brave and trustworthy lawman and a model of manly virtue. It was only the wrongdoers, and Kate, who seemed to disagree.

With the cattle season in full swing, Dodge City became an island of humanity in the middle of a sea of manure. The town was surrounded by acres of cow lots and stock-pens where thousands of head of Texas longhorns waited shipment to eastern slaughterhouses. By day, the sky was dung-colored with the dust the milling animals kicked up off the shaggy prairie. By night, the air was filled with the sound of their bawling, a mournful undertone to the rollicking clatter of saloon pianos and dance-hall fiddles that went on from dusk until dawn.

But then the rains came, spilling down from the sky so fast that the Arkansas River overflowed its banks right up to the back doors of the dance halls south of the railroad tracks, and the cattle business slowed up some. Thirty-eight herds were stuck on the far side of the Arkansas, and the cowboys who guarded them had to sleep out in the rain with the lights of Dodge just a frustrating flooded-stream away. There was sure to be trouble when those tired cowboys finally hit town, over-ready for some rest and relaxation, and Assistant Marshal Earp put out the word that he needed some extra deputies to help keep things under control.

Morgan was the first to apply for the job, and the first to be turned down. As the Marshal's younger brother, Wyatt explained, it would look like favoritism if Morgan got a paid position on the force before all the other applicants had been interviewed. Just wait awhile, Wyatt suggested. Maybe, if there's still room later on . . .

John Henry understood what Wyatt couldn't explain. Much as Morgan idolized his older brother, Wyatt, in his own quiet way, loved his younger brother even more devotedly.

But Morgan wasn't out of a law job for long. Taking Wyatt's refusal like a challenge, Morgan applied to Bat Masterson for a position with the County Sheriff's office instead, and was soon wearing a Sheriff's Deputy badge, showing the star around the saloons of Dodge like a medal of honor.

"I guess I showed Wyatt," Morgan bragged to John Henry, as he watched him buck the tiger at the Lone Star's best Faro table. "Showed him good. He thinks I'm just a kid! Sheriff Bat knows better. I can shoot as straight as Wyatt if I have to, and faster. Bat Masterson knows a natural-born lawman when he sees one."

"I thought you were a natural-born ladies' man, Morg," John Henry remarked, looking up from the game. "It's damn sure you're not a natural-born card player."

"Faro's too fancy," Morgan complained. "I like simple games. Give me a pretty set of dice . . ."

"A loaded set, you mean," John Henry said. "I don't believe I've seen you play with straight dice yet." Then, nodding to the dealer: "That looks like another winnin' bet for me, Sir."

"How the hell do you do that?" Morgan said, as John Henry collected his colorful stack of winning coppers: blues for the tens, reds for the fives, yellows for the ones. "It's like you're a mentalist or something, the way you always pick the winners like that."

"It's just trainin'. I've spent more time on the dealin' side of the layout than I have on the playin' side. That dealer can't deal a card I haven't already counted. I'll put ten on the red queen to win, Sir," he said, and remembered that the red queen had been Lottie Deno's favorite card.

"Well, like I said, I guess I showed Wyatt, treating me like that. You notice he didn't have any problem putting Virg on the force first thing. He no sooner hits town, then Wyatt's pinning a badge on him."

"You're digressin', Morg. Who the hell is Virg?"

"Virgil Earp, of course, our big brother. Didn't I mention they got in last night? Had to wait on the far side of the Arkansas until the river come down enough to cross. Eleven wagons in the outfit, and mostly it's all Earps: Pa and Ma, Newt and his family, Jim and Bessie and her gal, my sister Adelia, and our little brother Warren . . ."

"Another brother?"

"Ma breeds boys, that's what Pa says. All of them big and handsome, like me!"

"And not a bit vain, of course," John Henry commented, though if the rest of the Earp boys looked like Wyatt and Morgan, there wasn't all that much vanity to it. They were both handsome, strapping men, the kind other men admired and all the women fawned over. It was pleasant having such good-looking acquaintances and basking in some of the reflected glory. For though he'd had plenty of ladies call him handsome and take on over the Irish blue of his eyes and the gold of his hair, he knew he didn't have half the masculine, muscular charisma of the Earp brothers.

"So now Virg is here, and first damn thing Wyatt does as soon as he sees him is pin a badge on him, *Dodge City Police*. I guess it didn't look like favoritism to hire his big brother, like it would have to hire his little brother. Damn it, Doc, when's he going to stop thinking I'm just a kid? I'm twenty-eight years old, for hell's sake!"

John Henry looked up at Morgan and smiled. With his unruly head of russet hair, his easy grin and ready laugh, his love of playing games and chasing the girls, Morgan did seem more like an overgrown adolescent than the full-grown man that he was, especially when he stood in the shadow of his solemn older brother. And there was that other slightly mystical side of Morgan, as well, that made him seem like a wide-eyed innocent somehow in spite of his worldly habits. Even John Henry felt a little patronizing of him, though they were nearly the same age.

"I don't reckon he ever will stop treatin' you that way, Morg. From what I can see, Wyatt thinks he's your protector and he's not gonna do anything to put you in harm's way. He says your Mother's kind of fond of you, too."

"Aw, hell!" Morgan said, reddening with embarrassment. "Is that what it is? Is he still playing guardian angel? I swear, I learned how to climb years ago."

"You are a sorry story-teller, Morg! Why don't you start at the beginnin' for once?"

Morgan ran his hand through his tousled hair and gave an exasperated sigh.

"I was a little boy, not more'n four or five years old, and I tried to climb a big tree back of our house, the way I'd watched Jim and Virg doing. I climbed it pretty good, too, 'cept I didn't know how to get back down, so I was stuck up there and scared. I started yelling for Ma, and she came out of the house running, but she couldn't reach up high enough to get me down. That's when she sent Wyatt up to sit with me. *'Just hold onto him, Wyatt!'* she says. *'Don't let him fall! You hold on tight and don't let him outa your hands, no matter what. I'll go get Pa from out in the corn to come reach little Morgan down.'*

"'*Yes'm,'* Wyatt says, and that's just what he did. He shimmied up that tree and slipped his arms around me so tight I could hardly breathe, but he never did let go. Even when I got tired and started to slip, Wyatt just kept holding on, like our Ma said. And when I slid off that limb and fell all the ways down to the ground, Wyatt was still holding on. He fell right down with me, and by the time Ma come back with Pa, we were both lying on the ground with the wind knocked out of us, and Wyatt's arms still tight around me, holding on for dear life. Ma started screaming, thinking we'd both been killed for sure, but Pa just started laughing.

"Well, Morgan, looks like you got yourself a guardian angel,' Pa says, *'but it woulda helped if he'd had himself a pair of wings!'* Ever after that, Ma liked to call Wyatt my Guardian Angel, tell him it was his bound duty to hang onto me and see I didn't get into any more trouble. Ma had her hands full with little Adelia and baby Warren, and couldn't watch over me all the time, and she was afraid I'd get myself hurt or killed someways. I always was the wild one of the family, I guess, always getting into mischief."

"You remember all of that from when you were four years old?"

"I don't have to remember it," Morgan said, reddening again. "Ma tells that story on me every time we get together, reminds Wyatt it's his job to watch over me. And you know Wyatt, once he takes on a job he don't let go of it. Takes everything serious as God's word. But dammit, Doc, I don't need no guardian angel anymore! I wish he'd let me go on and grow up. I'd be a damn good lawman, if he'd just give me the chance."

"You've got that Sheriff's Deputy badge. Isn't that lawman enough?"

"You know county lawing's not the same as city lawing, not here in Dodge. What happens out in the county, anyway? The cows get loose or the cowboys run over somebody's crop. It's here in Dodge where the action's going on, right here in the gambling joints. This is where the gun-play happens," he said, fingering the six-shooter stuck down in the waistband of his trousers, legally carried with his new badge. "What good is being able to wear a pistol if you don't get to use it?"

John Henry let his Faro bet ride without him for a moment and gave Morgan another long look. "And that's just what Wyatt's afraid of, Morg. This is where the gun-play is. He doesn't want to lose you the way Bat lost his brother. If I were you, I'd be thankful I had a brother who loved me like that. I'd be thankful to have anybody care about me like that."

Morgan shrugged. "You got Kate, Doc. She cares a heap about you. That's something, ain't it?"

"Sure, Morg, that's somethin'," John Henry replied, turning back to his game, and feeling suddenly more alone than ever, standing on the outside of that warm circle of the Earp clan and wishing he could be one of them. "I've got Kate, all right. What more could I possibly want?"

Chapter Twelve

Dodge City, 1878

The Fourth of July came to Dodge City with all the usual revels: fireworks, dance hall brawls, patriotic gunfights between Yankee cattle buyers and Southern cowboys. It also brought a girl who swept Morgan Earp right off his bachelor feet and quickly ended his short career as a Kansas lawman.

John Henry wouldn't have believed that love-at-first-sight meeting if he hadn't seen it with his own eyes. But he was standing right there beside Morgan when it happened as he was making a purchase at the sales counter of the General Store.

"You keep buyin' that licorice, you're gonna need my services," John Henry had remarked.

"Can't help it, Doc, gotta sweet tooth. Always did, so says my Ma." Then he looked up and caught a glimpse of a dark-haired beauty behind a shelf of calico. "Gotta sweet tooth for something else, as well!" he said, giving the girl a grin.

It was no surprise when the girl gave him a smile back—Morgan was always catching the eyes of the ladies like that. The surprise came when Morgan stopped looking at any of the other ladies, caught up in that one moment by the charms of Miss Louisa Houston, granddaughter of General Sam Houston of Texas Independence fame.

Louisa was traveling with her father, Sam Houston Jr., the illegitimate son of the General and an Indian woman who'd fallen to the old man's charming ways. With his famous father's name and fondness for liquor and his Indian mother's dark-haired good looks, Sam Houston, Jr.

had charmed a few women himself, including Louisa's mother, a beauty who died soon after her daughter's birth and left the baby for Sam Jr. to raise. But though Sam didn't seem cut out for much besides drinking and carousing, he was a devoted father when it came to his little girl. Louisa Houston, darkly beautiful as her Indian grandmother, had been raised like a real princess, living in the nicest hotels in the frontier west and wearing the finest clothes her father's dwindling inheritance money could buy.

The Houstons had arrived in town just in time to join in the holiday festivities before heading on to Montana, where Sam Jr. was looking for some northern grazing land for his small herd of Texas cattle. And by the time they were packed again and ready to head on up the trail, the lovely Louisa had convinced Morgan to resign his Deputy Sheriff's badge and go along for the ride.

"So that's how it is, Doc," Morgan explained, when he dropped by John Henry's rooms at the Dodge House to say goodbye on his way out of town. "Louisa's leavin' with her father, and I can't let her get away, so I'm going along."

The day was early yet, not even ten a.m., and John Henry had been asleep still when Morgan banged on the bedroom door, though, thankfully, Kate was already up and gone to breakfast. She always made sure to have some cutting remark ready whenever Morgan came to visit, though she hated Wyatt most.

"I know I said I'd never let no woman tie me down," Morgan went on, as John Henry, still wearing the knee-length nightshirt he'd slept in, proceeded to shave and dress for the day. "But I'm not ashamed to say it, Doc: I'm in love! And if Lou will have me, I mean to marry her as soon as we get to Montana."

"You mean if Sam Houston Junior will have you," John Henry commented. "Sam's careful of that girl, I've noticed. And I hear he's got a regular arsenal on him. You know he learned to use a knife from Jim Bowie before the Mexicans got him at the Alamo? I'd be wary of becomin' target practice, if I were you." Then he wiped the shaving soap from his face, ran a handful of cologne through his sandy hair, and pulled off his nightshirt. Even in the near-hundred degree Kansas summer heat, a man had to dress properly: long flannel drawers under woolen trousers, cotton undershirt beneath crisp shirt bosom and starched collar and cuffs, round-collared vest buttoned under wool suit coat, linsey stockings inside ankle-high leather boots. He'd be sweating today before he even got out of his room.

"It's not Sam Junior I'm worried about, Doc. I can handle him all right. It's Wyatt I'm going to have trouble with. You know how he likes to keep an eye on me. I'm afraid if I tell him I'm leaving with Lou, he'll put up a stink and try to stop me, say I'm making a mistake, that we haven't known each other long enough to be going off and getting married."

"A week does seem mighty short for a courtship."

"I know, but I love her! What else matters? Besides, Wyatt didn't court Aurilla much longer than that himself. "

"You and your half-ass storytelling, Morg! When are you going to learn to start at the beginning instead of somewhere in the middle all the time? Who the hell is Aurilla?"

"Wyatt's first wife. Didn't you know? He met her in Missouri when we moved back there from California the first time. Aurilla Sutherland. Her father owned the hotel there in town, and Wyatt fell for her first thing. Had our Daddy marry them quick, as he was Justice of the Peace, but her father said who the hell was Wyatt Earp, and he'd be damned if he'd let his little girl run off with some young nobody. He even tried to get the thing annulled, but Aurilla was already in the family way, so they had to let the marriage stick."

"So what happened?"

"She died of fever before the baby came. All of Lamar was catching it, and it took Aurilla and the baby, too. Near to broke Wyatt's heart. Only time I ever seen him cry was at her funeral, and he was bawling like a baby. And then he just disappeared out of town for awhile, went over to Arkansas and got himself into some trouble there stealing horses. But he was so broke-up about Aurilla, you see, and damn near drinking himself to death trying to forget about it, so you have to excuse the horse stealing. It ain't like Wyatt to do something like that when he's in his right head."

But John Henry wasn't thinking about Wyatt's horse-thieving past. He was thinking about his own year of death-wish drinking, when he'd learned he had the consumption and life had seemed too bleak to go on living another day, when even the thought of Mattie's love couldn't comfort him, but only made his despair deeper.

"Poor Wyatt, I know how he must have felt . . ."

"But hell! Why should I care what Wyatt thinks? I'm a grown man. I guess I can get married without his permission!" Then he added with a sheepish grin, "Maybe you can talk to him for me, explain things? You're better with words than I am. You might even get the story straight and I'd forget half, or leave something out!"

"Sure, Morg. I'll talk to him for you, for whatever good it will do."

"Thanks, Doc," Morgan said as he put out his hand. "Well, it's been fun knowing you. Tell the crowd at the Long Branch to have a drink in my honor, all right?" Then he laughed—that happy, careless laugh of his. "Guess the boys will be laying two-to-one it don't last with me and Lou, but we'll prove them wrong, you'll see! We'll be rocking in our rocking chairs together, still in love like damn newlyweds when we're old and gray. I got a feeling about it. This one's the keeper for me. Wish I could be in two places at one time, though. I was looking forward to seeing some action around Dodge this summer, maybe get a chance to prove myself to Wyatt even. Guess I just got bad timing, huh? And Doc," he added, "there is one more thing I'd like to ask you to do for me."

"You name it."

"Keep an eye on Wyatt, all right? See he don't act too brave, get himself shot in the back or anything. I think maybe he's the one who's going to need a guardian angel with that bounty on his head."

Morgan was right about one thing: Wyatt needed someone to watch his back, though without knowing who was behind the rumored threats, it was hard to know what to watch out for, or when to be watching. So nobody was paying enough attention on the night of the first attempt on Wyatt's life, during Eddie Foy's vaudeville show at the Comique Theater.

Foy was a favorite with the Dodge City crowd—a strutting, swaggering little New Yorker with a brash sense of humor and a trunkful of offensive jokes about cattlemen—and the cowboys took an instant liking to him, showing their appreciation by capturing him and tying him up rodeo-style and riding him around town on horseback. And Eddie Foy, knowing a good audience when he saw one, laughed long and hard at the joke of it and turned the experience into new material for his twice-nightly show.

The Comique Theater was located at the back of Josh Webb's Lady Gay Saloon, and Eddie Foy's antics were just a background for the real entertainment there, as Sheriff Bat Masterson dealt Spanish Monte when he wasn't busy doing his law work. Having the County Sheriff as house dealer gave the place a slightly more respectable air than the other gambling houses in town, though from what John Henry could see, the Sheriff wasn't any more honest than the rest of the Dodge City dealers. Bat Masterson had fast hands and a slippery shuffle, and John Henry kept a steady eye on him as he dealt the cards. As a slippery card-dealer himself, he knew real competition when he came across it.

"Watch the deck, Sheriff," he cautioned. "I believe I saw a card or two trying to slide off the bottom there."

"Are you calling me a cheater, Doc?" Bat Masterson asked, his brown eyes flashing a warning and his neatly-barbered mustache twitching. "A false accusation like that could catch you a night in the cooler."

There was a politely mutual dislike between the two men, started when John Henry had first sighted the dandified lawman and continued when Masterson had discovered John Henry's outlaw past. But they still managed to play cards together amicably enough.

"Now, Sheriff," John Henry said blandly. "The games are town business, not county business, you know that. You'd have to get Marshal Earp to come arrest me, and as the Marshal is a personal friend of mine—"

"Why the Earps would choose a killer like you for a friend is beyond me."

"And how about your own friendship with that killer, Ben Thompsen?" John Henry asked. "He's twice the outlaw I am, yet I hear you two are bosom companions."

"Ben saved my life back in Sweetwater. Held off a lynch mob until I could get out of town. Does a man need more reason than that?"

"Ah, yes, the night poor Mollie Brennan died. I hear she was a sweet thing," he said tauntingly. Rumor had it that the Sheriff still carried a torch for the dead saloon girl, and was staying a bachelor in her honor. "Kate, my dear, why don't you refill my glass?"

With Morgan Earp gone, Kate had taken up her old place at his side in the gambling halls, and she seemed to be enjoying having him all to herself again. "Why don't you leave the cards and come dance with me, instead? Mr. Foy is about to call a quadrille."

"Gather 'round, folks!" Eddie Foy invited from the stage, "Choose your partners! Swing the right hand lady!"

"And miss out on beatin' our fine Sheriff at his own game? I wouldn't dream of it! Deal on, Sheriff Masterson. Kate, you go on and catch yourself a cowboy to dance with you. I am feelin' a winnin' streak comin' on."

"All balance left!" Foy called, "Alamon right!"

"I don't want to dance with a dirty cowboy," Kate said petulantly. "I want to dance with you. Don't you want to show me off in this new gown you've bought me?"

He was about to remind her that it was his gambling winnings that had paid for her new gown, and that if she kept expecting expensive gifts like that, she needed to let him play in peace, when his thoughts were cut short. A staccato of gunfire and a crash of window glass brought the dancing and the games to a halt.

Kate screamed and Bat said, "Drop!" And in a second, both John Henry and the Sheriff were lying face down on the dance hall floor. Kate took a moment longer to join them, struggling with her layers of ruffled petticoats and lace-trimmed satin.

"Damned Texans!" Masterson cursed as the firing went on. "Treeing the town again! Sounds like a whole army of them out there."

"Not an army," John Henry said, instinctively counting the shots. "Eight or ten, maybe, no more. Where's Wyatt?"

"He's out on patrol duty. Damn!" Bat said again, as a slug whizzed past his head. "He'll find them and put a stop to this soon enough."

"If they don't stop him first," John Henry said when a lull came in the shooting. "I've got to get out there and warn him!"

"What are you talking about?"

"That was a lot of lead for a howdy. It may be Wyatt in particular those Texans are gunnin' for, tryin' to collect on that thousand dollar bounty. Better lend me your pistol, Sheriff."

"Not a chance, Doc. We've got plenty of law around here without deputizing the likes of you. Wyatt can handle it, whatever it is."

There wasn't time to convince the Sheriff or retrieve his own revolver from behind the bar where he'd checked it earlier that evening, so he rolled over and grabbed Kate, running his hand up under her gathered skirts and along her smoothly curving thigh.

"Give me your derringer, darlin'! I'll take the rest of you later."

"No!" she said, and pushed him away, her eyes hot with anger and the derringer still snug inside her lace-edged garter. "Let them kill him. It's better than he deserves! I hope they collect every bit of that bounty!"

John Henry grabbed her shoulders and dragged her to her feet. "Damn you!" he cried, as the firing started up again, further down the street now, and answered by a volley of pistol shots and a blast from a shot-gun. "I could have been out there by now!"

"I'm just trying to protect you. You don't know the kind of men those bounty hunters are. You don't know . . ."

"And what do you know about it?" he demanded, a sudden suspicion taking him. "I swear, Kate, if you're hidin' something from me, I'll . . ."

"Let her go, Doc," Bat Masterson's steady voice commanded. "Or I will put you in the cooler."

And as John Henry's hands slid away from Kate shoulders, he saw the welts rising on her honey-colored skin.

But Kate put on a cool smile. "It's all right, Sheriff. He's just had a little too much to drink tonight, haven't you, my love? He wasn't really going to hurt me. There's no need to lock him up. Why don't I just take him home and let him sleep it off?"

"I am not drunk!" he said hotly.

"Maybe not, but you are acting dangerous," Bat Masterson said, "asking for my pistol and mistreating the lady like that. I think maybe you should go on home now and call it an evening. Ma'am, you let me know if he ever treats you hard like that again."

"Oh, I will, Sheriff," she said, purring like a cat with a mouse in its claws. "Come, my love. The night is young for us, yet. There's better games than this back in our rooms."

But lovemaking was the furthest thing from John Henry's mind. Kate knew something about those Texas bounty hunters, he was sure of it.

By the next morning, the whole town was talking about the shoot-up outside the Lady Gay Saloon, and how Marshal Earp and a few of his deputies had hurriedly saddled their horses and chased the Texans out of town. The Marshal had even managed to wing one of the shooters, a cowboy named George Hoyt, who fell wounded from his horse on a hill just south of the Arkansas River and was brought back to Dodge to be treated by the town doctor. The cowboy's wound was a bad one, the bullet severing an artery in his arm, and by the time Dr. McCarty had sewn him up again, Hoyt had lost a lot of blood—too much, the doctor thought, to have much chance of recovering.

The one thing Hoyt was strong enough to do was confess that the shooting hadn't been just an innocent treeing of the town, but was a hired job paid for by some big Texas cattleman looking for Wyatt Earp. Unfortunately, Hoyt died before saying who the cattleman was, and the *Ford County Globe* eulogized him in undeserved style:

> George was nothing but a poor cowboy, but his brother cowboys permitted him to want for nothing during his illness, and buried him in grand style when dead, which was very creditable to them. Let his faults, if he had any, be hidden in the grave.

"Let his faults damn him right to hell," was John Henry's comment, as he read the obituary. "And next time those boys come gunnin' for Wyatt, I'll be ready."

He glanced at Kate as he spoke, watching for her reaction, but she didn't flutter an eyelash. He'd already tempted her with pretty baubles, trying to get her to talk, and even threatened to kick her out if she didn't tell him what she knew of the bounty hunters. But Kate was as hard-headed as he was and insisted that she knew nothing more than she had already said.

"I only know that you are safe, my love. That's all that matters to me. You know how I love you, Doc."

He knew, all right. But knowing didn't make him feel any easier.

August came in a blaze of summer heat, 106 degrees in the shade wherever there was any. The Arkansas River that had been booming to overflowing just two months before now wallowed into a muddy stream that hardly gave enough water for the livestock to drink. John Henry, who didn't tolerate the heat well under the best of circumstances, could hardly make it across the street from the Dodge House to the Long Branch Saloon without the searing sun making him sick to his stomach and the blowing dust choking his lungs. If he hadn't promised Morgan that he'd watch out for Wyatt, he might have packed up then and headed on to Colorado for awhile, where the air was cool and clear. Even Sheriff Bat Masterson, with all his civic responsibilities, left town for a month, traveling to Hot Springs, Kansas where the mineral baths might cure the vertigo that had plagued him ever since his wounding at Sweetwater.

Then just as the whole town seemed about to dry up and blow away with the prairie wind, the rains returned, flooding the dry-bottomed Arkansas and turning the streets of Dodge into mires of mud. And with the rains came rumors that a thousand Cheyenne Indians had broken away from the reservation at Fort Reno in the Indian Territory, and were headed north to the Dakotas.

The Indians were led by the infamous Chief Dull Knife who was intent on returning his people to their ancestral lands, no matter what stood in the way. The killing started soon after they crossed over the Kansas line where two ranchers were murdered and left for the buzzards. In Comanche County, a gang of cowboys was shot down as they sat unarmed around their campfire. On the Salt Fork of the Cimarron River, a settler was shot in the neck, his wife was wounded, and their baby had a bullet put through its breast. In Meade County, a man's throat was slit from ear to ear. In Ford County, a Negro cooking breakfast for a cattle crew was butchered. Then just south of Dodge City, Dull Knife's band made a massacre, killing ten people, wounding five more, and slaughtering most of six-hundred head of cattle.

The residents of Dodge City were in a terror, expecting to be overrun at any moment by the bloodthirsty Cheyenne. And as the firehouse bell rang to call the citizens to arms, Mayor Dog Kelley telegraphed the governor to send weapons: *The country is filled with Indians.*

By the morning of the 20th of September, every farmer within thirty miles of Dodge had come into town for safety, and in response to Mayor Kelley's telegram, the adjutant general arrived with the first shipment of 6,000 carbines and 20,000 cartridges. His train was met by a mob of citizens and the Dodge City Silver Cornet Band, led by the Long Branch's own Chalk Beeson, and the local paper reported: *The scene at the depot reminds us of rebellion times.*

With the cavalry from Fort Dodge called out to help quell the uprising, and only nineteen men left at the fort to help defend the nearby town, Dodge City became an armed camp. Bawdy houses became shelters for the families of farmers come into town for protection, and good citizens joined in with cowboys and gamblers to go out in support of the army. The Santa Fe Railroad even outfitted a special locomotive to carry the civilian soldiers to suspected attack sites, with Wyatt Earp and Chalk Beeson leading a posse that rode the train to put out a range fire set by the Indians.

Kate was terrified and refused to leave the Dodge House Hotel, keeping a constant watch at the window for savages and drawing her derringer so many times in fright that John Henry decided he'd be safer somewhere else and headed for the Long Branch Saloon. Of course, he could have taken up one of those government carbines and gone out with Wyatt and most of the other men in town, but the thought of doing anything to aid the army didn't sit well with him. As long as the United States Cavalry still wore the hated Yankee blue, he couldn't bring himself to fight on their side.

So he was one of the only able-bodied men still left in town when Wyatt returned with some Indian prisoners, and Wyatt was the only lawman in town when cattleman Tobe Driskill and his cowboys hit Dodge a short time later, expecting to find the place empty and open for the taking.

John Henry was playing alone at the Long Branch Faro table, taking cards from Cockeyed Frank Loving, when there arose a commotion of pistol shots and breaking glass out on Front Street. His first thought was that the Indians were arriving to pillage the town, then he recognized the celebratory shouts of Texas cowboys, and he swore and dropped to the floor.

"Fool cowboys are at it again! Card playin' is getting damned dangerous in this town! Get down, Frank, unless you want a hole between your eyes."

The dealer did as he was told, cowering on the floor while outside the cowboys discussed in loud profanities what they ought to do to the Long Branch. John Henry gave a fleeting thought to making an escape by shimmying across the floor to the back alley door. Then one of the cowboys cursed and John Henry forgot all about escaping.

"Well, hell!" he heard the cowboy say, "it's Earp!"

"And this time he's going to get it!" another voice exclaimed. "You're such a fighter, Earp, here's your chance to do some. If he makes a move, boys, let him have it."

There was an assenting murmur from the crowd, then the first voice added:

"You white-livered son of a bitch! If you got some praying to do, get at it!"

It only took a moment for John Henry to make a leap to the bar where he grabbed the pistol he'd stashed there and another hanging by it. Then he crossed the saloon and pushed through the batwing doors while he cocked both pistols at once, taking aim at the surprised crowd.

"Throw 'em up!" he said, "high and wide, you damned murdering cow thieves!"

Before him, Wyatt stood empty handed on the board sidewalk, and past him in the street was a crowd of what looked to be twenty-five pistol-toting cowboys. And though Wyatt didn't even glance his way, John Henry's interruption had distracted the cowboys enough for him to jerk both his guns, cocking them as he swung them up from the holsters. So there they stood, Holliday and Earp, four guns against fifty. And to John Henry's eyes, the odds looked just about even.

"What'll we do with 'em, Wyatt?" he asked with a smile, as though the battle had already been won.

In reply, Wyatt took a single brave step toward the startled leader of the gang and laid the barrel of his Buntline Special over the cowboy's head. The man dropped like he'd been shot instead of buffaloed, and the rest of the cowboys stood in stunned silence.

"Throw 'em up!" Wyatt said to the rest of them. "All the way up and empty! Morrison's got his, and you're next, Driskill!"

Six-shooters clattered to the street as the cowboys' hands went skyward, but in the rear of the crowd, one Texan took a wild chance.

John Henry saw the cowboy's gun hand go up and yelled, "Look out, Wyatt!" as he leveled his own revolver and pulled off a shot just as the cowboy fired. The two reports roared almost as one, but a howl of pain from the back of the crowd told whose shot had taken effect.

"Sorry, Wyatt," John Henry apologized. "Reckon I only winged him. I was tryin' to kill him for you."

"Glad you didn't, Doc," Wyatt replied, as he waved the Buntline toward the rest of the crowd, herding them off to the calaboose. "I'd hate to have to arrest you for murder after you'd saved my life. Those boys were about to do me in when you jumped out the door. What the hell made you try a fool thing like that?"

"Morgan asked me to watch out for you. He figured you needed someone to cover your back. I was just doin' what he would have done if he'd been around."

"Morgan?" Wyatt said in surprise. "Morgan never would have made a play like that, nor Virg neither." Then he added with a nod of his head. "I guess you're the best brother I've got, Doc. I won't forget this."

John Henry would never forget it, either. Wyatt Earp had called him a brother.

Bat Masterson came to John Henry's rooms at the Dodge House Hotel the next week, limping as he always did, a painful reminder of the shooting in Sweetwater, and carrying a narrow box under his arm.

"I heard you're leaving Dodge," Bat said.

"You heard right. This Kansas dust is about to kill me. I'm going to Colorado where I can breathe. Besides, it looks like Wyatt's got things under control here now. The cattle season's about run out, and Morrison and Driskill will probably spread the word that Wyatt's too tough to collect that bounty on, anyhow."

Masterson nodded. "This county's already had enough trouble for one year. You know Dull Knife got away from the cavalry after all, headed up to the Cheyenne nation?"

"One more loss for the brave boys in blue," John Henry commented. "Can't say who I feel sorrier for, the fool Indians or the Army they made fools of."

"Still just as smart-mouthed as ever, aren't you?"

"Did you have somethin' you wanted to talk to me about, Sheriff?" John Henry asked irritably. "I've got a patient waiting to see me."

Bat sighed. "Listen, Doc. I know we haven't been the best of friends . . ."

"Nonsense, Sheriff. I'm friends with any man I can beat at cards."

"Let me finish what I have to say. It isn't easy for me to thank you."

"Thank me? For what?"

"For saving my friend's life. I could have been there with Wyatt, but I wasn't. I was off chasing Indians with the rest of the boys and didn't think about what Wyatt might be walking into taking those prisoners back to Dodge alone. If you hadn't happened to be there, he'd be dead now, and I can't afford to lose anybody else who matters. So, much as it goes against my grain to say it, I thank you for what you did."

Then he took the box from under his arm and lifted the lid. Inside was a shiny new Colt's .45, nickel-plated and pearl-handled, the kind of fancy firearm that only a dandy like Bat would buy.

"What's this?" John Henry asked, as Bat handed him the open box.

"It's a gift, just in case Wyatt ever needs your help again."

"I don't know what to say, Sheriff," John Henry said, and though his voice had a trace of his usual sarcasm, he meant the words. He couldn't remember the last time anyone had given him anything. Anyone but Kate, of course, who was always buying him presents with his own money.

"Don't say anything for a change. Just take it with my thanks. I ordered a couple of them from the Colt's company. Take it while I'm in the giving mood. And do us all a favor by trying to stay out of trouble with it."

"I always try, Sheriff. Haven't I been an exemplary citizen, here in Dodge? No brawling, no fighting, and only a minimum of public drunkenness."

"You've been all right, for Dodge. But I wouldn't go so far as calling you exemplary. You're still mostly a gambler living with a fallen angel."

"Kate's no angel!" John Henry said with a laugh. "Though I suppose that's why I've kept her around . . ."

"So where in Colorado are you headed? Maybe I should warn the marshal there that you're coming."

"I'm headed over to Trinidad, for starters, since the train runs that away now. Should be some fine gambling in that town with the Santa Fe coming in. Then maybe back up to Denver, open a dental practice there. They've got a gun ordinance now, so I'll probably never get a chance to use this pretty new pistol of yours, more's the pity. I have a fondness for nice firearms, you know."

Bat nodded. "That's why I figured you'd enjoy playing with this new toy. But Holliday . . ."

"Yes?"

"Play carefully. I'd hate to see your bad reputation cause your friends any trouble—especially Wyatt. Now he feels he owes you, he'll stick by you 'till the debt's repaid. No matter what it takes to repay it."

Chapter Thirteen

THE CITY LAY IN A NARROW VALLEY IN THE SAN JUAN MOUNTAINS OF southeastern Colorado, where the Purgatoire River crossed the Santa Fe Trail. The cowboys called the river the Picketwire, mispronouncing the French version of the original Spanish name, "El Rio de Las Animas Perdidas en Purgatorio." Everyone else just called it Purgatory.

But it looked more like heaven to John Henry, as the train from Dodge City rose up out of the dusty plains and wound into the green mountains that surrounded Trinidad.

"I saved a man from Purgatory, once," he mused to Kate.

"And just how did you do that? You're no priest."

"I rode a horse all night long, that's how, and nearly froze to death doin' it. My uncle was dyin' and I had to go all the way to Atlanta to get the priest to give him his last rites."

"You never told me you had a Catholic uncle," Kate said in surprise.

"I never told you a lot of things," he replied, as he touched the Claddagh ring on his little finger. Though Kate knew he wrote letters home to his cousin in Georgia, he was careful not to let her see the replies, with the envelopes addressed in Mattie's delicate feminine handwriting. Kate still thought his cousin was a man and he didn't plan to enlighten her any. "I almost became a Catholic myself, for instance. I never told you that either, did I?"

"You'd have made a good Catholic, with all that drinking."

"And you've made a bad one, if you were ever good at it in the first place. Surely you must know that our sleepin' together is a sin. We could both be damned, you know."

"You can be damned now, for all I care," she answered haughtily. "You're the one who's happy keeping a mistress. I'd be your wife, if you ever asked me."

He hadn't expected the sudden serious turn of the conversation, and he couldn't find the words to answer for a moment. It was true that Kate had been more like a wife than a mistress to him, traveling the hard miles up from Fort Griffin without complaining, caring for him during his sick spells, bearing him the only child he would ever have. But he didn't love Kate, not enough to marry her. Not the way he still loved Mattie.

"You wouldn't want to be married to me, Kate!" he said with a laugh. "I'd be a poor bet as a husband. I'd just die on you someday, leave you a wealthy widow, or a bust one, dependin' on my luck. And as I recall, I only promised to take you as far as Dodge City, anyhow. You're free to leave now, if you're tired of the way things are. Trinidad ought to suit you fine. I hear they have the most remarkable redlight district in Colorado."

"Are you calling me a whore?"

"That would be a case of the pot callin' the kettle black, I believe. I think you are a fine companion for a sportin' man, and more than adequate to my other needs. In fact, if this ridin' car had a sleepin' berth . . ."

"Go to hell!"

"You first!" he laughed. "Ah, Kate! You do look lovely when you're angry, with your eyes all on fire like that! It reminds me of why I wanted you in the first place, back in St. Louis."

"And why was that?"

"To see if I could tame your arrogant soul."

"That's one thing you will never do!" she said, tossing her head. But there was a smile behind her eyes, enjoying the battle. "I don't think I will marry you, even if you ask. You're not nearly my equal. I could have married a nobleman if my family had stayed in Hungary."

He smiled, too, intrigued as always by Kate's quick passions, so unlike Mattie's steady emotions that were like a balm to his troubled soul. Kate's passions fired his own, though there were times he wanted to kill her more than make love to her. But now he was only amused and toying with her.

"Yes, you're quite the princess," he said, "wearing all that finery your outlaw lover buys for you. I wonder what your old Hungarian family would think of you now with your face all painted and your bosom showing in the daytime?"

And all at once, Kate's haughty anger turned to tears, catching him off guard again.

"You are a cruel and heartless man!" she said with a sob.

The one thing John Henry couldn't bear was to see a woman cry, and he quickly took her gloved hand in his.

"Kate, I was only teasin'! I didn't mean anything by it. Do you think I'd stay with you if you looked like a street-walker? Why do you think I spend all this money dressin' you up, anyhow? Here," he said, pulling his own linen handkerchief from his vest pocket, "blow your nose. Your rouge is runnin'."

But as Kate opened the handkerchief, elegantly embroidered with his initials JHH, she saw the brown stain of old blood that wouldn't wash out.

"Oh, Doc!" she cried. "Why do we have to fight all the time? I don't want to lose you! I don't want you to die!"

"Everybody dies, Kate. Me and you and all the rest of the world, too. But I'm not dead just yet, so stop your weepin'. We're coming into Trinidad. You don't want to make your entrance with your face all a mess, do you?"

He could have stopped her tears all at once, he knew, by telling her that he loved her, and for a moment, he almost tried. Heaven knew he'd told enough other lies in his life. What difference would one more make? But heaven knew, too, that he'd made a vow to Mattie, and that one vow he meant to keep. Always, he had promised her. And though Kate was looking up at him with yearning in her eyes, he couldn't break that vow.

Trinidad was one of the boomtowns of the Santa Fe Trail, sprung up as a supply stop on the eight-hundred mile highway that ran from Missouri to the New Mexico Territory. The trail brought thousands of oxen-drawn prairie schooners driving along the two main streets of the town, and with the arrivals of the railroad from Denver in 1876 and Dodge City in 1878, Trinidad had quickly become the major shipping point for most of New Mexico, Arizona, and West Texas. The town boasted a population of 3,000 permanent residents, with eighty-eight stores, three hotels, a daily newspaper and mail, and the red-light district that was the wonder of Colorado.

But it wasn't Trinidad's bordellos that interested John Henry, and as soon as he got Kate and himself settled into a room at the swank new Southern Hotel, he headed up the street to the Exchange Club, the biggest saloon and gambling house in town. Though the Exchange had a reputation for violence, it also had a reputation for drawing some of the best-known sporting men in the west. Wild Bill Hickok had played there, and Frank and Jesse James. Some claimed that young Billy the Kid had tried his luck at the Exchange's gambling tables while running from the law in Lincoln County, New Mexico. With all that action, the Exchange was the kind of place where a gentleman gambler could rake in a bundle, and that's just what John Henry proposed to do.

The first night in town he won $200 on Faro; the second night he cleared $300 more on Spanish Monte and knew that he was on a roll. And though Kate pestered him about letting go of the games for an evening or two and getting a little rest after the trip up from Dodge City, he couldn't stop playing as long as things were going so well. He was riding on the wave of euphoria that a successful gambling spree always gave him, and he didn't feel like sleeping or eating or even making love.

But he did feel like drinking, both to celebrate his success at the card tables and to mask the growing pain in his lungs. The summer months in dusty Dodge City had been hard on his health and he was having more trouble breathing than usual, coughing and wheezing between every play. If it hadn't been for the blessed relief of the whiskey, he might not have been able to keep playing at all, streak or no streak. So by the end of his first week in Trinidad, he was $2,000 richer, tired beyond tired, and thoroughly soused, as well.

"Come on, Doc," Kate cajoled as he took another hand of cards and laid down his bet. The poker game in the Exchange Club had been going on for most of the day and into the night, and Kate was getting tired of waiting. "Let it go for awhile. Haven't we made enough money for one week? You need to rest."

"With you?" he said, looking up with blood-shot blue eyes. "That's funny, Kate! When did you ever let me get any rest, anyhow? You are a veritable virago in the bedroom. I'd get more rest right here on the green baize than in your eager embrace."

"Then come eat something, at least. Or take me shopping and buy me a new dress . . ."

"Ah! Is that what you're after? Well, hell, darlin'," he drawled, "why didn't you say so?" and he tossed her a wad of bills from the stack in front of him. "You go on ahead and get to shoppin' without me. I'm gonna stay on a little longer and see how much more money these fine gentlemen have to lose."

But although Kate took the money, sliding it down into the plunging neckline of her satin dress, she still persisted in trying to get him to give up his game. "You're going to make yourself sick, Doc. Take a break and come walking with me. Trinidad's not the place for a lady alone."

"Why, Kate! I'm surprised at you! Don't you still have that derringer tucked up inside your garter? If anybody tries to give you trouble, you just give 'em a little of what you've got between your legs!"

He always found himself immensely amusing when he'd been drinking and playing cards. Hilarious, Morgan had called him, and he had to agree. But Kate seemed to think otherwise.

"You're disgusting. I don't know why I stay with you."

"Then leave. But do so quickly, if you must. You're ruinin' my concentration on this fine hand of cards. Gentlemen, shall we play poker?"

Kate stood beside him fuming a moment longer before sweeping out of the gaming room, her head held high and her aristocratic nose in the air, and her dramatic exit wasn't lost on the other gamblers at John Henry's table.

Kid Colton, a scar-faced youngster who fancied himself another Billy the Kid, watched her with lusty young eyes and whistled in admiration. "That's a helluva woman, Holliday! Are you her pimp? I got $50 here I'll give you for a trick, if you're running her business."

Kate heard his words from the doorway and turned back haughtily. "What did you say?" she demanded. "What did you call me?"

"I said you're a helluva woman. Asked Holliday if he'd take a fifty for you. But I'll give it to you myself, if you'd rather. Don't make no difference to me. Long as I get a good lay for it."

"How dare you!" she cried. "Doc, you're not going to let him insult me like that, are you? You're not going to let him insult you . . ."

It was the personal insult, pointed out by Kate, that got John Henry's ire. Calling a spade a spade was one thing. But calling a gentleman a pimp was not to be borne.

He laid down his cards and said with a sigh, "Kid, you have put me in a difficult position. I'd rather keep beatin' you at cards than have to shoot you, but unless you apologize to Miss Elder and myself . . ."

"Apologize, hell! That was a damn good offer. The madams up on parlor hill don't make any more on a trick than that!"

"Then I shall have to challenge you to a duel in defense of Miss Elder's honor and my own." And as he rose to his feet, wobbly from a week of liquor, he waved his hand toward the other players at the table. "Gentlemen, may we have some room, please? Mr. Colton and I are about to have a duel . . ."

"You're crazy!" Kid Colton sneered, "crazy and drunk."

"Drunk perhaps, but only a little crazy," John Henry said, his drawl beginning to slur. Then he pulled open his suit coat and laid his hand on the pearl-handled revolver in his shoulder holster—Bat's revolver, special ordered from the Colt's Manufacturing Company. "Who's your second, Mr. Colton? You're gonna need him in a moment."

Kid Colton still seemed to think John Henry's growing anger was just a joke, as he sat unbelieving—and worse, laughing out loud.

"I'd like to see you try it, Holliday! They don't call me *Kid* for nothing. Ain't nobody faster on the draw than me, not even Billy the Kid hisself. Why, I bet I could take you with one hand behind my back." And as he reached toward his revolver, John Henry's new Colt's flashed and fired, the bullet slamming into Kid Colton's shooting arm and throwing him backward in a howl of pain.

"Well, I reckon Billy's reputation is still intact," John Henry commented, as he covered the startled crowd with his smoking six-shooter in one hand and swept up his poker winnings with the other. "Hold the door for me, will you, Kate darlin'? My hands are full."

Though John Henry had done his gentlemanly best to assuage both their honors, Kate was still fuming after their quick retreat to the Southern Hotel.

"I wish you had killed him for me. He deserved it, the bastard!"

"Watch your language, Kate. There's a lady in the room," John Henry replied, as he sat sprawled in an easy chair holding a glass to his aching head. The pleasant glow of the gambling was wearing off and he was beginning to have a raging headache.

"You had an easy shot at him," Kate went on as she paced the expensive carpet. "Why didn't you just put a bullet through his head and be done with it? Insulting me that way! Now he'll come back looking to settle the score and you'll just have to fight him all over again."

"He won't be comin' back again anytime soon, not with that shootin' arm. I did enough damage to teach him a lesson, anyhow. Besides, Bat asked me to stay out of trouble."

"Bat?" she said, stopping to stare at him. "What are you talking about?"

"Sheriff Masterson, back in Dodge City, when he gave me this pistol. He asked me to stay out of trouble, if I could, for Wyatt's sake. I reckon killin' was the kind of trouble in particular that he was talkin' about."

"Wyatt?" Kate said, her eyes flashing. "Always Wyatt! What about me? I'm the one whose honor was defiled! Damn Wyatt! I wish Larn's men had collected on that bounty and killed him back in Dodge."

"What did you say?" John Henry said, looking up sharply. "What do you know about Larn's men? I swear, Kate, if you do know somethin'..."

"I know plenty! I know it was Larn's money that was behind the bounty on Wyatt's head. I know it was Larn's men who tried to kill him back in Dodge. And I wish they'd done it!"

"That's a dangerous accusation to make. Are you sure of this?"

"Of course, I'm sure!" she said with a haughty laugh. "Who do you think told John Larn about Wyatt's nosing into his rustling, anyway? Who else knew what Wyatt was doing there in Shackleford County, except for you and me, or knew Larn well enough to pass the message on? It was me who told John Larn about Wyatt's detective work! And my only regret is that I didn't tell him sooner. Wyatt would be dead by now and out of our lives forever . . ."

"Damn your schemin' little soul to hell!" John Henry cursed as he flew from the chair and grabbed her roughly. "You almost got your wish, and got me killed, to boot! I ought to finish you before you can do any more damage!" And as he spoke, his hands slid up from her honey-colored shoulders to her perfumed neck. "I could kill you right now!"

"You wouldn't dare!" she said defiantly as his hands tightened. "You don't want to make any trouble, remember? For Wyatt's sake . . ."

"Damn you!" he said again, and let his hands fall away from her. "Get out of here! Get out of my life! Go back to the streets where you came from and leave me in peace . . ."

His words were choked off by a sudden tearing pain in his chest, sharper than any pain before, searing his lungs like fire.

"Doc?" Kate said, as he gasped and reached for the chair to steady himself. "What's wrong? What's the matter?"

But he couldn't answer her as his chest gave way all at once and the blood came up from his lungs, filling his mouth and choking him as he struggled to breathe.

"Doc!" Kate screamed again, reaching for him as he fell, and the world spun around him and went dark.

There was a voice hanging above him in the misty darkness.

"How long has he been like this?"

"Two days," Kate replied, her voice mingling with the other, a man's voice.

"And the bleeding? It was worse than this?"

"Yes. I was afraid to leave him to send for you. There was so much— clots and tissue."

"The lesions, no doubt," the man's voice said. "You are aware that he has the consumption?"

"I know," Kate said, "I don't need to hear about it. I just need to know what to do. My father was a surgeon. I can do whatever you tell me, Dr. Beshoar. Just tell me what to do for him, please. I can't let him die like this . . ."

"It won't be easy," the voice answered heavily. "You must take him down to New Mexico, to the hot springs in Las Vegas. There's a resort there that specializes in treating consumptives. The best doctors in the country visit to try out new treatments. There have been some remarkable cures . . ."

"But it's winter! He'll die if I take him over that mountain in the snow!"

"He'll die if you don't take him," the voice said. "Don't wait too long to decide."

Kate hired a wagon and team to carry them over the Raton Pass into New Mexico, joining on with a big freight outfit that was taking supplies to the military outpost of Fort Union. It would take a week or more for the wagon train to reach the fort, and Las Vegas was another day past that. They could have taken the faster route by Barlow and Sanderson Stage, four days direct to Las Vegas, but Dr. Beshoar warned that the jarring ride of the coach could start the bleeding again. Better to make a bed in the back of the wagon, he advised, and pray for a gentle journey.

But there was nothing gentle about it. The wagon, a white-canopied prairie schooner on iron-rimmed wheels, took every rut in the road with a thudding jolt that woke John Henry from his feverish sleep and set him off to coughing again. And in his fitful sleep, he dreamed he was back in Jonesboro again, with Mattie's cool hands wiping his fever-drenched brow. But it wasn't Mattie, he kept trying to remind himself. It was Kate, selfish and haughty Kate who was putting her own life in danger to take him to safety, and he clung onto her hand as if she could stave off the sickness and keep him alive.

"Doc, Doc," she whispered, as she hovered close to him in the wind-blown cold of the wagon bed. "You'll be fine, you'll see. We'll be in Las Vegas soon. The doctors at the hot springs will know what to do for you . . ."

Then the wagon would hit another rut, jostling him and starting the bleeding up again.

"Kate," he mumbled, coughing and retching into the bowl she held to his mouth. "Don't let me die . . ."

"Never!" she said, her voice as fierce as the howling wind all around them. "I will never let you die!"

And in the comfort of her courageous words, he slept again.

They were five days crossing the Raton Pass, the wagons crawling carefully forward to avoid the deep ravines that crisscrossed the mountain. At the bottoms of those ravines were the remnants of wagons that hadn't survived the crossing: wagon wheels and axles and harness-trees smashed to pieces along Raton Creek. To help the wagon trains make the crossing, someone had driven huge iron rings into the mountainside, and the wagons were tied down onto the rings, holding them back from careening out of control.

At the crest of the mountain, the outfit rested at the ranch of Dick Wooten, the shrewd owner of the toll road over the Raton Pass who charged two bits a head to make the crossing, collecting on every oxen, horse, sheep, and man who made the trip. It was his iron rings that made the crossing possible at all, and his hot coffee and hospitality that made it bearable. But Kate was impatient, waiting for the teams to be watered and fed, and she bent over John Henry, spooning some of her own coffee into him.

"Kate," he whispered, meaning to thank her, but she shushed him.

"Save your strength, my love. We've a long way to travel yet."

But with the Raton Pass behind them, the road became easier, the mountain falling away into long plateaus with the green paradise of New Mexico lying ahead.

The outfit stopped again at Willow Spring to water the horses, and camped out near the Clifton House before over-nighting at the trail town of Cimarron. John Henry spent the night in a real bed at the St. James Hotel there, and though there was noise all night from the bar-room below, he slept well for the first time in many days.

When the wagon train pulled in sight of Wagon Mound the next day, Kate roused him to see it for himself.

"The last landmark of the Santa Fe Trail," she told him. "The drover said it's the one thing every traveler prays to see, if they make it this far." And as she helped him to sit up, cradling him in her arms like a child, he had the grandest view he had ever seen: a single mountain rising up out of the rolling vastness of New Mexico, and looking for all the world like a huge prairie schooner with its canvas canopy blowing open in the wind.

"A wagon of stone!" Kate called it. "We'll tell our children how we saw it when we traveled the Santa Fe Trail together. We'll tell our grand-children, too, one day. You are going to get well, my love! You are going to live!"

The wagon train reached its destination at the military outpost of Fort Union, a circle of red sandstone barracks standing starkly against the blue New Mexico sky. But though Fort Union had a small hospital with a doctor on staff who treated travelers as well as the soldiers, Kate was determined to keep pushing on to Las Vegas.

"Just one more day," she promised him, as their hired wagon sepa-rated off from the rest of the outfit and rolled on in creaking solitude, following the tracks left by thousands of wagons gone before. The ruts were so deep in some places that they could be seen for miles ahead, two lines traveling off into the tall prairie grass, leading the way to Las Vegas and beyond to the trail end at old Santa Fe.

It was with wonder and relief that John Henry took his first sight of the green meadows around Las Vegas and the Church of our Lady of Sorrows, *Nuestra Señora de Dolores*, standing silently over the old Spanish plaza that was the heart of the town.

"*Gratia plena*," he mumbled, all of the Latin prayer that he could still remember. Then he added in the Spanish he had learned from Francisco Hidalgo as a child so long ago: "*Gracias, Catarina.*"

Chapter Fourteen

HE OWED HER HIS LIFE; THAT WAS THE SIMPLE TRUTH OF IT. WITHOUT Kate, he'd be dead in the ground in Trinidad, his passing mourned by no one but the gamblers who would steal his last belongings, and maybe the Earp brothers if they ever heard of it. And Mattie, he reminded himself. Mattie still loved him in spite of the distance between them; her constant letters proved that she did. But would she love him still if she knew about Kate, who had turned from his mistress into something more?

Kate had been his strength and his salvation in those awful days following his sudden illness in Trinidad. And sick as he was, he had been at her mercy, relying on her to do everything for him. Kate had made all the arrangements for their leaving Trinidad, getting him out before the law could get to him for the shooting of Kid Colton, and keeping him alive on the torturous trip over the Raton Pass and down into New Mexico. So he couldn't begrudge her signing the guest register at the Hot Springs Hotel as Dr. and Mrs. Holliday. Surely, only a wife would do so much for a man who had tried to kill her.

The Montezuma Hot Springs, named for the Incan king who supposedly took the mineral waters there, were located up narrow Gallinas Canyon a few miles to the southeast of Las Vegas. The springs bubbled up out of the rocky bed of the Rio Gallinas, steaming and smelling of sulfur and drawing visitors from all over the country to come sit in the shallow pools carved by the water. Near the pools, a bathhouse had been erected and the hot mineral water diverted into tubs and showers where an attentive staff provided the personal care the resort was famous for.

The regimen was simple: wash in the clear stream water then soak in the steaming sulfur pools, letting the minerals permeate through the vital fluids of the body. Modern medical practice held that the sulfur water would change the chemistry of the body, helping to fight off illness. Consumptives came by the droves, as did sufferers of a hundred other ailments, and some were even cured.

Above the stream and the springs, connected to the bathhouse by a narrow footbridge, was the new Hot Springs Hotel, elegant in native red granite with a main floor lobby and guest rooms on the second and third floors. From the white-painted verandah and balconies that wrapped the building, guests could take the clear mountain air and enjoy the healing view of the pine-covered canyon walls. But it was the smell of the place that John Henry would never forget: the hot sulfur pools stinking like rotting eggs; the sweet fragrance of the Piñon pines clearing his senses as he rose, crimson-skinned and sweating, out of the mineral baths.

He spent most of his days in the bathhouse or sleeping in his room at the hotel. He had little appetite, though Kate had trays of food brought up to him three times a day. It took all his strength just to keep breathing, inhaling the malodorous fumes as he bathed in the waters and prayed to be one of the miracle cures of Las Vegas. And when he wasn't bathing or sleeping, he sat in a slat-back chair near the window of his bedroom, looking out across the peaceful canyon and wondering how many more winters he would live to see such beauty. If it hadn't been for Kate, he wouldn't have lived to see this one.

Milagro! A miracle! That was what the attendants at the Hot Springs called his recovery. The doctors were a little more cautious, pointing out that the hemorrhaging of his lungs meant that more of the vital tissue had been lost, replaced with scarred pockets that would never heal. And though it did seem that he had obtained a remission of sorts, the bleeding under control and his breathing less wheezy, he would have to take better care of himself in the future. He would need to rest as much as possible, stay away from the tiring influences of late nights in the saloons and gambling halls, keep his drinking in moderation. But smoking tobacco could certainly do him no harm and might even help to exercise the lungs.

It seemed only proper to say a word of thanks to God for the miracle cure. His mother would have expected it of him, and Mattie would have been pleased to see him stepping hatless into the cold stone sanctuary of Our Lady of Sorrows in Las Vegas, lighting a candle like a practiced Catholic. He wasn't Catholic, of course, but the *Nuestra Señora de Dolores* didn't seem to mind, accepting his thanks in the smoky darkness and asking no explanation for his presence there.

Kate, however, was not so benign. Though she'd been raised a Catholic herself, she thought his sudden foray into religion a foolish show.

"It was me who saved you, not Our Lady," she said with something like jealousy. "Did she hire on with that freight team to carry you across the mountain? Did she nurse you in the snow? I'm the one who loves you, Doc, not the Virgin. As though you'd want a virgin, anyway!"

And though he could tell by the tone of her voice that she was waiting for some sarcastic word from him, agreeing that he was happier with her whorish behavior, he couldn't bring himself to say it. Being in that Catholic church had brought back memories of standing in the sanctuary of the Church of the Immaculate Conception in Atlanta the last time he'd seen Mattie, when all he'd wanted was her saintly heart. Kate might be his passion, but Mattie was still his love and always would be.

Still, he couldn't deny Kate's part in his cure, carrying him across the Raton Pass and down the Santa Fe Trail and staying by his side at the Hot Springs. So when she wanted to take expensive rooms at the Exchange Hotel on the Plaza in Las Vegas instead of more economical accommodations at a boarding house, he couldn't deny her. Besides, the view from the lace-curtained windows of their second floor suite was uniquely picturesque, looking out across the dusty plaza with its teams of horses and wagons and a windmill sporting a gallows.

That vivid reminder of the wages of sin should have kept him out of the gambling halls, but the Exchange Hotel was even pricier than the Hot Springs Hotel had been, where the $6 a day for room and board had cleaned out most of his remaining cash. He needed some money fast, and the fastest way to make money, in his experience, was to wager what he had on a game of cards.

He found a game quick enough at the Billiard Saloon across the plaza, and found himself in jail again soon after that. For Las Vegas, like Dallas, was trying to rid itself of the sporting element, at least in the part of town in sight of Our Lady of Sorrows. Kate's only comment was that Our Lady was no lady after all, taking his prayers and then taking away his income like that. But mostly, she was piqued at having to pack up her gowns and things and move on again, as John Henry paid his twenty-four dollar fine and bought two stage tickets to nearby Otero where he'd heard the gambling was easier and the town was looking for a dentist.

Nuestra Señora de Dolores, standing solemn in gray stone and Gothic towers on the hill above the plaza, kept her silence.

The town of Otero lay at the confluence of the Mora and Sapello Rivers, fifteen miles north of Las Vegas. It was a fortunate location for the village as the Santa Fe Railroad, building down into New Mexico Territory from Colorado, had chosen to lay tracks right through the middle of the place, so Otero would soon be a wide-open railroad town. Not that Otero was shy on business without the rails. As a stopping point on the Santa Fe Trail, the town had always had its share of commerce and was already busy enough that the town dentist was looking for a partner to help him take care of patients, and John Henry was glad to oblige.

The dentist, an Illinois man by the name of Fagaly, had a spare chair in his second-story room over a jeweler's shop, but it was the jeweler, not the dentist, with whom John Henry struck up an interesting acquaintance. His name was Billy Leonard, a New Yorker who'd come west looking for adventure, but had so far only found steady work repairing watches in towns up and down the Santa Fe Trail.

"Not the kind of excitement I was looking for," Billy Leonard complained, "though at least I've made some money at it. And made myself a name of sorts. The paper down in Las Cruces did a write-up on me last month, said I do first class work. Which opinion I agree with."

Leonard wasn't bragging, from what John Henry could see, for he did do fine work with watches, and could not only clean and repair the fixings, but make adjustments for heat, cold, and position as well. He'd even learned to put the same skills to use in the tooling of firearms, and had a nice little side business turning long-barreled Winchesters into carbines for saddle guns.

"Different kind of clientele, of course, in the gun business," was his understated comment. "When a man needs a Winchester retooled so's he can carry it sidearm style, you don't ask what he's planning to do with it."

There was a wistfulness to the jeweler's words, as though he were jealous of the adventures his creations were having while he repaired watches and set stones in ladies' neck pendants. But in spite of his longing for some adventures of his own, Billy Leonard hardly seemed the adventurous type. He was a small, slightly built man, with neat little features and longish yellow hair that curled over his shirt collar when he worked. Some folks might even have called him dainty, and Kate went so far as to say that Billy Leonard would have made a better looking woman than most of the whores in Texas, but John Henry chalked up her comment to womanly jealousy. She was just envious that John Henry spent more time in the dental office than he did in their room over a saloon, and talked more to Billy Leonard than he did to her.

Trouble was, now that he was feeling so much better, he was remembering what had made him want to strangle Kate back in Trinidad. Her meddling had almost gotten his friend Wyatt Earp killed, and no amount of gratitude for her nursing skills was washing that memory from his mind. So though he didn't think he could throw her out, he found he was more cheerful in the company of the watchmaker from New York than the woman who had taken to calling herself Mrs. Holliday.

Besides, Billy Leonard had a flattering interest in John Henry's work, often coming up the stairs to the dental office to watch him drill away decay or pull a rotted tooth. It was the gold work that most interested him, however, since he used some of the same techniques in his jewelry making, creating a wax cast then filling it with the molten metal in the process called the Lost Wax Method. Billy had even thought of a way to turn the process into another adventure of sorts.

"Seems like with this equipment handy, we could go into business melting down bullion."

"You mean gold bars?" John Henry asked. "And why would we want to do that?"

"So's they could be smuggled away after a robbery," Leonard said reasonably. "Seems like it would be hard to hide gold bars, but easy to secret away jewelry or dental foils. Then when it's safe and away from the law, you just melt it back down again into something more salable."

"You sound like you've given some thought to the matter, Billy. You plannin' to turn outlaw sometime soon?"

Leonard shrugged, a motion which made his yellow curls bounce around his too-pretty face, girl-like. "Not planning, exactly. More like daydreaming. From what I can see, it's the outlaws who have most of the fun around here, and the rest of us who do the work. And it's fun I was hoping to find when I came out from New York, not more of the same work I was doing before."

"It's the outlaws who do most of the jail time, as well," John Henry replied, "and get hung most often. Have you seen that gallows on the plaza down in Las Vegas? That's not just for show, you know. That's where they entertain stage robbers and the like—which is what I reckon you're imaginin' when you mention gold bars. Stage robbery's rough business and not something I'd be interested in givin' my life to. I'd rather play a safe hand and make my money at the gamblin' tables. Let the robbers steal the booty. I'll take my share when they wager it on a hand of cards."

It was a reasonable little speech aimed at ridding Billy Leonard of his suicidal thoughts of throwing in with stage robbery. Suicidal because Billy's own metal seemed to John Henry a lot like the gold they cast: bright and pretty, but soft enough to bend to a strong hand—which proved that Kate's evaluation of him was entirely wrong. Billy might have made a better looking whore than half the working women in Texas, but he didn't have anywhere near their strength of character from what John Henry could tell. And illegalities aside, successful outlawry seemed to demand a certain strength of character, at least.

Kate was less interested in his views on the qualities of the criminal mind than thoughts of what she'd be wearing to a benefit party at Henry and Robinson's Saloon and Dancehall. Just whom the benefit would be benefitting was never explained, but the highlight of the evening was to be a raffle for a violin—ten chances sold at $5 each. But though John Henry considered the wager a small price to pay for the chance of winning a violin, Kate found his expenditure extravagant.

"That's more money than you spent on this shawl of mine," she pouted as she primped in front of a washstand mirror an hour before the party. "People will think you're more concerned with winning a silly fiddle than in showing off your wife."

For all her years of struggle on the frontier and her selfless kindness in caring for John Henry in his illness, Kate was still a prima donna who demanded attention and fine things as signs of affection. The fact that she wasn't his wife and not entitled to such things by marital vows didn't seem to enter her mind.

"I am more concerned with winning the violin than in showing you off," he said honestly. "Whores get shown off. Wives are supposed to be sheltered from the lewd stares of society. And I fear that lewd stares are just what that dress is gonna gain you."

Kate's laugh showed that she hadn't taken on any wifely modesty when she borrowed his name for her own.

"I hope I do get stared at! What's the use of wearing all these corsets to shape my figure if no one notices? Might as well wear a fichu around my neck if there's no gentlemen trying for a peek down my décolletage."

There was a time when Kate's blatant worldliness would have charmed him, but with his renewed anger at her over the treachery with Wyatt, he could barely manage a sarcastic reply.

"Might as well wear the fichu then, as there's certainly no gentlemen here in Otero. Except for Billy Leonard, of course. He's mannerly enough to be sufficiently shocked at your Rubenesque display."

"He's more gentle than gentlemanly, looks like to me," she said, turning away from the mirror with a haughty laugh. "I wouldn't be surprised to see him show up tonight wearing a corset or two, himself. Which is another thing I'd think you have more concern for."

"And what might that be?"

"Your own reputation. They say you can tell a real gentleman by the company he keeps, and you've never been very good at picking the right kind of friends. First Wyatt and his pandering brothers, now that Nancy-boy Billy Leonard . . ."

He could have slapped her hard right then, left her roughed face bruised and her mouth bloodied for making such insinuations, but his own gentlemanly upbringing kept him from it. If she were looking for a fight, he wasn't going to give her the satisfaction, and his reply came in words as cold as hers were heated.

"I dare say you're right, my dear. But you've left one name off the short list of my friends: Miss Katherine Fisher Elder, the finest of all my base associations. You'll certainly add somethin' to my reputation tonight, goin' on my arm in that obscene gown of yours. No one could mistake either one of us for anything but what we are. Now powder yourself and put that derringer in your handbag. Henry and Robinson's isn't exactly the Planter's Hotel in St. Louis."

He had expected his words to hurt her, but was still surprised at the sudden catch of emotion in her voice and the tears that sparked at her dark lashes.

"And you're not the man I fell in love with there! I don't know why I even stay with you, you've changed so."

Her words allowed him no reply, since they were altogether too true. He was changed from the young man she had met there, having lost all delusion that his life was fair and his future bright. He wasn't the man she had known in St. Louis, but then neither was she the girl he had courted there. They were, both of them, fallen angels, having lost any expectation of heaven on earth. But maybe, in that, they were better suited to one another now than they had been before.

"Come, Kate," he said, reaching out his hand in reconciliation. "Let's not fuss with one another. You are fetching in that gown as always, and I shall have to fight off your admirers, even poor Billy Leonard should he be so foolish as to make advances on you."

"I wouldn't mind seeing you fight for me," she said, sniffing back her tears, "like King Menelaus fighting for Helen of Troy."

"And starting the whole Trojan War by doing it!" John Henry said with a laugh. "Kate, you really are an actress still at heart, living for the dramatic moment. You should have never left the stage."

"I never would have left the stage, except for you," she said with unexpected wistfulness. "I would have done anything for you, you know."

He believed that she very well might have gone to the gates of hell for him, if he'd wanted her to. It wasn't her fault that he hadn't wanted that kind of devotion from her. All he had ever really required of her was a warm bed and a comfortable companion. That would be enough, even now, if he could just forget what she had planned for Wyatt ...

There was a way to forget, if only for as long as it would take for her to remove all those corsets and petticoats and soothe him in the sweet perfume of her honey-colored skin, and he pulled her quickly into his arms.

"Let's not go off to the party just yet. The raffle's not till late, anyhow, and that violin can wait awhile. Truth is, I don't even know how to play one."

"Then why did you throw away all that money to win it?" she asked, as she pressed herself against the soft linen of his shirtfront.

"Because I have always wanted to learn to play—another unfulfilled dream. Like the whole rest of my life."

"Who needs dreams, Doc?" she said, willing as always. "Who needs dreams when we have this?"

It was forgetfulness for awhile, anyhow.

The social at Henry and Robinson's Dance Hall was like any saloon brawl: too many people crowded into the hot and airless room, too many hot tempers when the games didn't go well, too many heated words that led to fights and threats of more fights. But luckily for Mr. Henry and Mr. Robinson, co-owners of the only dance hall in Otero, the town had a peace officer to keep things orderly, and one who knew all about saloon altercations. For the new marshal of Otero, New Mexico was the old rowdy from Fort Griffin, Texas, Hurricane Bill Martin.

Hurricane had left his outlaw ways in Texas after being arrested in a barroom brawl and turning states' evidence against his former employer, the cattle-thieving sheriff, John Larn. Hurricane Bill's testimony turned the jury against Larn and led to the cattleman's lynching in the Shackleford County jail—and convinced Bill that his own outlaw days were better over. With the likes of Pony Diehl and Johnny Ringo still on Larn's side of the law, Hurricane Bill knew he'd be safer with a legal gun in his hand, just in case any of the old Fort Griffin gang came around looking for revenge. So Hurricane Bill left Texas and his famous past behind him, taking up the less dangerous vocation of town marshal of Otero.

Though he may have left his outlawry behind, he still looked like the old Hurricane Bill with his long tangled hair and bearded face and the buffalo skin coat he wore regardless of the climate. The only thing lacking in his appearance was the constant companionship of his old cohort, Billy Brocious—which was no great loss to the Marshal's new employers in Otero. Brocious had been a dangerous young man, and New Mexico was better off without him.

Besides, Brocious would no doubt have balked at the kind of work his former mentor was doing now: keeping watch over the benefit social at the dance hall and calling out the roll of the dice for the coveted violin. What would have surprised Brocious more was learning that Hurricane Bill had wagered on the violin himself, buying his own five-dollar chance.

The thought of Hurricane Bill taking up the fiddle and making music with those formerly murderous hands was enough to make John Henry hope the Marshal would win the raffle. It would make a good story to send home to Mattie, illustrating the influence of music in taming the wild beast, and he'd had precious little to write to her about of late. Since he hadn't yet told her about how he took sick again in Trinidad, he couldn't very well explain the miracle cure of the Montezuma Hot Springs or the life-or-death trek over the Raton Pass into New Mexico, and he certainly couldn't say that it was his mistress, Kate Elder, who had taken him over the mountain and up to the springs and was wearing his patience thin with her needy demands. The tale of the ex-outlaw turned violinist would amuse Mattie, and maybe make up in some small way for all the things he couldn't say.

But Hurricane didn't win the roll of the dice and neither did John Henry, the violin going instead to a local lawyer who actually did know how to play and spent the rest of the evening serenading the gamblers and their ladies. It was, all in all, the most civilized evening John Henry had spent in a long time. But it wasn't enough to convince him to make

Otero a real home, and when news came the next morning from Dodge City, he quickly sold his half-interest in Dr. Fagaly's dental office and packed up his things again.

"I don't understand why you have to go," Kate complained as John Henry folded his shirts into his valise on top of the trousers and stockings and undershirts already there.

"Because Bat Masterson needs my help, that's why. You should be pleased that Bat's even askin' for me, considering the low opinion he used to hold of us."

"Who cares what Bat Masterson thinks of us?" she said with a toss of her head. "He's little better than a muleskinner still himself. Besides, it's the railroad that's offering to pay, not Bat, himself. And what do you owe the Atchison, Topeka & Santa Fe, anyway?"

"Nothin', but I'm happy to take what they're offerin' to get the job done: $3 a day plus room and board."

"Three dollars seems like mighty little recompense for you to travel all the way back to Kansas just to play shotgun guard on the train."

"You're missin' the point entirely, Kate. I won't be guardin' the train, I'll be guardin' the rails while the Santa Fe and the Denver & Rio Grande wait for the court to decide which line gets the right of way through the Royal Gorge. It's all right there in the newspaper. You can study up on it while I'm gone."

"Why should I care which line gets the right of way? Let them both lay rail and stop this legal bickering. A train's a train, as far as I'm concerned."

John Henry sighed and tried to explain the situation.

"The Royal Gorge isn't wide enough for two sets of tracks, so only one company can have passage through from Colorado City to the mine country. Which means that only one company will make a profit off the ore that gets shipped out. A monopoly like that could force one or the other railroad out of business—which should matter a great deal to you, as the Santa Fe is comin' down into New Mexico and the Denver & Rio Grande is not. If the Santa Fe loses that mining money, she might have to stop building down this-away from Colorado and you'd be back to ridin' in stage coaches and buckboards again."

"I can ride in a buckboard all right, if I have to. I still don't see what the railroad needs you for. There's plenty of pistoleers up in Dodge City to hold the line."

"There are, and they're all goin' up to the Colorado to help Bat keep things orderly. He's got his hands overfull just now being county sheriff and agent for the Santa Fe both, and he can use a few extra guns. Last time the courts ruled and gave the Santa Fe a thirty-year lease on the rails, there was some real shooting involved. Bat's hopin' to avoid that this time, while keepin' the Denver & Rio Grande away while the court reconsiders the decision. It's as simple as that, Kate. And I'm goin' along for the ride."

He knew, of course, that it wasn't really an explanation of the situation that Kate was asking for. She could read as well as any woman, and the whole story was laid out in black and white on the pages of the *Otero Optic*, including Bat Masterson's invitation to all able-bodied shooters to join in his little army. What she really wanted was an invitation to come along, and he was determined not to give her one. Besides the fact that railroad work wasn't proper labor for women, he just plain didn't want her company on the trip. Since taking ill in Trinidad and the journey into New Mexico that followed, he'd had precious little time to himself without Kate watching his every move and making some judgmental comment upon it. He wouldn't have wanted that much togetherness with a wife; with a mistress it was beyond irritating.

And there was that other matter, as well—the hard feelings he still harbored over her plotting against Wyatt. Taking her back with him to Dodge would be uncomfortable in the extreme, even if Wyatt knew nothing about her ill-laid plans. Having her and Wyatt both in the same city would make John Henry feel like he was caught in the crossfire of a fight that wasn't quite over yet.

"And what am I supposed to do while you're away?" Kate asked when the invitation to accompany him wasn't forthcoming. "There's not much entertainment in Otero."

"Then buy a stage ticket to Las Vegas," he said, tossing her a handful of coins from his vest pocket purse. "I'm sure there's lots of ways for you to entertain yourself there. Or wear that red dress you had on last night, and maybe you can make some money for yourself."

It was the wrong thing to say, though he'd meant it as a backhanded compliment. In spite of their fuss the evening before, Kate had drawn plenty of attention in that dress of hers and would no doubt do the same in Las Vegas. But Kate didn't seem to appreciate his flattery, and flew at him in a rage.

"How dare you! How can you be so cruel after all I have done for you! How dare you treat me like a whore when I have been better than a wife to you! Go then, take yourself off to Dodge City and don't bother coming back! I won't be waiting here for you if you do! I'll go to Las Vegas, or Santa Fe even, but I won't stay another day in Otero!"

"Then I reckon this is goodbye?" he asked, hardly caring if it were. Kate had near worn him out with her tempers and tantrums, and he was looking forward to a long vacation away from her.

"Damn you to hell!" she said, turning on her heel and storming out of the room.

Somehow, it seemed an eloquent summation of their entire relationship.

Chapter Fifteen

DODGE CITY, 1879

HE HAD REMEMBERED DODGE BEING DUSTY AND HOT, AND IT DIDN'T disappoint him any in that respect. The temperature was ninety-six degrees in the shade the day he arrived, and the Arkansas River was just a muddy trickle of brown water and cow manure. Still, John Henry was glad to be back in the Cowboy Capital—after his angry parting from Kate, he was glad to be anywhere but with a woman. Not that Dodge had run out of ladies, of course. The red light district still seemed to be doing a brisk business, and Tom Sherman's dance hall was still filled with lovelies eager to please, for a price. But having had his own dance hall girl as a constant companion for the better part of two years, John Henry found it a relief to be alone again, and single.

Wyatt, thankfully, didn't even ask after Kate when John Henry found him at the Long Branch Saloon. The lawman had other things on his mind, like the lack of lawbreakers to buffalo and lock up in the cooler.

"Quietest cow season in as long as I can remember," Wyatt said, taking a thoughtful draw on his cigar. "It's this drought that's doing it. Texas cattle can't make it this far without water for the trail, which accounts for there being so few beeves this year. Which accounts for there being so few cowboys to corral, as well."

"Reckon that should give you more spare time for playin' cards," John Henry said with a smile. "Can't see anything wrong with that."

"Nothing wrong with card playing," Wyatt agreed, "when you've got the income for it. But if I'm not bringing in lawbreakers, I'm not getting paid. Same as when you're not pulling teeth."

Wyatt's sudden talkativeness came as a surprise, though John Henry was enjoying the conversation. In his recollection, the laconic lawman had rarely put more than two sentences together at one time, being the naturally quiet type, and now here he was speaking whole paragraphs at once. Must have been the lack of family around to talk to, John Henry reasoned, as Wyatt's brothers Morg and Virg had both left Dodge for better opportunities: Morgan following Louisa Houston up to the Deadwood, and Virgil heading off to the Arizona Territory.

"Hoping to find himself a better-paying law job," Wyatt commented on Virgil's move to the Territorial capitol of Prescott. "There's no money left in Dodge, that's for sure. What with the decrease in the cows and the cowboys, both, the city fathers decided they're paying us too much to keep the peace. Cut our salary back, last winter. If things don't pick up soon, I'll have to find a town with more snap myself. Which is why I took on to judge the Beautiful Baby of Dodge contest."

John Henry nearly choked on his whiskey. "You judged a baby contest?" The very thought of it was laughable, but he didn't let his amusement show.

"Paid five dollars. Didn't see as how I could turn down the opportunity. Wasn't really any judging to it, anyhow, just counting up the ballots to see who won. Besides, Jim Masterson had an idea of how to make it interesting."

"And how was that?"

Wyatt took another slow draw on his cigar, then said with something that almost resembled a smile, "We got the gamblers to buy up the most ballots, six for a quarter, to elect our own choice of Beautiful Baby of Dodge. Should have seen Reverend Wright's face when we announced the winner."

"You're as bad as your brother Morg at story-tellin', Wyatt," John Henry said with a laugh. "Get to the point."

"Point is, it wasn't even a baby that got elected. The boys chose their favorite whore. And not just any whore, but a big colored woman from one of the whorehouses south of the tracks. We called the name, but the Reverend says he don't know that name, so Jim and me went to bring her in. She was glad to come, knowing she was about to win $500 gold and didn't have to do a single night's work for it. Should have seen the Reverend's face," he said again, this time the suggestion of a smile lifting his golden mustache into something akin to a grin. "Best joke I ever took a part in. 'Course, the finer ladies of Dodge weren't too pleased by the winner, but she won the ballots fair and square. That's what comes of holding a Beautiful Baby Contest in a cowtown. They're lucky the sports didn't elect a cow."

John Henry smiled at the story, though he was more amused by Wyatt's uncharacteristic garrulousness than by the gamblers' little game. Dodge must truly be losing its snap for the serious-minded Wyatt Earp to spend his days playing practical jokes.

"I reckon you could make some money workin' for the Santa Fe," John Henry commented. "There's no whores up the Royal Gorge, but they're hirin' shooters."

"I'd go if I could get away from Dodge, but money in it or not, I've got this badge."

"Marshal Earp, you are absolutely antique in your fealty. I, for one, am lookin' forward to bein' paid for a pleasure trip in the mountains where the weather is more kind. This Dodge City dust-bowl is bringin' on my cough again."

He said it lightly, but the truth was that the dusty drought of Kansas was paining his lungs and making him fear he might be undoing the good the Montezuma Hot Springs had done him. So although he was enjoying Wyatt's surprisingly warm welcome, he didn't dare stay in Dodge overly long.

Wyatt wasn't the only Dodge City resident whose job kept him out of the Royal Gorge expedition. The Comedian Eddie Foy was back in town for the summer and too busy entertaining cowboys to consider serving the Santa Fe, though John Henry made a point to invite him along.

Foy was headlining at the Comique Theater again and spent his off hours at the Lady Gay Saloon that fronted the theater, and the owner, Josh Webb, was pleased to have the comic in his establishment, saying that Eddie added an atmosphere of New York class to the place. In return for the atmosphere, Josh gave Eddie his drinks for free—which encouraged both Eddie and his Dodge City admirers to drink even more. Eddie was careful, however, not to imbibe before a show so he could keep his comic wits about him, saving his carousing for the early morning hours when the Comique closed down for the day and he had the rest of the morning to sleep off his liquor. But Eddie couldn't very well decline a drink at a party in honor of the Santa Fe and the Dodge City boys going off in her defense, especially when his host was going along to Colorado himself as one of the leaders of the expedition. And it was, as John Henry pointed out to him, a cause worth considering.

"The Santa Fe bein' Dodge City's own railroad, so to speak, seems like Dodge owes her a little help."

"So they've hired you as a recruiter?" Eddie asked amiably, his rosy face glistening in the summer heat of the stuffy Lady Gay barroom.

"Somethin' like that," John Henry concurred. "Sheriff Masterson asked me to help get the word around, not that it needs gettin'. Seems like most of the sports in town are already hired on. Except for Marshal Earp," he added, "and Dodge City's favorite varieties star."

"Why, Dr. Holliday," Eddie said with a broad smile, "I didn't know you were an admirer! But I do appreciate the flattery, though I don't see how my joining in this little show will help the Santa Fe any. It's guns they're looking for, and I'm afraid I'm a powerful poor aim. Why, I couldn't hit the broad side of a barn if the cow painted a bulls-eye on it."

John Henry considered the problem a moment, then offered a reasonable solution. "Oh, that's all right. You can use a shotgun if you want to, so you don't even need to bother aimin'. The Santa Fe won't know the difference, and you'll get your pay, anyhow. And I reckon we could use some entertainment if things get slow between volleys."

"Tempting as the offer is, I believe I'll serve Dodge City best by staying right here and finishing up my contract with the Comique. The show, as you know, must go on, even without you fine sports around to liven things up. And it sounds like Marshal Earp may need my help to keep the cowboys under control—music, and comedy, having the gift of taming the savage beast."

"Not that there's all that many cowboys to control this season," Josh Webb put in, having overheard John Henry's little recruitment speech.

"Been so slow in Dodge this year, I'm thinking of selling this place and trying my hand elsewhere. Still, I'll thank you for not siren song-ing my floorshow away, Doc. Business is always better when Mr. Foy's in the place, and I need all the business I can get. Though I wouldn't mind some diversion, myself, along the way. Bound to be a scary ride, with a trainload of the meanest gunfighters around and nothing to do but enjoy the view."

"And not much view to enjoy at that," John Henry added, remembering the brown flatness of Kansas that lay between Dodge City and the browner flatness of southeastern Colorado. From what he could tell, it was good country for cattle and trains and not much else, and seven hours of staring at it from the inside of a stuffy railcar with the temperature right around a hundred degrees and nothing to do but sweat could set anyone's nerves on edge. When those nerves came with quick trigger fingers and loaded pistols, the climate could turn deadly.

"Which is why Sheriff Masterson asked me along," Josh said, seeming to share John Henry's thought. "He's made me a deputy, so I can show a badge if I have to. Won't be the first time I've gone along to help keep things orderly, just warmer this time out. Last time I was deputized, we went after the Dave Rudabaugh gang that robbed the westbound Santa Fe out of Kinsley. Miserable weather it was, snowing so hard we near lost our own trail, let alone finding the robbers. Had to hunker down a couple of days, waiting for the storm to pass, then just when the snow starts to settle, who should come riding up to our camp but ol' Dave and his gang like they was dropping by for a visit. They warn't, of course, just looking for a friendly fire somewhere in all that cold. Ours warn't the friendly fire they was thinking of, unfortunate for them. Sheriff Masterson didn't even wait 'till they was warmed again before putting them under arrest. But cold as they was, near froze themselves, they was almost glad to be going back to Dodge, bound up or not. So we took those train robbers in to justice with nary a shot fired. Which is how I hope this new employment will end. Don't mind so much being deputized and doing my civic duty when it all works out fine and happy. Don't always, though. Like when Marshal Masterson got shot outside the Lady Gay, right there on my own board walk."

He stopped talking then, getting a pensive look in his dark eyes, and John Henry respected his moment of silence. The Marshal Masterson he was talking about wasn't Bat, of course, but his brother Ed, the same man Wyatt had been mourning when John Henry first arrived in Dodge. Josh Webb had been friends with them all from his days of buffalo hunting along the Arkansas River when Dodge City was still just Fort Dodge and the buffalo herds had seemed endless.

Josh, himself, hardly seemed suited for such adventures, though he'd had plenty of them. He had a quiet, contemplative temperament and was so slow to rouse that, at thirty-two years of age, he still hadn't found a woman with whom he wanted to keep company, though he had ample selection from the string of cribs that lined the alleyway behind the Lady Gay Saloon. But Josh claimed he just had too much wanderlust in him to settle down, blaming it on his having been born across the Mississippi River from the Mormon town of Nauvoo, Illinois, spending his infancy watching wagon trains of the Saints moving west. Or maybe, it was the west itself that caused the wanderlust, calling to him from his youth. Whatever the cause, by the time he hit Dodge City, he'd already tried out the silver country in Deadwood and the gold country in Central City, Colorado, along with Texas, New Mexico, and most of the Indian Territory. But unlike John Henry, who'd seen most of those same places himself, Josh had gone of his own free will and not because he had the law at his back. In fact, he was hand-in-glove with the law most of the time, even when he wasn't wearing a deputy's badge. Steady, that was Josh Webb, which made him a good choice to help keep order on the trip to the Royal Gorge.

Steadiness was what it would take with close to sixty of the west's best gun handlers on the Santa Fe special as it steamed out of the station in Dodge City that hot day in June. For some of the boys, it was the first time they'd had a chance at being in a real War, and they took to it like Rebels going off to whip Yankees, whooping and hollering as the engine built up a head of steam. To John Henry, that Rebel Yell brought back memories of his childhood in Georgia where his hometown of Griffin had been the training ground for Confederate soldiers headed to the fight. He may have been too young to join with them then, but he was plenty old enough now, and this fight seemed just about right, to his mind.

The arrival of fifty gunfighters from Dodge City was enough to convince the few Denver & Rio Grande employees to turn over the roundhouse and telegraph office at Pueblo, and the boys congratulated themselves on an easy victory. But there were more violent skirmishes farther up the road: in Denver, the D&RG used a battering ram to force entry into the Santa Fe occupied general railroad offices; in Colorado Springs, they fired shots at the defenders; at Cuchara, two Santa Fe men were wounded and two killed before the station was surrendered. So there would surely be more fighting to come in Pueblo when the D&RG showed up to take back the roundhouse by force. But until then, it was sit and wait.

John Henry had never been good at waiting, being of a naturally restless disposition, and he found it particularly hard to wait in the crowded quarters of the Pueblo telegraph office where Bat had assigned him and Josh Webb guard duty. Though actually, it was him who was doing the guarding and Josh who was left in charge of the telegraph equipment, as he'd learned some Morse code somewhere in his travels and knew something about operating the wire as well.

"You know, the Royal Gorge isn't the only wonder along that part of the Arkansas," Josh Webb commented as they swapped stories and tried to stay awake. Besides the boredom of guard duty, they were both dozy from the summer heat that filled the telegraph office like a cook stove. "They've got sea monsters up there, too."

"You're ramblin', Josh. How could they have sea monsters when there's no sea for a thousand miles of here?"

"I didn't say they were live sea monsters, Doc. It's sea monster bones they've got up there. Found 'em in a rock quarry close to Cañon City. At first, they thought it was buffalo bones they were digging up, 'till the bones got to be too big for any buffalo you ever saw. That's when a professor from up in Colorado Springs makes a visit and says it's not buffalo bones, it's ancient monsters they're digging up. It was the newspaper that called 'em sea monsters. The professor called 'em *Dinosaurs*, but sea monsters sounds more interesting."

"So did the paper happen to explain how sea monsters got to the Royal Gorge?"

"Not in so many words. But the reporter did mention a Scottish legend about a lake creature that swims up an underground river from the North Sea. I suppose Cañon City's monster could have swum up an underground river to the Arkansas, aways back."

John Henry had to hold in a laugh, hearing Josh Webb's fanciful blending of science and mythology. For himself, he didn't believe in sea monsters any more than he believed in fairies. He did, however, know something about dinosaurs, having seen the reconstructed skeleton of a Hadrosaur at a museum in Philadelphia, its bones hung together with wire into a fantastical shape that defied belief—and yet there it was, bigger than life and impossible to disbelieve.

He'd had something of a trial of his faith, studying on that dinosaur, for his mother, he knew, would not have believed in the thing even if she had seen it with her own eyes. As the Lord had created the earth in six days and on the seventh rested from His labors, there was no time for anything as old as dinosaurs. She would have told him that they were just buffalo bones, bleached and hardened by the alkali desert, or the remains of Indian horses that had died before they found the cool waters of the Arkansas, and he would have believed her, as a child. But looking at those bones in the museum in Philadelphia, he knew for the first time that his mother may have been wrong about some things. It was a knowledge that had left him feeling unsettled somehow, and unfaithful to her saintly memory.

"So what do you believe, Josh? Do you believe the Lord created the world in six days and rested on the seventh, or do you believe in the dinosaurs?"

Josh Webb knit his dark brow and ruminated the question.

"Well, Doc, I suppose it all depends on what kind of days you're talking about. There's some days go by too fast, like when Eddie Foy is doing his variety show, and there's some days go by too slow, like sitting guard duty in this wire office. The hours are all the same, but they don't feel the same. So it wouldn't seem unreasonable to me if the good Lord had his slow days and his fast days, too, and maybe on some of 'em, he got more done than on others. Maybe it only seemed like six days of creation to Him because he was working so hard, whereas, to us it would seem more like six million years dragging by, waiting for the world to start. So I suppose I can believe in the Bible and the dinosaurs both, and not get confused between the two."

It was the best answer John Henry had ever heard on the matter, though it made no sense at all. And that, somehow, was a kind of comfort. Maybe life didn't have to make sense to be enjoyed. Maybe it was enough just to be living.

"I hear they have hot springs over there in Cañon City, too," John Henry said, thinking that a dip in a mineral bath might help to calm the cough that had come on him again in Dodge City.

"They do, down on the banks of the Arkansas. There's a nice hotel there, as well. Sheriff Masterson stayed there last visit we made for the Santa Fe. 'Course, the rest of us made do with tents down in the Gorge close by the tracks. Nice weather for camping, though, being springtime and all. I'd trade this stuffy office for a tent in the canyon right now. Suppose someone's got to guard the telegraph, though."

John Henry nodded, then had a thought. "Josh, you know how to operate this telegraph machine? I believe I would like to send a wire."

"You heard what Bat said: no messages in or out until he gives the order."

"This is a personal message, not railroad business. I don't remember hearin' Bat give any orders about that. Besides, seems like the Santa Fe owes us a free wire, at least, for keepin' their right-of-way open for them."

Josh had to concede the point, and he took a paper and ink pen from the telegrapher's desk. "It'll take me a bit to figure the code, being rusty as I am, but I'll give it a shot. Who's it going to?"

"Miss M.A. Holliday, Atlanta, Georgia. I believe my cousin would like to hear about the sea monsters."

They didn't learn until later that the Denver & Rio Grande had taken back the depot at Colorado Springs and was intercepting telegraph messages, which made Josh Webb worry that it had been their wire that tipped off the D&RG to the Santa Fe's position in Pueblo. But John Henry didn't see as how that could be possible, his message to Mattie having been the very briefest of wires and nothing whatsoever to do with the railroads. And during the heat of the battle that followed, even Josh stopped worrying over the matter.

The telegraph office was situated on the railroad platform at the north end of town, giving it a clear view back across the river and down Fourth Street toward the Victoria Hotel where the Denver & Rio Grande's hired guns were gathering. Even without that view, John Henry would have known they were coming, the sound of them carrying back down to the telegraph office like thunder carried before a coming storm. There were more than fifty of them, crowding the street as they marched toward the roundhouse, rifles fixed with bayonets that glinted in the summer sun.

John Henry took a stance at an open window, steadying his pistol hand on the window sill, while Josh positioned himself at the door, ready to bar the way.

"Do you think we can take 'em, Doc?" he asked as they cocked their pistols and took aim at the advancing army.

"No, but we can give 'em a little hell. You loaded up all around?"

If the Denver & Rio Grande men had come on orderly, waiting for a shout of challenge and reply, there might have been something like a fair fight. That was the way a siege was supposed to be, John Henry knew from his school days studying ancient wars. But the men of the D&RG hadn't been to the same school and came on like a mob, shoving their bayonetted rifles through the window glass and smashing their way into the telegraph office.

John Henry got off one useless shot through the open window, then spun around to see Josh Webb take a rifle butt across the face.

"Give way, Josh!" he cried. "Let 'em have the wire!"

Josh looked up, dazed and bloodied, and moaned as John Henry grabbed his arm, dragging him toward the back windows of the office.

After all his dreams of heroism and glory, his first battle was ended almost before it began.

The stand-off at the roundhouse didn't last much longer than that one-shot battle at the telegraph office, only long enough for Bat Masterson to make a deal with the Denver & Rio Grande's agent in Pueblo and turn the place over. It was a play that brought rumblings of a pay-off, though no one was bold enough to say such things right out in the open. Bat's claim was that he was a peace officer first and a Santa Fe agent second and he didn't want any casualties worse than Josh Webb's bloodied mouth and broken teeth. Besides, word had come down the line that the rest of the rails had fallen to the D&RG, so there wasn't much point in holding the roundhouse in Pueblo. The courts had ruled in favor of a shared right-of-way between the two railroad companies and that was a matter for negotiators, not hired guns.

For his part, John Henry was glad to see the thing ended, as he felt somehow responsible for Josh's damaged mouth. If he'd been backing up his partner instead of sighting his pistol, he might have sent that one shot into Josh Webb's attacker instead of wild into the crowd. As it was, the least he could do was offer to fix Josh's broken teeth for free—which, unfortunately, meant returning to Dodge instead of making a visit to the hot springs in Cañon City.

"So what do you think about making my new teeth out of gold?" Josh asked as they took the Santa Fe special back to Kansas, his words whistling through the empty space in his mouth like the Kansas wind whistled across the prairie. "I've always fancied gold teeth."

"Gold'll be fine," John Henry said with a nod, "and not much pricier than porcelain. You'll shine like a regular Midas."

Josh grinned at the thought, showing swollen gums and the bloodied space where his two front teeth had been. He'd been a mediocre looking man before; now he was downright homely.

John Henry sighed and pulled a deck of cards from his vest pocket. "You up for a game of poker? Got a long ride ahead of us, yet, and nothin' but this flat Kansas view for entertainment."

If Josh Webb wanted golden teeth, he could help to pay for them in poker winnings.

Josh sported that new dental work around Dodge the way Bat Masterson sported his Sheriff's badge—flashing it every chance he got like a medal of honor. Even Wyatt noticed, commenting that Josh's newfound vanity would be good for the dental business in Dodge, if the doctor planned to stay around.

"Free advertising," was the way Wyatt put it. "Not that there's all that much business in Dodge anymore."

"So why do you stay?" John Henry asked as they passed a wet afternoon in the Long Branch Saloon. The rainy season had finally come to Kansas, settling the lung-choking dust and turning the dirt streets into a reeking mass of mud and liquefying cow manure. There were few places as unpleasant as a cowtown in a rainstorm, and John Henry was having thoughts of an early return to New Mexico.

"Got a contract with the city fathers," Wyatt replied. "Can't leave until it runs out. Or until I find something worth breaking it for. As of yet, I haven't found anything better. But I'm looking. I'm always looking."

"You are dedicated, Wyatt. As for myself, I plan to be on the inaugural train from Trinidad to Las Vegas, which happens to be arrivin' there just in time for the Fourth of July festivities—Independence Day bringing the independence of a new mode of travel to the green meadows of New Mexico. A fortuitous time for the rails to be completed, don't you think?"

Wyatt let out a slow cloud of cigar smoke. "I think you think too much, Doc. But Las Vegas sounds interesting. Maybe I'll see you there."

Coming from Wyatt, it was as good as a guarantee.

Chapter Sixteen

LAS VEGAS, 1879

HE HALF-EXPECTED KATE TO BE WAITING FOR HIM AT THE RAILROAD depot when the Santa Fe stopped in Otero on its way to Las Vegas. It was, after all, the first train to roll down the newly laid tracks that far into New Mexico, heading on to Santa Fe, and its arrival was met with noisy celebration at every town along the way. But there was no Kate in Otero, nor had anyone seen her since John Henry himself had left town. There was no Kate in Las Vegas either, though it seemed that everyone else in town had come to the new rail station to hear the Governor welcome the era of steam travel to the meadows of northern New Mexico. But Kate Elder, who had called herself Mrs. Holliday in happier times, was gone as she said she would be.

John Henry was surprised to find himself actually disappointed not to see her there. It would have been amusing to share the celebrating with someone who appreciated a party as much as Kate did, and there was plenty of partying going on in the two towns of Las Vegas: the quaint Spanish village that surrounded the plaza and slept under the watchful eye of the *Nuestra Señora de Dolores*, and the jumble of tent saloons and boarding houses a mile away across the Gallinas River where the newly laid tracks of the Santa Fe stretched out into the meadowland. The old village was being called Old Town, while the railroad settlement was called New Town, but other than sharing the official name of Las Vegas, the two towns had nothing much to do with each other.

Even the celebrations held in the two towns of Las Vegas reflected the differing characters of the two communities. In Old Town, the arrival of the railroad was heralded with a fancy dress ball and speeches at the Exchange Hotel on the Plaza. In New Town, the party was an all-night affair of gambling and other vices.

John Henry didn't have any trouble deciding where to do his celebrating. For although Close and Patterson's Dance Hall, across from the new railroad depot, wasn't nearly as elegant as the Exchange Hotel, it had the attraction of twenty-five regular dancing girls and a commitment to entertaining everybody in the best possible manner—or so said the painted sign hanging over the bar. And by the amount of entertaining the place did that night, it was clear that saloons and dance halls were going to be the boom business of New Town.

John Henry had never owned or operated a saloon before, but the opportunity seemed too good to pass up. So within days of his arrival, he paid a call on the city fathers and arranged to lease three lots on Centre Street, the wide dirt avenue that led from the Santa Fe depot up toward the Gallinas River. And though the Holliday Saloon was nothing more than a big canvas tent with a floor of wood planks and a bar bill that boasted only beer and two brands of whiskey, it did well right from opening day.

He liked to think that it was his gaming tables that made the place so popular, but he knew that some of his quick success was owed to the serving girl he'd hired to help the barkeep with the drinks. Her name was Flor, a little Mexican from Old Town with wide dark eyes and glossy black hair and such a following among the railroaders that she kept the saloon busy just serving her admirers. "The Señorita," the customers called her, and began calling the saloon by the same name—which suited John Henry fine, as long as they kept coming in to buy his drinks and play at his tables.

While Flor took care of the customers, John Henry ran the gambling games, banking Monte and keno and acting as his own police. Although New Town had its small police force, there wasn't nearly enough law to keep the peace, so business owners had to do a little peacekeeping themselves—which John Henry took to mean that he was allowed to keep a pistol in his pocket. He was in good company, carrying a pistol or two, as even the Mayor of New Town packed a sidearm.

The Mayor wasn't really a mayor, just a sporting man who'd got himself elected Coroner for Precinct 29 of San Miguel County with jurisdiction over New Town and a tenuous authority over the local police, themselves mostly gamblers recently come to Las Vegas. They called the Mayor "Hoodoo Brown," and told how he was formerly of the western gambling circuit and most recently of a ranch on the Jones Plummer cattle trail in Kansas—though no one ever mistook him for a rancher. He had only come to own the place by winning it in a poker game, and only kept it long enough to break it up and sell it off to land-hungry homesteaders. "Land speculating," he called it, though others called it stealing, as Hoodoo was an expert card player and seldom lost on a wager of real estate. But John Henry had no reason to criticize the Mayor for using his skills to a profitable advantage; a man who could weasel a land deed out of a poker hand probably deserved to make a little money.

John Henry knew the story of Hoodoo Brown by rumor only, not having met the man himself, though he had met a few of the Coroner's hired guns: Chief of Police Joe Carson, Constable Jack Lyons, Deputies Bill Baker and "Mysterious Dave" Mather. Being sporting men like their boss, they had the best interests of New Town at heart and only interfered in the business of the saloons and gaming establishments when things got dangerous. And even then, they didn't interfere all that much, as John Henry learned on one hot evening toward the end of July.

He'd been doing well at the tables that day, taking in a good profit from his Monte bank and a neat percentage from the dice games as well, when Flor came to him complaining of personal trouble.

"It's *mi novio, Señor*, he wants me to go out with him."

"Well, tell him you can go when you're done workin'," he replied, not understanding why he should have to give permission for the tryst. What the girl did in her private time was none of his affair.

"No, *Señor*, he wants me to go with him now, out of the saloon. I told him to go away until later, but he won't go. He says if I don't come out, he will come in and get me. And *Señor*, he is very drunk today and I am afraid of what he will do to me if he does come in here. He gets very bad when he is drunk, *Señor*."

John Henry sighed and called to the barkeep to take over his Monte bank. Flor was right in what she said of her beau; Mike Gordon had already gained a reputation around New Town as a drunk and a brute and John Henry was bewildered as to what the girl saw in him. Still, a lady's request for protection couldn't go unanswered, and he pulled the pistol from his pocket, rolling the chamber to count the cartridges. One shot into the night sky would probably be enough to scare Mike Gordon away and let Flor get back to work serving drinks.

Mike Gordon was out in the street, as Flor had said, standing with wobbly legs and hanging onto a half-emptied whiskey bottle as though the liquor could steady him. He was also singing, though the sound was something more like a hound howling at the moon, and attracting an appreciative audience around him. A drunk was always good entertainment, even in a town with more than its fair share of them.

"Hey, Mike Gordon!" John Henry called out cheerily, and the man turned toward him unsteadily.

"Who's calling my name?" Mike asked, his words sliding together like slippery stones in river mud.

"Your lady-friend's employer. I'm gonna have to ask you to move on and take your singin' elsewhere, as Flor has work to do."

"Flor?" Mike Gordon asked, then he laughed. "You mean Flower! My little flower!" and he launched into another refrain of whatever it was he was trying to sing.

"He doesn't sound so dangerous to me," John Henry said to Flor, who had stepped out of the tent saloon and into the street behind him. "He seems to be in fine enough spirits."

"Fine for now, *Señor*," she whispered, keeping herself hidden behind him, "fine until you tell him I am not going with him."

"Well sung, Mike!" John Henry said with a smile, "but I must ask you again to move on. Your performance is distractin' Flor, and as I said, she has work to do."

"She has work to do, all right," Mike said, taking a break from his singing to swig at the whiskey bottle, "and I'm it. Come on out, little Flower, and give me something to sing about!"

"She's not goin' with you, Mike," John Henry replied reasonably, "but I'm sure a fine gent like yourself can procure other company to keep yourself occupied until she's through workin'. The way I hear it, half the whores in New Town have been askin' after you."

"They have?" the idea seemed as implausible to Mike Gordon as it really was, for to John Henry's knowledge, there wasn't anyone asking after Mike Gordon, except maybe the Magistrate when he did some real disturbing of the peace.

"That's right, Mike. In fact, there's some ladies down at Close and Patterson's right now, askin' for you. If I were you, I'd remove myself from Centre Street straight-away and get down to Railroad Avenue. A gentleman shouldn't keep a passel of whores waitin'."

Mike Gordon pondered a moment, then took a final swig of the whiskey.

"I guess you're right," he said, wiping his mustache, then running the same whiskey-wet hand through his greasy hair. "Better go find me them whores while they're willing and able. But you tell Flor I'll be back for her, y'hear? Wouldn't want my little sweetheart to think I forgot about her."

It was laughable, almost, how little sense one had to make to reason with a drunk, but when John Henry turned back toward the saloon, his laughter stopped before it could start. Flor was still standing behind him, and there were tears in her eyes.

"You see?" she said in a shaking voice. "You see how mean he can be?"

"But he didn't do anything to you. I sent him off to the dance hall. You'll be safe enough until he finishes with the women there . . ."

It was only then that he understood what she meant. It wasn't only in the supposed beatings that Mike Gordon was a brute, but in his well-known chasing after other women, as well. Yet somehow, John Henry hadn't expected the little Mexican girl to have the same feelings a real lady might have over such things. Was it possible that the girl was a lady at heart? Or were all women more the same than he had ever imagined? And following behind that thought was another memory: Kate's tears the day he had left for the Royal Gorge war.

"We're wasting good gamblin' time with this nonsense," he said in irritation, and Flor obediently sniffed back her tears.

"Si, *Señor*," she said with a hurried curtsy as she hustled back into the tent saloon.

John Henry watched the canvas door fall back into place behind her. If Flor weren't so good at bringing in customers, he'd fire her and hire another barkeep to help out, instead, and be done worrying about women entirely.

Mike Gordon came back later, as promised, but in worse spirits than when he'd left. His evening with the whores at Close and Patterson's had evidently not gone well, and he was determined to have Flor make up for his disappointments. And this time, he came armed with a shotgun and ready to take her by force.

"Flor!" he yelled, as he pushed his way into the tent saloon, setting the hanging oil lamp swaying over the gaming tables. "Your soldier's come back for you, and I mean to have you this time around!"

Flor looked up from the back of the room, dark eyes darting between Mike Gordon and John Henry.

"I am still working, *Miguel*," she called. "Besides, you're drunk. I don't want to go with you when you're bad drunk."

"I am drunk," he agreed, though he seemed more sober than he'd been before. But that was just the way the whiskey hit some men, making them jolly at first and steely later—and Mike Gordon looked to be getting steely in his resolve. "I am drunk," he repeated, "and you are coming with me."

But he was too occupied with Flor to notice John Henry off to the side of the saloon, pulling his own pistol and taking aim.

"Drop the shotgun, Gordon," John Henry said, "or take a bullet in the brain. You choose."

Mike wavered a moment, then let go of the gun, the whiskey making him bold, but not quite suicidal.

"That's an interesting way of impressin' a lady," John Henry commented, "but I don't think Flor's all that impressed. Now leave the shotgun here and get yourself out of my place. You can pick up your firearm tomorrow when you're not so drunk."

Mike turned slowly toward him, eyes fixed on John Henry's finger hovering over the trigger of his pistol. Then, bold but not stupid, he backed out of the saloon without saying another word.

"Well, I reckon that's enough excitement for one evenin'," John Henry said as he pocketed the pistol. "Flor, bring me two fingers of that Jack Daniels behind the counter. All this fuss is givin' me a thirst."

The little Mexican girl nodded and hurried to the bar. But as she bent down to find the bottle that John Henry kept special for himself, shots rang out in the street and a bullet came whistling in through the canvas wall of the tent saloon, lodging in the wood of the bar.

Flor screamed as she and the customers dropped to the floor. Only John Henry stayed standing, still waiting for his drink. He didn't have to ask to know that it was Mike Gordon doing the shooting, no doubt having grabbed another gun somewhere and turned it on the saloon. Then another shot sailed into the place, catching a customer in the leg as he cowered on the floor, and John Henry sprang into action.

He dove for Mike's abandoned shotgun and came up cocking it with one hand while he pulled his own pistol with the other. Then, both hands full of lead, he sprang to the canvas door of the saloon. With one quick glance, he saw Mike Gordon standing alone in the moonlit street reloading a six-shooter for another volley at the saloon, and he pulled up the pistol and drew a bead, firing off three shots before Mike could get his own pistol into play.

It was a bad setup for a shooting match, with the canvas tent door hanging in his way and one hand still holding the shotgun, but one of the three shots found its mark, and Mike spun around and grabbed at his shooting arm.

"I'm hit!" he screamed, dropping his six-shooter and looking with surprise toward the door of the tent. "I'm hit!" he said again, the reality of blood and broken bone somehow making its way through the fog of liquor. "Dammit, Flor, he shot me!"

"And I'll shoot you again if you don't go off and leave us in peace," John Henry said from behind the canvas, keeping his pistol aimed at the wounded man. "I have four shots left in my pistol and two charges left in this shotgun, and I'll gladly give you all of 'em if you dare fire another shot into my place."

But Mike Gordon wasn't listening to him, cradling his bloodied shooting arm and starting to cry.

"Flor!" he moaned, "I'm bleeding out here. Won't you come out with me now? I only wanted to take you dancing, and now I'm shot to pieces!"

"You're not shot to pieces, yet," John Henry replied, finding himself unable to feel any sympathy for a drunk with a deadly weapon. Behind him, the customer Gordon had hit was moaning as well, and Flor was kneeling over him with her apron stanching the bleeding.

"He needs a doctor, *Señor*. We must send someone right away."

"I reckon your boyfriend's gonna be needin' a doctor as well," he commented, but when he looked back toward the street, there was only moonlight and no Mike Gordon to be seen.

"Let him find a doctor for himself," Flor said bitterly. "I am glad to be rid of him. And grateful to you, *Señor*, for keeping him away from me tonight. I will light a candle for you tomorrow at *Nuestra Señora de Dolores*. But for him, I hope he dies."

While Flor lit her candle, John Henry had more practical matters to attend to. The gunfight with Mike Gordon had shown him how flimsy a structure a tent saloon could be and that it was time he invested in something more substantial. Wind and rain coming in around the edges of the tent walls were merely uncomfortable; gunshots tearing through the canvas and into the customers were downright dangerous. So he signed a contract with a local carpenter to build a real board and batten structure to take the place of his shot-through saloon, and paid out $45 in cash to get the job started.

The tent saloon came down on a Monday morning at about the same time that George Close found a body in the drainage ditch behind his Railroad Street dance hall. It was Mike Gordon, Flor's lover, dead of a gunshot wound to the arm. He'd bled to death seemingly, though a doctor could have saved him with no trouble at all. Now, his unnecessary death would be trouble for John Henry, for everyone knew that Mike Gordon had been shooting up the town in front of Doc Holliday's Saloon that

Saturday night, and someone's well-aimed answering shot had stopped the noise. So it wasn't surprising when the owner of the saloon was subpoenaed as a witness in the Coroner's hearing into the untimely death of poor genial old Mike Gordon. What was surprising was how a town's perceptions of a man could change just because he was dead.

The Coroner's hearing was held in the dining room of the Exchange Hotel on the Plaza in Old Town Las Vegas, a place John Henry knew well, having paid good money to live in luxury there after his miraculous recovery at the Hot Springs. But he hadn't lived there alone, and as he stepped into the chandeliered lobby where the afternoon light filtered through fancy lace curtains, he couldn't help but think of Kate. She had loved the Exchange, with its shiny brass beds and deep feather mattresses, it's printed artwork adorning papered walls, its long windows looking out over the Plaza where the hanging gallows stood encircled by a white picket fence. The Exchange, he realized, was much like Kate in some ways: elegance in the midst of trail dust and wagon trains, ease and comfort in the face of affliction.

He had never thought of Kate and comfort in the same breath before, except when she was nursing him back to health. But she had been comfortable, in her way, standing by him when other women would have been long gone. It was her companionship, mostly, that he was missing, he decided, and the comfort of having another human being near. It was a comfort that would be welcome this afternoon, as he walked into the dining room of the hotel and faced a crowd of spectators—hearings on suspicious deaths being close to hangings as entertainment in Las Vegas.

He found a seat on a curved-back dining room chair and looked around the room, noting the number of sporting men in the audience. He was in good company, at least, if anything untoward came of the hearing. Still, he couldn't help but wish he'd brought along someone for moral support. His thoughts were interrupted by the arrival of a red-haired, red-faced stranger.

"You must be Doc Holliday," the man said, not bothering to offer his hand in a proper introduction. His hands, in fact, were already occupied with a pencil and sheaf of paper on which he scribbled as he spoke.

"I am," John Henry said. "And who do I have the pleasure of addressin'?"

"Kistler," the man replied brusquely, "Russell Kistler, Editor of the *Otero Optic* and soon to be Editor of the *Las Vegas Optic* as well. Currently working as a court reporter covering murder cases in San Miguel County."

"Then you're in the wrong courtroom, Mr. Kistler. This isn't a murder case."

"Oh?" the newspaper reporter said, voice and pencil poised in midair. "And why do you say that?"

"Because Mike Gordon wasn't worth murderin'. Ask any of his limited number of friends."

"I have," the reporter replied, "and they all think you killed him, shooting out the door of your saloon."

"I didn't have a door on my saloon last Saturday night," John Henry said coolly. "It was nothin' but a tent until two days ago, so I'm afraid Mike's friends must have it wrong."

"And who do you think shot him?" the reporter asked.

"I think that's a question for the Coroner," John Henry answered, noting with irritation that the reporter scribbled down those words, too.

"And what do you think of our acting Mayor and Coroner?" Kistler questioned, ready to write down another reply.

"I haven't had the pleasure of meetin' him yet," John Henry replied carefully, "though I hear he has the best interests of New Town at heart. And you may quote me on that."

"Oh, I already have," the reporter said with a smile.

It was a smile John Henry didn't find comforting, and he was almost relieved to hear the Constable's cry of attention.

"All arise for the honorable Hoodoo Brown!"

John Henry's irritation at the annoying reporter turned into amusement at the ridiculous ceremony being afforded the Coroner. He was, after all, just another sporting man with an outlandish nickname and little qualification for a legal career. But the laughter left him as the Coroner swept into the room, bedecked in judge's robes and jeweled finger rings that sparkled as he took up the gavel.

"That Hoodoo Brown's quite a dandy, ain't he?" a man beside him whispered. "Where do you suppose they dug up such a daisy?"

John Henry stared at the Coroner, his reply coming out in a hoarse whisper. "St. Louis," he said, hardly believing the words himself, "on the Levee in St. Louis . . ."

If the man looked at him quizzically, he didn't notice. His mind was racing back to a night when he'd played poker with the cunning owner of a saloon on the cobblestoned levee in St. Louis. He could still see the signboard hanging over the saloon door: a man fighting an alligator and losing. He could still hear the echo of riverboats sliding past and the warning of a river man whose words echoed in his memory: *Hoodoo be black magic, and that man in there, he be hoodoo, too, he be bad luck . . ."*

Hoodoo, the Jamaican had called him. Hoodoo Brown folks called him now, but it still meant the same thing: bad luck. For the Coroner of New Town Las Vegas, the man who had come to make a charge of murder in the death of Mike Gordon, was the man John Henry had played poker against at the Alligator Saloon back in St. Louis, the gambler named Hyram Neil.

It had been seven years since John Henry had wagered his inheritance and lost, leaving St. Louis without making good on the debt. And for most of those seven years, he hadn't given Hyram Neil a second thought. But now it came back to him all at once: the youthful arrogance that had made him think he could beat a sophisticated sporting man; the horror of realizing he hadn't beaten him after all and had lost his family's property; the fear that Hyram Neil would come to collect on the debt and deal him worse than a creditor. And now, he was face to face with Neil again and the gambler had the power to make him pay at last, or punish him, at least, for not paying up.

The Coroner's dark eyes took in the room and John Henry felt himself flinch under their appraising gaze. Surely the man would recognize him and remember the debt he'd never paid. But Neil's glance only flickered past him, showing no more interest in him than in any of the other men the room. And even when the name of Doc Holliday was called as a witness in the hearing, the Coroner's face seemed as undisturbed as the slow-moving waters of the muddy Mississippi River. But like the Mississippi, where treacherous shoals and twisting currents lay hidden beneath the surface of the water, a poker player's face hid his real thoughts—Hyram Neil was, above all things, a poker player.

John Henry put on his own poker face to answer the Coroner's questions, hoping to look as unruffled as Hoodoo did.

"Yessir, Your Honor, I own a saloon on Centre Street. Next door to Heran's Saloon, except for an alley in between."

"And how long have you owned this saloon?"

"Just a month, more or less. I bought the lot and had a tent put on it, like they do down in New Town. Though the tent is gone now since I'm havin' a board saloon built in its place."

"You must be prospering, Dr. Holliday," the coroner said, and John Henry answered warily.

"I'm doin' all right. Prosperity bein' a matter of interpretation, I reckon."

"And were you in your saloon on Saturday evening last?"

"Yessir, I was."

"Describe the evening, if you would. Was it a clear night?"

"It was."

"And was there a moon overhead?"

The question was ridiculous, since everyone in the courtroom surely knew the weather and the phase of the moon that night.

"Yessir, there was. A three-quarter moon, as I recall."

"And what was the mood of the customers in your saloon?"

"Cheerful. Whiskey has a way of makin' men cheerful."

There was a ruffle of laughter in the room, but the Coroner ignored it and went on. "And your employees, were they cheerful as well?"

"They were cheerful, too, for the most part."

"And by that, do you mean to say that some of your employees were not in a cheerful state?"

"I only have two employees, and one of them was less than cheerful."

"And which employee would that be?"

"My waitress, Flor Hernandez."

"And what was the cause of her unhappiness?"

"Some trouble with her lover, as I suppose. One never knows for sure with women."

Again there was laughter from the crowd, ignored by the coroner.

"And the lover you mention was the late Mike Gordon?"

"Yessir."

The Coroner paused to write something on the papers in front of him, and John Henry noticed newspaper reporter Kistler doing the same. Then the Coroner looked up again, his dark eyes glinting.

"As I hear it around town, Dr. Holliday, you were Flor's lover and Mike Gordon was your rival for her affections. Cause enough for you to kill him."

The laughter in the courtroom turned to a sudden silence.

"I believe I would like to speak with a lawyer," John Henry said carefully. "I would like to be represented by counsel."

It was a reasonable enough request in any other court of law. But in New Town Las Vegas, the Coroner was the law and he set his own rules. And surprisingly, Hyram Neil laughed.

"Come now, Dr. Holliday, that won't be necessary! This isn't a trial and you haven't been charged with anything. This is only a hearing to find whether there is cause to make a charge. Now, why don't you tell me your version of the story and let me decide your fate?"

It was as unattractive an offer as he had ever received, yet he had no choice but to accept it and say everything he knew about the shooting, from Mike Gordon's first appearance in the street that Saturday night to his last words to Flor. But, true as John Henry's story was, it was only his word against Hyram Neil's and no guarantee of justice. And as he waited for the court to consider the story and render judgment, he remembered the words his uncle Will McKey had spoken long ago: What a man could prove and what he got accused of were two different things—and sometimes all it took was an accusation to ruin a man's good name. Or his life, John Henry thought as the moments dragged on and the Coroner still considered.

The silence in the courtroom was broken only by the pencil-scratching of Russell Kistler who was, no doubt, relishing the drama and readying it for the front page of his *Otero Optic*. And still the Coroner held his silence, considering.

John Henry had heard that kind of silence before, in the tense moments of a high-stakes poker game. And suddenly, he understood: Hyram Neil was playing poker and about to raise the stakes.

"Ladies and Gentlemen of the Court," he said at last, "this is a difficult matter to decide. As our witness tells it, the death of Mike Gordon is a simple case of excusable homicide, as the shooting was done by way of a police act to protect the customers in an established place of business. But as certain other sources tell it, the shooting was more than a police action. It was, in fact, a premeditated and efficiently accomplished act of revenge. It was, in fact, murder in the first degree."

John Henry glanced out the long windows of the dining room toward the Plaza and the gallows waiting there, and shivered in spite of the summer heat. Hyram Neil had raised the stakes, all right, and he had nothing left to play.

"However," the Coroner went on in measured tones, "since this is such a difficult matter, I feel it my duty to give careful consideration to the situation. Court is hereby adjourned until ten o'clock tomorrow morning." The slam of his gavel on the makeshift judge's bench rattled the water glasses and the windows in their casements, making the gallows outside seem to come alive.

Hyram Neil was hanging him already, just by leaving him hanging.

In his dreams that night he was back in St. Louis, playing cards down on the levee. He knew the place was the Alligator Saloon because there was an alligator sitting across the table from him, making wagers in the wavering light of a hanging oil lamp. But try as he might to find a winning play, he kept losing to the grinning monster before him.

But the alligator didn't eat him, which seemed like a good sign, and as he shaved and dressed the next morning and took a drink to steady his nerves, he hoped the dream was right.

Russell Kistler met him at the door of the Exchange Hotel, maddeningly cheerful about the morning's coming events.

"Well, you're famous in Otero already, no matter how the hearing goes. The judge called the trial so early yesterday I was able to get the type set in time for this morning's press. 'Course today's story could make the headlines, too, depending on Hoodoo's call."

John Henry wasn't sure how he was supposed to react to such exciting news, but was sure he didn't much like reporter Kistler.

"I'll try not to disappoint you," he commented as he pushed past the newspaperman and made his way into the dining room—more crowded this morning than it had been the day before. If Hoodoo did make a murder charge and the thing came to a real trial, they'd have to build a new courtroom to accommodate all the spectators.

But Hoodoo Brown didn't make any charge at all, and instead, had his constable Jack Lyons read the court's brief decision that there wasn't enough evidence to make a charge against anyone—yet. As soon as something turned up, or was made to turn up, the case could come to a hearing again. But John Henry was too relieved at the temporary stay of execution to worry over what might come in the future, and when Russell Kistler asked for his comments for the readers of the *Otero Optic*, he could only shrug and say, "I reckon I'm lucky."

But as made his way back out of the Exchange Hotel and into the summer sunlight, the warm wind seemed to carry a sound like a haunted laugh:

That man be Hoodoo, mon. Good luck with that man be bad luck.

As reporter Kistler had said, the story of the unsolved murder of Mike Gordon made the morning paper in Otero, and went from there to every other town in the Territory. It was just the kind of thing Russell Kistler liked to write about, extolling the excitement of life in New Town Las Vegas and warning of the dangers of too many sporting men and not enough police. Kistler, it seemed, was on a crusade to clean up New Town while promoting its growth. In his vision of things, New Town would soon overtake Old Town as the real Las Vegas and leave the Plaza and the *Nuestra Señora de Dolores* in a sleepy siesta.

It was the newspaper article that brought Kate back to Las Vegas, the story of the murder of Mike Gordon having been picked up from the *Otero Optic* and reprinted in the paper in Santa Fe.

"I was hoping to see you hang," she said tenderly on the afternoon that she swept back into town and found him at the Senorita Saloon. "I'm sure you deserve it for something or other, even if you didn't shoot Mr. Gordon."

"Oh, I shot him, all right," John Henry replied, his tone matching the sarcasm of her own, "but I don't consider that I killed him. He'd still be alive if he'd been sober enough to find a doctor. His own fault for drinkin' too much and tryin' to tree the town. I was only doin' my civic duty in protectin' my establishment. But I suppose the paper neglected to mention that part."

"I don't recall," Kate replied, pulling off a soft leather glove and running her hand across the construction dust that covered the bar. "So you've given up dentistry for something more sophisticated, I see."

"Not entirely. I'm just makin' a little money off the railroad boom. I'll get my tools out again when things quiet down."

"And how was Dodge?" she asked, as though they were having a real conversation instead of preparing for a duel.

"Muddy. But Colorado was nice, though I had to hurry back before I could see much of the Royal Gorge. It wasn't exactly a pleasure trip."

"Wasn't it?" she said, one brow artfully raised. "You seemed quite pleased to be leaving me."

"I was, at the time," he replied, letting the almost imperceptible pause convey his meaning. If Kate had come to reconcile, he was willing. If she had only come to spar, he was willing to do that, too.

But her own momentary silence showed she had caught his intent.

"Otero got dull," she said with a stage sigh, "and Las Vegas never did interest me much. So I went on to Santa Fe and auditioned for a role in the theater company there. I was about to accept a part in a new play they're staging when I noticed the story in the newspaper. Of course, I had to come and see if the shooting outside Doc Holliday's Saloon had anything to do with you. The newspaper said there'd likely be a hanging once the culprit was discovered."

"So that explains why you're wearin' your best gown," he commented, though her attire was more suitable to a fancy party than a frontier strangling. She was wearing a bosom-baring frock of midnight blue satin with black velvet trim, an outfit entirely wrong for the season, but entirely fetching on her—which she knew, of course.

"I thought you should see me looking well before you died," she replied, but there was a light in her eyes that said she was enjoying the repartee.

And so was he, having missed the kind of cat-and-mouse conversations Kate was so good at. "Well, I am sorry to disappoint you in regards to the hangin'," he said. "But if it's any consolation, I did think of you while I was away."

"And now that you're back?"

He smiled wryly. "It's hard not to think of someone who says she wants you dead, but dresses like she hopes there's plenty of life in you yet."

"But it's really the undressing that proves the life in a man," came her quick reply, and by the way she smiled when she said it, he knew she'd be proving him again soon enough.

Kate's comment on the sophistication of keeping bar for a living inspired him to make another real estate deal: he purchased the eight-foot alleyway between his saloon and the building next door with the intent of planting a dental office on it. Eight feet wasn't much space across, but it was enough to set up a chair and a dental engine, especially since his saloon could serve as waiting room and laboratory. During the slow afternoons, before the real gamblers and drinkers came around, he could amuse himself by doing a little dentistry—and appease Kate that their life was still something more than cards and booze. And to prove his acceptance of her return, he had her name added to the deed as well, though the judge questioned his intent. After all, a man didn't have to share his property with a real wife; why make such a legal entanglement with a woman who only pretended to be Mrs. Holliday? But John Henry was resolute: add her name to the deed regardless of who was pretending what. He knew that he could never offer what Kate really wanted, but he could give her part ownership in his land, at least.

The Senorita Saloon reopened for business on the second Saturday evening in August, and on the following Tuesday, its owner was arrested for keeping a gaming table. In any other town, he'd have considered the fine just a normal business expense, a license fee of sorts for the privilege of banking bets. But when the gaming charge was followed the next day by a warrant for his arrest for carrying a deadly weapon, he knew there was more to it than just license fees. It was Hoodoo Brown who was finding excuses to have him arrested again and again, playing a kind of shell game with John Henry's life—and keeping him wondering when Mike Gordon would rise from the dead to seek his revenge.

Kate thought his suspicions unfounded. "Why would he have you arrested just to pay off an old debt?"

"Not to pay it off," John Henry explained, "to settle up. I ran out on him and now he's gonna take his revenge, one arrest at a time."

"But you said he never even spoke to you after the hearing, and didn't really speak to you there either. What makes you think he remembers you at all? Why, I passed him on the street yesterday and he didn't take any notice at all, and I used to be a big star back in St. Louis."

To hear Kate tell it, she'd been the toast of every town along the Mississippi instead of just a varieties actress with a mostly male following. The truth was, she had never quite made the big time and probably never would. Even her supposed starring role in the Santa Fe theater company would have been nothing more than a chorus part. But he had no need to tarnish the silver-lining of her dreams, so he let her remember herself as the West's Greatest Actress. What did her past matter now, anyhow?

His own past, however, mattered a great deal. In spite of Kate's assurances to the contrary, he knew that the coroner wasn't quite through with him yet. It was one of those things only another card player would understand: the wariness that came from a half-seen glance across a table, a second-sense foreboding that ran under the skin. Hoodoo Brown might be arresting him on proper grounds, but Hyram Neil was finding opportunities.

Hoodoo's harassment only lasted a few days, however, before the town was taken over by the excitement of a robbery on the Barlow and Sanderson Stage. The stage was on its regular route from Santa Fe to Trinidad, carrying payroll for the military post at Fort Union, when it was set upon near the village of Tecolote, eight miles from Las Vegas. According to the driver, three masked riders came alongside the coach flourishing shotguns and commanding the express messenger to open the treasure box and throw down the payroll bag. As it was a small payroll and not worth endangering the lives of the passengers, the messenger did as he was told and the robbers rode away satisfied—but not before the driver recognized the masked bandits as three lowlifes from Las Vegas.

Though the robbery was County Sheriff's business, the Coroner was quick to send his own police to aid in the chase—an irony not lost on the residents of New Town. For it was common knowledge that the three robbers had also done work for Hoodoo Brown, which made it seem unlikely that the Coroner would make any real attempt to apprehend them. More likely, he was sending his police to lead the county sheriff off the trail, and would be paid for his efforts out of that stolen military payroll. And when another Barlow and Sanderson stage was robbed a week later, the irony seemed like proof that something mysterious was going on in Las Vegas—especially when the driver identified the bandits as three of Hoodoo Brown's underlings.

This time, the stage company didn't leave the investigation to the local authorities, but brought in their own man to make the chase, a part time officer of the law from Dodge City by the name of John Joshua Webb.

Josh was still proudly sporting his shiny gold tooth when he walked into the Senorita Saloon, though his smile was lacking.

"Seems like the old Dodge City gang has just moved on down here, or at least the lesser aspects of it," he told John Henry over a short glass of whiskey, Josh never having been one to drink to excess, especially when he had business to conduct. "Fact is, so many of the gang have left town, the Lady Gay isn't doing much business at all anymore. Trouble with a cowtown: when the cows are gone, so are the cowboys, which leaves things quiet and poor. Which is why I took this job with the express company to make a little money on the side. But the express won't pay if I don't find their robbers."

"And you think both robberies are connected?" John Henry asked. "Couldn't they just be random highwaymen takin' advantage of the summer weather?"

"Could be," Josh replied, "but the express ain't going to wait around and find out. They've lost two payrolls in a week, and that's too much. They keep losing money like that, folks won't trust to have them ship anymore."

"So where do you reckon to find these robbers?"

Josh considered a moment, looking around as if wary of overhearing ears. "Fact is, Doc, I was hoping you could help me with that, which is why I stopped by your place first. You've got your ear to the ground, most of the time. I figured you could give me the heads-up on what's going on in this town."

John Henry took a sip at his own whiskey glass before answering.

"I'm afraid I'm in a bad position to help you out, Josh. Seems the guilty parties already have an interest in seein' me in distress, and I don't want to give them anymore cause. But I can tell you that what looks like law around here is more like a cover for law-breakin'. The rest you'll have to cipher for yourself."

Josh nodded. "That's pretty much what I expected, what with the names that keep turning up on the express wanted list. I'm just surprised they haven't tried to rob the train as yet."

"The stage is easier, you know that. You only have to down a horse to stop a coach. But I wouldn't put it past this gang to try the rails next. Seems like they're gettin' mighty cocky and self-assured. 'Course, the way they keep gettin' away with things, maybe they have some Jamaican luck on their side and a cause to be so cocky."

"Jamaican luck?"

"That's right," he said, keeping his eyes on his whiskey glass. "I heard about it back in St. Louis, from a colored down on the levee. He told me that Jamaican luck is bad luck. He had a name for it, even." He paused, as if waiting for the word to come to him, then shrugged. "Can't remember what it was, just now. But that's the thing you're lookin' for, Josh. You find that Jamaican luck, you'll find your bandits."

He didn't dare say more, but knew that if anyone had enough imagination to figure out the clue, Josh Webb did, black magic not being all that strange for a man who believed in sea monsters.

Though Kate claimed to have no jealousy over John Henry's rumored romance with Flor, she still fired the girl the first chance she got. John Henry had been away from the saloon that evening, trying his own gambling hand at Close and Patterson's down by the railroad tracks, and by the time he got back, Flor was gone and Kate was serving the drinks instead—and wearing a look that said she wasn't going to be challenged over the arrangement. So it was Kate, not Flor, who got the pleasure of pouring for Hyram Neil when he came into the saloon later that evening, looking for a poker game. At least, Kate acted like it was a pleasure, flirting and trifling with Hoodoo Brown as if she had a real interest in him.

"I'm only being nice to the customers," she said, when John Henry mentioned her surprising behavior. "Seems like you'd want a high roller like Hoodoo Brown to be happy in your saloon, so he spends more money. But you act like you want him out of here."

"I do want him out," John Henry said under his breath. "I wish he'd leave Las Vegas altogether, and I wish you'd stop playin' up to him."

Kate smiled and slid her arm around his neck. "Are you jealous, my love?"

John Henry brushed off her seduction. "Just cautious, that's all. Neil is still tryin' to settle up with me somehow. I can feel it, and I don't want to give him any advantage in doin' it. And your flirtations don't help any, encouragin' him."

Kate's arm slid back down and her smile turned to a frown. "I suppose I can flirt with anyone I want, as long as I'm still a single woman."

It was the same old complaint she'd always made and that he always tried to ignore. Make Kate his wife? It was a ridiculous thought.

"Why, Kate, if I were to marry you, I wouldn't have a mistress anymore. And a sporting man can't be without a mistress; it doesn't look right."

For a moment, she seemed torn between crying and slapping him, then she tossed her head and laughed.

"Then you can't complain when I flirt with other men! And I happen to find Hoodoo Brown quite charming in spite of your guilty notions about him. He's only come here to play cards, not seek revenge."

She said it with such a dramatic flair that he almost laughed himself, until he glanced toward the gaming tables and saw Hyram Neil looking his way, dark eyes glinting. He'd seen those eyes before, in the alligator dream. Hoodoo was after him all right, he had no doubt of that.

But there wasn't any black magic in the saloon that night, only card games, and the Coroner left with a respectable profit and nothing more; although, when he came back the next night and the night after that, even Kate began to wonder why he had taken such a liking to Doc Holliday's Saloon.

"It's you, my dear," John Henry said, taunting her. "He's recognized you, after all, and is challengin' Silas Melvin for your affections like another stage-door Johnny."

"And you're still jealous of Silas!" she said with satisfaction. "But Hoodoo won't be fighting you for me, not now."

"And why is that?"

"Because he's going to be busy fighting Marshal Joe Carson instead. From what I hear, Mrs. Carson agrees with me about the Coroner being charming, and he thinks the same of her."

"Marshal Carson isn't a man to fool with," he said, remembering the impressive physical presence of the leading lawman in Las Vegas— two-hundred fifty pounds, at least, packed onto a frame something over six feet tall. "Seems like suicide to fool with his wife."

"The Marshal doesn't know about it just yet," Kate replied. "Joe's been out with your friend Josh Webb, chasing those stage robbers while his wife philanders with Hoodoo."

"So how did you happen to come upon this information?"

"Women's intuition," Kate said smugly. "Some things I just know."

"Well, it's knowledge you ought to keep to yourself, Kate. A story like that could get someone killed, true or not."

"Oh, I hope so," she said. "It's been altogether too quiet around here so far."

Kate's quiet was good news for John Henry's business, as it meant the gaming tables at the Senorita ran undisturbed nearly night and day. And whenever a gambler came in with a toothache or a broken bit of bicuspid, Dr. Holliday ushered him into the lean-to dental office next door for an extraction or a new gold crown. There were some days when the dental office brought in more than the gaming, which made John Henry feel almost like a professional man again.

When he wasn't doing dentistry or playing the games, he was up Gallinas Canyon taking the water cure for the consumption. And it had been a real cure, the attendants at the hot springs all assured him, as his lungs sounded so clear that there surely must be no remains of the disease. John Henry wanted to believe them, and there were days that he did as he lay in the sulphureted water smelling the pungent perfume of rotting eggs and Piñon pine. There were days that he stepped from the bath into a waiting wrap of Turkish toweling to be swaddled and set to dry in the clear mountain air and felt almost his old self again. And on those days, staring up at a sky of startling blue broken by the evergreen of the pine-covered mountains, he felt like he might live forever. Twenty-eight years old he was that summer, with the whole rest of his life before him still.

In the quiet of the canyon, he missed the next excitement that came to town when the Barlow and Sanderson stage was robbed again and another payroll stolen. But this time, Josh Webb was near enough to follow the clues. The robbers—Frank Cady, Slap Jack Bill, and Bull-Shit Jack—had colorful names but not very bright minds, as they went straight from the sight of the robbery to the nearest bar to start celebrating their success. By the time they returned to Las Vegas, they were happily inebriated and telling everyone who would listen that they had robbed the Barlow and Sanderson and got to keep all the money minus the portion paid to the men who had set-up the scheme.

Josh didn't have to do much to bring them in, only buy them a few drinks and listen admiringly to the story. Then without so much as pulling his pistol, he genially escorted the boys out of Close and Patterson's Dance Hall and up Main Street to where there was another big party, so he told them—the location of the party being the county jail, where the sheriff was equally happy to entertain them and hear their tale.

As for the planners behind the robbery, catching them wouldn't be so easy. According to the robbers' drunken story, the masterminds were Mysterious Dave Rudabaugh and Joe Carson, the town marshal of Las Vegas.

Josh had crossed paths with Rudabaugh before, but he doubted the outlaw's involvement in the Las Vegas hold-up as Dave was known to be back in Kansas at the time and far from the meadows of New Mexico. As for Marshal Joe Carson, that was business Josh didn't want to get mixed into. The express company had promised to pay him for arresting robbers, not cleaning up the law in Las Vegas, and he had already made good on that deal. Leave it to the citizens of the town to clean up their own corruption; he was headed back to Dodge City to see after his Lady Gay Saloon.

Josh had said that Dodge City was clearing out and heading down to Las Vegas, and that seemed to be true, with most of the refugees coming by way of Pueblo and Trinidad on the newly completed southbound rails of the Atchison, Topeka & Santa Fe. They were the sporting men who traveled light and took up temporary residence in the hotels and brothels around the railroad depot of New Town and swelled the crowds in the Centre Street saloons. The family groups mostly took a different route, moving by wagon train with all their homely belongings and traveling slow along the old Santa Fe Trail. Where the trail ended at the Plaza in Old Town, they made a campground, ringing the square with the white canopies of the prairie schooners and drawing water from the well below the hangman's gallows. And so the divergent populations of Old Town and New Town grew with their separate citizenry: family folk in their campground around the Plaza; sporting men and dance halls girls in the boomtown down around the depot, and neither mixing much with the other. So it was an unusual evening when one of the denizens of Old Town took a walk down the hill and over the Gallinas River bridge to pay a social visit on one of the denizens of New Town.

He was a long lean fellow, so tall that he had to bend his head to get through the door of the Senorita Saloon, though he didn't try to accommodate the space by taking off his hat. To the contrary, he kept his hat on his head as if needing to shade his face from the fading rays of the sun. Or needing to hide himself somehow, John Henry thought, as he watched the man step into the saloon. But it was impossible to hide such height or such natural swagger, though the man didn't mean to make a show of himself. He was, indeed, the least showy man John Henry had ever known, a quiet self-deprecating soul who somehow kept bringing fame to himself. And John Henry knew in a moment, just by the way the fellow shed a tall shadow, that Wyatt Earp had come to town.

Wyatt was his usual laconic self, as short of words as he was long of body, and John Henry had to work to get any kind of conversation out of him.

"So you packed up and brought the whole family along with you?" he asked, and Wyatt nodded under the shadow of his hat brim.

"All that was left in Dodge: just Jim and Bessie and their kids and me and Celia. Virgil's already moved out, gone to Arizona to try his hand there. Owns a sawmill up above Prescott."

"And Morgan?" John Henry asked. "Any word since he went off to get married?"

Wyatt shrugged, which said more than any words would have. Wyatt had never cottoned to the idea of his brother's union with Miss Louisa Houston, considering her more ornamental than useful in a wifely way. Wyatt's own taste ran to the sturdy independent type of woman, and Louisa was more southern belle than prairie flower. But his opinion hadn't quelled Morgan's infatuation with the pretty Louisa, which was something of a stumbling block between the brothers. Wyatt was accustomed to being trailed by Morgan like an eager puppy following a hunting dog, but in this thing, Morgan had taken another lead.

"So what are your plans from here?" John Henry asked, ambling away from the undiscussed subject.

Wyatt touched a hand to his hat, settling it back a bit on his head, signaling his willingness to entertain the topic. It was an unthinking action, John Henry suspected, but it was always the same: Wyatt with hat down low over his face closed himself off from the world; Wyatt with hat pushed back allowed the world in. Funny how you could grow to know a man just by the way he wore his hat.

"We're traveling, going to Arizona Territory to pick up Virgil and Allie. Then we're headed down to the silver country."

"Why, Wyatt, I never figured you for a miner!" John Henry said with a laugh. "Since when did you get interested in silver?"

"Since Ed Shieffelin staked his claim down on the border. The Tombstone mines are the richest in the whole United States, or so says

Virg. He's been keeping an eye on the boom since he got to the Arizona Territory, and he figures we can follow the mines to some good business opportunities."

"Such as?"

"Milling, for one thing. That's what Virg's been doing in Prescott. A new town's got to have fresh lumber milled. Plus transportation for the wood and whatever else needs transporting. Which is why I've been thinking of turning our prairie schooner to transport use, after we get there. A wagon's a big investment to just retire when the traveling's done, and I know something about the shipping business. Used to drive freight out of California, when I was boy."

"The Earp Brothers Express," John Henry said, trying out the idea. "Has a ring to it. Though I never figured you for a freighter, either."

"It's not the freight I'm interested in," Wyatt countered, "just the business. There's money in it, and that's my aim. I've been looking for a money-making business, and I think this may be it."

"You'll need a good guard, if the roads there are anything like the roads around here. You heard Josh Webb was hired by the Adam's Express to chase stage robbers?"

"I heard something of it. But the way I see it, the Earp Brothers have something the Adam's doesn't."

"And what's that?" John Henry asked, though he already knew the answer.

"The Earp Brothers," Wyatt replied with something like a smile, the most humor he ever showed. "Between me and Virg and Morg, we've got three of the best guns around. That ought to do."

"If you can get Morgan out of Montana," John Henry said, pointing out the most obvious difficulty in the endeavor.

Wyatt nodded. "Which is why I came to see you, Doc. I was hoping you might help me write a letter to Morg, convincing him to join us. You're good with words and writing and all. I was thinking that if you wrote Morgan, you might convince him to leave Sam Houston's party and join back up with us again."

"So you want me to play Cyrano, read poetry from balconies on your behalf?" John Henry said, considering.

"There's no need for poetry," Wyatt replied, his literal mind missing the literary allusion. "I figured you could paint a pretty picture of the silver country, make it seem appealing to him."

"I reckon I could, if I'd seen the place myself. But the closest I've been to Tombstone is a summer south of the Texas border, and there wasn't any silver there that I could see. I'd just be makin' up stories: '*The streets of Tombstone, paved like Heaven in bricks of precious ore*,' perhaps, or '*the undulating hills where the silver shimmers like veins straining at a whore's breast. . .*'"

He'd meant the fanciful lines as an example of the foolishness of the plan, but Wyatt nodded in seeming appreciation.

"Stories will do, if they get Morgan back with the family. 'Course, if he heard you were coming along, he'd have that much more reason. He always was partial to you."

"Why, Wyatt, are you invitin' me to join your caravan?"

The sarcastic tone was meant to cover his surprise. Having Wyatt ask for his help in writing a letter was one thing; having him extend an invitation to go along with the family was quite another. He was flattered by the first and flustered by the second, and hardly knew how to answer. But one thing he did know: he couldn't leave Las Vegas and the hot springs up Gallinas Canyon. After returning from dusty Dodge City with a relapse of his cough, he'd spent every free day soaking in the springs and drinking the mineral water, taking the cure. He couldn't take a chance of having another relapse that might not be so quickly overcome.

But he couldn't say all that to Wyatt, admitting how fragile he sometimes felt. Wyatt wouldn't understand something as unmanly as that.

"I'm asking you to come along, if you're interested," Wyatt went on. "If Tombstone turns out to be what Virgil says it is, there'll be plenty of opportunity to go around."

"Well, I do appreciate your thinkin' of me," John Henry replied with a calculatedly casual tone, "but I'm already knee-deep in opportunities here. Las Vegas is boomin' and just right for a man of my many talents. Besides, Kate would hate the desert. She likes to be close to the dressmakers in case she needs new ruffles and such."

He threw in the words about Kate as an afterthought, to lighten the conversation, and wished as soon as he'd spoken that he hadn't.

"So you're still with Kate? I never took you for a saint, Doc."

"No saint, just payin' up on a debt," he said, for hellion or not, she had saved his life. "Besides," he added by way of explaining, "she's good with the saloon clientele, keeps the sporting men occupied while I take their money." Although the Senorita Saloon wasn't much of a theater, Kate could make an audience out of any crowd. And thinking of the way she had saved him and traded away her acting career for a boomtown saloon, he had a sudden surge of compassion for her. It wasn't love, not in the way he had feelings for Mattie, but there was something special in his feelings for Kate.

"Well, suit yourself," Wyatt said, downing the last of his drink and pushing his hat back down low on his head. "I'll be back along tomorrow or the day after that, if you're still willing to help me write that letter. May even take in a poker game, if there's some rollers in the crowd."

"Why, Marshal Earp, I'd be happy to have you lose your money in my saloon. It would be a real honor."

"And what makes you think I'm going to lose?" Wyatt asked, eyes squinted against the thought.

"'Cause I'll be the first to ante in," John Henry replied with a smile.

September brought another visitor to Las Vegas, this one even more unexpected than Wyatt. For the last person John Henry figured on seeing was someone from his own far-off past and his days as a respectable Atlanta dentist. Though, if he had to have a former friend see him in his current sporting life, Lee Smith was the right one to see him.

Lee had been the owner of the Maison de Ville Saloon during John Henry's Atlanta days, and had been interested in Western investments even then: railroads, banks, iron and coal. Now he was traveling the west looking for interesting new opportunities, which was what brought him to Las Vegas that fall on a scouting trip down from Colorado and into the silver southwest. But it was a newspaper article about his upcoming adventure, published in the *Atlanta Constitution*, that had brought him to Doc Holliday's Saloon in Las Vegas.

When the Holliday family of Atlanta had read of Lee Smith's intended itinerary, they'd sent him a note asking him to visit their cousin in New Mexico should his travels take him that direction—or more precisely, it was Miss Mattie Holliday who had made the request. She knew of Lee Smith by reputation only, never having ventured into his Maison de Ville, but she knew the family was acquainted with him and used that social connection as reason to send him a politely worded request—

"*As you may have heard, my Uncle Henry Holliday's son, our cousin John Henry, has been on an extended tour of Texas and the west. He is currently a resident of the city of Las Vegas, New Mexico Territory where he practices his profession of Dentistry . . .*"

That was the way Lee Smith remembered her words, anyhow, when he told them to John Henry upon his arrival in New Town—where he was more than a little surprised to find Dr. Holliday not only practicing dentistry, but keeping bank at a Faro table in his own saloon, as well. In fact, his surprise had started when he first got off the southbound Santa Fe at the depot in New Town and checked into the Mackley House Hotel where he asked if the clerk could direct him to the dental office of Dr. John H. Holliday.

The clerk looked mystified at first, then laughed as if the traveler had made a clever joke. "You mean Doc Holliday's place? Well, Sir, I can direct you to his treatment room, if it's pain relief you're after." Then he said that Dr. Holliday could no doubt be found at a place called The Senorita, a block or so up Centre Street. It wasn't until Lee found the saloon by that name with young Dr. Holliday running the games that he got the joke.

It was a reunion so amusing to Lee Smith that he told the tale again and again to every sporting man and at every game he happened into: how young Dr. Holliday, heir of the esteemed Holliday and McKey families of Georgia and an expensively educated professional man, should have chosen the same career as he himself had chosen who had no fine family or professional education to stand behind him.

John Henry didn't mind so much Lee's recitations to the only somewhat interested gamblers of Las Vegas. What concerned him was the possibility that Lee would return to Atlanta and share the same story with the newspapers there—or worse, with Mattie. Lee found John Henry's double vocation of dentistry and saloon dealing merely amusing—Mattie would not be so favorably inclined. But as it turned out, he should have worried less about Mattie and more about Las Vegas.

The little lean-to dental office he had built next to the saloon kept him interestingly occupied when he wasn't busy banking Faro or joining in a poker game. As always, he found his dental practice to be pleasurable in a way he couldn't have made anyone else understand, and though some might say that it was a sadistic streak that made him enjoy causing pain to his patients, he didn't see it that way at all. In fact, he more often put them out of pain than caused them the same by removing a damaged or decayed tooth and replacing it with something more serviceable.

But it was for himself, mostly, that he enjoyed practicing. He liked the craft of his profession, being able to do something with his hands and know he was doing it well. It was just too bad that there was no one around who could really appreciate his work—not that he was the only dentist in Las Vegas, of course. He was just the only one working out of a saloon in New Town, which gave him a somewhat limited professional association. And that was a shame, when he was doing such fine work as he was just now, crafting a gleaming porcelain and gold bridge for a railroader who'd lost his two front teeth in a saloon fight. The railroader, a big Irishman with more brawn than brain, had chosen to use only his fists, while his opponent had pulled a pistol and shoved the butt end of it into his mouth. The Irishman lost his teeth, but the other man lost the fight, going down in a heap of bruises and groans. It was the luck of the Irish, the man said, that the loser had a wad of greenbacks in his pockets which he took as winnings—and which he was happy to give to Doc Holliday to make him look presentable again.

John Henry was happy to take the hard-won money, and happier to take on the dental case, which was far more challenging than the usual fillings and extractions that occupied his occasional work hours. And so it was that he found himself engrossed in carving and excavating and making plaster impressions, and ignoring what was going on in his saloon on the other side of the doorway until a boisterous voice drew his attention. Most days, the hubbub of the Senorita's bar and gaming tables was just a pleasant background sound to the louder whir of his dental drill, but on this late September afternoon, even the drill couldn't drown out the sound of a man's laughter as he told an old story to anyone who would listen.

The man was Lee Smith, of course, holding court somewhere in the saloon like he used to hold court in his Maison de Ville in Atlanta. His voice, from long years of speaking across the noise of his own saloon, had learned a resonance that carried it to every corner of a room. He might have made a name for himself on the theater stage, John Henry mused, the way his voice carried through the thin walls of the saloon like it was carrying across the footlights, though the tale he was telling would never make for good drama. He was recounting, in what John Henry heard as dully accurate detail, the history of the Holliday family in Georgia and how he came to be associated with them all.

"Yessir," said Lee, "I was pleased to see John Henry here following in the family footsteps, goin' into the liquor business. A stable sort of livin', I've always found it to be. No matter the economic turn of things, there's always call for a good saloon. In fact, the worst times is oft the best of times for a saloonkeeper, as bad times make a man needful of a good drink. Then the good times come and what's a man gonna spend his money on but another drink? Yessir," he said again, as though proving a point, although no one could be heard disputing him, "there's no business better suited to a stable and satisfying lifestyle than sellin' drinks across the bar. 'Course the Hollidays have known that from way back. As I recall it, there was a Holliday saloon in Georgia in the frontier days when the roads cut through the Indian nation to get from one white town to another. Though, in those days, they weren't called saloons, a fancy sort of name that came later. They were taverns back then, part hotel and part drinkin' room, and welcome wherever they were established. That was the first business of John Henry's Grandpa Bob Holliday, and they say a finer tavern keeper you never did meet: friendly, fast on the pour, full of talk. Like me! So the way I see it, John Henry comes by the saloon business naturally. What's that you say?"

There was a pause as though Lee were listening to a question, which he then readily answered.

"That's right, they came into some money after those days. Came from land, mostly. The Holliday boys—I'm talkin' John Henry's father and uncles now—were smart about the women they married. All of them married into families of some substance, at least as to bein' landowners. And Henry Holliday—that's John Henry's father and a longtime friend of my own—and his brother John, they married best of all. Both of them wed planter's daughters, so they got the slaves along with the land when it came time for the inheritances to be doled out. 'Course they lost the slaves after the War, but they kept most of the land. Henry did, anyhow, and kept buyin' up more when he relocated down toward the Florida border."

There was another pause, but whether for another question or for Lee to take a drink to wet his throat, John Henry couldn't tell.

"Oh, I'm sure there's still plenty of that property left, even so. But the real money isn't in property anymore, it's in commodities. It's his Uncle John, himself a Dr. Holliday, who's the wealthy one now. He made the smart move to Atlanta just when it was boomin' and settled himself and his businesses there. Bought an old general store and turned it profitable, then made some investments. The Holliday money now is in jewelry and silver and such things—easier to trade than land down in the swamps."

Another pause, a longer one this time.

"Inheritance? Well, I suppose he does. There was quite something to it at one time between the land and the other properties. I'd say there's plenty of inheritance left. Why do you ask?"

John Henry couldn't hear the answer, though he had stopped the foot-treadle that kept his dental drill smoking away and excused himself from his patient, near enough done to be dismissed for the day anyhow, and stepped into the barroom to see whom it was that Lee Smith was entertaining in such eager fashion.

At first glance, he saw only Kate at Lee's poker table, sitting beside him in all her satin and finery. No matter the time or the company, she always dressed like she was on her way to some fancy dress ball or an opening night on the stage, and this afternoon was no exception as she sat decorating the room and hanging on Lee's every word. But it wasn't Kate that Lee was addressing himself to, but one of the players in the poker game, a man with his back to the wall and his face toward the door, guarded. And though John Henry couldn't see his face, he knew by the man's hands who it was that was asking after his inheritance—they were gambler's hands, decked out in jeweled rings and with a pearl-handled derringer resting beside them.

It was Hoodoo Brown who was playing poker with Lee Smith that afternoon, and who was encouraging his talk of the Holliday family properties. And it seemed to John Henry, as he stood there taking in the sight and calculating the situation, that Hyram Neil had come back like the alligator in his dreams, sniffing around dark river water and looking for something to eat.

"Oh, there he is now,' Kate said, glancing up and seeing him listening, "the hero of our little drama. Why don't you come join us, darling, and tell us if what Mr. Smith is saying here is true. I had no idea you had such fine family connections."

"My connections are tenuous, these days," he replied with a cool he didn't feel, "and my fine family is far away with nothin' to do with my present circumstances."

It was then that Hoodoo Brown turned around, his dark-mustached face sporting a smile that glinted like the dark jewels on his gambling hands.

"But it's your past circumstances that interest me, Dr. Holliday. For I seem to recall a certain wager made by you with your family's property back in Georgia as collateral. A wager you lost then left without honoring, though I remember quite clearly your signing a promissory note guaranteeing payment on the same. I wonder what your fine Georgia family would think about that? I wonder if they would be pleased to hear that their dear relation is both a bad gambler and a bad debtor, and that he still owes me what he promised: his inheritance."

His words had been spoken with such modulated tones that only those sharing his gaming table heard him. But that was sufficient.

"Is this true, John Henry?" Lee Smith breathed out incredulously. "It's one thing, followin' in the family footsteps and ownin' a drinkin' saloon, but wagerin' your family's hard-earned wealth . . ." And for once, Lee Smith was beyond words.

But Hyram Neil had enough to fill the stunned silence.

"Oh, I assure you my words are every bit the truth. In fact, I'm sure I could produce that promissory note for you to take back to Georgia, if you'd like. Perhaps Dr. Holliday's fine and upstanding family there would be better about honoring a debt than their dissembling relation has been."

"No –" John Henry said weakly, his voice revealing the dread Hoodoo's words put into him. If that promissory note, signed by him one drunken night in a St. Louis saloon, should find its way back to Georgia, he'd lose whatever respect his family still had for him—and whatever affection Mattie still had for him, as well. If she ever came to know the truth of his circumstances. . .

"No," he said again, this time decisively. "I will make good on that debt myself, Mr. Neil. You don't have to trouble my family."

Hoodoo looked at him a long appraising moment before speaking.

"Well, then," he said, "I accept your pledge, in spite of your past lack of fidelity. But how do you plan to repay the debt? Have you a large bank account from which to draw the money? Have you, yourself, the kind of property holdings your inheritance boasted?

"He's got this saloon," Lee Smith put in unhelpfully. He didn't need Hoodoo finding out how meager his assets really were, and decide to send the promissory note off to Georgia after all.

"But it's cash I've got mostly," he said quickly, "my winnings from all these poker games. The house takes a cut, as you know, and business has been brisk since the Santa Fe came to town."

Kate looked at him with raised brows, surely knowing his deceit. For though he always had money for the clothes and baubles she demanded, they were still living in a rented boarding house room and not in the more elaborate Exchange Hotel that she would have preferred. But she was ever an actress at heart, and said with dramatic flair:

"Yes, Mr. Neil, business has done very well. Why, I recently returned from a little trip down to Santa Fe, inquiring after purchasing a theater company there. Doc has always wanted to buy me one for my own. Haven't you darling?"

The words came like sugared syrup out of her prettily painted lips, so sweet that John Henry almost believed them himself. And he could have kissed her right then for being clever enough to see a role and play it to his advantage.

"Yes indeed, my sweet. I look forward to seein' you on the stage again. But I think Santa Fe is too small an audience for your talents. Why don't we try for San Francisco instead, just as soon as I clean out Mr. Neil here in a little poker game? Unless he thinks he's game enough to beat me again and win back what he thinks I stole from him . . ."

His only hope, as he could see it, to save himself from disgrace in the family—and in Mattie's eyes—was to make Hyram Neil agree to another poker game and then to beat him at it. But would the alligator take the bait?

"That's a helluva deal," Lee Smith put in, this time his comments coming with more welcome. "John Henry here's quite a poker player. It would take a real sport to beat him at his own game."

Neil gave another one of his long appraising looks, as if measuring out a meal. "Well then," he said again, "shall we call it my promissory note against the wagers in a friendly poker game? You win, I return the note to you. I win, I take everything you put up against me. Fair enough?"

Fair didn't even enter into it.

Neil offered his own fresh deck for the game, which John Henry, of course, declined. He'd resealed too many marked decks himself to fall for such a common ruse. So, in the end, they sent out for a deck and a dealer from another saloon, taking equal chances—then John Henry shuffled and Neil cut, and they were both satisfied.

They played a few small-stakes hands at first, getting a feel for the game and gathering a crowd, as well, and by the time the real contest began, the saloon was busier than it had ever been, and John Henry was making money on the drinks even before he made money on the cards. Though it wasn't money he was after on this night, but a reckoning. He hadn't understood, last time they'd played, the difference between playing the cards and playing the man, and Neil had taken him for everything he had and more. Now he understood that it didn't really matter what hand a man was dealt, if he knew how to wager and raise and bluff his way around it. And in that, poker was much like life.

There was something else that John Henry hadn't known before: that every poker player gave himself away somehow, and all an opponent had to do was pay attention until he figured out the signs. Some men sucked in their breath when a bad card was drawn, some did the same thing for a good card. Some men chewed their cigar too eagerly, or blinked their eyes nervously, or got an itch on their nose when things were going well—or perhaps when things were going wrong. Some men sweated and dripped perspiration from their brow onto the baize when they were about to lose a hand and an important pot, while others sweated when they were about to win. But everyone had some response to the stress of the game, and the best players watched for those signs.

Hyram Neil, however, seemed inscrutable. His black eyes glittered whether he was winning or losing, his face a stony calm no matter what the turn of the cards. Indeed, his whole person seemed in repose as he played, only his hands moving as he fanned or tucked the cards, as he fingered his jeweled rings.

John Henry played with his own ring, the one Mattie had given to him as they'd stood together in the stained-glass light of the Church of the Immaculate Conception. It had become something of a talisman to him, a comfort when things got difficult. Even little Lenora Seegar had commented on it, noting that he played with it all the time, and asking where he got such a small ring, too small for a man's hand. It had been nearly too tight to slip over his knuckle at first, but as the years had gone by, his fingers had grown thinner like the rest of him, and the ring slid around easily, turning circles as his thumb reached across his palm to play with it.

When the final deal came, they were evenly paired, well-matched players, luck and skill working for both of them. "Five cards to you, Doc," said the dealer, "and five to you, Mister Brown. Wagers, please."

John Henry picked up his cards and considered them: a pair of Queens and three small cards. It was an acceptable hand that could become three-of-a-kind or even two pair on a lucky draw, or stay a pair if the draw brought him nothing useful. But even a pair could win him the game, if he could figure out what Hyram Neil was thinking.

Neil took his own cards, his face stony as always, his eyes sharp and shining as obsidian. And then came the wagers: Neil's being another note, promising to relinquish all claim to John Henry's inheritance property in the form of land or cash or any other conveyance; John Henry's a collection of other valuables, with his pearl-handled revolver and his diamond stickpin, along with Kate's derringer taken against her will from its hiding place in her lacey garter.

"Wager with your own things!" she said angrily, as John Henry slid a hand under her satin skirts and reached along her thigh for the little revolver.

"I am," he said, retrieving the derringer and laying it down on top of the other items in the pot. "I believe it was my money that paid for this, like most everything you're wearin'."

She stiffened to show her anger but didn't argue, taking the reminder that if he did well at the gambling tables, she would do well herself. But Neil seemed unimpressed by the offering.

"Come now! A derringer? I can buy my own pocket pistols. I don't need to steal your lady's protection."

"So what did you have in mind?"

Neil took a glance around the crowded saloon that looked more prosperous this night than it usually was. "How about the deed to your place here?"

"You want me to put my property up against my own property?" John Henry asked, incredulous. There was no end to the man's bravado.

"Not yours anymore," Neil replied. "Your inheritance is legally mine now, remember? So it's your property against mine, for now, at least. After this hand, it will all be mine."

Such confidence would have cowed him, times past, but watching Hyram Neil fan his cards, John Henry wasn't cowed at all, for he suddenly knew how to beat the alligator. As he played with the Irish ring on his little finger, mindlessly twisting at it, so Neil played with his own finger rings, caressing the diamonds and the emeralds whenever he had a good hand of cards—and leaving them alone when he did not. And the fact that Neil wasn't playing with his rings, stroking them with satisfaction as he did on a good hand, showed that the dealer hadn't dealt him well.

"Wagers, gentlemen?" the dealer asked.

"Kate, write me a note for the saloon," John Henry said. Then he added with a purposefully heavy sigh: "I reckon it's not all that much of a prize, anyhow . . ." as if he really thought he might be losing it. All part of the show, the play of the game.

Neil nodded, acknowledging the wager, and the dealer stacked the deck on the baize, cutting it halfway and separating the cards into draw and deadwood.

"Gentlemen," he said, "how many cards would you like?"

"I'll take three, please," said Neil, dropping his unwanted cards onto the deadwood and slipping the newly dealt ones into his hand without a flicker of expression.

"And I'll take two," John Henry said, keeping his own face as emotionless as Neil's. He'd wagered on his two Queens, hoping for three of a kind or maybe another pair at least on the draw, but got nothing useful. And though he didn't let his disappointment show, he caught himself reaching thumb to little finger for the comfort of Mattie's ring—caught himself and stopped. If he were watching for Neil's giveaway, then Neil was surely watching him, as well.

Across the table from him, Neil was still stony-faced, still not toying with his jeweled finger rings. And John Henry knew, through his own years of poker playing and his stint as a Denver card dealer, what was going on in Hyram Neil's mind: should he fold now, give up the pot and its promised land and money? Should he raise the stakes, bluffing and hoping that John Henry would get nervous and fold instead? And if he did raise, how much did he want to risk, if John Henry had a better hand?

He wasn't surprised when Neil said at last, "I believe I'm all in," and opened his money purse to sweeten the pot, one last ploy to frighten his opponent.

John Henry had nothing much left to wager but his dental equipment, and he told Kate to write another promissory note. He was going to win big or lose big, one or the other, and he was gentleman enough to allow Hyram Neil the same opportunity. So with everything on the table, he said coolly, "I call."

The dealer nodded. "Show your cards please, Mr. Brown."

Neil's always expressionless face didn't quiver as he laid out his hand: a pair of fives and nothing much more, easily bested by the pair of Queens that John Henry showed.

"Well, I believe it's congratulations, Dr. Holliday," Hyram Neil said smoothly, as though he'd given up pocket change in a parlor game instead of losing what he'd been wanting for years. Then he turned to Kate, taking her hand and raising it to his lips and said, "It's been an enchanting evening."

Although he'd beaten Hyram Neil at last and put his troubles behind him, John Henry still spent a couple of sleepless nights battling bad dreams. This time, the alligator was slinking along in the dark water at the edge of the levee, watching him and waiting for one misstep, mouth open and ready to bite.

Kate, who said his sleeplessness was disturbing her own rest, took to sleeping in her dressing room, which meant that he was alone when a visitor came knocking early one morning. He groaned and slid out of bed, standing shakily and not bothering to draw on his dressing gown before answering the door.

Josh Webb was back in town and standing in the doorway, hat in hand and looking uncomfortable. "We got trouble, Doc," he said in a hushed voice, as if someone might be listening.

"What is it now?" John Henry asked wearily. "Stage robbers again?"

Josh shook his homely head. "Stage robbers would be better," he said. "It's the rails this time, Doc, like you said it would be. The robbers held up the southbound Santa Fe. Took a payroll bag from the mailcar—$5,000."

John Henry let out a whistle. "Well, Josh, sounds like you've got your work cut out for you. Who do you suppose did it?"

"It's not who I suppose. This time it's who I know. I finally figured out that riddle you gave me, but that don't make it any easier. Remember you told me to find some Jamaican luck and I'd find the robber-chief? Well, I was down at Close and Patterson's the other night when a trainload of travelers comes in. Rich folks from the east, I reckon, talking about their adventures. And the last place they visited was the islands past Cuba. It's magic out there, they said, full of mysterious doing and voodoo. But they didn't say voodoo exactly. It was hoodoo they called it, bad luck and such. Well, my ears picked up at that, remembering what you told me. It's Hoodoo Brown that's behind the robberies, isn't it? The robber-chief is Hoodoo Brown, the Mayor of Las Vegas as he calls himself."

"Congratulations," John Henry said cheerfully, as though Josh had just won a spelling bee. "Now all you have to do is bring him in and your job is done."

"But it's not him I gotta arrest this time," Josh said, looking even more uncomfortable, "even though I know he's the one behind it. But he says different, naming names and making accusations."

"Naming his own men?" John Henry commented in surprise. "That doesn't sound like his style."

"It ain't his own men he's naming, Doc. It's you."

"Me?" John Henry said with a laugh, "a train robber? And when would I have had time to do this dastardly deed, between runnin' my saloon and doin' my dentistry? Ask Kate where I've been, if you're brave enough to wake her. She's a mean woman when she hasn't had her night's rest."

"It's not me you gotta convince, Doc. I don't think you'd bother robbing a train when you got easier means of making money. But what I think don't much matter. It's what a jury's gonna think, if Hoodoo makes a charge. And from what I hear, he's getting ready to make one."

And then, John Henry realized what was happening. Hyram Neil, having lost out on his winnings once in St. Louis and again in Las Vegas, was going to take his vengeance at last. In a town full of people who already considered John Henry a killer, it wouldn't be too hard to find a jury that would consider him a train robber, as well. And once Hoodoo had made the train robbery charge stick, he could easily invent evidence that the killing of Mike Gordon was really a murder after all, and hang him for both crimes.

"So what do I do, Josh?" he asked, all the warmth of sleepiness gone in a sudden shiver of cold fear.

"I'd get out of town, if I was you, and soon. But I wouldn't make any big show of it, more like sneak out, I'd say. If he knows you're going, he'll have his road agents stop you, or worse."

He didn't have to ask Josh what his imaginary mind was thinking up this time. It seemed his good luck at the poker table had been hoodoo again, and this time it was deadly.

He knew what he needed to do, and hoped it wasn't too late to do it. Wyatt had invited him to join the Earps on the journey into the Arizona Territory, and he had laughed off the invitation when it was made. The last thing he'd wanted to do was make a long trip across the open desert, riding for weeks alongside a plodding wagon train. His health seemed to take a turn for the worse just imagining such an effort. But the last thing he wanted now seemed like the one thing he needed: a way out of Las Vegas without drawing attention to his leaving. There were hundreds of wagon trains traveling along the Santa Fe Trail, passing through Las Vegas on their way to wherever else they were headed. No one much noticed their coming or going, other than to make a quick profit off the provisions they bought to supply their outfits. No one would notice John Henry joining in with one of those wagon trains headed west into the desert—at least that was his hope.

It didn't take him long to find the Earp caravan, their wagons still camped at the Plaza in Old Town, though by the looks of things they'd be pulling out soon.

"The weather's cooling," Wyatt explained when John Henry found him and inquired after their impending departure, "better climate for desert traveling."

"I reckon," John Henry replied. "So how long do you figure on drivin' before you have to stop to provision again?" Wyatt's wagons, he noted, were already neatly filled with barrels and boxes and odd household belongings. There was even a rocking chair, positioned so as to take in a nice view of the landscape they were leaving behind.

"Virgil says we can make it to Prescott all right, if the weather holds. We're hoping to get there before the snow starts, it being up toward the mountains and all."

"Any word yet from Morgan?" John Henry asked, trying to keep the conversation seemingly light. If Wyatt had been surprised to receive his visit to Old Town, he didn't show it. But then, Wyatt didn't show much of any kind of emotion anyway, surprised or not.

"No word, yet," he said with a shrug as his hefted a bag of sugar into the wagon bed. "Not sure he even got that letter yet, up there in Deadwood. If he's still in Deadwood. That was his last known whereabouts, or Sam Houston Junior's, anyhow."

Wyatt didn't mention any thanks for John Henry's hand in writing that letter, which he, himself, considered a small masterpiece of creativity. But he hadn't come to discuss literature.

"I've been thinkin' about your offer, Wyatt," he said, trying to sound casual. "I've been thinkin' maybe I'd like to try my hand in Arizona after all, give another locale the pleasure of my presence."

Wyatt glanced at him a moment, then nodded. "We leave at dawn. You planning to ride along or bring your own wagon?"

He hadn't actually thought that far into the matter in his haste to find Wyatt and his relief at locating him still in Las Vegas.

"I reckon I'll just ride," he said, and started figuring the cost of buying a horse for the trail. A horse and saddle would set him back a bit, along with a bed roll and whatever saddle provisions he could carry for himself. As for his dental equipment, he'd have to arrange to have that sent along to him later, once he got himself settled somewhere, an arrangement that seemed to be turning into a routine. Then there was the matter of the management of his saloon. He couldn't very well just walk away and leave his business to tend to itself, and wondered if maybe Josh Webb would be interested in buying in or buying him out altogether. Josh had been considering making Las Vegas his permanent location now that Dodge City had dried up and his own Lady Gay Saloon wasn't bringing in the money that it used to.

"And how about Kate?" Wyatt asked, interrupting his plans. "Will she be coming along, as well?"

He'd given even less thought to Kate than he had to the horse he'd ride out of town.

"Not this time," he said easily, certain that Kate would have no interest in a long wagon train crossing the desert, especially one led by Wyatt Earp. This time, it would be just himself he was having to please.

Kate, however, had other ideas when he arrived back at their boarding house room and began packing up his belongings.

"I can travel as well as you," she said in an angry voice that didn't do much to cover her hurt. "Though, I'd rather you'd have bought tickets on the train to Santa Fe, instead. We could travel on from there to anywhere, even San Francisco."

"And why would I want to go to San Francisco?" he asked, irritated at being corralled into such a conversation when he had more important things on his mind. If he didn't get himself out of Las Vegas, fast and quiet, it wouldn't much matter where else he went. Hyram Neil had let him slip away once before; he wasn't likely to lose him again.

"So I can act on the stage there," she said petulantly, "like you said the other night. I know we've talked about going back to St. Louis, or even to New York, but San Francisco would be fine by me. San Francisco would be like heaven compared to anywhere else we've been . . ."

"San Francisco will be like hell, if Hoodoo follows us there. For me, at least, though you might find the show entertainin'. As I have tried to explain to you before, he isn't one to lose gracefully. But I don't intend to hang for his greediness."

"But why do you have to go with Wyatt?" she said, with something more than anger or hurt mounting in her voice. "Why can't we just go off alone?"

"I'm safer travelin' with a group, if trouble comes along. Wyatt's a handy man with a gun, as you may have noticed. Why, he tried to hold off a whole gang of cowboys by himself, back in Dodge City, until I happened along to help him. I believe he'd do the same for me, if it came to that."

"So you're trusting your life to him, when it's me who's already saved you?"

There was a surprise of something like tears in her voice, and he stopped his packing for a moment to console her.

"I know what you did for me, Kate, and for that I thank you. I know I could have died back there in Trinidad if you hadn't brought me down here to the hot springs. It's a miracle, the doctors keep tellin' me, the way I've healed so well. And there wouldn't have been a miracle at all if you hadn't arranged for it. But I don't think you can help me out of this trouble. This time, I need Wyatt."

It was hard admitting that he needed anyone, especially to Kate, and harder to admit that it was Wyatt whom she seemed to hate out of pure jealousy. But he didn't have time to worry about Kate's extravagant emotions if he planned to stay alive. After all those nightmare dreams of alligators and dark water, he felt like he was about to go under at last.

"Then let me come with you!" she said fervidly, as he turned his attention back to folding shirts into his valise. "I know I've caused you trouble where Wyatt is concerned. But you know how I feel about you; you know how I love you . . ."

She was always saying it, so much that the words hardly meant a thing to him anymore. But this time, there was something like desperation in her voice, like she was holding on and sliding away at the same time.

"Please let me go along, please . . ." she said, and this time the tears filled her eyes and spilled over onto her red-rouged cheeks.

He could stand up to her stubbornness, answer her anger with his own, even hit her when she slapped at him in a fury. But he couldn't take her tears.

"All right," he said with a sigh, "all right. Though I don't know where we'll put all your gowns and shoes and such. Hell never did see a hellion better dressed than I've made you. Pick out what's best in all that," he said, gesturing toward her overflowing dresser and the trunks that held the rest, "and pack it up as fast as you can. I'm off to buy some horses. I suppose you'll be wantin' another white-blazed thoroughbred you can name Wonder."

She looked up at him in surprise. "You remembered the name of my horse?" she said, her tears drying up as fast as they had come.

"I remember everything about you, Kate. Even the parts I wish I could forget."

He might as well have said that he loved her, the way she smiled at him in triumph.

They left Las Vegas the next morning, pulling out with Wyatt's wagon train in the dark hour before dawn. There were seven of them in that outfit: Jim Earp and his wife and daughter, Wyatt Earp and his common-law wife Celia, and Dr. J.H. Holliday and the former actress who called herself Mrs. Holliday. And if anyone in the still sleeping town had roused at the sound of their wagons and animals passing by long enough to take a look at them, there would have been nothing unusual to notice at all, just another wagon train headed on down the Santa Fe Trail.

But there was something unusual about it, at least to John Henry's way of thinking—something ironic even. For while he had first gone west as a wanted man, running from the law and hoping to lose himself somehow, now he was running from the robbers and riding with the law instead, and feeling like maybe he'd finally found himself. He might not be every bit the gentleman anymore, not like he'd been in Georgia, but he wasn't an outlaw anymore either, and his friendship with Wyatt Earp was proof enough of that.

Author's Note

Dance with the Devil IS THE STORY OF A QUEST, AS YOUNG DR. JOHN Henry Holliday arrives in Texas looking for a new start while dealing with old demons: his love for a woman he can't have, his troubled relationship with his father, his double addiction to gambling and alcohol, and his death sentence of consumption. Although Western legend paints Doc Holliday as a cynic who didn't care if he lived or died, I had a hard time believing that a 23 year-old young man just starting into professional life would be so world-weary already. Instead, I imagined him as a young Aids victim who gets a fatal diagnosis at the prime of his life and goes through all the stages of grief before realizing that he isn't dying just yet, but living until he dies. And the facts of Holliday's life support that theme, as he starts what seems to be promising new career in Dallas before spiraling out of control into a life of liquor and legal trouble as he wandered the Western frontier. It wasn't until he left Texas behind and followed Wyatt Earp to Dodge City that he regained something of his old life, practicing dentistry in the Cattle Capital and, according to Ford County Sheriff Bat Masterson, staying out of trouble.

It was Bat Masterson's recollections of Doc Holliday, combined with the memoirs of Doc's mistress Kate Elder, that shaped this book, telling a much different story than the later inventions of novelists and screenwriters. Bat had known Doc in Dodge City and Denver and Tombstone and wrote about him as part of a series of articles for *Human Life Magazine* in 1907. Bat's version of Doc's history was reprinted in newspapers across the country at a time when other people who'd known Holliday were still alive and could have disputed the facts—but no one ever did. Neither Wyatt Earp nor Kate Elder, nor any of Doc's other associates countered Bat's stories, and so they stand as his first authoritative biography. And according to Bat, it wasn't sickness, but a shooting that made Doc leave Georgia and head west.

As Bat tells it, near to the South Georgia village where Holliday was raised there was a little river where a swimming hole had been cleared, and where he one day came across some black boys swimming where he thought they shouldn't be. He ordered them out of the water and when they refused, he took a shotgun to them and "caused a massacre." His family thought it best that he leave the area, and so he moved to Dallas, Texas. Although the story of a *massacre* isn't likely, there are some interesting points to Bat's account: Holliday did, in fact, live in a village in South Georgia, the town of Valdosta, near where there is a little river called the Withlacoochee, along which his family owned some land and a swimming hole. Where would Bat have gotten such details, if not from Holliday himself? And when the family was later asked about the episode by a reporter, they said that Holliday had fired over the boys' heads, not at them—but they did not deny the shooting. Having a perfect opportunity to deny the event and protect the family name, they did not. As for the story of Doc leaving Georgia for his health, that tale was first told nearly fifty years after he died in a novelized account of the life of Wyatt Earp called *Wyatt Earp: Frontier Marshall*. Although none of Doc's contemporaries ever said that he left Georgia for his health, the fiction has been repeated so many times that it's become part of his legend.

Following the facts instead of the legend lead me to an important discovery in Dallas: the legal case around Doc's New Year's Day shooting scrape, a story that appeared in the *Dallas Herald* of January 2, 1875:

> *"Dr. Holliday and Mr. Austin, a saloon-keeper, relieved the monotony of the noise of fire-crackers by taking a couple of shots at each other yesterday afternoon. The cheerful note of the peaceful six-shooter is heard once more among us. Both shooters were arrested."*

Because of the light tone of the news article, other writers had assumed that the incident was treated lightly by the law and that Holliday was laughed out of town. But before I was a novelist I was a trained paralegal and knew that where there was an arrest, there was also a legal paper trail. So I started my search for the paperwork of the New Year's Day shooting in the Dallas County Court records stored in a series of boxes in the Dallas Public Library. With the assistance of my friend and fellow paralegal VelDean Fincher, we found the original charge listed in the Minutes book of the Court: Case #2643, Assault to Murder, which carried a penalty of 20 years in the State Penitentiary. Clearly, this was no laughing matter. But how was the case resolved? Although several legal aides in Texas told me that those court papers no longer existed, I knew in my bones that they did and kept searching, and found the records in another set of boxes in the State Archives in Austin:

January 25, 1875

2643

State of Texas vs J.H. Holliday

Assault to Murder

On this day came J.G. Colin, District Attorney pro tem for the State and the Deft. J.H. Holliday in his own proper person, and by his Attorney and this cause coming now for trial the parties announced themselves ready and the Deft for the plea says he is not guilty and thereupon came a jury with J.H Daniels and eleven others who being duly empanelled and sworn after hearing the evidence and argument of Council and receiving the charge of the Court retired to consider their verdict and came and returned into court the following Verdict: We the jury find the Deft not guilty. It is therefore ordered adjudged and decreed by the Court that the Deft J.H. Holliday go *hence without day and of this cause stand fully acquitted.*

In this serious case Doc Holliday was not only taken seriously but found not guilty—and he was not laughed out of town. And when he did leave Dallas and later return, his only legal charges were for gambling in a house of spirituous liquors, for although the movies show things differently, betting on cards in a saloon was generally against the law in the Wild West.

The facts of his day-to-day life in Texas were drawn from city directories and newspaper articles, along with an interview he gave to a newspaper in Colorado, where we first learned that he had attended the Dallas Methodist Church and joined the local Temperance Union and spent some time in the North Texas town of Denison. What he didn't talk about in that interview was his fight in Breckenridge, which was reported in the Dallas papers, or his shooting of a soldier in Fort Griffin. That was another story from Bat Masterson, though Bat gives the location as the military post town of Jacksboro. But as there was no soldier killed in Jacksboro during Doc's Texas years, Bat may have just gotten the location wrong. There was a soldier killed in the post town of Fort Griffin while Doc was there and shortly before he left Texas for Denver, where he lived under the alias Tom McKey—running from a killing would certainly explain his taking an alias until things cooled down. The fact that the man killed in Fort Griffin, Private Jake Smith, was a black Buffalo Soldier seems to support the story of the shooting on the Withlacoochee, showing a pattern of racial violence not unusual in the Reconstruction South.

It was also in Fort Griffin that Doc took up with Hungarian born Mary Katherine Haroney, known in the West as Kate Elder—though according to Kate she had first met Doc a few years earlier in St. Louis when he was a newly graduated dental student practicing dentistry "on Fourth Street, near the Planter's House Hotel." Kate's reminiscence was part of a series of letters she wrote to an Arizona newspaper reporter in the 1930's, but as she was just a woman in a man's Western world her story was pretty much ignored. I had ignored it myself, as everyone knew that Doc Holliday had never been in St. Louis and Kate's memories were likely confused by old age. But when I went to Philadelphia to research Holliday's time in dental school, I discovered that he had a classmate there who was from St. Louis and who had returned to that city after graduation, where he had a practice on Fourth Street near the Planter's House Hotel—the very location Kate had mentioned in her letters. Of all the cities and all the addresses she could have imagined, she had picked a place actually linked to Holliday's early life, which gave credence to her memoir.

It was also from Kate that I took the story of Doc's sudden illness in Trinidad and the harrowing covered wagon journey over the mountains to the healing hot springs at Las Vegas, New Mexico, but it was my own research that uncovered information about Doc's Las Vegas saloon. I had written to the clerk of the San Miguel County Court three times asking for a copy of the original deed and three times been told that no such record existed. Although Holliday's property ownership in Las Vegas was mentioned in the local paper, the usual legal proof of ownership seemed strangely missing. So I booked a flight to New Mexico and went to see for myself if the deed existed. And there it was carefully recorded in the County Deed Book: Dock Holliday's deed to a saloon on Centre Street. The misspelled name had made the clerk miss the record.

But I wasn't alone in researching Doc's lost years between Georgia and Tombstone. My friend and fellow author Dr Gary Roberts (*Doc Holliday: The Life and Legend*) has spent years delving into old newspapers and trying to piece together the scattered facts that add up to a story. I thank him for his generous sharing of his research and his support of my own work. We never saw a conflict between his biography and my historical fiction, as we approach the history of Doc Holliday from our own areas of expertise, trying to breathe life into the legend. I also thank author Casey Tefertiller for his research and encouragement through the years—his *Wyatt Earp: The Life Behind the Legend* remains the best biography of the lawman who became Doc Holliday's favorite friend. If Bat Masterson expressed dislike for Doc, it may have been because Doc so clearly favored Wyatt over all the other men he knew. Even Kate was jealous of Doc's affection for Wyatt, a factual element that added to the fiction of *Dance with the Devil*.

Many thanks to the archivists and historians who aided in my own work: the late Susan McKey Thomas (*In Search of the Hollidays*), Doc's cousin whose family history work started my own research and who became my dear friend over the years; Joan Farmer of the Old Jail Art Center, Albany, Texas; Harold F. Thatcher, City of Las Vegas Museum and Rough Rider Memorial Collection, New Mexico; and Dr. Arthur W. Bork,

Prescott, Arizona, who knew and interviewed Kate Elder and shared his recollections with me. Family & friends who were my first readers and stalwart supporters: Patricia Petersen, Samuel Shannon, Sterling Felsted, Jennifer Felsted, Heather Shannon, Ashley Wilcox, Ross Wilcox, Mack Peirson, Daniel Mikat, Michael Spain, Melinda Talley, VelDean Fincher, and Dr. Dorothy Mikat. Special thanks to Laura Pilcher, copyeditor extraordinaire, and to Dan and Sally Mikat for giving me long quiet weeks to write at their home on Mackinac Island, Michigan. And especially to Erin Turner, Editorial Director of TwoDot Books, for giving new life and a new look to Doc Holliday's Wild West story.

Finally, thanks to my late mother, Beth Wanlass Peirson, who was my best research assistant as we traveled the West in search of Doc Holliday, and to my husband and favorite dentist, Dr. Ronald Wilcox, who paid for all the trips and watched the kids while I was traveling, and whose understanding of the pride of profession helped me to understand John Henry Holliday, D.D.S. Without you, Doc's story would have remained just a legend.

—Victoria Wilcox
Peachtree City, Georgia

About the Author

Victoria Wilcox is Founding Director of Georgia's Holliday-Dorsey-Fife House Museum (the antebellum home of the family of Doc Holliday, now a site on the National Register of Historic Places), where she learned the family's untold stories of their legendary cousin. Her work with the museum led to two decades of original research, making her a nationally recognized authority on the life of Doc Holliday. She is the author of the documentary film *In Search of Doc Holliday* and the award-winning historical novel trilogy *The Saga of Doc Holliday*, for which she twice received Georgia Author of the Year honors and in 2016 was named Best Historical Western Novelist by *True West Magazine*. She has lectured across the country, appeared in local and regional media, guested on NPR affiliates, and was featured in the Fox Network series *Legends & Lies: The Real West*. She is a member of the Western Writers of America, the Wild West History Association, Women Writing the West, and the Writer's Guild of the Booth Museum of Western Art and has been a featured contributor to *True West Magazine*. In the summer of 2017, she joined actor Val Kilmer (*Tombstone*) as guest historian at the inaugural "Doc HolliDays" in Tombstone, Arizona, site of the legendary OK Corral gunfight.